WILLOWTREE PRESS, L.L.C.

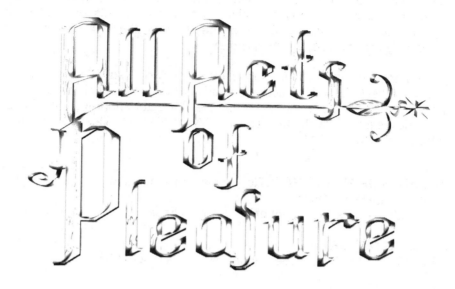

All Acts of Pleasure

A ROWAN GANT INVESTIGATION

BOOK TWO OF THE MIRANDA TRILOGY

A Novel of Suspense and Magick

By

M. R. Sellars

E.M.A. Mysteries

ALL ACTS OF PLEASURE: A Rowan Gant Investigation
A WillowTree Press Book
E.M.A. Mysteries is an imprint of WillowTree Press

PRINTING HISTORY
WillowTree Press First Trade Paper Edition / October 2006

For information, contact WillowTree Press on the World Wide Web:
http://www.willowtreepress.com

ISBN-10: 0-9678221-3-0
ISBN-13: 978-0-9678221-3-6

Cover Design Copyright © 2006 Johnathan Minton

Cover Photo Copyright © 2006 On The Edge Photography

Cover Model: Ms. Gwendolin "Wendi" O'Brien

Author Photo Copyright © 2004 K. J. Epps

10   9   8   7   6   5   4   3   2   1

PRINTED IN THE U.S.A.
by
TCS Printing
North Kansas City, Missouri

Books By M. R. Sellars

The RGI Series (*in order*)

HARM NONE
NEVER BURN A WITCH
PERFECT TRUST
THE LAW OF THREE
CRONE'S MOON
LOVE IS THE BOND *
ALL ACTS OF PLEASURE *

Forthcoming in the RGI Series

THE END OF DESIRE *

* Denotes *The Miranda Trilogy*

ACKNOWLEDGEMENTS

Once again I find myself with the monumental task of thanking those who made this installment—and in some cases even the entire RGI series—possible. As I have said before, with each book I write, the list of people I feel compelled to thank grows, and eventually, this roll call will take up an entire volume in itself. Still, my good and true friends are very important to me, so this "thank you" list has become like a moral imperative for me. That said, if I happen to miss someone, I hope you understand that it was unintentional, so please accept my apologies in advance. I'm getting old and my brain doesn't always work the way it is supposed to.

Finally, while I may simply run down this list like an *Oscar* winner getting the "wind it up" signal, please know that you all made this possible through your love and support (and in more than one instance, your complete insanity...)—

In all seriousness, however, it is of utmost importance with regard to this particular book that I present a big thank you to *eDNA/Genetic Technologies, Incorporated* and *Genelex Corporation* for the background info on DNA and genetic identification. And, in that vein, especially EXTRA HUGE props go out to the entire team at *Genetree*—not only did the folks at *Genetree* give me info, they actually went out of their way to help me make sure my plotting and methodology were sound, and for that I owe them big. Thanks y'all...

Now, on to the usual list of suspects, all of whom are very dear to me...

Dorothy Morrison—all hail the mighty "Box of Joe"
Sergeant Scott Ruddle, SLPD—don't you just hate that?
Roy Osbourn—don't worry, it'll keep ya' regular.
Trish Telesco, Ann Moura, A.J Drew, Aimee, and Aubrey; *Mystic Moon Coven, Dragon Clan Circle* and *The Grove of the Old Ways*; Duane, Amy, Angel & Randal, Chell, Scott & Andrea...All of my good friends from the various acronyms: F.O.C.A.S.M.I., H.S.A., M.E.C., S.I.P.A, I.M.P., etc. (And even the acronyms that have since disappeared)...Patrick & Tish, Lori, Beth, Jim, Dave, Rachel, Doug, Duncan, Kitti, Tracy, Edain, Boom-Boom, Kevin, David, Bella, Annmarie, Marie, Kathy, Shannon, Denessa, Annette, Boudica, Imajicka, Owl, Breanna, Anne, Maggie, Gail, Phyllis, Zita, Heather, Lorna, Linn, Jerry, Mark, Christine, Kristin, Velvet, Rollie, Gil, Hardee, Z, Charlie, Cindy, The Chunkmeister, Johnathan, and probably twenty or thirty more...
My parents—you know...I wish you were here.
My daughter—there's never a dull moment where you're concerned...
My wife Kat—all that mushy stuff times three...
Gwendolin, EK, and *The Evil One*—love you all...
Firestorm Publicity Services for keeping the blaze going...
The gang at CAO for the *MX2* and entire *Brazilia* line of cigars...
The Drover in Omaha, Nebraska for the killer steaks!

Paper plates, sporks, wet naps, big paper clips, corkboard, fishnet stockings, hot sauce, butterscotch pudding, applewood smoked bacon, scotch, gin, vodka, green olives, and bologna (the deli kind, not that pre-packaged stuff)...

And, as always, everyone who takes the time to pick up one of my novels, read it, and then recommends it to a friend.

For
Ken Vanlieu

I'm pointing, looking confused
and giving you the "Columbo salute"…

See you on the other side, my friend.

AUTHOR'S NOTE:

Dear Reader,

If you have been following the *Rowan Gant Investigations*, you already know that this book, *All Acts of Pleasure*, is for all intents and purposes part two of a much larger three-part story. It all began in the sixth book in the RGI series, *Love is the Bond*. That installment more or less took on a life of its own and very quickly grew beyond the confines of the covers betwixt which the words were sandwiched. Of course, most of you are already aware, that particular part of the story ended in a gut-wrenching cliffhanger. I have the angry emails and letters to prove it. However, you also know that said cliffhanger set the stage from which *All Acts of Pleasure* could springboard, just as it, in and of itself, will propel you into *The End of Desire*, the eighth book in the RGI series and third book in what is now being referred to as *The Miranda Trilogy*.

However, because of the fact that this is an ongoing series, you will find that this novel will cover some familiar ground in order to refresh your memories. This minor rehash of events is also intended to set the stage for those who may not have read *Love is the Bond*. Why? Because someone out there will pick up this novel and read it out of sequence. Guaranteed. It happens every time a new RGI novel hits the bookstores, and there is nothing I can do except say, "Hey, you! Yes, you! Start at the beginning of the series! Or, at the very least read *Love is the Bond* before you read *All Acts of Pleasure!*"

There. I said it. Unfortunately, I know someone out there is going to ignore me, but at least I gave it a try. Therefore, I am now blameless. (In my mind, at least.)

Another important note—you will find that *All Acts of Pleasure* is somewhat different. Not radically, but a little. While all of the books in the series are truly about the characters and their relationships with one another, this installment is even more so. In it, you will explore not only the selfless depth of a couple's love for one another, but also crisis in a close friendship, and desperate issues with family as well.

Fear not, the fabric of the Rowan Gant saga remains intact—I simply splashed some different colors upon it this go around. I had no choice as this story arc within a story arc is taking us across three separate novels, and that simply requires a change of palette to keep things vibrant and alive.

Also, of note—just because, *The End of Desire,* the novel that is to follow this one, will wrap up the *Miranda Trilogy,* it does not herald the end of *The Rowan Gant Investigations* as a series. The RGI stories will continue for some time to come. It is just a basic fact that sometimes a particular character gets a little big for his or her britches (or skirt) and demands some extra verbiage upon the pages. We all saw this happen with *Eldon Porter* in *Never Burn a Witch* and *The Law of Three.* It seems that *Miranda* just happens to be one of those characters with a life, mind, and major attitude of her own. She's demanding, to say the least, and try as I might, she isn't letting me ignore her need to complete this arc before allowing me to move on. In a sense, you could say I am at her mercy just like her victims in the story.

At any rate, I hope that you find *All Acts of Pleasure,* as well as the entire trilogy, enjoyable, and that they give you a little more of a peek into the lives of these characters, most especially *Felicity* and *Miranda.* I know that writing them has opened my eyes a bit wider, and I'm the one who created the characters to begin with. In fact, I sometimes wonder if I am actually writing these novels, or merely taking dictation.

One final thing: As promised, questions will be answered. But, remember, I never swore an oath that I wouldn't raise a few more.

Brightest Blessings!

THE USUAL DISCLAIMER:

While the city of St. Louis and its various notable landmarks are certainly real, many names have been changed and liberties taken with some of the details in this book. They are fabrications. They are pieces of fiction within fiction to create an illusion of reality to be experienced and enjoyed.

In short, I made them up because it helped me make the story more entertaining—or in some cases, just because I wanted to do so.

Note also that this book is a first-person narrative. You are seeing this story through the eyes of Rowan Gant. The words you are reading are his thoughts. In first person writing, the narrative should match the dialogue of the character telling the story. Since Rowan (and anyone else that I know of for that matter) does not speak in perfect, unblemished English throughout his dialogue, he will not do so throughout his narrative. Therefore, you will notice that some grammatical anomalies have been retained (under protest from editors) in order to support this illusion of reality.

Let me repeat something—I DID IT ON PURPOSE. DO NOT send me an email complaining about my grammar. It is a rude thing to do, and it does nothing more than waste your valuable time. If you find a typo, that is a different story. Even editors miss a few now and then. They are no more perfect than you or me.

Finally, this book is not intended as a primer for WitchCraft, Wicca, or any other Pagan/magickal path. However, please note that the rituals, spells, and explanations of these religious/magickal practices are accurate. Some of my explanations may not fit your particular tradition, but you should bear in mind that your explanations just might not fit mine either. That's why it's called diversity.

And finally, yes, some of the Magick is "over the top." But, like I said in the first paragraph, this is fiction…

Let *Her* worship be within the heart that rejoiceth;
for behold, all acts of love and pleasure are *Her* rituals.

Paraphrased from
The Charge of the Goddess
As attributed to Doreen Valiente

Thursday, December 1
2:47 P.M.
New Orleans Public Library, Main Branch
Louisiana Division, Archives
New Orleans, Louisiana

PROLOGUE:

Steady rain was falling, relentlessly spattering the windows that looked out onto a small third floor courtyard.

Rain was probably the last thing this city needed at the moment. Especially when one considered that the floodwaters, which had invaded the streets and neighborhoods in the aftermath of Hurricane Katrina, had only recently been pumped back to from whence they came.

Of course, Mother Nature was on a roll, and she had every intention of hurling more water down upon the dampened city, whether it needed it or not. Fortunately, however, she also had a soft spot for this magickal place, so this go around the precipitation was merely a steady soaking instead of a violent downpour.

Inside the library the unmistakable funk of mildewed carpet, coupled with countless strains of mold, filled the air. The stagnant aroma relentlessly intermingled with the rich, "academic" smells of paper and ink, both old and new, decaying and preserved. Not one inch of the building was immune as the ventilation system pumped the malodorous air throughout.

Even upstairs where the archives resided on the third floor of the building, well above the highest point the floodwaters had managed to reach, the smell was still only of slightly lessened intensity. This fact was most likely due to its competition for dominance over the tang of oxidizing microfilm rolls and sporadic wafts of warm ozone.

The telltale whine of a laser printer whirred upward, increasing in pitch until barely audible, revealing the source of the second of the sharp olfactory notes that stood out against the pervasive, flat mustiness. With a series of clicks and a plastic rattle, it spit out a piece of paper then hummed back into idleness.

The piece of computer equipment occupied a low table next to a copier, located directly across from the main desk, all of which was just a short walk from the elevator. A few feet beyond the office equipment was the far corner of the information counter. There, the room made a sharp turn, wrapping around the rear of the empty courtyard.

Perpendicular to the wall opposite the windows, shelves stacked with genealogical records and census data stood at attention, lined outward in perfect formation. At the far end of that dogleg, which terminated the L-shaped room, a man was hunched over, barely visible behind the back-to-back rows of chest-high metal cabinets.

He straightened upward and gently placed a hand-sized, square box atop the cabinets then peered back downward over the rim of his eyeglasses. After a moment he began moving slowly to his right, fixed gaze scanning intently. A few seconds later he came to a halt and tugged at the front of the sheet metal cube before him.

A drawer rolled out on full suspension slides, the decrepit ball bearings rattling complaints into the relative quiet of the room. Stepping backward, he extended it fully and then began carefully running his index finger across the contents. It took only a few seconds before he selected yet another of the cardboard boxes and extracted it from the shallow bin. Then, elbowing the drawer shut once again, he gathered the first container along with a tattered steno pad and headed back toward the center of the dogleg where the microfilm readers were set up in short rows.

Activity had been minimal in the archives earlier in the day. Other than himself, there had only been what appeared to be a few students researching projects and an elderly couple who were obviously on a quest for a lost ancestor. What that had meant was that there were plenty of readers to go around.

But, that was earlier, and unfortunately, things had changed. The number of warm bodies occupying the third floor had increased dramatically over the past hour or so, and it was now becoming commonplace to need to wait your turn.

The man peered up and down the stubby ranks, checking the backside of the furthest stand of machines and found none free. With a tired sigh, he trudged over to a table and started to pull out a chair. The wait could be short, or it could be long. One could never tell.

"Excuse me…Sir?" A feminine voice came into his ears just as he'd edged the seat from beneath the table.

He turned to find a very blonde and very young-looking woman motioning to him with one hand as she spun a crank with the other in order to rewind the film she had been viewing.

"Yeah?" he grunted.

"I'm done here, if you need the machine," she replied.

He took notice of the fact that her voice held none of the affectations of the area he'd grown accustomed to hearing since he'd arrived. In that sense, she seemed almost as out of place as he felt. Still, she was young, clad in blue jeans and a hooded sweatshirt, with a nylon backpack sitting on the floor next to her chair. His sluggish brain added up the evidence at hand and came to the conclusion that she was probably a college student from out-of-state.

"Yeah, thanks," he replied with a shallow nod. His voice was a tired drone, which all but broadcast the fact that he was surviving on nothing more than coffee and very little sleep.

He nudged the chair back beneath the table then walked over to the side of the reader and waited patiently. The young woman removed the spool and stuffed it back into a box then gathered her notebook. Hefting her book bag from the floor, she slipped it onto one shoulder then stepped to the side and gave him a quick smile.

"You kind of have to coax it a bit sometimes," she offered. "It sticks every now and then."

"Yeah." He nodded. "I had to use this one a little earlier. Thanks."

"Soooo…Genealogy?" she asked.

He grunted, "Huh?"

He had already dropped a spool of aging film from the box into his hand and was pushing it onto the feed spindle when she asked the question, so he wasn't really paying attention. In actuality, he was thinking about the fact that, until today, he hadn't done research via microfilm since he was in college, and that had been longer ago than he cared to remember. He mentally "hmmphed" as the memory passed and mutely attributed the interaction with the young student as triggering it.

"I was just wondering if you were maybe doing genealogical research," she continued, undaunted by his inattentive demeanor. "You know, investigating your roots. That sort of thing."

"Yeah," he glanced back at her and replied with a tired nod. "Yeah, I guess you could say it's something like that."

He returned his gaze to the front and pressed the plastic spool inward until he felt it snap into place then tugged at the free end of the celluloid. He could literally feel that the young woman was still standing behind him for some unknown reason. He briefly wondered if he should reach back and check for his wallet, however, what she was exuding definitely didn't feel malicious. In fact, unless he missed his guess, it felt like a strange mix of curiosity and arousal. At any rate, since no hairs were rising on his neck and no alarms were going off inside his head, he mentally shook it off and tried to ignore her.

She didn't let him.

"Yeah, I figured as much," she finally said. "I've been watching you."

He looked over his shoulder at her again. "Yeah? Why's that?"

"Well, I mean…" she paused and shrugged. "You look kinda old to be a student."

"Thanks," he replied flatly, a complete lack of sincerity haloing the word.

He turned back to the machine and continued on with the task at hand, threading the film under the glass and hooking it carefully into the take-up reel.

"Oh, that wasn't meant as an insult," she offered.

"No big deal. I wasn't offended. I realize I'm old as compared to you. That part of my brain still works."

Though their voices were already held low, she dropped her own down a notch and infused it with a cloying sweetness that bordered on an attempt at sultry. Shifting her stance, she leaned in toward the man and cocked her head as if sharing a secret with him. "The truth is, I really like older men…a lot…know what I mean?"

Now the hairs on his neck actually were starting to pivot upward. There certainly wasn't what you would call a sense of physical danger by any means, but he knew the conversation was taking a turn down a path he didn't want to follow.

He stopped what he was doing and hung his head. With a sigh he finally said, "Please tell me you aren't trying to pick me up."

There was an audible shrug in her voice. "Well, hey… You're kind of cute. I was thinking maybe we could go get a cup of coffee or something and see where things go from there?"

He turned to face her. "I'm betting I'm old enough to be your father."

"Yeah, probably. So what? That's the point."

He started to reply to the last statement but thinking it better left alone simply objected with, "I'm also happily married."

"Yeah. Okay. But, she isn't with you right now is she? You've been alone since I've been here."

"Actually, she's the entire reason I'm here at the moment, but that's not the point…"

"Hey, I won't tell if you won't."

"Look, young lady…"

"Erika," she interrupted, holding out her hand. "And you are?"

He ignored the gesture but returned with a sigh, "Rowan."

"Rowan. That's an interesting name. I like it." She continued to hold her hand thrust forward.

"Thanks," he replied, still avoiding the offered appendage. "So listen, Erika, you've got to know that you're playing a dangerous game here. You have absolutely no idea who I am."

After a thick silence she finally pulled her hand back. "Yeah. Well, that's part of the turn-on too."

"Uh-huh. Well, I could be some kind of sicko for all you know."

"You look pretty safe to me."

"Most sociopaths do," he said. "And, I've actually got some experience in that area."

"Really? How so?"

"Trust me, you really don't want to know."

She paused for a moment, giving him a once over, then said, "Okay. So, tell me. Are you a 'sicko'?"

"Again, that's not the point."

She stuck out her lower lip in an exaggerated pout. "So what is it then? Are you just not into blondes?"

"Listen, Erika, is this some kind of game show? Is there a hidden camera somewhere? Because, honestly, I don't have time for this."

She chuckled. "You're funny too."

He let out another heavy sigh and held up his hands. "All right, look, I'm flattered...At least I think I am...Anyway, this just isn't going to happen. Understand?"

She blinked and gave her head a quick shake as if reality had just rapped her on the back of the skull. "You're serious."

"Yes. Yes, I am."

"You really don't want to..."

"No. No, I don't."

"Well...Okay. It's your loss."

"I'll just have to take your word for that."

"Well, you know..." she started as she opened her notebook to a fresh page and began fishing a pen from the spiral binding. "I could give you my number in case you change your mind..."

This time he did the interrupting. "That isn't necessary. I won't."

She paused then shoved the pen back down and closed the notebook. "Okay. Well, never know until you try." She shrugged and added, "Good luck with whatever you're doing there, I guess."

"Yeah. Thanks. You too."

After staring at him curiously for a moment, she shook her head then turned and walked away.

This was the second time he'd been propositioned in as many days, and it was something he wasn't particularly used to having happen. He wasn't sure if it was his obvious emotional state or what. Vulnerability was exuding from every one of his pores and he knew it; he had just hoped that the rest of the world wouldn't notice. Of course, maybe it was something in the water, so to speak, and women here just had a thing for worn-out, middle-aged men with greying hair and ponytails. Whatever it was, he could certainly do without the aggravation right now.

He shook his head then tried to forget about it. If the rest of this day continued along the same fruitless vein, as had the morning, he still had quite a bit of searching to do. And, even then, he knew he might not find what he was looking for because, to be honest, even he didn't know quite exactly what that was.

Cocking his head over against his shoulder and staring at the image on the marred base, he wound the film a few frames forward and found a reference point. Quickly glancing to the side, he checked a note he had scrawled on the steno pad then looked back to the dimly luminous image. He started to crank the winding lever, stopping and giving it a hard rap to engage the slipping gears once again before continuing. After a moment he slowed, advancing frame by frame until he found the date he sought.

Twisting the projection head, he turned the glowing reproduction of the over one hundred-fifty year old newspaper so that he no longer had to hold his own head at such an odd angle. Seating himself, he adjusted the magnification and fiddled with the focus until it was as good as it was ever going to get, which wasn't exactly sharp by any stretch of the imagination.

With determination he scanned the hard to read blobs, picking his way between scratches, dropout, and the just plain low quality print of the day. He was on the verge of giving up and moving on when his eye caught something familiar. He pulled on the positioning bar and moved the frame in enough to center it and then drew a bead on the type that had commandeered his attention.

Tilting his head up and gazing through the lower half of his bifocals, he focused on the words. Then, with one finger he slowly traced along beneath the lines of text, his lips slowly but silently moving as he read to himself.

Then, he read the lines again.

And, again…

After the third time, he sat back in the seat and let out the hot breath he had unconsciously been holding within for the duration. Slowly he ran the palm of his hand across the lower half of his face then pushed his glasses up and closed his eyes as he pinched the bridge of his nose between his thumb and forefinger. After a moment, the man let out a quiet chuckle that could have been born of subdued elation or exhaustion-induced insanity, even he didn't know which.

When he finally opened his eyes again, he looked at the page just to make sure the words were really there then muttered aloud to no one in particular, "Miranda, you bitch."

Two Weeks Earlier
Thursday, November 17
12:16 P.M.
Saint Louis, Missouri

CHAPTER 1:

"**M**y heart is pounding in my chest so hard that I can hear it... And I don't mean like that thudding rush of blood you get in your ears when your heart is racing. I mean I can literally hear this frantic thump echoing in the darkness.

"Then, just all of a sudden I gasp for breath. I guess it's the panic that makes me do it, I don't know. Anyway, the air is foul. There's this...I don't know...something like a stench of death, rotting meat, and maybe even excrement all mixed together. It's so thick it seems to coat the back of my tongue. You know what I mean? And then I feel this sudden need to vomit..."

I paused for a moment to gather myself, staring off into space as the steam from my breath quickly dissipated before me. The temperature was hovering right around freezing, several degrees below normal for Saint Louis in late November, but then the weather here was always an enigma. However, ruminating on the offbeat weather patterns was something I didn't have time to do. I had something much more important, and unfortunately, far more horrifying to contend with. I was already beginning to think the latter was an understatement.

Thus far, the retelling of my recurring nightmare had been just as bad as living it each night. I had hoped that voicing it to a sympathetic ear might be liberating, which is why I was here, now, putting myself through this. However, instead of manifesting as a freeing experience, it was just serving to make my head hurt and my stomach churn.

Next to me, Helen Storm shifted against the balcony rail and lit another cigarette. "So, is that when you wake up, Rowan?"

What the outside observer might see as a casual conversation was in actuality an impromptu therapy session. Helen was a psychiatrist, and odd as it may seem, this was pretty much how all of our sessions happened. Outside, rain or shine. Whether it was frigid and windy, as it was now, or hot and muggy in the dead of summer, it didn't matter. We would always be outdoors, with her chain smoking and me nursing a cigar.

Whenever we were in the building where her office was located, as we were today, this particular spot was exactly where we could be found. Standing out here on the large, partially covered corner balcony that had been set up as a smoking lounge for several of the upper floors.

Unusual, yes, but there was a familiarity between us that allowed for the less than formal setting; in fact, it all but demanded it.

Helen had come into my life during a period when I truly thought I was going insane. In fact, at the time, I was fairly sure that I had already been delivered to madness' doorstep. Of course, discovering that you can communicate with the dead can tend to do that to a person, and at that point I had already been living with that very affliction for quite some time.

To be truthful, I hadn't been falling all over myself to talk to a psychiatrist when it was suggested. My immediate assumption was that I would be labeled insane, instantly medicated, and carted off to the land of straightjackets and padded rooms. However, considering that the deceased individuals with whom I had been having conversations were all murder victims, and I'd been spending an inordinate amount of time helping the police track down their killers, I needed to vent to someone. I had been seeing things that seasoned cops had trouble dealing with, and I had been experiencing them on a far grander scale than photographs or even the physical crime scene. I saw through the eyes, and felt through the bodies, of the victims.

No, these were things that truly didn't need to remain shuttered away in my subconscious.

In the end, a good friend of mine who was a Saint Louis city homicide detective, and also happened to be Helen's brother, had argued that I needed to at least give her a chance. Of course, my wife had been directly involved in the "intervention" as well. Between the two of them, the pressure on me to seek outside help dealing with my "gift" had been relentless.

Fortunately, they had won the skirmish because Helen's counsel had seen me through some very pitch darkness, both then and countless times since. In fact, her understanding ear and uncanny ability to guide one through his or her own psyche had developed into an invaluable resource.

On top of that, she had also become a very good friend.

"Rowan?" she repeated, somewhat louder than before.

The tone of her voice, rather than the volume, managed to prod me back from the edge of introspection, and I gave her an apologetic glance. "Sorry…it's all just a little intense."

"I understand," she replied. "Take your time."

"It's okay. I'm fine."

"All right then…is this the point in the nightmare when you wake up?"

"No," I answered, staring at the ash on the end of the cigar hooked beneath my index finger. I consciously tucked the double Maduro roll of tobacco into the corner of my mouth and slowly drew, only to discover that it had gone out.

"Please continue," Helen urged. "If you are ready to do so, that is."

I let out a heavy sigh. Truth be told, I wasn't really fine, and I was far from ready. Moreover, I definitely wasn't excited about revisiting this terror, but I was already right in the middle of the tale, so it was a little late to turn back. Besides, this was the whole reason I had come to her to begin with, so holding it all inside was the last thing I needed to do.

"So…anyway…I try to force the feeling away," I continued, hesitantly at first. After a deep breath I made myself dive straight into the rest of the story. "So, I try, but I'm too weak, apparently, even to do that. I feel myself heave, but it's not like I double over. I'm lying on my back, and I kind of just jerk in place because I can't really move. I'm restrained somehow. Anyway, nothing comes up, except bile. I guess that's what it is because I feel a burning in my throat, and then I start to gag.

"At this point I start to notice that all of my muscles are pretty much screaming. It's like I'm stretched beyond my limits, and now they're all starting to cramp. I know that if I can just get up and move it will stop. But, like I said, I'm restrained and I can't. It's at that moment of realization that I always hear them. And then, the panic just starts all over again."

"Them?"

"The footsteps. At first they sound like they're in the distance…almost like they're below me…but somehow I know they aren't going to stay there. I know they're going to come closer. I don't know why I know, but I just do. And, here's something odd—they aren't new to me. It's as if I've heard these very footsteps countless times before. So, you would almost think that I'd be used to them, but I'm not. Either way, as soon as they start, my heart jumps and begins pounding even faster."

Helen cocked her head to the side in a thoughtful pose then interjected, "Perhaps it is your familiarity with them that triggers your panic."

"Makes sense. You're probably right."

"However, I suspect you have already thought of that."

"Yeah. I guess I did."

"All right. Go on."

"Anyway, the footsteps start, and I force myself to listen. Before long they do start coming closer, just like I knew they would. What's weird is that they sound excited and cruel at the same time. I don't know if that makes sense…I mean, I know they're just footsteps and all, but there seems to be this whole mix of depravity and even arousal in the sound…"

"It is not unusual to apply emotions to ambient noises, Rowan," Helen offered. "It is a normal function of the subconscious. Sound will easily evoke an emotional response. If it did not we would have no need for music and sound effects in movies. Of course, the particular pairing you mention is most assuredly…shall we say, different."

"Yeah, exactly. It definitely seemed odd to me except that what I've been dealing with recently… Well, the circumstances make them fit together in a way."

"I see. So, is there more?"

"A little," I said with a nod. "This is when I realize…no…actually it's more like I *remember* that there are others here with me…I guess I'm just suddenly reminded of it when I hear them because they hear the footsteps too. But, when they hear them, they start whimpering and crying."

I felt myself shudder physically as the words spilled out. Out of reflex I thumped the heel of my palm against the top of the railing as if the gesture could make it all go away. With a quick snap of my head I exclaimed, "Gods! They always sound so terrified that it…I don't know…I really can't describe it…I…I…Dammit!"

"Calm down, Rowan," Helen instructed. "Take a breath and relax."

I did as she told me and forced myself to settle. Finally I said, "All I can say is that their terror just fuels mine, and that just makes my panic grow."

"A natural response."

"Doesn't make it any more pleasant…anyway, then, of all things, I start praying. As frightened—and I mean flat out petrified—as I am, I don't cry like the others. I don't moan. I don't whimper…I just start to pray."

"To whom are you praying?"

I knew exactly why she asked the question. She was fully aware that my personal leanings didn't fit with the generally accepted concept of prayer. The fact of the matter being very simply that I was a Witch, a card carrying Pagan. I was a practitioner of magick and follower of an alternative religious path commonly known as Wicca. The idea of me praying was about as far left of center as it could get.

I shook my head. "I don't know. God I guess, believe it or not…Yeah…I know…doesn't make much sense, does it? Me, a devout Pagan praying to God."

"It is not as if you do not believe in a duality of Godhead, Rowan. As I understand it, in your path you have both a God and a Goddess."

"Yeah, but I get the feeling it's not *that* God I'm praying to."

"Perhaps in this nightmare you are not yourself, but rather someone else."

"I gave that some thought," I replied. "But, usually in the dreams I'm myself. It's when I have a waking vision that I actually channel the dead and take on their memories and such."

"However, I recall that you have spoken to the dead in your dreams. Correct?"

Helen was truly one of the few individuals with whom I could discuss these things without being looked upon with a jaundiced eye, as evidenced by what she had just said to me. I suppose it was her Native American heritage that made her so open to the idea that I really did communicate with those who had departed this realm.

The truth is, I sometimes had trouble believing it myself. Witches aren't what you read about in fairy tales or Shakespearean plays. Practicing magick and following a Pagan religious path, while an alternative to the societal norm, didn't automatically make you some kind of psychic medium. In fact just about any other Pagan could tell you that I, and those like me, were an anomaly. While the mental exercises that come with the territory may have enhanced some type of latent ability I had always possessed, Witches, in general, simply didn't go around talking to dead people.

Why did I get to be so lucky? Who knows? All I can say is that "why me" had become a personal mantra over the past few years.

I gave Helen a shallow nod after considering her response to my explanation. "Yeah, but I'm obviously not doing a lot of speaking to anybody in this one."

"This is true."

I waited a moment then added. "Well, there is one thing I know for sure, and that's what I'm praying *for*."

"And, that would be?"

"I'm ashamed to admit it, but what I'm praying for is that this time it won't be me. As selfish as that sounds, I want her to hurt someone else and not me."

"Her?" Helen asked, cocking her head to the side once again and raising an eyebrow.

"I don't know," I replied with a shrug then dug into my pocket for a lighter. "It's like the arousal and callousness with the footsteps. I just have this overwhelming sense of a female presence in connection with the terror and pain. There's definitely a woman at the root of it, but I couldn't begin to tell you who she is."

She clucked her tongue then gave her head a shake, looking at me with an expression that said she had reached a conclusion she was not yet ready to share. Not in direct terms, anyway.

"I do not believe that is entirely true," she said.

"What do you mean?"

"I mean perhaps you do not know for certain who she is, but you have a definite suspicion. That suspicion is exactly why you are here talking to me now."

I huffed out a heavy breath as my response. I was feeling only a small amount of relief at unloading the painful information to begin with, and I wasn't sure if I wanted to take things the direction Helen was now heading. Of course, her high-powered perception was the very reason I sought her out; it just wasn't always comfortable being under the polished surface of her lens.

Pressing on, I tried to bypass the inference. "Yeah, well...anyway, to answer your earlier question, that's when I wake up...and, my heart is pounding in my chest; thudding against my ribcage so hard I can literally hear it. Just exactly like in the nightmare."

"And, is that always how it ends?"

"Pretty much. Most of the time, anyway." I nodded. "There've been a few times when it went a bit further. I'll hear a creak of an opening door, and then the footsteps will actually make it into the room with me. Then, the wailing and crying of the others gets louder, but that's pretty much it. It's never progressed beyond that point. Not yet, anyway."

"And, you never see her? The woman?"

"See? No. Feel, yes."

"Does she feel familiar?"

"Can't say for sure. Maybe."

"Are you certain of that?"

I lifted my shoulders then allowed them to drop. "Yeah. Okay. She feels familiar."

"Mmmhmmm," Helen pursed her lips and nodded as she made the noise. "And, how often did you say this is recurring?"

"Never less than twice a night since it started, and that was right at a week ago today. Last night was the worst yet. I can remember waking up five times in a total panic, but there may have been more. I'm not sure. That's pretty much why I called you this morning. It just keeps getting worse…Oh, and I'm not sure if I said thanks for fitting me in by the way."

"Of course, Rowan," Helen replied. "That is never a problem."

"Well, I took a chance. I wasn't sure if you would be taking some time off after your father's funeral or not."

Her father's recent passing had been another of the reasons I had endured the nightmare as long as I had.

"We all grieve in different ways, Rowan," she said, leaving the sentence to stand on its own as an explanation. "Speaking of gratitude, I appreciate that Felicity and you came to the service. I am certain that my brother did as well."

"It's the least we could do…and, I'll take your word for it about Ben. We haven't really spoken lately."

"Because of the investigation? I know he has been very busy."

"That's my guess. He hasn't returned any of my calls."

"I would not be too concerned. As I said, we all grieve in different ways. Delving into his work is simply Benjamin's way."

"I hope you're right," I returned. "Either way, thanks again for fitting me in."

"Well, keep this between the two of us, but even had I taken time off, I would have managed something for you. I have learned that when you feel the need to call me, it is not to be taken lightly."

"I'll take that as a compliment, I think."

"It was, in a manner of speaking."

She didn't embellish her reply and that wasn't unusual, so I didn't press the point. Since I seemed to have been moderately successful in diverting the topic from her earlier succinct insinuation, I finally relaxed a bit. Seizing the opportunity, I relit my cigar and puffed on it thoughtfully then gave the business end a quick inspection to make sure the glow was relatively even. Satisfied, I stuffed the lighter into my pocket and leaned back against the rail.

"So," I spoke after an extended pause. "What do you think about the nightmare, Doc? Anxiety? Chemical imbalance? Or, have I finally just lost it?"

She let out a thin "hmph" but kept her attention focused on the cigarette in her hand. I wasn't bothered at all by the wordless reply because I knew it simply meant she was still digesting everything I had been saying over the past quarter hour. Of course, knowing her as I did, I should have realized that it also meant I hadn't really changed her course at all.

After a moment, she spoke. "It is most certainly anxiety, but you already knew that. However, the truly important question here is 'what do *you* think', Rowan?"

"Well, that sounds like a typical response right out of the therapist handbook," I commented with a chuckle.

She let out a small laugh as well. "Yes, I suppose it does, but since you attempted to circumvent my earlier observation, I am now electing to pose it to you as a direct question."

"Caught that, did you?" I grunted the question.

"Was there any doubt that I would?" she countered.

"Well, I was hoping…"

"Rowan, we both know that in your case there is more to this nightmare than a bad horror movie or too much anchovy pizza for a midnight snack."

"Now, see, I was hoping you would tell me that's exactly what this is."

"But, you know better than that, do you not?"

I let out a resigned sigh before I gave her the answer. "Yes, unfortunately, I do. For one thing, I don't watch horror movies. I see enough of it without them."

"Exactly my point."

"Yeah, well, even so I was still hoping we couldn't rule out the anchovy pizza."

"You are evading again, Rowan."

"Uh-huh, I know. Can you blame me?"

"No, I do not suppose that I can. However, you also know that with me you cannot get away with it."

"Yeah, you're right."

"Good of you to notice," she replied, a hint of faux-conceit in her voice that was almost instantly replaced by measured seriousness. "Now, tell me…who do you believe the woman in your nightmare to be?"

"Honestly, I think she's probably the woman who killed Hammond Wentworth and Officer Hobbes."

"Really?"

"You sound surprised."

"No, not surprised," she returned with a shake of her head. "Disappointed."

"About what?"

"About the fact that you are still trying to evade my question."

"I'm not sure I follow, because I'm fairly certain I just answered it."

"You gave me an answer, but you did not tell me the truth."

"Come again?"

"Rowan, be honest. We both know that you did not seek me out to tell me you believe you are having nightmares about an unidentified killer in an ongoing murder investigation. As insane as it may sound to the general populous, for you, that is the norm. No, there is a vastly deeper issue here that you cannot begin to overcome until you admit to it."

"Okay," I returned with a shrug. "Since we seem to be on completely different pages here, would you like to share your insight?"

"Borrowing your analogy, we are both on the same page and you know it. You, however, are choosing not to read what is upon it." Helen shook her head and peered back at me with obvious sadness in her expression. "You know, Rowan, for someone with the depth of intuition you possess, it amazes me how difficult you can elect to be at times, especially when it comes to your own sanity."

I raised my eyebrows and harrumphed softly. "Yeah. You aren't the first person to make that observation."

"I am certain of that."

"So...you're going to make me say it, aren't you?"

"We cannot discuss this fully until you do."

"I don't want to."

"All right, start there. Why not?"

"Because if I do...well, if I do then that might make it real. I can't let it be real. Hell, I came here so you could tell me that it's not."

"I understand that."

"Okay then. So you obviously know what it is. Just tell me I'm being paranoid, and we'll be done with all this."

"Me telling you what you want to hear will not fix the issue. You know that, Rowan."

"Okay, so what will?"

"You facing your fear."

"Facing my fear? Are you kidding? Haven't I faced enough of those for one lifetime?"

"Actually, my friend, you have come nose to nose with more fears than anyone I know, and I commend you for that. But, by the same token, you have turned and run from just as many, if not more."

"Some of them just don't need facing, Helen."

"Perhaps you are correct. It is true that some fears are transient. However, this one is not, and it will haunt you if you run from it. You know this. That is why you are here now."

I slowly twisted around and looked out at the scattered clouds in the sky. It was now a given that we were going to veer down this road whether I wanted to or not.

"All right," I finally agreed as I hung my head. "I'm afraid the woman in the nightmare might be Felicity."

CHAPTER 2:

Felicity.

Felicity Caitlin O'Brien, to be exact—my wife, and unequivocally the greatest love of my life.

It sickened me that this vile thought could even cross my mind. And, that exact thought was also the very reason why I had gone to great lengths to hide this recurring nightmare from her.

Normally, I could tell Felicity anything. Close simply wasn't strong enough a word to describe our relationship. We were without a doubt, soul mates, and not in the new-agey, soft-focus sense of the overused catchphrase. There was a depth of connection between the two of us that transcended normal bonds of love and friendship.

"Good," Helen announced calmly after a brief pause. "Now we are progressing."

"I'm glad someone thinks so," I mumbled.

"Tell me, why do you think the woman in your nightmare is Felicity?"

"I said *might be*."

"Yes, you did. However, that does not answer my question."

"I don't know."

"I think that you do."

"Well maybe you're wrong for a change."

"Perhaps. No one is ever correct one-hundred percent of the time," she admitted. "However, I would hazard to say that this is not one of the times when I have fallen from my pedestal." She made an overt show of rocking back and forth as if checking her footing. "No, it feels quite solid. I am still up here."

I couldn't help but crack a thin smile at her theatrics. I knew that while she was serious, this brush with humor was her attempt at bolstering my mood, which was sinking rapidly. What made it even more effective was that it was so out of character for her.

"Well," I began, allowing the brief levity to push me into a fragile sense of security. "It's complicated. How much do you know about what has been happening with the Hammond Wentworth homicide?"

"Very little," she replied. "Benjamin has not spoken of it except to say that you and Felicity had been helping."

"Nothing else?"

"He did let slip that the two of you were somehow involved in an incident last week that became somewhat of a problem. However, he did not provide any details."

"Incident," I echoed. "That's one word for it."

"Well, I will admit that when you called I suspected that it had something to do with what Benjamin had mentioned. The nightmare, I had not foreseen, however it is obvious to me that there is a connection."

"Well, there's no denying that," I answered with a heavy sigh then took a pull on my cigar and rolled the smoke around on my tongue. After letting it out in a slow stream, I regarded the dark cylinder as I twisted it between my thumb and forefinger. Finally, I looked up at Helen who was waiting patiently. "So, do you have enough time for me to start at the beginning?"

Without speaking she reached into the pocket of her coat and extracted her cigarette case. Snapping it open, she peered into the top then closed it and returned it to the pocket.

Looking back at me she said, "I have a little more than a half pack with me. I think we are good."

I shook my head and almost allowed myself to chuckle at the seriousness with which she had delivered the reply. Had the situation been different, I suspect I wouldn't have been able to keep from laughing outright.

"Okay, I'll try to keep it as short a possible," I began. "About two weeks ago, right at the height of the flu epidemic, Felicity got a call from Ben. Apparently there was a high profile crime scene that needed photos."

"Judge Wentworth," Helen interjected.

"Exactly."

"I know Felicity is a photographer, but why did Benjamin call her? Is that not something that should have been handled by the police?"

"Under normal circumstances, yes. But, the flu had pretty much taken the majority of the Crime Scene guys out of commission. Felicity has evidence photography training, and she's on the short list of freelance contractors the department calls for specialized techniques, like infrared, painting with light, that sort of thing. Anyway, since the scene was high profile, and the Crime Scene Unit was on a skeleton staff, they decided to bring in a freelancer, so they would know all of the bases were covered."

"Ahhhh," Helen nodded. "And, Felicity got the call."

"Pretty much. From what I understand, they went down the list and she...actually I...was the first one to answer the phone."

"I see. Sorry to interrupt. Please, go on."

"Not a problem. Anyway, I'm sure you've probably seen some of the news reports, so you're aware that Wentworth's body was found in a motel in a bit of a compromising situation?"

"Yes, of course. As I recall it had something to do with bondage, did it not?"

"Yeah. Apparently Wentworth was into the whole kidnap and torture game. No biggie in my book. I mean, whatever does it for you as long as it's between consenting adults. Problem is, it looks like something went way south with the scenario because he was found with the back of his head sprayed all over the bathroom wall."

Helen held up her hand, "Please...consider yourself free to spare me those sorts of details unless you really feel them to be important."

"Sorry," I apologized. "I didn't realize you were squeamish."

"Only about certain things, but that is all right. Continue."

"Okay, well our first thought was that he had been purposely executed, but something didn't feel right about the scene to either Felicity or me."

"What were *you* doing there?"

"Helping Felicity."

"Helping her, Rowan, or trying to protect her?"

I looked over the top of my glasses at Helen. "Does anything get past you?"

"Usually, no."

"Okay, guilty. Either way, I was there and the whole scene just felt weird. You could actually sense the sexual arousal and such in the room, but that wasn't what struck us. The bizarre thing was that there was no lingering sense of fear, like you would expect if the whole scenario had been a real kidnapping. Still, Ben didn't rule it out because the whole thing could have been a setup. Plus, while he listens to me when I say I have a feeling, as we know, not everyone else does.

"Anyhow, since Wentworth was actually known to have a history with prostitutes that had been getting swept under the carpet for a while, he looked into it. After doing a little digging, it came to light that the whole kidnap and torture victim fetish was his particular kink. So, things added up in that respect, but there was still something weird going on."

"How so?"

"Felicity," I said in a matter-of-fact tone. "She started acting strange. It began with her acting…well…kind of…I guess the only delicate way to put it is sex starved. She was just plain insatiable. And, if that weren't enough, she turned into a complete bitch."

"Bitch?" Helen echoed. "That is certainly not a word I would have ever expected you to use in conjunction with your wife, Rowan."

"Tell me about it, but that's what happened. She would actually get herself aroused by berating me, or in some instances, by actually physically abusing me."

"I believe I see a rather obvious connection with your nightmare now."

"Yeah," I grunted. "Kind of brings it all into focus, doesn't it? Anyway, it was at about this time that I found out my dear, sweet wife actually has a history with the BDSM community."

"Yes."

"Yes?" I repeated, slightly puzzled. "You don't seem particularly surprised by that."

"Actually, I was already aware of it."

Slight puzzlement became brow-furrowing confusion. "I'm sorry? I'm not sure I heard you correctly."

"Remember, Rowan. Felicity has sought my counsel as well. She shared her proclivities with me quite some time ago."

"Well, that's interesting," I said in a mild huff. "Because she never bothered to tell me."

"Until now, obviously."

"Well, yeah."

"And did she give you a reason why she did not tell you before now?"

"What she said is that she was afraid I might not be open to the idea and that I would stop loving her."

"Yes. That was her concern when she spoke of it to me."

"But, she knows me better than that."

"Does she?"

"Of course she does."

"Contrary to what you may believe, Rowan, everyone has secrets. They do not necessarily keep them secret to harm or injure. Sometimes they do so in order to protect. You are a perfect example."

"Me?"

"Yes, you. How often have you lied, or simply twisted the truth, in order to protect Felicity from what you perceived as harm?"

"That's different," I objected.

"Actually, no it is not. You are simply too close to see that."

"Maybe," I half-agreed. "But she lied to me about our relationship."

"No, Rowan, she did not. She simply repressed one of her own desires in order to protect her relationship with you. She never lied."

"You're splitting hairs."

"No, I am stating a fact."

"Okay, fine," I said with a nod. In my heart I knew she was correct, so further objections wouldn't do any good. "So, what else did she tell you?"

"I am not at liberty to discuss that. Her sessions with me are confidential, as are yours."

"But you just…"

She cut me off. "I simply told you something you already knew, because she had told you herself. Please, do not ask any more about things you know I cannot discuss. Now, continue your story."

"I'm not sure that I'm comfortable with that, given what you just…"

"Rowan, you need not worry. Your wife adores you, which is the very reason she repressed this aspect of her sexuality to begin with. Believe me when I tell you there is nothing else you need to know. Now, please…go on."

"Well, I don't really see the point…"

"I, however, do."

"Okay," I huffed. "Anyway, things really escalated a couple of days later when Officer Hobbes was found dead in a motel. This time there was absolutely no question about the whole B and D, S and M thing. All of the trappings were right there in plain sight. But, this time there was a new twist to the scene. Artifacts were present that lead me to believe some sort of convoluted Voodoo ritual had taken place."

"Voodoo?"

"Yeah, Voodoo. Well, a horribly bastardized version of it really. I'll leave out the gorier details since you asked me to, but let's just say it was twisted. What happened in that room may have started out as consensual sex play, but that's not how it ended. It also didn't have anything to do with true *Vodoun* religious practice…it was just sick…

"What's even worse is that once again there was an overwhelming sense of female sexual arousal permeating the room. Almost to the point of being stifling—for me anyway. It was then that I was absolutely positive the killer was a woman and that she had literally gotten off on torturing this man to death."

"You felt it deeply, didn't you, Rowan?" Helen asked.

The tenor of her question told me she already knew the answer, but I gave it to her anyway. "Yeah. From both sides of the fence, actually."

I paused and absently attempted a drag on my cigar only to find that it had gone out once again. Instead of relighting it, I simply fiddled with the band, twisting it in an endless circle.

"Anyhow," I continued. "Felicity had a meeting with a client that morning, so she didn't go to that crime scene with me. But, while I was standing there talking to Ben, she just suddenly showed up. The problem was, it wasn't really her. She was acting haughty and abusive to everyone, calling herself Miranda, and had even started speaking with a heavy Southern drawl. That's about the time I started doing the math and figured out she was being possessed by a *Lwa*."

"Low-ahh?"

"Kind of a high ranking ancestral spirit in Voodoo culture. They are more or less the pantheon of Gods and Goddesses that *Vodoun* practitioners worship. During rituals they will invite *Lwa* into their bodies. They call it being *ridden*, and the practitioner is then called the *horse* for the particular spirit. That's basically how the ancestors speak to them from the afterlife.

"The thing is, though, *Lwa* aren't evil beings that run about torturing and killing. In a rudimentary sense they are messengers. Because of that, I figured that this particular spirit wasn't a generally accepted *Lwa* but instead had to be one that this person elevated to Godhood in her own mind."

"Thank you for the primer. However, I still do not understand what this spirit has to do with Felicity? Why would it choose to possess her?"

"That's the sixty-four thousand dollar question, Helen. I'm not sure either, but I can tell you that Felicity was being *ridden* by someone or something who wasn't particularly friendly, and that's when the so-called *incident* occurred.

"In a nutshell, after physically assaulting me and managing to twist the situation such that it got me arrested instead of her, my wife disappeared. Well, actually while Ben was getting me out of jail, she went home and changed clothes."

"That seems to be an odd thing to do."

"Normally, I'd agree, but given where she was heading, it actually made a bizarre kind of sense. So, anyhow, Ben called Agent Mandalay and asked her to stop by our house just on the off chance that Felicity went there. When she arrived, Felicity was in fact still in the house, but things went south. Felicity—actually at that point, Miranda—assaulted Agent Mandalay, somehow managed to get the upper hand then took her weapon and really did disappear for a while.

"Obviously, we managed to find her but only after several hours. And, this is why the change of clothes—she went over to a fetish nightclub on the East side, picked up a guy, and took him back to a motel."

Helen looked at me, a note of concern in her face. "But, surely she did not kill him, did she?"

I shook my head. "No. The *Lwa* jumped ship before she got that far. She did manage to do a serious number on him with her high heels, though. Literally trampled him until he was bloody and unconscious."

"Do you have any idea why the possession ended so suddenly?"

"Actually, that's typical for a *Lwa* possession. They pop in and pop out. Although, I don't have an answer for why this one didn't complete its task before it left. I suppose it could be because taking over Felicity had to be some kind of accidental collateral possession—because she doesn't practice Voodoo and certainly didn't consciously invite it in, that I'm aware of.

"In fact, prior to showing up at the Hobbes crime scene, she would tend to fight it whenever she would realize an attack was happening. Of course, that was before I had a handle on what it actually was, so I wasn't much help in that department. Anyway, I suspect she was still trying to fight it to some extent even then, so I guess it was kind of like a host rejecting a transplant or something of that sort. But, that's only a pet theory. Either way, I'm just glad she didn't kill the guy."

"How serious did his injuries turn out to be?"

"She hurt him pretty bad," I replied. "He spent a day in the hospital, which I'm sure I'll end up getting a bill for. But, when the cops talked to him, he refused to press charges against her. Seems he actually liked getting stomped on by her so much he wants to 'submit to Mistress Miranda' again. He somehow even managed to make the connection between Felicity and the pseudonym. Probably from the cops would be my guess since he was actually being urged to press charges. Anyhow, he got her business number and has called several times."

"I am sure that is disconcerting for Felicity."

"Yeah. She was a bit freaked out at first. After the fifth or sixth time though, she just switched on a whole alpha female persona and *ordered* him to stop calling her. That seemed to do the trick, for now at least."

"Obviously you think he will call again."

"He seemed pretty fixated on her, so, no, I'm not going to rule it out."

"Does this bother you?"

"Well yeah, stalkers are not something you take lightly. And, even if he isn't dangerous it's just plain annoying."

"No, Rowan. What I mean is are you jealous?"

I thought about that for a moment. I hadn't really considered jealousy as a possibility, consciously anyway, so I weighed it carefully before responding.

"I don't know, to be honest. I don't think I am. I mean, she was being *ridden* by a *Lwa* when the encounter happened, so it's not like she was cheating on me. However, she did tell me that when she snapped back to reality, she was so aroused that she didn't exactly stop right away."

"And, naturally, that concerns you," she remarked.

"Maybe a little. But, the sudden exit of a *Lwa* tends to leave the *horse* disoriented. Even if she thinks she knew what she was doing, she didn't really know what she was doing. Does that make sense?"

"Of course. However, that was not the aspect of jealousy I was asking about."

"Okay, so why else would I be jealous?'

"Because, in a sense this man is fulfilling your wife's sexual fantasies and you are not."

"Feeling a little direct today, Helen?"

"Am I not always direct?"

"Yeah, I suppose you are. For the most part."

"So?"

"So, I really haven't given it that much thought."

"Yes, Rowan, you have."

"Okay, so yeah. I have."

"And?"

"And, yeah," I shrugged. "Maybe I am a little jealous."

"Have you spoken to Felicity about it?"

"No."

"You need to."

"Yeah, you're probably right. I will when things calm down a bit."

"Good," she offered with a nod then extracted a fresh cigarette and lit it before changing the subject. "So, what about Constance? Is she well? She seemed to be fine when she attended the funeral service with Benjamin."

I hadn't even given thought to calling Agent Mandalay, Constance, when I had spoken of her earlier, even though we certainly knew one another well enough. I suppose I was so caught up in the story that the informality hadn't had a chance to creep in. Of course, it stood to reason that Helen would use her first name since the petite federal agent had been in an on-again, off-again relationship with her brother for more than a year.

"She's fine. Felicity mainly just managed to stun her enough that she could get her own handcuffs on her," I explained then quickly added, "Don't spread that around."

"Of course not. Are there going to be any repercussions?"

"I don't think so. Constance actually pulled some strings and so did Ben, so there weren't any charges filed. However…"

I felt, as much as heard my own voice trail off into silence.

"However, what, Rowan?"

"Your brother told me something when we were out looking for Felicity that night. Apparently, they found long red hairs at both crime scenes. The Wentworth scene could have been a fluke since she was physically there taking the photos, but she was never actually inside the room at the Hobbes scene, and they were there too."

"Did he tell you they were definitely from Felicity?"

"No, but they took a few samples from her for comparison when they had her in custody, and we haven't heard anything yet. In fact, ever since that day we've been *persona non grata* as far as the investigation goes. They've made no secret of the fact that they consider Felicity a "person of interest", but they haven't gone so far as to call her a suspect. At least not yet."

"I see," Helen said with a nod then turned her head and proceeded to look out at the broken cloud cover.

"Anyway, that's the story. And, that's when the nightmare started. And, like I said, it's just been getting worse since."

"So," she said after an uncomfortable pause. "Now, you believe Felicity is leading a double life and actually killed those two men."

I looked back at her with complete incredulity twisting my features. "Hell no! Where in the world did you get that?"

"So, then why is it you told me you think Felicity is the woman in your nightmare?"

I opened my mouth to reply but closed it quickly. I felt my face relax into a chagrined half smile as the realization dawned on me that I had just been the victim of a carefully guided psychological play. The truly embarrassing part was that I had cast myself in the lead role without realizing it, and all Helen had done was sit back and direct.

"Face my fear, huh?" I grunted.

"Sometimes we use swords, sometimes we use words," she replied with a shrug. "So, I take this to mean you have managed to reason yourself out of the silly notion that the cruel specter you have been battling nightly is in reality your wife?"

"Yeah," I replied with a nod.

"She may have a proclivity toward sexual dominance and mildly sadistic play, Rowan, but certainly within limits. She is no monster. You know that."

"But, the nightmare does mean something…" I ventured.

"I am certain it does. For you, they always do. You simply need to listen to what it is saying and not what you were afraid it might be inferring."

"There's just a bit of a language barrier, Helen. Dead people don't always use words quite the same way you or I do. They like to tell their tales with strange imagery and convoluted verbal references that come across as bizarre parodies of reality."

"Yes, I know."

"Yeah, well you wouldn't happen to have a *dead-to-living* dictionary laying around would you?"

"No, but given your wealth of experience in that realm, perhaps you should consider writing one."

"I doubt if it would sell."

"You might be surprised."

"Yeah, maybe. So, let me ask you something. Why didn't you just tell me I was being paranoid like I asked you to do in the beginning?"

"Because, Rowan, you would not have believed me if I had. You did, however, need someone to listen so that you could figure out for yourself that which you knew all along."

"Yeah. I guess you're right," I said. "Even so, I still have this nightmare to contend with."

"Yes, but now you can meet it on your own terms."

The relief began to fade as I felt murky shadows folding around me once again. That seemed to be the way of my life most of the time, gloomy and overcast with occasional brief periods of warmth and light. I just wished those periods of brightness would last a little longer.

"You know, Helen," I said as the weight of the ethereal darkness pressed in on me. "I have a terrible feeling that things are going to get a lot worse before they even think about getting better."

"Is that a feeling, or an intuition, Rowan?"

"A lot of both."

"I hate to say this, but I fear you are correct."

"That's not exactly comforting, Helen."

"It was not meant to be."

Friday, November 18
1:27 P.M.
Saint Louis, Missouri

CHAPTER 3:

I suppose having only three repetitions of the horrifying night terror was better than the quintuplet I had experienced the night before I visited with Helen. I'll admit I would have preferred none at all, but I wasn't going to complain. I'd take what I could get, and a reduction in frequency was as good a place as any to start.

The lower rate of recurrence wasn't the only positive note either. While the panic that always accompanied the nightmare didn't dissipate one iota, at least I didn't wake up imagining that it was my red-haired wife standing just out of my sight while harboring cruel intentions. And, even though I supposedly reasoned that out on my own, I definitely credited Helen with getting me there with my sanity intact. Or, what there was of it I suppose; because I wasn't always sure I qualified as fully *compos mentis*.

However, even though I no longer envisioned Felicity as the physical embodiment of my fear, the fact remained that the presence I felt was still undeniably female, and she was disturbingly familiar.

I was actually starting to consider making an attempt at lucid dreaming. Programming myself to remain aware and in control of the subconscious vision. Not so much for the purpose of directing the events as was the usual reason for the exercise but more to keep myself at the center of them. Or, even on the periphery for that matter. I simply wanted to watch from one point of view or the other. It really didn't matter which it was, just as long as I could stay immersed enough to once again take a cue from Helen, and "face my fear." I needed to see who this mystery woman was, if that was even possible.

Unfortunately, I'd have to dwell on that exercise a bit later because right now there was very little room for it inside my skull. I had plenty of things to deal with at the moment, and the list didn't seem to be getting any shorter. But, that was only one of the reasons for my lack of focus. The biggie was the fact that at this given moment in time my head felt like it was about to split open and spill its contents unceremoniously onto the desk before me.

I had already tossed down a handful of aspirin in an attempt to dull the throb. That had been almost an hour ago, and I was now considering adding some more to the mix. The problem was that while the first dose hadn't touched the pain in my skull, it had done an excellent job of making my stomach churn. Of course, my stomach had already been twisted into a knot to begin with, most likely because I knew this type of headache all too well.

It wasn't normal. It went far beyond off-kilter brain chemistry, sinuses, or even the immobilizing cranial thud of a bad hangover. In fact, I was pretty sure that even a deeply sickening, hangover-induced headache might have felt better right about now.

Like a fool in denial, however, I still kept trying to convince myself that it was nothing more than lack of sleep and eyestrain brought about by the numerous hours I'd been spending in front of my computer. The cold truth was, I knew better. The constant ache was just as ethereal in nature as the recurring nightmare, and it was another prime indicator that something unpleasant was going to happen. I just didn't know what or when, and no one on the other side was talking.

I shook my head gently, regretted the action, and then wondered for a moment at my own thoughts. Whenever *they* were talking, I wanted nothing more than for *them* to go away. But, when *they* fell silent, I practically begged *them* to say something, anything— especially at times such as this. It was a typical love-hate relationship between not so typical partners.

Of course, I often thought that what would make the most sense was for me to have never heard their tortured voices at all. To have never pierced the veil between the worlds, effectively becoming a conduit for the dead. It's not like it had ever brought me anything but grief.

But, there was nothing I could do about that now. I'd tried shutting the imaginary door several times, but its latch was broken and it wouldn't stay closed. Apparently, the dead were going to be waltzing in and out of my head right up until I permanently joined them on their darkened side of the threshold. Maybe then I would get some peace. Who knows? Maybe once I died it would be my turn to annoy some poor bastard back here in the land of the living who also happened to share my particular vexation. Of course, if that happened it would pretty much mean I had met a violent end, just like all of the spirits who chose to speak to me. I really couldn't say I was able to find any sort of positive spin hidden anywhere in that thought.

I pushed the unsavory musing aside and struggled to bring my attentions fully upon the task at hand, that being research. Running the computer cursor down a list of menu items, I settled upon the one I was looking for and clicked. After a moment I sat back and waited, as even though I had a fast Internet connection, the remote server doling out the requested page didn't seem to be in a particular hurry to comply.

Ever since Felicity's episode with the *Lwa* possession, I had been trying to find out everything I could about Voodoo—as well as anything related to it—and there were still a good number of questions for which I needed answers. I suppose for that reason the process had actually become more than mere research. In its own way it was a ruthless obsession. If I wasn't working or taking care of some chore around the house, I could be found reading, searching the web, or making calls to purported authorities on the subject in hopes of gathering more information. With both Felicity and me cut out of the loop on the Wentworth and Hobbes homicide cases, as well as her being a subject of that ongoing investigation, it was all I had left that I could do.

I certainly understood why we had been shut out, but that didn't mean I had to like it or like that my friend was now ignoring my calls. In fact, even though Helen had reassured me on that point, I still found it very disturbing.

Of course, it only stood to reason that we would be more or less disavowed given that the microscope was now aimed at my wife. They couldn't very well have us being privy to what they might be looking for to use as evidence against her. Not that I believed there really was anything for them to find, mind you, and I was certain their legwork would soon prove that out. Still, I simply couldn't sit idly by and wait for them to finish because I also wasn't necessarily willing to trust the police in this specific endeavor.

The fact is, there were some serious underlying issues at play. I had begun consulting for the Greater Saint Louis Major Case Squad somewhere around five years ago. Ever since the first time the tortured spirit of a murdered young woman had chosen to slap me across the back of the head with an ethereal two-by-four and beg my help. It hadn't been easy getting someone to listen, even my close friend, Ben. But, eventually he had come around, as well as a few others within the local law enforcement community. Since then, I'd racked up more than my share of unwanted press clippings, but that was something that came with the territory. Headlines like "Self-Proclaimed Witch Solves Serial Murder Case" tend to sell papers. Unfortunately, it got to be my not-so-smiling face displayed beneath the bold type.

The real problem, however, was that while there were those who realized I could be a benefit, I also had some extremely vocal detractors. There were more than a few who felt my ethereal visions were just parlor tricks and bids for attention. Others literally claimed it to be the work of Satan. Those were the ones who even went so far as to publicly denounce me purely because of my chosen religious path.

Under different circumstances I would have just tried to ignore them like I usually did, but this was a completely different situation. It was largely because of the fact that some of these individuals held fairly high-ranking positions that I wasn't convinced of a fair and impartial investigation. In my mind, finding the real killer was the best way to be sure Felicity wouldn't get railroaded as a way of getting to me. I tended not to voice that too much because I knew that it sounded like the convoluted plot of a Hollywood conspiracy thriller, but the truth is that it was pretty much my life in a nutshell.

On top of it all, my need to clear Felicity hadn't completely overshadowed the fact that a terribly sick sociopath was still out there.

A sexual sadist none of whose games were safe, sane, or consensual. It didn't take an advanced degree to surmise that she was going to kill again. Since I knew for a fact the police were looking in the wrong place and were showing all the signs of continuing to do so, it fell to me to do something about it before she produced another victim.

Adding up everything I already knew, it seemed that finding out all I could about Voodoo would be the best course of action under the circumstances. I hoped that the knowledge would provide the clues necessary to track down the person responsible, and some of the primary leads I was following were the symbols, called *veve*, which were left behind at the second scene.

I'd had no trouble identifying two of them as belonging to generally accepted figures within Voodoo practice, those being *Papa Legba* and *Ezili Dantò*. The third, however, remained as elusive as a real steak in a vegetarian restaurant. The best I'd been able to determine was that it had been patterned after a symbol widely used within the bondage community. Not surprising, I suppose, given the mind-set of the killer, even though her version of the lifestyle was twisted and grotesque. Still, that didn't give me the name of a *Lwa*, and that missing bit of information just fueled my need to know. If the *veve* didn't belong to a generally accepted spirit, then there had to be more to it. There had to be something special about that ancestor that might lead me to the killer.

Certainly, something else I wanted to know was whether or not Felicity's preternatural incident had actually been her body being used as a *horse* by the *Lwa*. I was almost certain that it was, but there was still a small, nagging doubt. What if it was something else entirely? I couldn't imagine what that might be; however, I couldn't deny that she had been known to channel both the dead and the living herself, just like me. Her brush with that affliction was something for which I blamed myself because she had opened herself up to the other side of the veil when trying to protect me. And, as I had discovered, once they had their foot in the door, it was all over. They were unwanted houseguests with no intention of ever leaving.

Still, channeling was one thing. In this case what she had done was completely out of the park, at least in my experience. Either way, the thing that troubled me even more was whether or not it was going to happen again, whatever the cause turned out to be.

Therefore, it was for those reasons, and a number of others, that I once again found myself sitting in front of my computer, books piled about me, and the contact page of a university's website glowing on my screen.

I suddenly noticed that the page was now finished loading, and the screen had been refreshed. In fact, it probably had been for several minutes because, in truth, I had just caught myself staring off into space. I rocked forward in my desk chair and looked at the blurry lines of type displayed against a muted background.

I rubbed my eyes then pushed my glasses back up onto the bridge of my nose. I blinked hard, trying not only to focus but also to forget the headache that was still raging inside my skull. Finding what I was after, I picked up the telephone handset and put it against my ear. Glancing between the phone and my monitor, I punched in the number listed on the web page before me. Before it even began to ring at the other end, I rocked back in my chair and began idly moving the mouse across the surface of my desk as if doodling on a notepad. A moment later, the buzzing tones abated and were followed by the sound of the phone being taken off-hook.

"Louisiana State University Department of Sociology," a woman's voice eventually drawled into my ear. "How may I direct your call?"

"Doctor Rieth's office, please," I replied.

"Please hold."

I continued watching the pointer as I nudged it around the screen. My real attention, however, remained focused on the hollow sound of the phone as I waited for the transfer to occur.

A minute or so passed before there was a dull click at the other end and a new voice issued from the handset. "Doctor Rieth's office, this is Kathy, may I help you?"

"Good afternoon, Kathy," I said as I rocked back forward and straightened my posture. "Is Doctor Rieth in by any chance?"

"No sir, I'm afraid she's gone for the holiday break. I'm her assistant, can I help you?"

It hadn't even dawned on me that Thanksgiving was less than one week away at this point. Considering that, I was probably fortunate to have reached anyone at the university at all.

"No offense, but probably not," I replied. "I'm calling from Saint Louis, and I need to speak with the doctor about something in her book, *Voodoo Practice in American Culture*."

I glanced at the corner of my desk where the tome was resting atop a pile of other books, all with the same general subject matter, Afro-Cuban religion and mysticism.

"I'm sorry, sir, but all queries regarding Doctor Rieth's books should be made via the University Press," Kathy replied, launching into a decidedly prepared sounding spiel. "The address can be found…"

"I understand that," I spoke up, truncating her instructions. "Please understand that I'm not looking for an autograph or trying to dispute her or anything like that. I'm doing some research regarding a murder investigation here, and I think she might be able to help me."

There was no reply from the other end, but I could still hear background noise, so I knew she hadn't hung up.

"Hello?" I said.

"Yes, I'm here," the assistant replied. "I'm sorry. Where did you say you were calling from again?"

"Saint Louis, Missouri, why?"

"Just curious. Doctor Rieth received a call a year or so back from a police officer in South Carolina regarding a murder investigation."

My curiosity was immediately piqued. "Really? Do you remember any of the details?"

"No," she replied. "And, honestly, I really shouldn't have said anything."

"That's okay, I won't tell," I replied half jokingly then moved on rather than risk alienating her. "Is there any way I can reach Doctor Rieth? It's very important."

"I'm afraid not," she replied. "She is scheduled to return the Monday after the holiday however."

I wasn't excited about the wait, but it was just that time of year, so there was little I could do. I went ahead and asked, "Do you think it would be possible for me to leave a message for the doctor then?"

"Yes sir, I can certainly do that," she answered. "Which police department are you with again?"

"I'm actually an independent consultant," I explained then took the truth and wrapped it into an interwoven pretzel before relaying it to her. "I'm currently working with the Greater Saint Louis Major Case Squad."

It wasn't a complete lie, but I hoped that the doctor didn't elect to verify my story because under the current circumstances, I was betting no one would be willing to back me up.

I finished giving her my contact information and bid her a pleasant afternoon before hanging up and pondering what the young woman had just let slip. Hopefully, if and when Doctor Rieth returned my call, she would be willing to share a bit more about what she had consulted on in South Carolina.

I picked up a pen and jotted a quick note about it in a steno pad I had been using for keeping track of my research. I heard the dogs barking outside and wondered for a moment if they were wanting back in the house. I started to get up, but they quieted down before I could get completely out of my seat, so I figured it must be a taunting squirrel or simply a passerby. When I settled back into the chair, however, a familiar prickling sensation crawled across the back of my neck as I felt my hair pivoting at the roots.

I reached up and rubbed the offending spot as I looked around the room. I couldn't imagine a reason for the brief attack of shivers. It faded quickly so I tried to put it out of my mind.

Returning to the materials I had at hand, I shuffled through the stack of books on my desk and withdrew another one, heavily laden with bookmarks protruding from the end, and flipped it open to the copyright page. I was just about to begin typing in the publisher's website address in search of contact information for the author when I heard the doorbell ring.

Now I had my answer as to why the dogs had been barking.

I knew Felicity was downstairs in her darkroom and probably wouldn't be able to answer it. In reality, most of her work these days was digital and didn't require the somewhat antiquated processes of chemicals and light sensitive papers. However, I had the impression that my wife was finding the familiarity and closeness of her analog workspace a comfort in the wake of her recent experience. Put simply, she was hiding from the world, and while I was willing to condone it for a brief period, I wasn't going to allow her to do it forever. But, at this particular moment, I wasn't going to press the issue.

I tossed the book back onto the pile and pushed away from my desk. I found that I had to skirt around Dickens, our black feline, who had elected to take a nap almost immediately in front of the office door. He opened one yellow eye and regarded me silently as I stepped over him, but other than that he didn't even twitch.

I was making my way down the stairs when the doorbell pealed once again in a rapid staccato.

"Hold on!" I yelled, not that I really expected anyone outside to hear me. "I'm coming, I'm coming..."

I skipped the last couple of stairs near the bottom, making the turn at the landing, and almost jogged across the living room. With a quick turn of my wrist, I unlocked the door and swung it open.

My friend, homicide detective Benjamin Storm was standing on my front porch, along with someone else I thought I recognized as a member of the MCS but to whom I couldn't place a name. Neither of them looked particularly happy, but I didn't need to see their expressions to know something was wrong. The warning signs had been there for a while now. I had just been too absorbed, and even more unwilling, to pay attention to them.

Ben reached out and pulled the storm door open, looking at me quietly for a heartbeat or two before saying, "Do you mind if we come in, Row?"

I definitely didn't like the sound of his voice, and my skin started prickling once again.

"That depends, Ben," I replied evenly. "Do I have any choice in the matter?"

He reached up and smoothed his hair back, looked down at the porch briefly, then back up to my face. "Actually… No."

"Do I need to call our attorney?" I asked.

He returned a shallow nod. "It'd be a good idea, Row."

What transpired in the fifteen minutes following that simple statement set a series of events into motion that, if they didn't kill me, would undoubtedly leave an indelible scar upon my life, and the lives of those I loved.

CHAPTER 4:

"**D**ammit, Ben!" I screamed. "Talk to me! Why won't you tell me what the hell is happening here!"

"Rowan, you know damn good 'n well what this is about!" my friend shot back. "A dead federal judge and a dead copper."

"Bullshit! Politics is what it's about," I snarled at him. "Who's behind this? Albright?"

I almost gagged on the name of the cop whose life's mission seemed to be anything that involved making my very existence unbearable. Captain Barbara Albright, self-appointed leader of the "God Squad."

Of course, there you had it, plain and simple.

When you took into consideration the fact that she was an old school, fundamentalist Christian with a badge, and I was a Neopagan Witch who consulted for the police department, we were bound to clash. The problem was, it was even worse than that. In plain truth we weren't just at polar opposites; in many ways we seemed almost to be one another's arch nemesis. Unfortunately, she tended to take that idea very seriously and more often than not would push things way too far.

She had already interjected her opinions and views into the current investigation, casting aspersions on both Felicity and me. Out of all of my detractors, she had been the one I most feared would skew the investigation. Given how vocal she had already been, it stood to reason that she would be behind this action. However, in my estimation, her habit of pushing things too far had just turned into shoving them completely over the edge and gleefully watching them fall.

"Look, I already said this a dozen times," my friend spat in reply. "Ya' got the goddamned warrants right there in your hand. Read 'em!"

I barked in return as I waved the sheaf of legal documents in the air, "And, I've told you every time you said it that I already did and they don't tell me a fucking thing."

"Well, try readin' 'em again!"

Ben stared back at me, grimly silent on the heels of the shouted order. I had to keep my head tilted back to meet his gaze, as he stood six-foot-six and was, therefore, better than a head taller than me. He carried himself on an overtly muscular frame that often made him seem larger than life, and in a sense, almost heroic.

His classic, angular features, which not only broadcast his pure Native American heritage but also served him well in forming his handsome visage, were now creased into a hard scowl. The deep lines made him look less like my friend and more like the stoic "Injun on the warpath" from an old Western. All he needed were some feathers and face paint to make the caricature complete.

In fact, a travesty is all that was left of him in my mind, for at this particular moment, even though his dark eyes were betraying his own turbulent mix of emotions, any sense of heroism I envisioned in him had long since fled. To me, he had become no more than a threatening obstacle standing dead in the middle of my path.

He sighed heavily then shook his head and cast his eyes toward the floor. Out of reflex he reached up with a large hand to smooth his jet-black hair. This was a mannerism I'd seen countless times, and it was something he always did whenever he was thinking hard on a subject. I stood watching him, and in the wake of the motion, I could see salty flecks of grey that I knew for certain had been there for quite some time but now seemed to be appearing right before my eyes. It was as if he was visibly aging as he stood there.

Under the circumstances, I think perhaps we both were.

I waited for a healthy measure, or at least I think I did. I know I tried. Unfortunately, my patience was as thin as the dry, paper-like skin of an onion right now and even more brittle. I wasn't interested in giving him time to think about anything. I wanted answers and I wanted them ten minutes ago.

"Tell me what's going on, Ben!" I repeated my demand for the umpteenth time.

"GODDAMMIT, ROWAN! I CAN'T!" he shouted then suddenly slammed the heel of his fist hard against the doorframe before repeating in a near whisper, "I just...can't."

Whether we were getting somewhere or not, I couldn't say, but this was the first time he had given me a response other than "you know" or "read the warrants."

My friend looked over his shoulder through the glass of the storm door as it slowly worked its way toward obscuring the view by fogging over with condensation. After a second he looked back at me and muttered, "Jeezus fuckin' Christ, Row...don'tcha think I wanna tell ya'?"

I didn't let up. "You sure as hell aren't acting like it."

"Sonofabitch! Dammit...I...Jeez...I...It's...Shit! Fuck me! Dammit, Row, I just can't!" He stuttered through the sentence as his morose tone ramped back into anger.

Mine, however, had never ramped down. "That's not good enough!"

"Well it's gonna hafta be for now!"

Ben Storm was probably my second best friend walking the face of the planet—period, end of story. However, at this instant I was within a hair's breadth of planting my fist square on his chin replete with every last speck of strength, anger, and unfettered malice I could muster. Never mind the fact that it would probably be the one and only shot I would get before he pummeled me into the middle of next month, or even that he was a cop with a gun and a similarly armed partner sitting in a vehicle in my driveway. Right now, none of that mattered to me.

What did matter, more than anything, was what had brought the two of us to the brink of a violent, physical confrontation such as this. And, that, beyond any shadow of a doubt, would be my best friend. Not my *second* best friend, but my first, and absolute, *best* friend—a petite, redheaded, Irish-American woman whose name was typed prominently upon the warrants.

And, the thing about my dear and lovely wife that had me on the edge of committing assault against Ben was the fact that I had just stood here in my living room and watched him place her in handcuffs then recite to her the Miranda rights of silence.

Miranda.

Now there was irony in all its glory considering that one simple word, the name "Miranda", had everything to do with the head-on collision my life, my friend's life, and moreover, my wife's life had just become.

Our screaming match was far from over, and since it was my turn I shouted back, "Something, Ben! You've got to be able to tell me *something!*"

"I told you, I CAN'T!"

"Fuck that! What you mean is you WON'T!"

"Goddammit, Rowan! What I mean is I CAN'T! Do ya' really think I like this any more than you do?"

"Ben, you just arrested my wife for murder! You can't just do that then walk out like nothing's happened! You've got to give me some answers here!"

He huffed out a breath then dropped his forehead into his hand and allowed it to rest there for a moment before pushing his palm back through his hair once again. This time, he left the large paw clamped onto his neck and began working his fingers against the muscles.

"I wish I could."

"Well, answer me this: Why aren't you arresting me too?"

"We ain't got a reason. But trust me, it was mentioned."

"Dammit, you don't have a reason to arrest her either!"

"I'm afraid we do, Row."

"What is it? Tell me."

"Look," he offered. "I'm not even s'posed to say this, but all I can tell ya' is there's hard evidence that Firehair might be the one that killed Hammond Wentworth and Officer Hobbes."

I found myself offended by the fact that he called her Firehair. The use of the friendly moniker he had long ago dubbed Felicity with seemed inappropriately familiar under the circumstances. Considering what he had just done, I didn't feel he had that right. I started to say something but decided against it before the words could leave my throat. No matter what my visceral response to it, the truth is, the hypocrisy I saw in his use of the nickname really wasn't what was important right now.

Instead, I focused on the crux of what he had just said and made a demand. "What kind of evidence? Surely not the hairs you said they found at the Wentworth scene."

"I can't say, Row."

"Well, whatever it is, it's bullshit and you know it. She didn't kill anyone."

"I…she…crap…" he muttered.

"Dammit, Ben, think about it! If she killed Wentworth and Hobbes, then why didn't she kill that character she picked up at the club?"

"I dunno. You tell me. For all you know she might've if things had gone different."

"No, she wouldn't have and here's why—because she didn't kill any of them. I told you what was going on. She was possessed by a *Lwa* that night."

"Dammit, Row, that's not gonna fly an' you know it. Not with my superiors and sure as fuck not with a court."

"It's still the truth."

"Yeah. Maybe."

"Maybe?" I snipped. "So now you don't believe me either?"

"I didn't say that."

"Yeah, well from where I'm standing you haven't said much, period."

He didn't reply. He just kept working on the knotted muscle in his shoulder.

"So, what's this hard evidence?" I pressed, returning to my original query. "Tell me."

"I've already said more than I should."

"Damn you, Ben," I growled.

He sucked in a quick breath and pulled his hand from his shoulder, stiffly jabbing his index finger toward me. His eyes glowered as his face hardened once again, and his mouth opened in preparation to deliver some manner of angry ripost. However, no sound issued from him even though his jaw slowly worked at forming the words.

After a tense exhale he lowered his hand and shook his head. With a sad note underscoring his words, he mumbled, "Yeah, Row. Damn me. That's fine. If it makes ya' feel better, go ahead an' damn me all ya' want."

We stared at one another in almost total silence for a handful of heartbeats. I couldn't think of anything else to say. I wanted answers I wasn't going to get, even from my friend. With that avenue closed to me, I was suddenly feeling very flustered. I suspected the only thing keeping me from losing any semblance of rationality I still maintained was the seething anger that filled my very being.

For that very reason, I clung to the outrage like a lifeline.

Ben turned and glanced out the fogged door once again, pushing it open for a moment to get a better view. When he looked back to me, he broke the silence. "The guys from the CSU just pulled up. Their gonna hafta search the house."

"I pretty much got that from the handful of papers. What are they looking for?"

"Look at the warrant. It's all listed."

"I did and it's pretty goddamned ambiguous, Ben."

"Yeah, well that's how they write 'em."

"Obviously. So what are they really looking for?"

"I can't tell ya'. You should know that."

"Uh-huh, that seems to be your answer for everything right now."

He shook his head. "They're lookin' for evidence, Row. Evidence."

"Dammit, Ben. This is wrong and you know it."

"Call your lawyer," he said. "And light a candle...or burn some incense...or whatever the hell you Witches do. 'Cause I'm tellin' ya' now, Felicity's gonna need it."

"This isn't over, Ben."

"Jeezus, Row, believe me...I hope like hell you're right."

"I want to talk to her before you go," I demanded.

"She's already in custody."

"Yeah. No shit."

"What I'm sayin' is that means I can't let ya' talk to 'er. Not now. Not yet."

"Bullshit! Get out of my way. I'm talking to her."

"I just told ya', you can't," he replied in a far more stern tone, punctuating it with a shake of his head. "Don't make this any harder than it already is."

"The hell I can't!" I shot back as I started forward.

I didn't get very far.

I was stopped cold as the palm of Ben's hand thudded hard in the center of my chest. I wasn't surprised that he would do something of the sort, but I also had no intention of letting it stop me for very long. I instantly lashed out, swinging my right arm wide in a roundhouse punch.

Of course, I should have realized that he would be expecting it. As turbulent as the past few minutes had been, he had probably been waiting for me to do something stupid all along. And, stupid was putting it mildly.

My friend's left arm shot upward out of trained reflex, sliding against mine and deflecting my angry fist harmlessly away. With a quick thrust of his right, he pushed me hard. Since my wildly careening punch already had me off balance, it didn't take much for him to launch me backward across the room.

I stumbled a pair of steps before completely losing my footing, and a split second later sharp pain shot through my buttocks as they impacted the floor. That sensation was almost instantly followed by a stab of agony lancing into my left elbow when it came down against the hardwood, and finally there was a dull thunk on the back of my head from striking the arm of the chair. That last blow didn't exactly do wonders for my already throbbing grey matter.

I heard myself yelp, and then I started to scramble upward but only came a few inches off the floor before dropping back down with a heavy thud. Dull pain was radiating from my tailbone up through my lower back, and my nerves were more than just a little jangled.

"Jeezus! Fuck me! Goddammit, Rowan!" Ben sputtered with more than enough anger to fill the room to capacity. "GOD DAMMIT! GOD DAMMIT!"

I was definitely stunned from the fall, and my ears were now ringing, so his tirade came at me as a muted string of syllables. Fortunately, I didn't feel any queasiness or a blackout coming on, so I didn't think I was truly injured.

However, I just kept sitting there, motionless, letting my rage work as an anesthetic for all the pain, emotional as well as physical.

Ben's tone ratcheted down the scale from anger to remorse in the span of a single sentence. "Awww, Jeez, Row…Man…What'd ya' hafta fuckin' go an' do that for?!"

I assumed the question was rhetorical, not that I had really intended to answer him if it wasn't. Still, I couldn't help but throw one of his earlier comments back in his face.

"I think you know," I spat.

"Jeezus…Are ya' okay?" He stepped forward as he spoke, extending his arm and offering me a hand up.

I simply shrugged away from him.

"Row…"

"Fuck you, Ben," I told him.

"Dammit, Row, this…"

"Get out of my house," I ordered, my voice a low growl, fully devoid of any compassion. "Just...Just get out of my house."

He stood there, looking down at me with abject sadness welling behind his eyes. What just happened was something neither one of us was going to be able to fix, at least, not right at this moment. And, the way I was feeling, I wasn't sure if I ever wanted it fixed. I had a sickening notion that I was going to need every bit of my anger just to get through what was coming, and that was assuming that I was going to make it through at all.

The silent pause continued with us both staring at one another, him pained, me incensed. I allowed it to continue for what seemed a full minute but was in reality probably no more than a scant few seconds.

"You heard me you sonofabitch!" I finally screamed. "Get the fuck out of my house!"

With a dazed shake of his head and one last look of sadness, he turned and headed for the door.

CSU technicians were already coming into the house as Ben was lumbering out. One of them shot me a concerned look, glanced over his shoulder at Ben's back as he disappeared down the front steps, and then returned his gaze to me.

"Are you okay, sir?" he asked.

"No," I snipped.

He reached his hand toward me and started to ask, "Do you need..."

"No!" I cut him off, my tone still livid. "Just leave me alone!"

He shook his head and muttered a sarcastic "Excuse me" as he took a step back then turned away and joined up with the other techs as they began fanning out through my home.

I didn't bother to drag myself up from the floor until I heard Ben's vehicle back out of the driveway then speed away, taking my entire reason for living with it.

CHAPTER 5:

"This isn't good," Jackie's voice hummed from the earpiece of the phone.

Our attorney had patiently listened to me as I relayed to her the story of Felicity's arrest, interrupting me only when necessary to ask for clarification on particular facts. Then, following a proverbial pregnant pause at the end of my diatribe, those three words were all she said. Unfortunately, they were far from what I wanted to hear.

Jackie had a habit of thinking out loud, and I'm certain that the comment was nothing more than her rhetorically voicing her thoughts. However, I was still at least five notches beyond pissed off, not to mention the fact that a handful of crime scene technicians were turning my house into a disaster area all around me as I stood there. Therefore, I was really in no mood for listening to someone tell me something I already knew. Especially when it wasn't helping to fix the problem.

"No fucking shit," I spat into the handset. "Are you billing me for that? Because I already had it figured out on my own."

"Okay," she returned, far more calmly than I expected. "The first thing you need to do, Rowan, is settle down. Biting people's heads off isn't going to help the situation. Especially when the head you're biting off is mine. I'm on your side, remember?"

"Yeah, well you'll have to excuse me. I'm still trying to pry a knife out of my back that was put there by someone else who was supposed to be on my side."

"Your friend the cop? The one who arrested Felicity?"

"I wouldn't exactly call him my friend. Not now. Not after this."

"You might need to take a step back and look at it from a different perspective, Rowan."

"I'm not so sure that there *is* another perspective on this."

"Oh, I don't know about that," she replied. "Think about this. You're in a big city where they usually frown on having police officers arresting their friends. You aren't in a small town where everyone knows everyone else, and there's no choice in the matter. It would be better for the department to avoid a conflict of interest like this."

"Yeah, so what's your point?"

"My point is that your friend probably had to pull some' major strings to be allowed to make the arrest rather than allowing someone else to take her in. He most likely saw what he was doing as a favor."

My reply was so sharply edged with sarcasm I'm surprised I didn't cut my own tongue. "Yeah, some favor."

"I suspect he was trying to spare you from the anguish of having strangers show up and haul Felicity away."

I stayed silent for a moment and thought about what she had just said. I finally replied, "Well, I guess he did make it a point to repeatedly tell her not to say a word. The other cop with him wasn't real excited about that at all."

"You need to give your friend some credit, Rowan. I'm sure he was only doing what he thought was best for his friends, given the situation," Her statement was punctuated by an electromechanical "ding" in the background then the hollow quality that had surrounded her voice disappeared. I could hear a droning background noise and assumed she must have just stepped from the elevator in her office building and was on her way past the decorative waterfall in the lobby.

"Maybe," I replied. "But, this is wrong and he knows it."

"Yes, I'm sure that he does. But, obviously she was going to be arrested anyway given the fact that a warrant was issued. So, who would you rather have had do it?"

I didn't think she really wanted an answer to the question so I just grunted.

"Now, the reason I said this isn't good is the fact that they even had a warrant to begin with and that they came and got her on a Friday."

"What's that got to do with it?"

"Well, first off arrest warrants aren't typically issued on felony cases if there is probable cause. Especially where violent crime is concerned. The arrest is simply made and the charges get filed. The warrant is just paperwork that happens during the process as a matter of course.

"Someone is definitely dotting I's and crossing T's on this one. Being very cautious and official about it. So, that tells me one of two things. One, they don't have much of a case so they are playing it by the book..."

"That's a good thing, right?" I interrupted hopefully, a sudden brightness in my voice.

"If that's the case, yes," she answered then proceeded to extinguish my momentary glow. "However, it could also mean that they are pretty certain they have a smoking gun, and they're just being careful because of their long time affiliation with you as a consultant.

"Either way, one thing is perfectly clear. She is no longer simply under investigation. She's been moved up from person of interest to prime suspect."

"Damn."

"Of course, we won't know for sure what is going on until I can get there and get a read on the situation."

"Whatever it is, the one behind it has got to be Albright," I mumbled. "She's a bureaucrat with a badge and she hates both of us. She's tried to pull stunts before, and I can just about guarantee you she'll do whatever it takes to make this stick."

"Well, whoever it is, they're playing for keeps. Warrants aren't issued on whims. They've got *something* they think is damaging, or she wouldn't be in custody right now."

"Okay, so what about it being Friday? What's up with that?"

"The courts are closed over the weekend, Rowan, and it's..." she paused for a moment. "...It's already after two in the afternoon. Given the nature of the arrest, I seriously doubt I'm going to be able to do much in the way of getting an emergency bail hearing. Unless there was a bail amount on the arrest warrant already."

"I don't remember seeing one."

"I'm not surprised. It would be pretty much unheard of in a homicide case, and with this being a high profile double murder charge…so, anyway, what it all means is that I'm afraid Felicity is going to be spending the weekend, at the very least, in jail. To be honest, Rowan, probably longer. Bail in a homicide case like this is going to be unlikely, and even on the off chance we can get it set, it will be exorbitant."

"I don't care. I've got money."

"We could be talking millions, Rowan, and even though you'll only need ten percent in cash, it could mount up."

"I can cash in our IRA's if I have to."

"I understand, but remember it could all be a moot point. Like I said, bail might not even be an option depending on what they have."

"Dammit!" I spat. "You aren't telling me what I need to hear."

"Actually, yes I am. I'm just not telling you what you *want* to hear."

"Yeah. Okay. Fine. So what now?"

"Now, I need to ask you a question."

"What?"

"You aren't going to like it."

"Yeah, so why should my day suddenly start getting better?" I returned sarcastically. "What's the question?"

I heard her take in a deep breath, and a second later she hit me with the last thing I expected. "Is Felicity guilty? Did she kill those men?"

"Hell no! How can you ask me that?! What happened to being on my side?!"

"It's my job, Rowan. I have to know what I'm up against and whom I'm defending. You're absolutely certain she's innocent?"

"Yes," I returned harshly. "And don't ever ask me that again."

"I won't. Not you. But you need to understand that I'm going to have to ask Felicity the same thing."

"And you'll get the same answer."

Here we had a slight problem. And, that problem came in the form of the fact that I wasn't entirely sure I was telling the truth with that last comment. The night Felicity had been taken into custody at the East side motel, the suspicious fingers were already being pointed and the investigation underway. When I discussed it with her, she had told me that she wasn't even certain in her own mind that she hadn't committed the crimes. The *Lwa* possession had caused substantial blocks of time to be missing from her memory, and that frightened her. It didn't do much for me either, but I still knew she was innocent. Why, when the police apparently had evidence to the contrary, I couldn't say; but the fact remained that I knew it beyond any doubt in my mind.

Unfortunately, something else I knew was that my wife was still harboring distrust in her own sanity. And, because of her personal history within the bondage and D/S subculture, she was finding it easy to convince herself that perhaps she really was the killer. The truth was, when Jackie asked her the question, she was very likely to say, "I don't know." What was even more frightening was that it was going to be a bit before Jackie got there. Given Felicity's mental state, depending on what she was told by the police between now and then, her answer could well be "Yes. I think I'm guilty."

That single possibility, all by itself, scared me as much as anything ever could right now.

"Find a way to get her home, Jackie. I know that's asking a lot, but I need her home. I need her home NOW."

"I'll do what I can," she offered. "But, you need to be prepared for this."

"Prepared?" Incredulity filled my voice. "Okay, then why don't you tell me how I'm supposed to prepare myself for my wife spending time in jail on a bogus murder charge."

"I wish I knew, Ro..."

The end of her sentence was truncated by an annoying beep issuing from the earpiece of my phone. Lately, I had been ignoring the call-waiting when it chimed in, due to a recent resurgence of mysterious hang-ups that had been plaguing us off and on for the past few years. Under the circumstances, however, I thought it might be a good idea to answer it this time.

"I've got another call coming in. Can you hold for a sec?"

"Listen, I'm almost to my car," she replied. "Why don't you go ahead and answer the call. I'll get back to you when I get to the police station and have a handle on things."

"Don't you want me to meet you there?"

"Absolutely not. There's nothing you can do at this point, and emotionally you're a bomb looking for a place to explode. You'd do nothing but cause trouble and make things worse. Just stay right there while they're searching the house, and don't do anything stupid."

The insistent beep chimed in again.

"What do you mean?"

"I mean just stay there and don't do *anything*," she instructed, heavily emphasizing the last word. "I need to concentrate on your wife right now, so I don't need to be worrying about you too."

I answered in a clipped tone. "Yeah. Fine. Okay. Later."

I didn't wait for her to say goodbye. I reached out and stabbed the off-hook switch on the telephone's base with my finger, held it for a second, and then released it. A second later I heard the telltale click rattling in the earpiece as the call I had just been on was disconnected.

"Hello?" I said into the mouthpiece.

"Rowan," a familiar voice floated into my ear. "How are you doing?"

I sighed, half from relief and half from frustration. It obviously wasn't a hang-up, but it also wasn't someone calling to tell me this had all been a terrible mistake either. Of course, logically I knew that wasn't going to happen, but under stress we tend to create fantastic resolutions for situations simply in order to maintain hope, and that was but one of the happy endings bouncing around inside my skull at the moment.

"I've been better, Helen," I replied, my tone flat.

"I know, Rowan. Benjamin just called and told me what happened."

"I suppose he wants you to find out if I'm still mad at him," I quipped.

I knew I shouldn't be taking my anger with her brother, and the situation, out on her; but I just couldn't help myself. The way I saw it, everyone in my path was a potential enemy at this point.

"Actually, Rowan, no, he does not. I believe he is fully expecting you to be angry with him for some time to come. He has resigned himself to that."

"Very astute observation on his part," I asserted. "Mainly because he's right."

"He was forced to make an extremely hard decision."

"Well, I've got some bad news for him. He decided wrong. Felicity is innocent and he knows it."

"I am speaking of his decision to handle the arrest rather than allow someone else from the department to do so."

Apparently, Jackie had been correct. Still, it didn't change the fact that he had led my wife out of the house in handcuffs.

"Yeah, well, he just might have been wrong on that count too."

"Be that as it may, it really is not my point, Rowan."

"I'm listening."

"He is concerned."

"Yeah, well no offense, Helen, but I've got other things on my mind right now, so if he's looking for absolution tell him to try a confessional."

"He is not concerned about forgiveness. He is worried about *you.*"

"Could've fooled me."

"Rowan," Helen's voice took on a stern quality I wasn't used to hearing when speaking with her. "Stop this. I know that you have a dire situation with which to cope. And, after our talk yesterday I think that I, better than anyone, know the stress you have been facing lately.

"I want you to understand that I am certainly not begging sympathy for my brother. However, as both a therapist and as your friend, I am telling you that you simply must let go of some of this anger."

"I can't, Helen. It's all that's keeping me afloat right now."

"In the short run, I would say that is a good thing. However, I know you, Rowan. You will not let this subside, and you will continue feeding it. If you do that, then it is no longer a good thing. It becomes unhealthy."

"Well, we all have our addictions, don't we?" I replied, making a veiled reference to her chain smoking. "I guess this one will be mine for the time being."

I was sorry I made the stab as soon as it came out of my mouth, but what was done was done. I'm certain she caught my meaning, she was too smart and far too quick not to. Still, she graciously ignored it. I suppose she was used to people lashing out when under stress.

"If so, then I suspect you will again be needing my services when you finally sink," she told me in an almost purely clinical voice. "Because trust me, you are going to be hitting the bottom very fast and very hard. I am serious, Rowan. *Very* hard."

"Then I suppose I'll just have to hope you can dredge me up and put me back together when the time comes."

"I believe we will both be hoping for that," she offered and then paused. I could hear her let out a small sigh before continuing, "You are a very stubborn man, Rowan. I hope you realize that I did not call to argue with you."

I closed my eyes and shook my head. For the first time in the past few hours, the motion didn't cause me excruciating pain. My headache had mellowed down to a dull thud for the moment, but I wasn't expecting it to stay that way for long.

"I know, Helen," I told her. "I'm just not in a very good place right now."

"I know. And trust me, Benjamin is truly concerned for your well being right now. As am I."

"Join the club. That seems to be the order of the day."

"Did you have the nightmare again?" she asked, momentarily switching the subject.

"Yeah. Three times last night."

"And, how did you feel?"

"Scared."

"Yes, but what about the other issue. The one involving your wife."

"It's a non-issue."

"Good. Your faith in Felicity is going to be monumentally important in the coming days, Rowan."

"Yeah," I grunted. "Tell me about it."

I happened to look up toward the stairs as I made the comment and noticed a crime scene technician on his way down, arms filled with books.

He called past me to another tech in the living room, "Looks like we've got something here."

I could see that the "something here" he had in hand was every text on Voodoo and Afro-Caribbean Mysticism I had purchased, or checked out from the library, in the past week.

"Those are mine," I called out to him.

He continued down the stairs, ignoring me completely.

"I said, those are mine," I stressed. "I just bought them."

Helen was calling to me from the earpiece, "Rowan? Rowan, what is wrong?"

The technician finally shot me a glance and shook his head. "Sorry sir. Now they're evidence."

My hand was already moving to hang up the phone even as I spoke. "Helen, I've got to go."

CHAPTER 6:

"**E**xactly which part of 'I just bought those' are you having trouble understanding?" I barked. "And, if you'll look closely you'll see I got a few of them from the library as well."

My objections had gone unheeded for the most part, and me simply being angry was starting to become me being flat-out, livid pissed. Even as I spoke, the stack of books was being placed in a paper evidence bag.

"Dammit! You aren't taking those!" I almost shouted.

"Calm down, Mister Gant." The lead crime scene technician tried to soothe me as his subordinate continued the process of securing the evidence, tagging it, and adding a description to the log.

"Calm down? My wife's been arrested, you're tearing my house apart, and now you're going to take something that belongs to me and has nothing to do with this, all so you can use it against her? Calm down my ass!"

I would have simply pushed the man aside and gone after the technician who was actually bagging the books, but the situation had recently taken on a new layer of complexity. That layer came in the form of two uniformed Briarwood police officers who were presently standing in very close proximity to our heated disagreement. They had arrived at the house within a scant few minutes of the evidence technicians and had been quietly surveying the goings on from the middle of the dining room ever since. Until now, that is.

When they originally showed up, I assumed it had something to do with cooperation between jurisdictions. Keeping each other in the loop, professional courtesy, that sort of thing. While that was probably true to a large extent, they were now quite obviously providing security for the team that was legally ransacking my home.

"Mister Gant, I'm sorry but the books clearly fit the description of items listed on the warrant."

"Listen to what I'm telling you," I stated once again then exaggerated the enunciation of my following sentences as if speaking to a small child. "They. Do. Not. Be-long. To. Her... They. Be-long. To. Me."

"I'm sorry." He ignored my patronizing comment and splayed out his hands in surrender to some higher power as he made the apology one more time. "But, we have to take them."

"No. You don't."

His tone became harder and he shot back, "Look, the warrant has been served, and it's my job to execute it per the instructions of the court. The books fit the description on the list, so the books go with us. It's that simple and there's nothing I can do about it."

"Sure there is. You can stop spouting this Nuremberg nonsense about following orders, engage your brain, and give them back to me."

"Okay, now listen to what *I'm* telling *you*," he instructed. "Because this is the last time I'm going to say it. You aren't getting the books back. As of this moment they are evidence. Now, up till a few minutes ago, you've been cooperative and we definitely appreciate that. But, if you're going to start interfering, I'm going to have to ask you to step outside."

I shook my head and stared back at him as if he'd lost his mind. "Bullshit. I have the right to be present during the search."

"As long as you aren't obstructing the search, that's true. But, you're getting very close to crossing that line."

"So, just because you and your crew can't use a little common sense, you're going to kick me out of my own house?"

"If that's what it takes."

"Gods! What is it with you people?! Does the fact that I just bought those books have no bearing on this at all?"

"Look, if that's true, and you have receipts to prove it, you can take it up with Major Case and the prosecutor."

"Maybe so, but right now I'm taking it up with YOU," I returned.

In reality, I'm sure he was correct. If I could provide receipts, which I could, at the very least Jackie should be able to negate the effect of the books as evidence. In fact, she could probably get them thrown out altogether before it even went that far. But, I wasn't willing to take that chance because with the situation as it was, our attorney's ability to accomplish that feat was by no means guaranteed.

Ominous shadows were lurking somewhere in the background of all this. Someone, or maybe even something, was trying very hard to stack the deck against Felicity. That much had become painfully apparent over the past hour. I certainly wasn't about to let anything I was holding in my own hand be used in that process if I could help it.

"That's it, I'm done with this," the crime scene technician replied with a wave of his hand before looking over to the Briarwood cops. "I have a job to do, and this man is preventing me from doing it. Would you guys like to take it from here?"

"Sir," one of the uniformed officers spoke up. "Why don't you step outside with me for a bit?"

The tech had turned back to face me, and I was now holding him locked in a stare down, so I snapped an acrid reply without breaking my gaze. "Why? Because I don't want to."

"Sir, that wasn't a question. It was a strong suggestion."

"Your suggestion is noted."

"Sir, it was a *very strong* suggestion. Under the circumstances I can make it an order."

"What? You people aren't happy with just arresting my wife? Now you're arresting me too?"

The officer replied, "No sir, you aren't being arrested." After a short pause he added, "Not yet, but if you keep going the way you are, it's a very good possibility. So, why don't you do like I suggested, and just step outside with me where you can cool off for a few minutes?"

Before I could manage to formulate another snide remark, I flashed on the recent conversation with Jackie. The words "don't do anything stupid" rang through my head at full volume and made me take pause. As much as I wanted to lash out at all of them, to just go stark raving berserk, the fact remained that getting myself locked up wasn't going to help Felicity at all.

I dwelled on the realization for a moment then huffed out a resigned sigh and ended my unblinking glare at the technician. With an agitated shake of my head, I looked over at the officer and grumbled, "Yeah, fine."

"Good call," he replied.

He was standing close enough to me that when he'd spoken I'd easily been able to pick up the odor of burnt tobacco on his breath.

"You smoke, right?" I asked.

"Yeah, why, I got bad breath?"

"No, because I need a cigarette."

I hadn't really given much thought to the comment, any at all, really. It just came tumbling out of my mouth in place of something far more caustic. Still, all I could manage to do was give an internal shrug when it dawned on me what I had just said.

As we headed for the door, the officer pulled a pack from his pocket then tapped it across his index finger before holding it out toward me.

Whether it was out of reflex or because I truly did feel like I needed one, I don't know, but I reached over and pulled the proffered smoke from the pack and stuck it between my lips.

"You want to grab a jacket?" the officer asked.

A sarcastic quip escaped before I could subdue it. "Why would I want to do that? I'm supposed to be cooling off, right?"

"Yeah. Right," he returned.

Without another word I pushed the door open and headed through with him on my heels. As I'd suspected, neighbors had positioned themselves to watch the show. Since it was still early enough in the afternoon, there weren't as many peeking from behind curtains or lethargically walking dogs as there could have been. But, it was a good bet that phones were buzzing with news of yet another incident involving the police at "the Witch's house". I'm sure my ears should have been burning.

It was only a few moments later that a van emblazoned with the logo of a local television station pulled up and parked on the opposite side of the street. As usual, I wasn't going to be immune from the jaundiced spotlight of the media either.

"Damn TV people," the cop muttered and then offered, "We can go out back or sit in the car if you want."

"That's okay," I replied with a slight shake of my head. "It's not the first time they've pointed their cameras at me, and I doubt it will be the last."

"Guess the neighbors are having a field day," he grunted.

"Yeah, probably," I agreed. "You'd think they'd be used to it by now."

I didn't expand on the history of flashing lights and news vans that had been positioned in front of my house over the years, and he didn't ask. He probably already knew all about it anyway. In fact, it was entirely possible he had been one of the many cops to have graced my doorstep in the past. After a quiet moment I pulled the cigarette from my mouth and inspected the still pristine paper and tobacco on its end.

"Got a light?" I asked before tucking it back between my lips.

He dug in his pocket then withdrew a disposable lighter and handed it to me. I gave it a quick flick with my thumb and touched the flame to the business end of the smoke then handed the stubby metal and plastic device back to him.

As we stood on the porch, and I took the first drag on the nicotine and menthol laden tobacco, I simply yielded to the idea that I was once again re-adding an old vice to my list.

If circumstances were different, given my earlier jibe, I suspect Helen would have found it thoroughly amusing.

CHAPTER 7:

The crime scene unit had been gone for something on the order of fifteen minutes now, and I was still trying to figure out how they could possibly manage to lay waste to someone's home as quickly as they had in this case. All in all, it had taken them just under two hours to accomplish what I can only imagine would have taken a busload of sugared up toddlers an entire day to do.

The emotional response to the specter of the destruction even seemed to transcend the boundary between human and house pet, as evidenced by our cats—Dickens, Emily, and Salinger. At the moment, they were sitting in a loose semicircle on the coffee table, perusing the mess. Earlier, they had found places to hide away, as they always did whenever we had unfamiliar visitors, and had only ventured back out now that the commotion was done and gone. Watching them from across the room, it looked for all the world like they were having an impromptu emergency meeting. It was as if they were trying to come to some conclusion about the scene before them that would make sense to their feline brains. Every now and then they would look at one another then at me, nervously twitch their tails or ears, and then go back to swiveling their heads around the room, yellow-green eyes open wide with a glaze of curiosity and perhaps even fear.

I couldn't blame them. Our house was, in a word, trashed. The only way I can explain the spectacle that greeted me upon re-entering my home was that it looked as though everything had been the victim of a very strong, but somewhat considerate earthquake. I say considerate because nothing appeared to have been broken, at least not that I could see. However, no matter where I looked, there was obvious visual evidence of the search.

Furniture had been moved out from walls and instead of being put back was simply left sticking out at odd angles. Books were piled on the floor instead of resting in their rightful places on shelves. Even

DVD and videocassette cases created a haphazard mound on a chair after having been opened, inspected and discarded.

That disaster was merely the living room, and I knew for a fact that they hadn't contained themselves there.

Now I was getting angry all over again. Although standing on the front porch with the Briarwood officer had calmed me considerably, I couldn't quell the renewed surge of rage as I looked at the mess and realized that not only had the books been pulled from the bookcases but so had all the items we kept on the shelf we used as our altar. I tried to keep telling myself that they most likely had no idea that they were desecrating objects of religious significance—literally violating what was deemed by our faith a sacred space. But, no matter how many times I repeated it to myself, it wasn't an easy sell, mostly because I had recognized a couple of their faces. They were people I had worked with at crime scenes before. People, who knew who I was, knew that I was a Witch, and had heard me speak about such things before.

And, even if that wasn't enough, I knew for certain that one of them had attended a class I had taught for the police department on recognizing the difference between religious activity and cult coercion. A portion of that workshop had specifically addressed altars and their importance to practitioners of alternative religions. At the very least, *he* should have known better.

Of course, if I were the paranoid type, I would bet that Albright had something to do with that as well. The fact is, whether my suspicion was born of paranoia or not, she probably did.

When I finally managed to dampen my newly inflamed rage, I left the cats to their huddle and moved toward the back of the house to continue my own assessment of the chaos. In retrospect, I probably should have waited a little longer because what I found only served to ignite my smoldering temper once again.

My heart all but skipped a beat, and I felt a hot rush of blood fill my face the moment I saw our bedroom. If the front of the house had been the victim of an earthquake, this room had been pummeled by its big brother as well as every other disaster imaginable. The contents of the dresser and chest of drawers now resided in a scattered heap on top of our bed, and along with that was anything that might have been stored away in the matching nightstands. While the majority was carelessly piled, a small portion of it actually sat in something remotely resembling stacks. I had a feeling these existed only because it had been easier for them to take those particular items out of the drawers that way.

The clothing that had once occupied the walk-in closet was tossed in crumpled heaps across the footboard of the waterbed. Garments that had once been methodically arranged by Felicity according to color, length, and a number of other factors that fit her personal system of organization, were now nothing short of a giant pile of laundry.

Everything else from the closet looked as if it had been vomited out across the floor. This included every pair of shoes my wife owned, and trust me there were more of them than I wanted to count. Those, along with several rectangular boxes where some of them had once made their homes, formed a colorful debris field expanding out from the mirrored doors which were themselves hanging wide open. It looked much like a disastrous accident had occurred in the middle of a shoe store stockroom.

On the far wall, through the bathroom doorway, I could see that the medicine chest had pretty much been ransacked. Judging from the terrycloth mass I spotted on the floor just in front of the double vanity, the linen closet hadn't been spared either.

Standing here surveying the blatant deconstruction of our lives, I didn't even want to think about what the office, or even worse, my wife's darkroom and files, looked like right about now. There was so much strife here on the main floor that I wasn't entirely certain I could stomach going upstairs or downstairs just yet.

At this point, however, there was no doubt in my mind that someone, whether it was Albright or not, had instructed the crime scene technicians to lay waste to our home. I'd been involved in far too many investigations and had seen how these things were normally done. What I saw staring back at me now definitely wasn't an example of standard procedure.

My rising anger eventually gave way to a cold swell of depression, and I simply hung my head. After a moment I pushed a pile of shirts aside with a distracted swipe of my hand then slowly settled myself onto the edge of the bed.

I couldn't begin to say exactly what all had been taken, with the exception of the books and a handgun that was registered to me. The only reason I knew about the weapon was because they had seen fit to tell me they were going to confiscate it for the time being. I didn't know why, but I had already discovered that arguing with them over the books didn't do any good, so I didn't bother to object.

I also knew for a fact that some of Felicity's clothing and shoes had been removed because I saw them being loaded into evidence bags while I was standing on the outside looking in. From what little I overheard, intimate garments had been of particular interest and in fact, were even specifically listed on the warrant. I'm sure the reasoning for that probably had everything to do with the sexual nature of the crimes.

Even though I knew my wife wasn't one to be easily embarrassed, I certainly didn't know how she would react to a handful of strangers looting her lingerie drawer. For some reason, the fact that they had encroached upon this particular sanctity made me feel more violated than any of the other things they had manhandled and then absconded with. Surprisingly, even the desecration of our altar no longer mattered in the face of this. Odd, considering that they weren't even my undergarments, but I was in a very protective mode right now. Anything that violated Felicity was, to me, patently unforgivable.

I heard a damp snort and looked over to see our English setter staring at me with sad eyes. Taking a tentative step forward, he nudged my hand then nuzzled in and brought his head to rest on my thigh. I absently stroked his crown and gave him a half-hearted scritch behind the ears. Usually, Quigley the Australian cattle dog was hot on his heels, but last I'd seen him he was sitting in the dining room looking just about as confused as the cats.

Our animals were as close as we had to children—not that we hadn't tried for one of our own species. Unfortunately, Felicity's only pregnancy to date had been abruptly terminated by a physical altercation between her and a murder suspect who was making a getaway attempt. Since then, even though everything checked out for both of us according to doctors, we hadn't had much luck in the conception department.

In truth, it was probably a good thing that we didn't have children because I had the feeling that right now I would be completely lost. I could easily comfort a dog with a few pats on the head even if he could still sense that something was amiss. On the other hand, I had no clue what I could possibly tell a child that would quell his or her fears in a situation such as this.

"Mommy is going to go with the nice policemen for a while," just didn't seem to me like it would do the trick. And, right now, saying something like "Don't worry, everything is going to be okay" could very well be a flat-out lie. Primarily, because I wasn't so sure that it was going to be okay. On top of that, I knew that my own mental state wouldn't be particularly healthy for a child to endure either.

I looked down at the dog, only to find his large brown eyes peering back up at me. As he watched, the small sprigs of hair that passed for eyebrows began rocking back and forth on his expressive face then his tail began slowly thumping against the side of the bed.

"Kind of a mess, isn't it, buddy?" I mumbled, turning my head and looking around the room while my hand continued automatically stroking his fur.

My brain was more or less chasing itself around in a circle at this point. What I felt like I wanted to do right now was to jump in my truck and head down to the police station. But, that was just the surface reaction. What I truly wanted more than anything else was Felicity back home, safe and free of this insanity. Short of "busting her out," there wasn't really much I could do to make that happen. At least not by showing up there and causing a scene, anyway. Since Jackie had told me to stay put, I had no choice but to fight back the urge to make a beeline for Clark Avenue downtown.

Our attorney was certainly right about one thing. I would definitely cause more trouble than anything else, and I knew that. I just had to trust her to take care of this, but that was becoming harder to do with each passing moment. A quick glance at the clock told me that better than two hours had passed since she had told me she was on her way to the police station, and I still hadn't heard anything from her. I suppose that in the grand scheme of things, two hours isn't really that much time, but for me it had already been an eternity.

As I continued looking around the room, my eyes fell on a picture frame resting in a niche on our headboard. From all outward appearances, it was apparently the only thing that hadn't been touched by the uncaring hands of the crime scene technicians. The frame was small but intricately designed—the kind of heirloom that readily evokes sentimentality at first glance. Centered within its rectangular border was a semi-candid shot of Felicity and me.

I stared at the photo, studying it to the exclusion of everything around me. Though I had pretty much forgotten that it was there, I remembered the snapshot well. It had been taken at a party some years before. My petite wife was perched on my lap with her arms around my neck, and mine were encircling her waist, hugging her close. We were both grinning, obviously filled to overflowing with the happiness of the moment. The vivid memory played back inside my skull as I recalled the gathering. What stood out most of all was the fact that only moments before that particular photo had been snapped, we had all been playing the "trust game". In essence, it was an old pseudo-psychological exercise where you demonstrate your trust in your partner by falling backwards into their arms. We had all really just been clowning around, but in truth, there was an underlying seriousness to the results.

Almost all of the people at the get-together had faltered to some extent, much to one another's chagrin. However, Felicity and I had fallen freely into one another without hesitation and without so much as a flinch of doubt. I hadn't thought much of it at the time, as it simply seemed natural, but in the final analysis these were acts of absolute, blind faith. We both knew that neither of us would allow any harm to befall the other. I trusted her, she trusted me.

Trust. A concept I had only recently been forced by my overactive psyche to revisit. Fortunately, the reminder had taken hold and flourished.

I trusted in the fact that I knew Felicity was innocent, and moreover, I trusted her. Just as, even at this moment she was trusting me. Trusting me to take care of her, to get her out of this mess. But, instead of honoring that trust, here I was perched on the edge of the bed, feeling sorry for myself because she wasn't here.

I'm not sure how long I had been sitting there staring at the photograph. To be perfectly honest, it could have been a minute, or it could have been five. My perception of time was so far off kilter that I probably wouldn't have known the difference between the two even if I had been watching the clock instead of the picture.

However, when my epiphany finally forced my reticent gaze to loosen its grip on me, I slowly turned back to the canine using my lap as a pillow and looked into his eyes again.

I shook my head and muttered to him, "Dammit…What the hell am I doing here? Watch the house. I've got to go."

I had already shrugged into my coat and tapped in the code to set the house alarm when the phone began to ring.

CHAPTER 8:

"Hello?" I barked into the phone, stretching the handset's cord almost to its breaking point while I spoke.

The warble of the alarm system's countdown tone was speeding up as it approached its armed state. I knew if I let it get that far I'd end up setting off a motion detector, and then I'd have cops crawling all over my house yet again. Extending as far as I could I leaned across the chair and quickly stabbed in the master code then punched the off button, sending the raucous electronic beeping into silence.

Unfortunately, as annoying as the tone was, I would have preferred it to what I heard coming back at me across the phone line.

"You bastard!" An angry, heavily accented voice struck my ear with the insult. "What have you done?!"

This was absolutely the last thing I needed at the moment, but I couldn't say that I hadn't been expecting it all along. I just wished that I'd checked the caller ID before snatching up the handset with such haste because now I was committed to the call even though this definitely wasn't the time for it.

My father-in-law Shamus O'Brien had never made a secret of his dislike for me. Ostensibly it was due to my religious beliefs, and given his tirades, I had no reason to doubt they truly were the cause. In fact, he had stated on more than one occasion that he was firmly convinced that it was I who had corrupted his only daughter. The fact that she was already following a Pagan path long before I met her didn't seem to have any bearing on his conviction either.

With my public identity as a Witch having become even higher profile over the past few years because of my involvement with the police, what had long been at least an outward tolerance of me on his part had slowly and surely waned. Given his staunch, though distorted views, I wasn't at all shocked that he would blame me for Felicity's current predicament.

I tried not to let myself react to his immediate attack and instead fought to remain composed, answering with a simple, "Calm down, Shamus. Believe me, I'm just as upset about this as you are."

"Why should I calm down, then, you bastard?! Felicity is all over the news. They're callin' her a murderin' psychopath."

"I know they are."

"And then what do I see? You, you bastard. Just standin' there chit-chattin' with the police and smokin' a cigarette. Standin' there for the whole world to see, just like it's another day. Just like nothing's happened!"

Suddenly my decision to remain on the front porch instead of hiding out on the back deck away from the news cameras didn't seem very prudent. I had probably known subconsciously that it would come back around to bite me, I just hadn't given any thought to which set of teeth were going to be sinking into my flesh. Of course, I suppose that mystery was now solved.

My gut reaction was to snap back at him, but I forced myself to offer an explanation instead. "I think you're misinterpreting what you saw. I had a half dozen crime scene guys tearing this place apart, and I'd just been ejected from my own house for fighting with them. I was trying to calm down before they arrested me too."

"*Cac capaill*! They should have arrested you *instead* of my daughter!"

"No, they shouldn't have arrested either of us."

"*Damnú ort*! What did you do to her?!

The Gaelic curse wishing damnation upon me wasn't unfamiliar. Felicity was prone to slipping into the old language whenever she was angry, just like her father was doing now. In fact, her personal list of favorite vulgarities mirrored his, so I'd heard most of them before. Of course, the imprecations usually weren't directed *at* me as they were in this case.

"I didn't do anything to her, Shamus. You know that."

"Aye, I don't believe it. You and your godless cult did something to my colleen. You brainwashed her and forced her to do some Satanic sacrifice or something, didn't you!?"

He didn't even give me a chance to respond to the ludicrous accusation before starting in again.

"ANSWER ME, YOU BASTARD! THAT'S WHAT YOU DID, ISN'T IT?!"

"Listen to me, Shamus," I interjected sharply. "Number one, she didn't kill anyone, much less get forced to do anything against her will. Number two, you sure as hell aren't going to help her situation if you go around telling everyone that she did do it but only because I forced her to."

There was a brief pause, and I hoped that I had managed to get my point across to him. When he finally spoke again, he was somewhat more reserved, though you could tell the anger was still seething behind his words, just waiting for a chance to escape.

"Why didn't you call me? Why did I have to hear about this from the television, then?"

"I've been just a little busy, believe it not." I couldn't keep the sarcasm out of my tone. "As you noted, my wife just got arrested."

"Well, what are you doing about this?" he demanded without actually acknowledging what I had just said.

"I'm trying to find out what's going on myself. Our lawyer is already at the station…"

He interrupted, "Aye, is he any good, this lawyer of yours?"

"He's a she and yes, she's good."

"Aye, well it doesn't really matter. I'll be sendin' my own then anyway."

"Shamus, don't turn this into a bigger circus than it already is. If Jackie doesn't think she can handle this, she'll be the first one to say so. Then, if I need to, I'll hire another attorney."

"I'll be sendin' mine," he repeated flatly.

I started to object again but decided against it. At least he seemed to have calmed a bit and was apparently trying to be constructive instead of just placing blame and swearing at me.

"Fine," I told him. "Just tell your attorney to get in touch with Jacquelyn Hunt. She's got the lead on this, and we don't need any confusion causing problems."

"I'll tell him your girl is there, but I'll be wanting him to take over."

"Shamus... Dammit...Can't you...Sheesh!" I stammered out a halting mish-mash of verbiage as I tried to beat down the desire to climb through the phone line and throttle the man. I knew he wasn't going to listen to me, and this whole conversation was about as futile as trying to empty an ocean with a teaspoon and a paper cup, so I decided it was time for it to end. "Listen, I'm going to have to get off the line here. When you called I was just heading out the door to go down to the police station myself."

My bid for a quick exit did nothing more than set fire to his temper once again.

"Don't you dare!" he snapped. "You stay away from my daughter. You've done enough to her already!"

It had become a violent internal struggle for me to keep an even temper during this conversation. I thought I had been more than reasonable with him, even if we had been under the best of circumstances. There was no doubt, however, that the current conditions were a far cry from the best.

I simply couldn't hold my tongue any longer, and my own anger rose to the surface, "Dammit, Shamus. She may be your daughter, but she's also my wife!"

"If I have anything to say about it, she won't be for much longer!"

Confusion filled my voice. "Excuse me?!"

"Don't play stupid. I've figured you out. I know you've brainwashed my daughter and turned her against me. I've already talked to someone about taking care of it!"

It only took a fraction of a second for his words to sink in. "You've got to be fuc... Deprogramming? Is that what you're talking about, Shamus?! Deprogramming?!"

"They call it exit counseling and thought reform therapy."

"They call it that when it is done by an ethical, licensed therapist and the subject is willing," I spat. "If you kidnap her and do it against her will, it's deprogramming, pure and simple."

"It doesn't matter what you call it."

"It sure as hell matters that she doesn't need it," I countered. "Not to mention that it's also illegal."

"I don't care about that. She needs to be rescued."

"From what? Who? Me?"

"Aye."

"Have you lost your goddamned mind?"

"No, but apparently you've taken my daughter's from her, and I'm going to get it back. And then once she's in her right mind, she'll be getting you out of her life, of that you can be sure."

That was it; I'd had enough. "Listen up you son-of-a-bitch, don't you even think about doing this!"

"Go hifrean leat!"

"You want me to go to hell, Shamus?" I returned, quickly translating the epithet he'd just screamed at me. "Well I've got some happy freaking news for you, I'm pretty much already there, and you just helped with the trip. I've got to go. Bye."

I could hear his voice screaming from the handset even as I slammed it back onto the base. What I picked up of the stream of Gaelic was yet another condemnation I'd heard before, and it roughly translated into him wishing "scorching and burning" upon me. Well, I sure wasn't going to call back to break the news to him, but he definitely wasn't the first to offer up that curse, so he could just stand in line.

I closed my eyes and sucked in a deep breath, huffing it back out angrily as I tried to settle myself. Lashing out, I slammed the heel of my fist against the underside of one of the empty bookshelves. The impact generated a hollow thud followed by a resounding crash as the shelf lifted off the adjustable pegs then slammed back down. For some reason, the wooden rectangle skewed downward and slid out onto the floor, narrowly missing my foot. The resulting clatter startled the cats and made them jump, which in turn caused them to knock a stack of books from the coffee table and onto the floor. The clamorous chain reaction sent them skittering throughout the house to their secretive hiding places. The dogs, however, took the opposite tack and both came to investigate the small crashes but more or less took it in stride.

I picked up the shelf and tried to re-install it, and that's when I discovered that the reason it had fallen was that the impact had sheared off one of the forward adjustable pegs on the uprights. I reached up and slid it onto the empty shelf above for the time being then shook my head and turned, starting back toward the alarm keypad on the wall across the room. Before I could take the first step, however, the peal of the telephone's ringer filled the room.

My anger really hadn't had time to drop off, and it immediately welled in me once again. I twisted back in a flash, snatching the handset up and placing it to my ear as I shouted, "What?! Did you think of some other curse to throw at me?!"

There was a hollow buzz but no reply came from the other end. I couldn't imagine that Shamus would be shut down by the comment, so I allowed my gaze to fall down to the caller ID box. I didn't get a chance to offer up an apology right away as a confused voice finally broke the relative silence.

"Rowan?" Jackie asked.

"Yeah, sorry," I returned. "I just got off the phone with… Screwit…Never mind, what's going on? Were you able to get her out?"

"She's still in processing," she replied. "They're almost done, and then I'll be able to get into a room with her."

"She's not coming home tonight, is she?"

"No, Rowan, she isn't. She's likely not coming home this weekend at all."

My voice dropped almost to a mumble as I closed my eyes and rubbed my forehead, "Dammit, Jackie..."

"I told you to prepare yourself for this."

"I know."

"Look, I called for a couple of reasons. First, to give you an update, and second, to ask a couple of questions."

"About what?"

"I called in a favor and managed to get a little bit of information about what's going on. It's not much, but it's a place to start. So, what I need to know is if Felicity does any traveling alone."

"What do you mean?"

"Like for her job. Does she ever go out of town without you?"

"Well, yeah. She's one of the top freelance photographers in the country. She gets jobs all over the country. Why?"

She pressed on, ignoring my query. "Has she ever been to Myrtle Beach, South Carolina that you know of?"

"Yeah, I'm pretty sure she has," I replied impatiently then demanded again, "Why?"

"Without you?"

"Yeah, I think so. Why?"

"Specifically, about a year ago, maybe? Somewhere around the beginning of December?"

"Yeah. I don't remember for sure, but yeah, I think she took a trip around then, so could be." My edginess ratcheted up the scale and I took on a harsh tone. "Jackie, just what the hell is this..."

I stopped cold with my mouth hanging wide open. Before I could even consider finishing my sentence, the conversation with Doctor Rieth's assistant flashed through my brain. Two and two joined forces to create four, and that became the sum of all my fears, which then punched me square between the eyes.

"Rowan?" Jackie queried. "Are you still there?"

"Yeah," I finally replied, my voice barely above a whisper. "Yeah, I'm here."

"Listen, the information I obtained could be wrong, but the rumor is the police have hard evidence placing Felicity at the scene of a somewhat bizarre homicide in Myrtle Beach, South Carolina that happened in December of last year."

"What evidence?" I asked quietly.

"I don't know that yet," she replied.

The dull ache at the back of my head was now returning in force. It wasn't going to take long for it to fill my skull and make itself right at home for the duration. I closed my eyes once again and sighed.

"Well, they're right about one thing," I offered flatly. "The same woman committed that murder as did the two homicides in Saint Louis. But, Felicity is NOT that woman."

"I believe you, Rowan," Jackie replied. "But you need to understand that I'm not the one we need to convince of that fact."

CHAPTER 9:

"I thought I told you to wait at home?" Jackie said, glaring at me with the best stoic attorney face she could muster plastered across her features.

"I got lonely," I replied.

"Don't be a smartass, Rowan," she snapped. "I've got my hands full here, so I really don't need to be babysitting you."

"I don't recall asking you to."

"Let me refresh your memory," she snapped. "You asked by showing up here."

"Hey, don't get mad at me."

"How can I not? I just had a detective drag me out of the middle of an interview with your wife."

"Then you should go yell at him."

We were standing in the lobby of police headquarters at the corner of Clark and Tucker in downtown Saint Louis. I'd been here more times than I cared to count, but usually I was escorted straight in by Ben and at times, even treated like just another one of the cops. This afternoon, however, was vastly different. I had been detained here at the main entrance, and Jackie had been brought out to see me. It was immediately obvious that she wasn't thrilled about it. Of course, she also hadn't been aware that I was on my way here, and I had purposely neglected to mention it before hanging up the phone earlier.

"Right now I'd rather tell him to just shoot you," she hissed, still trying to keep her voice low. At the tail end of the comment, she let out a heavy sigh and shook her head in exasperation.

"From the reception I got, I'm guessing you wouldn't have a problem getting him to take you up on the idea," I replied.

"What did you expect, Rowan, a marching band and a parade? You're the husband of a murder suspect who is currently detained in this building, and you come blazing in here like everyone is supposed to clear a path for you. Wake up, will you?!"

Jackie was in her mid-fifties but looked more like she was hovering somewhere in her forties, even when sporting the flat expression. She was the sole attorney in a wildly successful one-woman shop bearing her name, although she did have a small support staff consisting of a paralegal and a part-time receptionist.

I'd heard rumors that she'd been offered partnerships in some rather prestigious local firms more than once but always declined in favor of the autonomy that allowed complete control over her caseload. I wasn't at all surprised, because she wasn't one for taking direction. Giving it, yes. Taking it, definitely not.

"Hey, I'm trying to help here," I appealed, attempting to change my approach, though in a halfhearted sense.

"Well, you definitely aren't. Helping, that is."

My bid at toning down my temper didn't last, and I snarled my reply. "Yeah, well you don't appear to be helping all that much either."

She tossed back a shock of platinum blonde hair and fixed me with her hard gaze once again. Physically, she was really closer to Felicity's height than mine, but wearing her ever-present designer heels, she came right to eye level with me. The stature elevating shoes along with her reputation for relentlessly tearing apart cases—and even other attorneys if necessary—until she came out on top are what had garnered her the nickname "the pit bull in high heels." She would instantly feign annoyance anytime she heard someone call her by the moniker, but secretly, I think she actually liked it.

After a pause she punctuated her cold stare with a calm but brutally caustic reply, "That's because I'm out here dealing with an asshole instead of being allowed to do my job."

"Listen, I…"

She cut me off before I could finish. "No. Just shut up and YOU listen for once. If that last comment had come out of any other client's mouth, I would have packed my briefcase and headed home. But, I've known you way too long, and I know that you're actually a pretty nice guy. I'm writing this all off to the stress you are under, but believe me, I'm only going to write off just so much.

"Besides, the reality of the situation is that I'm representing your wife right now, not you. So, I suggest you count yourself as damned lucky I'm still standing here."

"Yeah, but..." I started.

"I'm not finished," she spat, cutting me off. "Now, what you need to do is start listening to me and stop acting like some kind of maniac. You sure as hell aren't making any friends right now, and you're trying my patience to say the least."

"But why can't I see her?" I demanded, still trying to circumvent her tirade.

"That's easy. I could have told you that on the phone if you'd bothered to ask. The short list is A: She's under arrest for two, and quite possibly three counts of first degree murder; B: You aren't her attorney, I am; and C: Right now you're acting irrationally and the police have some genuine concerns for your mental stability, as do I."

"Bullshit. I'm fine."

"Then like I said, start acting like it and listen to me for a change. Go home. Sit on your hands. Don't talk to anyone, especially not the press, and just wait for me to call you. End of discussion. Is that clear?"

I shook my head. "I can't, Jackie. Not right now. Not after what they did to the house."

"What they...What did they do to your house?"

"It's trashed. They totally wrecked the place."

Now it was her turn to do the head shaking. "Did they destroy anything?"

"No...I don't think so...Not that I could see, anyway, but it looks like a tornado went through it."

"Did you happen to notice what they took?"

"Some of Felicity's clothes, my handgun, and some of my books on Voodoo for sure," I rattled off my own short list. "I tried to tell them the books were mine..."

"Are they?"

"Yes. I just bought them. And, checked some out from the library."

"The books from the library shouldn't be a problem. We'll just have to contact the branch where you checked them out, and that should be enough to get them disallowed. What about the books you purchased? Do you have proof of when you bought them?"

"Yes. I have the receipts."

"Then don't worry about it, they won't be an issue. Anything else?"

I nodded. "I know there was other stuff, but I can't remember what. They gave me a voucher, but I haven't really gone over it..."

"Great...Okay, fine. We'll address that later. Have you got your cell phone with you?"

I rummaged in my pocket to check then nodded. "Yeah."

"Okay, why don't you go find someplace to get a cup of coffee, and I'll call you as soon as I know something."

"Are you..."

"Yes, I'm sure," she interrupted, finishing the query for me. "Now just go and let me do what you're paying me for."

"Yeah, okay," I answered with a nod.

Her enumerated reasons for keeping me out of the loop had effectively shut me down for the time being. On top of that, my befuddled emotions were now batting me back into depression territory. I knew I was probably shifting back and forth between sounding insane and coming off like a frightened child, just like she said I was, but I couldn't help it. I was still trying to get a handle on what was happening, but that handle kept staying just out of my grasp.

"You'll call the minute you know something, right?" I asked, desperate for reassurance. In fact, my voice had an almost pleading tone to it.

"Yes, I'll call. Now go."

I gave her another nod then turned and started toward the front door of the building.

"Rowan," she suddenly called after me.

I stopped and turned back to face her with a questioning look.

"Just coffee, no booze, okay?"

I involuntarily screwed my face into a confused expression then said, "You know, it's not like I have a drinking problem or something."

"I didn't say you did, but I know you, and in your present state, if you drink you're definitely going to be a problem. Trust me. No alcohol, okay?"

"Yeah, okay." I gave her a nod then started to turn back toward the door but stopped myself. "Wait, Jackie…"

"What?" she asked, her voice sounding strained as she tried to hide her obvious aggravation.

"I forgot to tell you. My father-in-law is taking it upon himself to send his own attorney down here with orders to take over the case."

"Do you know who the attorney is?"

"Sorry, no."

"Do you want his attorney to take over?"

"No."

"Then as long as Felicity is of the same opinion, don't worry about it. Just let me handle it."

"It's possible Shamus, her father, might show up himself."

"He's not going to get any farther than you have, so like I said: Don't worry, just let me handle it."

"Okay…And, Jackie…Thanks."

"Yeah," she replied as she turned, calling over her shoulder, "You know the old line about the bill, right?"

I watched her disappear into the elevator then continued on my way through the front doors then out onto the sidewalk. The wind was picking up, whipping along the street as it cut its way between the buildings. I could feel the encroaching cold as a burning sting against my cheeks, but even so, I didn't bother to zip up my coat, simply leaving it wide open to the wintry chill.

I knew I had to do what Jackie said, but I couldn't get excited about climbing into my truck and putting any more distance between Felicity and me than there already was. While I'm certain "the pit bull" would have been happier if I would at least go a few blocks away, I set my sights on the small diner directly across the street which boasted the bizarre name, Forty.

Residing just to the side of the entrance to City Hall's parking lot, I knew for certain the place was a hangout for cops. Not just because of its proximity to the station but also due to the fact that I had once commented to Ben about the odd name. In response he had explained that 40 is the Saint Louis city police radio code for a meal break.

Even though I wasn't holding members of the local law enforcement community in very high regard at the moment, I decided I could bear sitting at the lunch counter with a cup of java. As long as I kept to myself, I figured I should be okay. After waiting for a pair of cars to pass, I stepped out onto the asphalt and jogged across the street.

I had only been sitting at the counter for around ten minutes, my hands wrapped around a ceramic mug and eyes gazing unfocused at my reflection in the black liquid, when the hair on the back of my neck began to prickle.

Amid the drone of chatting patrons, sizzling grills, staticky radios, and even ringing phones, a painful sound pierced my ears, launching me back out of the depression and square into the middle of anger once again.

"Yo, Carl," Ben Storm's voice called to someone behind the counter. "Ya' got that order I called in ready yet?"

CHAPTER 10:

"Heya, Storm, yeah..." the man replied. "Got yer eats right here."

I shot a quick glance in the direction of the voices and saw Ben standing near the register only a dozen or so feet to my right. He was angled away from me, and given his relaxed posture I got the impression that he hadn't seen me when he came in, even though he had to have passed within two or three feet of me at the most.

"Lessee, I got a Reuben, two bacon cheeseburgers, and a chicken salad on wheat." The cook listed the order while parking a large sack on the counter between them." With a chuckle he added, "You hungry or somethin'?"

"Not really," Ben responded to the joke. "This is just a snack ta' get me through."

"Yeah, right, you sure you don't want any fries or some drinks wit' dat?"

"Nahh, this is good."

The logical side of my brain was telling me to keep quiet and shrink into the shadows. This diner was literally right next to the last place on earth I needed to get into an altercation with him. And, considering the clientele here, being right next to police headquarters was for all intents and purposes just like being in the squad room itself. Of course, those were just the facts I should be paying attention to. The truth is, I had a terrible habit of allowing my emotional half to override the practical aspect of my personality, and that was when I usually got myself into trouble.

I tilted my head forward and struggled with the two sides as they competed for dominance over my actions. For the moment, I had myself nailed down, and I was fairly certain I could stay that way for a bit. The problem was, I didn't know exactly how long that bit would be.

"Okay, so what's the damage?" Ben asked.

"Seventeen-thirty-two," Carl replied.

He handed him the money while adding, "Jeezus. You tryin' ta' retire early?"

"Yeah, I wish. Lemme get yer change."

"Keep it," Storm told him and then quipped, "Buy yourself somethin' nice."

"Yeah, funny. Thanks."

"Not a problem. Catch ya' later."

"Not if I'm careful."

"Uh-huh. Who's funny now?" Ben chuckled, reaching out and grabbing the bag of sandwiches. "Later."

"Yeah, later."

I immediately shifted in my seat, trying to remain inconspicuous but not actually look like I was hiding. The stool directly next to me on my right was currently empty, which would give him a clear view of me when he turned this way to leave. The seat on my left, however, was filled with a uniform clad patron, and I was concerned that too much fidgeting would just attract unwanted attention from him. If that happened then I definitely wouldn't have a chance of going unnoticed.

Of course, it didn't help at all that my anger was steadily rising, effectively nudging the pragmatic approach to the situation off into the wings. If Ben didn't get out of here soon, I wasn't going to be hiding; I was going to be up in his face.

I shut my eyes and kept them squeezed tight as I endeavored to slowly breathe my way through this, grounding and centering my energy in order to keep calm. Surprisingly, the bid to maintain control actually seemed to be working, and I could feel my shoulders start to relax as I continued the practiced breaths, in through my nose and out through my mouth, all the while visualizing a solid connection with the earth.

Hopefully, I only needed to keep this up for another minute or so and it would all be moot. Once he was gone I was certain the surge of negative emotions would subside. I waited, focusing on my breathing as I listened for the door. The rattle of the bell finally hit my ears just as I was letting a slow stream of air out between my lips. I was actually beginning to think I might make it through this without incident. Of course, it was at right about that moment when I was blindsided.

I really should have felt him standing behind me. Any other time I'm sure I would have, but I suppose I was too busy concentrating on not flying off the stool and attempting to actually land the punch he'd avoided earlier in the day.

Either way, I knew my luck was depleted the moment I heard his voice coming at me from just over my right shoulder.

"What're ya' doin' down here, white man?" Ben asked, a jumbled mix of concern, remorse, and even trepidation wrapped tightly about the words.

"Waiting," I returned without looking up. I held my voice even, but there was no mistaking the disdain in my tone.

"Mind if I sit here for a minute?"

"Free country." I took a sip of my coffee and struggled to contain myself as I felt my face flush with heated anger.

There was a thick tension between us as he placed the sack onto the counter then dropped his frame onto the stool and leaned forward on crossed arms. I could feel my heart pounding in my chest, and the growing thump reverberated in my ears amidst the rush of blood. I actually started counting the beats as we sat there, making it almost to fifty before he elected to speak again.

"You really shoulda stayed at home, Row," he offered.

While my brain was debating whether or not to reply, my mouth disassociated itself from the process and ran off on its own. "Your guys didn't exactly leave me much of a place to stay."

"Yeah…" he grunted then paused a moment. "I heard a rumor. Sorry. They don't usually do that."

"Yeah, I know. Been there, got a t-shirt. Remember?"

"Yeah."

"So I guess I just get to be the lucky one then, huh?"

"I have a feelin' it was a request from on high."

"I pretty much figured that out too. Perfect opportunity to screw with the Witch, huh?"

"Somethin' like that."

"Seems like a pretty popular pastime for you cops today."

He purposely avoided replying to the jibe, asking instead, "You need a hand cleanin' up?"

"If you're the one offering, then no."

"Actually, I can't…But, maybe I could get…"

I interrupted him. "Oh yeah, I forgot. Seems you can't do much of anything these days."

He sighed. "I'm not happy 'bout this, Row."

"Funny. Doesn't seem to have affected your appetite."

"Stop bein' such an asshole, Rowan," he returned. "It just so happens the Rueben's for Firehair, an' the chicken salad's for your mouthpiece. And they ain't on the department's dime either."

"Am I supposed to say thank you or something?" I made a show of reaching for my wallet. "Or do you just want the cash?"

"No. An' put your fuckin' wallet away…I just thought ya' should know I'm tryin' ta' take care of Firehair best I can."

"Like when you cuffed her?"

"I can't have this conversation with ya' right now."

"Big surprise."

He huffed out a heavy sigh and then paused for a moment before shifting in the seat and picking up the bag. "I better get these back over there before they get cold."

"You do that," I chided, and as usual I couldn't leave well enough alone, so I quickly added, "When you placed the order, I sure hope you remembered to ask for plenty of arsenic. You wouldn't want to miss a chance to poison her too."

"All right! Fuckit!" Ben spat, dropping the sandwiches and slamming his fist down hard on the counter.

Pushing back, he stood up quickly. I looked over out of reflex and saw him reach to his belt. With a tug he pulled his gold shield from it and then slapped it onto the counter next to the sack of food. In another quick motion, he shoved his hand beneath the folds of his jacket. I heard a quick snap, and a moment later he laid his Beretta alongside the badge and sandwiches.

He was attracting attention from plenty of others, and I started mutely chastising myself for allowing my mouth to countermand my brain.

Ben shot a quick glance to the side and shoved the items toward another cop as he barked, "Watch these for me, willya, Anderson?"

"There a problem?" the uniformed officer asked, starting up from his seat, as were several of the others who were within earshot.

"No," Ben snapped loudly enough for all to hear as he grabbed me by the collar and yanked me backwards from the stool, causing me to spill coffee across the counter. "I just gotta go finish somethin'."

"Hey!" I yelped. "What the hell are…"

"Shut up!" he ordered, whipping me around like I was nothing then shoving me toward the door.

"Yo, Storm, don't kill 'im," one of the cops shouted across the diner, punctuating the comment with a laugh. "Way too much paperwork."

"Hey," another added. "At least the meat house is right across the street. Won't have far to go to drop 'im off."

I knew from personal experience, the "meat house" he was referring to was the medical examiner's office that sat immediately next door to police headquarters.

"You want me to call the paramedics for him?" yet another officer quipped.

"Everybody just stay put," he ordered again. "This's personal."

"Goddammit, Ben!" I was growling as I continued my futile attempt to twist out of his grasp.

"I said shut up!" he shot back, shoving me through the now open door and out onto the sidewalk.

With a rough yank he guided me around the side of the building, pushing me along as we went.

"What the hell are you doing?!" I demanded, but my words seemed to fall on purposely-deaf ears.

As we rounded the corner, he gave me a final hard shove, sending me stumbling into the side of a dumpster. Free of his grasp, I wheeled around to face him, rage continuing to surge through me.

"Take your coat off," he ordered as he stripped out of his own and tossed it into a heap against the building.

"You're kidding," I snipped. "You're not happy with just fucking my wife over. Now you want to kick my ass too?"

"Take your coat off," he repeated, ignoring my question.

"What for?" I demanded.

"'Cause, dumbass, you can swing harder if ya' haven't got your goddamn coat on, now take it off."

I reluctantly shrugged off my coat and tossed it against the building as he had done with his. Why I bothered I really didn't know. Whether I had the coat on or not, it wasn't going to make any difference. He had height, weight, training, and even more importantly, first hand experience over me. There was no way I could come out of this without broken bones and blood loss at the minimum. At least it was cold outside, so I guessed when I folded, I could use the parking lot as an interim full-body ice pack until the ambulance arrived.

It's not that I wasn't going to defend myself, mind you, but I also wasn't stupid. A no win situation is just that. Somebody isn't going to win. And, I knew with absolute certainty that it was me who was in the "no" column when it came to a "win" in this instance.

I stood there, staring back at Ben, building as much hatred as I could in hopes that I would at least get in a shot or two before he clocked me and total darkness fell upon my world. Once again, I could feel my heart hammering in my chest as the glare locked between us.

Contrary to his instructions, not everyone had stayed inside, and there was now a small gathering of uniformed and plainclothes officers alike forming behind Ben. He didn't seem to have a problem with it, and truth is, he probably expected the audience. Train wrecks always attract spectators, and that was pretty much what was about to happen.

I couldn't say for sure because I wasn't paying very close attention to them, but something told me wagers were being made within the group. I didn't imagine they were giving me very good odds.

"Well, what the hell are ya' waitin' for?" Ben finally said. "Come on. Let's have it!"

"Have what?!" I snapped.

"Come on! Take your shot!"

"What?" I snarled. "You really expect me to throw the first punch right here in front of a bunch of cops?"

"Everybody heard me say this is personal, right?" he called over his shoulder.

A disjointed chorus of "yeah's" and "whatever's" issued from the handful of onlookers.

"So then I guess you want me to swing first just so you'll have a clear conscience when you beat the shit out of me?"

"Wake up, Rowan. I've got no intention of hittin' you, ya' fuckin' idiot! You're the one that's got the issues here! Now come on! You been wantin' ta' hit me all goddamned day, so just do it and get it over with!"

Incredulity flowed into my voice, unevenly mixing with the anger that had already claimed the space. "You're going to let me hit you?"

"Ain't that what I just said?"

"And you aren't going to hit me back?"

"I am if ya' don't hurry the fuck up and do it!" he shot back. "Now come on!"

I didn't wait for him to repeat the invitation again.

CHAPTER 11:

"Feel better now?" Ben asked, following the question with a hard groan.

"A little," I said, inspecting the ends of my fingers where they protruded from beneath a stained cloth. "I don't think it's broken."

We were currently parked in a booth back inside the diner, him positioned so that he was facing the door and me on the opposite side of the chipped and uneven table. The burgers from the sack were sitting before him, still folded neatly into their paper wrappers. He hadn't touched them except to pull them from the bag before sending it across the street with one of the other officers.

At this point, I wasn't entirely sure if he was going to eat them or just look at them longingly, as he was still holding an ice-filled dishcloth pressed against the side of his face. Of course, I wasn't in much better shape considering that I had its frigid twin wrapped around my hand.

After a moment he grunted. "Yeah, well I wasn't talkin' 'bout your hand."

"Oh, you mean..." I replied, pantomiming a right cross.

"Uh-huh."

"Truth?"

"Yeah."

"Right now I'm still thinking about it."

"That's fuckin' great," he huffed, voice brimming with sarcasm. "So much for takin' one on the chin."

"How about you?" I asked.

"Hey, I'm not the one with the issues."

"Okay, but I meant your jaw."

"Oh...hurts like a sonofabitch."

While the crux of my own pain was localized dead center on the knuckles, it was still radiating up my forearm, past my elbow, and stabbing into my shoulder at odd intervals. Much to my surprise, the explosion of rage had somehow served to negate my inherent clumsiness; so, as it turned out, I couldn't have landed a punch any squarer onto Ben's jaw if I had mapped the angle and trajectory with precision instruments.

Of course, in addition to that, not really knowing for sure that he wasn't going to retaliate once I struck, I had gone for broke with that first swing, putting everything I could muster behind it—hatred, anger, strength, and weight. The problem was, as much as it actually ended up hurting him, for me it had still been pretty much like I had slammed my fist into a brick wall. At least, that's how it felt to my throbbing hand.

He squinted back at me with one eye, reaching up and working his jaw with his right hand while still keeping the ice pack pressed against it with his left.

"Jeezus, white man…" he half-groaned. "Where the hell'd ya' learn ta' punch like that anyway?"

"You, as I recall."

"Oh yeah…" he muttered.

We sat in silence for a short span then I asked, "So what do we do now?"

"That's up ta' you, Row," he answered with a sigh. "I've given ya' all I got. If you wanna keep hatin' me then there's nothin' more I can do about it."

"It's not that I want to, Ben," I offered.

"Coulda fooled me."

"Look…My head's not in a very good place right now. I'm sorry."

"Yeah, I can tell. You talk ta' Helen?"

"Yeah," I grunted. "She told me you thought you were doing us a favor."

He gave his head a shake. "I did, but I'm not talkin' 'bout that. I wanna know have ya' talked to 'er about you? About what's goin' on inside *your* head."

"A little."

"A little ain't enough, Row."

"Yeah, I know," I agreed. "But there will be time for that once I clear Felicity."

"How're you gonna do that?" he asked.

"I don't know yet."

"Well, I gotta tell ya', Kemosabe. I don't either, 'cause no matter how ya' slice it, it don't look good."

"Uh-huh. That's all I seem to be hearing from you, my attorney, and everyone else."

"Sorry. Just bein' honest."

"Are you telling me that even you think she's guilty?"

He closed his eyes and shook his head, waiting a measured beat before answering. "I don't want to, but…"

I waited for him to finish the sentence, however, he simply allowed his voice to trail off.

"But what, Ben?" I finally asked. "Can you honestly say that you think Felicity is a killer?"

"Under different circumstances, no."

"So what's so different about the circumstances now?"

"The cards just ain't fallin' in her favor, Row."

"Last I recall you had nothing other than circumstantial evidence at best."

"I'm afraid it's gotten a little more complicated."

"Complicated how?"

"I can't really get into it, Row."

"Damn you, Ben," I spat in a low voice. "Don't keep doing this. You can't dangle that shit in front of me then clam up all over again. Tell me what's going on."

He looked at me with a pained expression that definitely wasn't a by-product of the ache in his jaw and then reached up with his free hand to rub his neck.

"What the hell," he muttered. "They've prob'ly hit 'er with it by now anyway. The hair samples from the scenes matched with…"

I immediately cut him off, countering what he was going to say. "...I already told you there's a logical explanation for that."

"Let me finish..." he held out his hand to stop me. "They didn't just match the samples from the two scenes here. They also measured up with hairs lifted from a homicide in Myrtle Beach that happened around a year ago."

Now I knew what the evidence was Jackie had mentioned earlier.

I offered a cold rebuttal. "A couple of hairs aren't conclusive, Ben. Even I know that. So does your crime lab. That's thin and they know it."

"You're right, they aren't," he agreed. "As far as just comparison goes. But when ya' combine 'em with a DNA match, they suddenly take on a lot more weight."

"So, you're telling me Felicity's DNA matches to evidence found at a crime scene in South Carolina?"

"And the two homicides here. Yeah, I'm afraid so. That's the word anyway."

"That's ludicrous."

"Maybe so, but from what I'm hearin' it's still a fact."

I shook my head and stated flatly, "Well, there's a simple explanation for that too. It's a mistake."

"I wish it was, Row. But, I asked around. After they ran the two here, they sent samples to Washington. What I got told was the Feebs ran 'em three times. Plus, they got the sample direct from Myrtle Beach and ran that comparison, not us."

"I don't care," I spat. "They're still wrong."

"Look, Rowan, I don't wanna believe it either."

"Then don't."

He sighed and cleared his throat then sat back against the seat in the booth, regarding me silently. He tossed the ice pack onto the table then gingerly pressed his fingers along his jaw line, wincing slightly but remaining silent.

"She didn't do it, Ben," I appealed once more.

"Okay, Row," he spread his hands out in front of him in mock surrender. "Who did then?"

"I don't know, but I'm damn sure going to find out."

"How?"

"To start with, I'm going to track down a *Lwa*."

"Row…" he shook his head. "Listen, I know you're convinced this evil spirit Voodoo thing has got somethin' to do with this…"

"And you aren't?"

"I dunno. Not quite like you are, I don't think."

"Well, were there signs of a Voodoo ritual at the crime scene in Myrtle Beach?" I demanded.

Based on my earlier conversation with the young woman at the university in Louisiana, I knew it was a safe bet his answer would be yes. Still, I didn't want to show my hand just yet. I needed for him to tell me himself.

"That's not the point, Row…"

"There were, weren't there?"

"Yeah, there was, but so what? They're just gonna say that connects it with the Hobbes murder here. And that's not ta' mention the fact that there was plenty of evidence that the whole kinky sex thing was involved."

"It does connect them, Ben," I replied. "But, you've still got the wrong woman. I don't know how many times I have to say it— Felicity did NOT do this."

"Row, are you forgettin' what she did to that asshole she picked up in the club?"

"She didn't kill him."

"Yeah, well she damn near did."

"She was possessed at the time. You know that."

"I know you keep sayin' it, but dammit, Row, it doesn't make it true."

"So now you're calling me a liar?"

"No, what I'm really tryin' ta' say is *so what*? I wanna believe ya', but come on…how're ya' gonna prove she was possessed?"

"Like I said, by finding the *Lwa*."

"And then what? You gonna have a nice chat with it and convince it to confess? Somethin' tells me even you ain't that good at the hocus-pocus, Kemosabe."

"This *Lwa* is either a personal ancestor or someone who ended up on an altar by mistake, Ben. If I can track down the *Lwa*, then I've tracked down the real killer."

"Do I hafta remind you that we can't arrest an evil spirit? Not to mention that you're never gonna get a court ta' listen to ya' with a story like that."

"I don't mean the spirit itself. What I'm saying is the *Lwa* needs a corporeal being in order to manifest physical actions on this plane."

"Do what?"

"It needs a body. It has to possess someone in order to commit the murders."

"Yeah, well, I hate ta' tell ya' this but you just got finished tellin' me that it possessed Firehair. Ain't ya' kinda diggin' your own hole for her with that approach?"

"Hers was a collateral possession, Ben. Felicity doesn't practice Voodoo. Hell, she doesn't know any more about it than I did when this all started. No…this *Lwa* is sitting on an altar somewhere, and the practitioner who belongs to it is your killer."

"That's a great theory, Row, even if it is all *Twilight Zone* and shit…but, even if ya' could get a judge ta' listen to ya', you're still forgettin' one thing."

"What?"

"The DNA. It's the smokin' gun that puts Firehair at all three scenes. I dunno how you're gonna get around that, even if ya' do find this whacked out ghost you're chasin'."

"I still say they're wrong, Ben," I insisted.

"Row, I told ya' they ran it three times."

"So maybe they got the samples mixed up."

"That's not real likely."

"Maybe not, but it's possible."

"Yeah, well anything's possible, but you're grabbin' at straws here."

"Well, the only other explanation is that someone purposely tampered with the evidence."

"Actually, the other explanation is that she's…"

"Don't say it," I snarled.

"But…"

"I said, DON'T SAY IT."

"Yeah fine… So, what you're tryin' ta' say is that…well…'you know who' is the one who did this?" He deliberately used the verbal evasion in place of Albright's name. Considering the location, and recent shifts within the department, he couldn't really be sure about the exact loyalties of all of the other cops in the diner. An outright mention of her wasn't what you could term a stellar idea; of course, anyone who might be listening and knew my history could have figured out exactly whom he meant.

The truth was, Ben had already taken a huge risk simply by being seen talking to me at such length. Once word made it up the chain of command, he was probably going to have hell to pay, especially considering that I now suspected he had done more than just call in markers to keep himself involved in this case. In fact, he probably owed more favors than I wanted to know about.

"Can you think of anyone else with a reason?" I asked.

"Jeez, Row, I know you two are at odds, but to go so far as to frame Felicity?" He shook his head. "That's pushin' a whole 'nother envelope."

"Are you forgetting she tried to use me as bait for Eldon Porter? And, as I recall she was actually overheard saying that if I got killed in the process…what was it? Something like, too bad, so sad?"

"Yeah, but she had a way outta that. She could get caught real easy if she tampered with evidence. Besides, like I said, there were tests done at the Feeb's lab in DC anyway."

"So? The evidence still originated here."

"Yeah, but not the evidence from Myrtle Beach," he reminded me. "It went from them to DC. Never even saw Saint Louis, much less her."

"Speaking of Myrtle Beach, how did that even get into the mix to begin with?"

"NCIC hit," he explained. "The bondage aspect along with the ritual stuff. When our two homicides got entered into the computer, that's what got spit back out."

"Great."

"Yeah, well, I didn't wanna tell ya' this, but you're prob'ly gonna find out sooner or later. The homicide in South Carolina wasn't the only hit."

"What are you saying?" I knew full well what he had just implied, but I couldn't stop the words from tumbling out of my mouth.

"NCIC returned seven other unresolved cases in various states that have similar characteristics, datin' back as far as oh-three. The kinky shit, the mutilation, and in a couple of 'em some of the Voodoo stuff..." He allowed his voice to trail off as he ran through the list.

"Are they trying to say Felicity committed all of these murders?"

He nodded. "They're definitely lookin' into it. Right now Myrtle Beach is the only department to provide physical evidence that links. That, and they can positively place her there in the city at the time of the murder from the subpoenaed airline records."

"Dammit..." I muttered.

"Just so ya' know, they're followin' up on all her travelin'. Even if they don't get any more matches with physical evidence from the other states, if they can show that she was in those cities around the times of the other murders...Well, circumstantial or not, put it together with what they already got, an' it's gonna make a major impression on a jury... And, it ain't gonna be a good one, Row."

I pondered what he had just said and felt my blood run cold. Instead of getting answers that would help me clear Felicity, I was just getting more and more signs pointing directly to her guilt. However, they were all detours I didn't intend to follow. I knew my wife was innocent; I just had to prove it to everyone else. Given what Ben had told me over the past few minutes, it was obvious that I needed to do so very soon.

"You know that question you asked me earlier?" I finally asked.

"Which one?" he grunted.

"About if I was feeling better," I replied.

"Yeah, what about it?"

"Well, I thought about it and right now I want to hit you again."

CHAPTER 12:

Intent and want can be very fickle concepts. More often than not, they are two completely different things, even though we might try to convince ourselves they are one and the same. This is true for both the practice of magick and everyday, mundane life as well. Right now just happened to be one of those classic instances of diametric opposition.

Put plainly and simply as possible, no matter what I had just said, I really had no intention of taking another poke at Ben. He knew that, and so did I. In fact, I'm fairly sure my fist couldn't have handled it anyway, so the verbal jab would simply have to suffice.

On the other hand, *want* is a very strong emotion in and of itself. Considering that I felt like the man whom I had long called my friend was still at odds with me and wasn't listening to reason, I definitely *wanted* to gift him with a black eye to go with the welt on his jaw.

Of course, having established that as being out of the question, and what with me being a magickal practitioner, I had to admit that other forms of retaliation had crossed my mind. For instance, if a bag of coffin nails were in my possession at the moment, I'd be hard pressed not to go ahead and slip a handful of them into his coat pocket along with a few muttered words of disdain. Not to kill him as one might surmise but just to make him miserably ill for a while. Either way, it was an act that wouldn't exactly adhere to the generally accepted concept of "Harm None", but what the hell. I had already thrown a punch in the physical realm; I might as well go for broke and take a swing in the ethereal.

All things considered, I suppose it was probably a good thing I didn't really have those nails handy.

Of course, whether I wanted to admit it or not, the situation was without a doubt one of those proverbial Gordian knots. If I took a moment and put myself in Ben's place, I'm sure that what I was calling "reason" certainly sounded like an outlandish fantasy. And, as usual, that pretty much seemed to be the way of things in my peculiar world. It was no wonder he used the term *Twilight Zone* in reference to me as often as he did. My life definitely played out like a marathon episode with no end in sight.

Still, I didn't make any secret of the fact that even I didn't consider the overabundance of ethereal happenings in Felicity's and my life to be normal. But, be they normal or not, that didn't make them any less real. I suppose it came down to the fact that I was just far more open-minded with regard to accepting that the events simply were what they were, and no amount of rationalizing or postulating on my part could change that. To paraphrase the worn out truism, magick happens. Much to our dismay, however, it just isn't always the magick we want.

Fortunately, as I sat there mutely pondering what items might be readily available that I could substitute for coffin nails, common sense got a much-needed boost from the insistent warble of my cell phone. Shadowy emotions were instantly shoved onto the back burner once again, and considering just exactly how dark they had been getting, that was a very good thing.

"Rowan Gant," I said into the mouthpiece as soon as I dug the device from my pocket, thumbed the answer button, and tucked it up to my ear.

"Rowan, it's Jackie," my attorney's voice came back across the line. "Where are you?"

"At Forty, the diner right across the street. Do you want me to come over? Can I get in to see Felicity now?"

"Just stay right where you are," she replied, circumventing my second question. "I'll be there in just a few minutes and we can talk about that."

The line clicked off without so much as a goodbye, so I hung up and laid the phone on the table in front of me.

"Lawyer?" Ben asked with a thrust of his chin toward the device.

"Yeah, apparently she's on her way over here right now."

"Well, then I guess I'd better get outta here," he replied, gathering up his coat. "You're gonna wanna talk to 'er without me around."

I shot a quick glance to the side and then over my shoulder. In less than five seconds I counted three cops who were easily within earshot, and those were just the ones wearing uniforms. I looked back over to Ben and said, "Yeah, well, we'll probably want to go somewhere else to talk anyway."

"Yeah," he grunted as he slid out of the booth and stood up. "Prob'ly not a bad idea."

Ben slipped into his jacket, shrugged it up onto his shoulders, and then took a moment to adjust his holster rig beneath its folds. Even after he was finished, however, he continued to stand next to the table, staring out through the window at Clark Avenue and the half dozen or so squad cars diagonally parked against the curb in front of police headquarters. After a quiet moment, he looked down toward me with a thoughtful stare.

"Listen…Row…Are we gonna make it? I mean…Is this…"

"I'm still pissed at you, Ben, if that's what you mean," I replied, meeting the clumsy question head on. "That's not going to go away overnight."

"Yeah…" he mumbled. "I pretty much figured that. But what I wanna know is are we gonna be able to make it right between you an' me?"

"I honestly don't know yet."

"Fair enough," he sighed. The heavy breath seemed to broadcast a sense of depression. He waited a second then added, "So, is there anything I can do ta' fix it?"

"Yes. You can help me clear my wife."

He shook his head slowly. "I dunno what I can do on that front, Row."

"I'm not sure either, but it might help if you'd just start believing she's innocent."

"Yeah." He let out what might have been a curious half-chuckle. "Well, I know you're not gonna believe this, but Constance told me the same thing a coupla' hours ago."

I had been wondering how she was doing. The last time I had seen her was at the funeral, and she had been just as distant as Ben. I assumed it had to do with the ongoing investigation, but considering her run in with "Felicity in Miranda's clothing," I couldn't help but worry that her forgiveness had worn off. Based on what Ben had just stated, obviously, it had not.

"So, she believes Felicity is innocent?" I asked.

"Yeah, actually, she does," he replied with a nod. "And she's been lettin' everyone who'll listen to 'er know it."

"Good to know we still have someone on our side."

He ignored the overtone of the comment and responded purely to its face value. "Yeah, well I gotta tell ya', the water she's swimmin' in is startin' ta' get real hot."

"Is she in a lot of trouble?"

"Not yet, but after the toes she stepped on ta' get Firehair released and make the assault charges disappear…well, put it this way, she's runnin' short on friends and long on enemies."

I hadn't had much room to house any compassion for others over the past few hours, but Constance truly had gone out of her way to make some potentially damaging charges against my wife vanish into thin air. I was aware she had called in some favors, but at the time, I had been so wrapped up in the situation that I had no idea she might be seriously jeopardizing her career in the process.

"Is it really that bad?" I asked.

"Let's just say if she ain't careful she might end up dustin' off 'er law degree for use in the private sector."

"I didn't know…"

"And you still don't. I wasn't s'posed to say anything to ya', so just…ya'know…keep it to yourself."

"Yeah…Okay…" I agreed.

Ben snorted and shook his head before saying, "Just a feelin'."

"What?"

"That's what Constance said… The reason why she doesn't think Felicity is the killer. It's *just a feelin'*."

"Sounds familiar."

"Yeah, well she's probably just gone shoe shoppin' with Firehair too many times. Some of that spooky ass shit musta rubbed off on 'er."

"You say that like it's a problem."

He harrumphed. "I got enough a' your *Twilight Zone* stuff in my life as it is, Row. Don't need ta' be datin' one of ya' on top of it."

"I seem to recall you telling me awhile back that cops get feelings about things too…inexplicable hunches. 'Hinky feelings' I think is what you said."

"Uh-huh, yeah. Guess I shoulda known tellin' ya' that would come back ta' haunt me."

"Are you saying you don't really believe it?"

"You know better'n that."

"So maybe you need to listen to your gut, just like she is."

"My gut ain't talkin' right now."

"But Constance's is, and she believes Felicity is innocent even after everything that happened." I offered the words more as an admonishment than a question.

"Yeah, Row, I get it. If Mandalay thinks she's clean, why can't I?"

I didn't reply. I didn't really feel the need to because he had said almost verbatim what I had been thinking.

Ben turned his face back to the window and stared into the growing darkness of the evening as he let out a long sigh. "Like I said, white man. My gut's not talkin'. I'm just not gettin' a feelin' on it, either way."

"Then give her the benefit of the doubt."

"I'm tryin'…" He shook his head. "Believe me, I'm tryin'…"

"Maybe it's just that you're too close."

"Yeah, maybe."

After a long pause I offered, "Felicity once said something about you that you might like to know. She told me she felt that when it came to your friends you were loyal to a fault."

"I try."

"Well, I've never had a reason to disagree with that assessment...until now."

"Ya'think I'm not feelin' guilty enough about it on my own, Row?"

"Maybe you are," I replied. "But I think we both know I'm not in a terribly forgiving mood right now."

"Yeah," he grunted. "No shit."

The bell on the diner's door jangled, and I glanced back over my shoulder to see Jackie coming through the opening.

"Well, your mouthpiece is here," Ben offered as he scooped the still-wrapped burgers from the table and cradled them in one large hand. "Guess I'd better go so you two can talk."

"Don't give up on Felicity, Ben," I returned. "Just...just believe."

Without looking back down, he spoke in a low voice that sounded almost like a plea. "Gimme somethin', Row. Dammit, just gimme a reason I should *believe*."

"You don't need a reason from me, Ben," I replied. "You already know in your heart that she's innocent. You just have to stop being blinded by the evidence."

"I'm a cop, Row. We live and die by the evidence."

"Then stop being a cop for a minute. Stop looking at what someone else is calling evidence and take a long, hard look at the truth."

Saturday, November 19
10:05 A.M.
Saint Louis, Missouri

CHAPTER 13:

I gave up and simply stopped paying attention to the angry voice that was currently bellowing from the speaker of the answering machine in the living room. Given that it was my father-in-law, calling yet again to place blame and scream epithets at me, I didn't feel that his diatribe warranted very close consideration on my part. It wasn't as if I hadn't already heard everything he had to say more than once. I'd even made the unfortunate mistake of blindly picking up on the initial ring the first two times he'd called, so I'd twice been on the receiving end of every name and insult he could think of—and, some that I suspected he'd just made up. Of course, my grasp of Gaelic extended only as far as my wife's commonly used phrases, so I couldn't be positive about anything other than the fact that he'd repeatedly damned me to hell for all eternity.

I'd already told him once that as far as I was concerned, I was already there, and the past twenty-four hours had definitely seemed endless. I didn't bother to repeat it.

After that second round, I'd learned my lesson and just started screening the calls, allowing the machine to handle his ongoing tirades. There was nothing I could tell him that he didn't already know, and I was just as frustrated as he could ever be. Probably more so when you considered that last evening Jackie hadn't even waited to get out of the diner before breaking the news to me that I wasn't going to be able to see Felicity until today; and that would only happen if she could call in a favor or two and get a judge to sign off on it. Needless to say, I hadn't taken the news well at all. Of course, I'm sure she had expected that fact, and it probably had quite a bit to do with her decision to tell me while standing in a diner full of cops. Still, even then I made a scene, but in the end there was nothing I could do to change the harsh reality, and all that I accomplished was to get us kicked out.

After that, things took a turn for the worse, which was something I hadn't really thought possible. As if the first piece of painful information wasn't enough, Jackie was now completely unwilling to discuss any further details of the case with me. My own wife, it seems, had requested that everything remain under the umbrella of attorney client privilege for the time being, and since I was neither attorney nor client, I was completely removed from the loop. Had she dropped that bomb on me prior to us getting kicked out of the diner, my explosive response probably would have ended up getting me arrested.

The insult topping it all was that I wasn't even privy to her reasoning behind subjecting me to the information blackout. Each of these things, in turn, had dumped their own load of distress onto my already strained emotional state. Adding all of them together was just about to put me over the edge, and I still honestly don't know how I managed to avoid having a bigger meltdown than I actually did.

I was momentarily snapped out of my introspective haze by an angry click popping loudly from the speaker in the front room. Shamus had once again ended his call by slamming down the phone. If I was lucky, maybe this time he had broken it and wouldn't be able to call back for a while.

Of course, that wouldn't necessarily bode well either. At this point, I had lost track of how many times the man had phoned just this morning. He had pretty much reached critical mass, and I had a bad feeling he actually might be ceasing the relentless calls very soon anyway. I say a bad feeling because I figured once he stopped, it wouldn't be long before he replaced phone calls with a face-to-face attack. I feared he would soon be knocking on my door, and a physical confrontation with my wife's hot-tempered father was something I really didn't want to deal with right now.

I didn't actually fear him; it was the situation itself I wanted to avoid. He was nowhere near as big as Ben, so I could pretty much guarantee that we would both end up going to the hospital, and that wasn't going to help anyone, least of all, Felicity. Don't get me wrong,

I certainly wasn't looking for another fight, but if it came in search of me, I wasn't about to turn and run from it either.

The thought prompted me to look down at the back of my right hand. It was slightly swollen and had already started taking on a reddish-purple cast. I ran the fingers of my left hand over the bruised knuckles and noticed that it was definitely sore. Still, I suspected I would be able to ignore that if the need presented itself.

I sighed and bent to the bathroom basin then cupped my hands beneath the running faucet. Once they started to overflow, I pressed the handfuls of cold water against my face. Of course, most of it either ran between my fingers or dribbled along my arms to turn my shirtsleeves into a soggy mess, but I didn't care. Wet clothing was the least of my worries right now.

Looking back up, I stared into the mirror at the dampened, haggard visage now living in the silvery, reflected world. Its eyes were sunken and bloodshot, stubble shadowed its cheeks and neck, and its face sagged with exhaustion. I kept telling myself that all of those properties applied only to *it* and not to *me*, because I simply didn't have time to feel like *it* looked. Of course, I had learned long ago that denial would only get you so far; but, that wasn't going to stop me from riding it all the way to the last stop.

The peal of the pendulum clock in the dining room had died away several minutes ago, but using the memory of the evenly spaced tones as reference, I did some quick math. The product of the equation was a number which told me I hadn't slept in better than twenty-four hours, a fact that readily explained at least part of my current state of being.

It wasn't that I hadn't tried, mind you. I knew I needed rest, and I had actually set out to get some. The problem was, every time I closed my eyes I saw Felicity. While that was something I would normally consider a pleasant thought, the countenance that filled my waking nightmare was the one that had been burned into my mind when last I saw her being led out of the house.

What painted the inside of my eyelids was her face contorted into a mask of fear, paler than her ivory skin could possibly be. Her eyes were wide and imploring. Her lips were trembling as she called to me. As an added bonus, the visions came complete with an endlessly looping soundtrack of handcuffs snapping tight around her dainty wrists.

I could still hear her voice echoing in my ears as she pled for me to stop this from happening. And now…well, now for some reason, she was shutting me out, and that certainly didn't help the pain at all.

I let out another sigh as I felt the emotion well deep inside me once again. The sadness was so overwhelming, I felt like sitting down on the floor right where I was and crying until I couldn't cry anymore. But, that simply wasn't going to happen. I knew it wouldn't do any good because sometime around midnight I had given it a try, and now, I just didn't have any tears left to give.

An even hiss filled my ears, beckoning me once again into the land of lucidity. I looked down and noticed the water was still running, so I twisted the handle to shut it off then reached for something to dry my face. Exiting the bathroom, I trudged through the bedroom while blotting my damp skin with a hand towel. I had to pick my way around various obstacles, as I hadn't yet cleaned up the mess left in the wake of the search. That is, other than to push the pile of clothing on the bed off to the side when I tried to lie down and sleep. I was just stepping into the hallway when the telephone began to ring once again.

Only a few minutes had passed since Shamus' last screaming fit, but he'd had a tendency to deliver them in clusters, so I was sure it was probably him for the who-knows-how-manyeth time today. I was so sure, in fact, that I didn't even bother to head for the bookshelves to look at the caller ID box, electing instead to finish drying my face and then simply stand at the end of the hallway surveying the carnage that still graced my living room.

Following the third ring, the answering machine kicked on, burping its greeting into the room once again.

"You have reached the Gant and O'Brien household, please leave a message…" The voice was followed by a shrill tone then a staticky pause.

Finally, in the wake of the beep, an authoritative voice issued from the speaker. This time, however, it was distinctly feminine and possessed of a heavy Southern accent.

"I am calling for a Mister Rowan Gant," the woman announced. "I picked up a message from my office that he was trying to reach me. My name is Doctor Velvet Rieth, and I can…"

Midway through her first sentence I was already in motion, stumbling frantically through the room as the dogs and cats scattered before me. I hadn't even needed to hear her name to have guessed exactly who she was, and this was a call I had not only been waiting for but desperately needed.

Something told me this woman was holding a vital clue that would help me clear Felicity. What it was and why I believed it to be so, I couldn't say. It was just one of those feelings, and I knew better than to ignore them.

"Yes, yes, I'm here…" I yelped into the handset, cutting her off before she could finish the message and hang up. "Hold on just a second…"

For some reason the answering machine hadn't cut off as it normally should, and a loud squeal had burst from the speaker the moment I lifted the receiver. I was now fumbling with the buttons to switch it off but meeting with no success whatsoever. Frustrated by my frenzy-induced klutziness, I quickly gave up and yanked the power plug from its base with a violent jerk.

Quiet fell in behind the sudden termination of the racket, and I returned my attention instantly to the handset.

"Doctor Rieth? Are you still there?"

"Mister Gant?" she replied.

"Yes, I'm Rowan Gant. Sorry about the feedback there. It's kind of an old answering machine."

"That's okay," she said and then added. "I'm sorry, but do I know you? There's something very familiar about your name."

"No, Doctor, I'm fairly certain we've never met."

Considering that I had recently heard my name mentioned on the national news in conjunction with Felicity's arrest, I was trying to tread cautiously. I desperately needed information from this woman, and I didn't think it would help if she knew my wife was an accused serial killer.

"Hmmm. Are you sure? I'd swear I've heard your name before."

"There's a British comedian named Rowan who's fairly popular," I offered. "Maybe that's where there's some confusion."

"Maybe so…" she allowed her voice to fade thoughtfully.

There was a brief pause, but from the tone of our exchange, even given the pleasantries, I got the overwhelming feeling that she was somewhat dispirited that I had actually answered the phone. Still, that could simply have been my own mood overshadowing my judgment. After all, she did call back on a Saturday, so surely she was expecting someone to answer. That was unless, of course, she thought she was calling a business number and was hoping for voicemail.

As my sluggish brain was trying to make sense of what were probably exhaustion-blunted perceptions, she spoke again.

"Are you there?"

"Yes. I'm here. Sorry."

"Well, I picked up a message from my office saying you had some questions regarding my book and a murder investigation?"

"Yes, that's correct, I am…"

She cut me off before I could continue. "Okay, first off, if you found my book at a murder scene, I don't know what to tell you. It wasn't me. Second, there are no human sacrifices in Voodoo practice. And, third, if you found a doll with pins in it at a murder scene, you're barking at an empty tree, and you need to call someone else."

I wasn't sure if she was testing me, or just looking for a quick out to end the phone call, but I definitely no longer thought I was just being paranoid about her humor. She actually sounded exasperated, as if she'd had those very questions posed to her countless times before. Whichever it was, or even if it was both, I met the commentary with a firm reply.

"Of course, Doctor Rieth. First, no, your book wasn't found at a crime scene, at least, not that I am aware of. Second, if I thought I was dealing strictly with a human sacrifice, I would be contacting a Hindu mystic, not that I would expect him to condone it, of course.

"And, finally, as to dolls and pins, if that were the case, I would want to talk to a Witch since poppets are actually a product of traditional WitchCraft and not *Vodoun*."

I definitely wasn't going to tell her that the Witch I would be consulting would be me. At least, not quite yet.

This time, once I finished speaking, there was a much weightier pause at the other end of the line. Still, I made no move to fill its void, instead remaining silent and waiting for her to respond.

"Obviously you've done some homework," she finally replied.

"I try to stick to the facts whenever possible."

"You'll have to excuse me," she offered. "When it comes to the subject of Voodoo, I'm not used to dealing with well informed cops much farther north than Baton Rouge."

"Actually, I'm only a consultant," I said, sticking to the twisted version of the truth I'd given her assistant just in case she was still feeling me out.

"Close enough when it comes to this sort of thing." There was an audible shrug in her voice. "So what makes you think Voodoo is involved in your case, Mister Gant?"

"Several things, actually," I replied. "A couple of *veve* for one. A victim profile and method of killing for another."

Her standoffish air had dissipated quickly once I had proven my acumen on the subject of alternative religions, but she had remained staunchly businesslike. Now, her demeanor abruptly cascaded into one of urgent and uneasy curiosity. "Which *veve*?"

"*Ezili Dantó, Papa Legba,* and one which has yet to be identified."

There was no mistaking the note of trepidation in her voice when she spoke. "What does that one look like? The unidentified *veve.*"

Her reaction, combined with what Ben had said the night before, all but confirmed my suspicions. Out of a mild sense of paranoia, I decided to test the theory.

"What do you think it looked like, Doctor Rieth?" I asked.

"Why?" she asked, a startled note in her voice.

"I just get the feeling you might have seen it before."

"Look, I don't have anything to do with..."

"Calm down, Doctor. I never said you did. Please, just indulge me for a second. What do you think this third *veve* looks like?"

"Well, I'm really afraid it might look very similar to a stripped down, simplified Celtic triskele. Basically, a circle with three centrally joined arcs radiating from the center out to the circumference, and a dot located within each third."

"Yes," I agreed. "That's pretty much exactly it."

"The bondo-*veve,*" she muttered, almost too quiet for me to hear.

"Excuse me?"

"Sorry," she replied. "It's just a nickname. Bondo-*veve.* I call it that primarily because the symbol itself..."

"...Is used by the bondage and S and M community." I finished the sentence for her then added, "So, I was right. You've seen it before." The last sentence was spoken as both a statement and a question.

"Yes, I'm afraid I have."

I went out on a limb. "From a homicide in Myrtle Beach?"

"Yes, and from one in New York as well. At both of them the police found the three *veve's* you've mentioned as well as obvious signs of some sort of sadomasochistic sex play. But I suppose you already knew that."

The reference to New York only took me slightly by surprise since Ben had mentioned that there were several other states with unsolved homicides that were possibly linked. He just hadn't told me actual names or any real details. Now I had a line on at least one more. Still, I decided not to let on to Doctor Rieth that I hadn't known about it until now.

"Pretty much. So, can you tell me which *Lwa* belongs to this *veve*?" I asked, voice hopeful.

"I'm afraid not. That's the reason for the nickname. The only time I've ever seen it is in connection with those two murders…and, now apparently this one."

"Actually we have two homicides here we believe to be connected, but the *veve* was only found at one of the scenes."

"Good God," she mumbled again. "So I suppose this really is what the FBI types call a serial killer."

"Yes, I suppose it is."

"Well," she said, seeming to regain some of her composure. "I'm not sure what it is I can do for you. Even if I could identify the *veve,* I don't know that it would be any help."

"Actually, it might. From what I've researched, I would have to guess that this symbol is being used to represent a personal ancestor."

"I'd be inclined to agree with you, and that's what I told the other departments. Not that they seemed particularly interested in the arcane facts at the time. They just kept calling it a cult crime."

"That's an easy out for things they don't understand. Trust me, I've dealt with that very same attitude here myself. But, back to the *veve*…I would think that if we could track down that particular ancestor, perhaps we could find the person who has it on her altar."

"So you think the killer is a woman too?"

"Is that what you were told by the other departments?"

"They weren't willing to share that speculation, but the evidence they told me about seemed to indicate such."

"Here too. So you're a bit of an amateur sleuth I take it?"

"Not really. But, I can put two and two together."

"Well, I'm afraid the math gets a bit harder from here on out."

"Well, Mister Gant, I'll count myself lucky that I'm not in your position then. But, as I said before, it seems to me that you've done quite a bit of homework on this. I wish my students were as dedicated to their studies."

"Let's just say I've got an important motivation. And, yes, the local librarians and occult bookshops know me pretty well right now."

"I'm sure...well...I'll admit you have a good theory. If you could find the ancestor then maybe you could track down a descendent. But, even that could be a dead end because it assumes that the person who has placed this spirit on her altar and elevated it to the status of *Lwa* is actually a direct descendent. In all likelihood she's of no relation whatsoever, and that would put you back at square one."

"True, but right now I'm more or less at square zero."

"I understand, but like I said, I honestly don't know where you would even start to look for this ancestor."

"Actually, I have a few ideas."

"Okay, then no offense, but what do you need me for? You definitely seem to have a better handle on this whole situation than the other police departments."

"Well, to be truthful, the main reason I called is that I have some questions about something you covered in your book on Voodoo."

"You mean about something other than the *veve*'s?"

"Yes. Specifically what I'm interested in is possession by *Lwa*."

I could hear what sounded like a frustrated sigh at the other end then she said, "Yes, it really happens."

"Believe me, I don't doubt that."

"Then what exactly did you need to know about it?"

"Well, what prompted me to call you is that in your book you mentioned instances of secondary or collateral possession."

"You actually read it, didn't you?"

"Not all, but quite a bit of, yes."

"Amazing…so what's your question?"

"Well, you're actually the only authority on Voodoo I found who even mentioned collateral possession by *Lwa*."

"Probably because it's an exceptionally rare occurrence."

"But it happens."

"Yes, it does. But, as I said, it's extremely rare. *Lwa* don't just hop from *horse* to *horse* for no reason."

"I'll accept that, but let's say we have an instance where it does occur. Do you think it's possible for an unwitting subject to accidentally become a *horse* for a *Lwa*?"

"I believe that's pretty much what I just said, isn't it?"

"Let me rephrase that…what I'm talking about is someone who is completely oblivious."

"So when you say 'unwitting' you really mean it. As in someone who is totally out of the loop?"

"Yes. Completely. Someone who's not even a practitioner of Voodoo."

"Well, my initial reaction would be to say, no. However, I suppose that given the right circumstances just about anything is possible." She paused for a second before adding, "Hmmm…but, no, it's not very likely."

"But, it's still possible, correct?"

"Like I said, I suppose anything is possible under exactly the right circumstances. Now, please excuse my curiosity here, but what has *Lwa* possession got to do with these homicides?"

I'm not sure if for some reason I had developed a sort of implicit trust in Doctor Rieth during this short conversation, or if I just needed someone to listen to me. Maybe it was both, maybe it was neither. All I know is that my original plans to conceal my motives for this call were instantly negated as words came rolling out of my mouth before I realized what I was doing.

"Early yesterday afternoon my wife was arrested and charged with them."

CHAPTER 14:

If Doctor Rieth's earlier pauses were weighty, the one that now followed my spontaneous confession overloaded the scale. I instantly began to wonder if revealing that particular fact had been wise. Of course, the decision had to have been made subconsciously because it had never been my intention to take the conversation down this dark alley at all. But, here we were and there was no backing up. All I could do about it now was hope any damage I'd just done was manageable.

"So you lied," she finally said, her original reserved tone tightly coiled about her voice once again as anger replaced curiosity. "You aren't really working with the police, are you?"

"Yes and no," I replied.

"Tell me, Mister Gant…if that's really your name. Are you answering the questions in order, or simply objecting? Because those two words are mutually exclusive."

"That's really my name, and a little of both, I suppose," I told her. "Yes, I lied to you, sort of."

"Sort of? Either you lied or you…Oh, why am I even talking to you?! Good day!"

"No, no, wait!" I begged. "Please, just hear me out!"

"Why?" she spat. "So you can lie to me some more?"

"No. No more lies, just the truth from here on out. I promise."

"Forgive me, but just how will I know that you're really telling the truth? So far, you haven't exactly established a good track record on that point."

I puffed out my cheeks and exhaled heavily as I tried to think of a halfway reasonable response for the extremely reasonable query. Unfortunately, there wasn't one, so I simply said, "I guess you'll just have to trust me."

I'm fairly certain that if she hadn't been stunned by the reply, she would have laughed and hung up. Luck, however, fi seemed to be throwing me a bone, so to speak, and the ta apparently worked in my favor.

"That's asking a lot considering how this started, Mister Gant."

"I know, but I'm desperate and I need your help."

"Why me?"

"Like I said, from the research I've done, apparently you are one of the very few authorities on Voodoo, if not the only one, who believes collateral possession by *Lwa* is possible."

"That's because I've seen it happen."

"Then I came to the right person."

"Are you trying to flatter your way out of this? Because I hate con men."

"No, Doctor Rieth, you have no idea how serious I am about this. My wife is being charged with murders she didn't commit, and I intend to prove it."

Again the clicking semi-silence of the open line filled the earpiece. I wanted to continue pleading, but I'd played all the cards I had, which in reality amounted to a hand anyone else would have folded. The woman at the other end of the phone had no earthly reason to help me, and I knew that. What's more, I was fully aware that she knew it as well; so continuing to run off at the mouth wasn't going to do me a bit of good.

"Okay," she finally said. "You've got two minutes to convince me that I should keep listening to you. But I'm warning you, even if I don't just hang up on you in the middle of this, I'm going to check out your story."

"Sounds more than fair," I agreed. "And, thank you. First off, my apologies for the lie. I just wasn't sure if you'd talk to me otherwise. In reality, it wasn't a complete lie; it was more of a half-truth."

"Semantics."

"Yes. Well, the part about me being a consultant was absolutely ... I work with the local authorities as well as the FBI on cases ...re non-traditional religious artifacts and symbology are found or ...ught to be involved.

"When I told you I was working with the police, that's where it got a bit fuzzy because at the moment I'm not. However, I was up until a week ago. I was originally…"

"Wait a minute," she said, interrupting. "You're in Saint Louis, correct?"

"Yes."

She began repeating my name in a low voice, mumbling the syllables in repetition. "Rowan Gant…Rowan Gant…That's where I've heard of you. I knew it! I knew your name sounded familiar. You're that guy…you're the Witch…"

"I don't know about *the* Witch, but yes, I'm a Witch."

"No, I mean you're the one who caught that psycho a few years ago, aren't you? That crazy who was going around accusing people of being Witches and then killing them…" Her voice trailed off into a murmur once again. "What was his name? Something Parker…or maybe Palmer…"

"Eldon Porter," I volunteered, knowing all too well to whom she was referring. "And, actually, the police caught him. I was just…bait…more or less."

"I think someone forgot to tell that to the media because it was all over the national news."

"Yes, well you really shouldn't believe everything you see on TV."

"As a rule, I don't, but I seem to recall the FBI themselves crediting you with being instrumental in the capture."

Dredging up those events from my past wasn't going to help my mood by any stretch of the imagination. I had made some very heavy sacrifices to end Porter's spree—a bloody orgy that had seen the deaths of several innocent people, among them two of my friends and coven mates. I had far too pressing a matter at hand to wrap myself up in that pain yet again.

"No offense, Doctor Rieth, but those are some memories I really don't enjoy revisiting...besides, there's the issue with my wife and I would..."

"Oh, yes. Certainly. I understand completely. But, I have to admit that your credibility just got an enormous boost."

"Well, that's good to know," I returned. "I would have played that ace from the outset if I had known it was one."

"So, let me get this straight," she ventured. "Your wife has been arrested and charged with these murders, and if I'm following your line of questions to me, you believe she was being ridden by a *Lwa* when they were committed? And, furthermore, that the *Lwa* is the actual entity responsible for the killing?"

"Close. I do think Felicity was being ridden, but I definitely don't believe she committed the crimes, while possessed or at any other time. It was someone else entirely."

"But, I get the feeling you still think the *Lwa* is directly responsible?"

"Yes."

"I don't want to burst your bubble, but since you did read my book you should have picked up on the fact that *Lwa* don't purposely cause harm. Granted, they certainly get used as an excuse by individuals who would like for you to believe...for lack of a better phrase, the 'devil' made them do it...but, that really isn't the case."

"I know that, but I have a strange feeling that this *Lwa* is different. I'm certain that it actually is somehow driving or directing what the killer is doing. And, that it temporarily possessed my wife, otherwise she wouldn't have exhibited the behavior she did. The way I see it, if this *Lwa* was riding someone who was actually willing, then the murders aren't a stretch at all."

"Well, even if you're correct, and some particularly malevolent spirit has been elevated to the status of a personal *Lwa* by a practitioner of Voodoo, that person must be insane. In any case, you're still in the same boat. There's no way you're going to convince anyone to put an ancestral spirit on trial, Mister Gant."

"That goes without saying. But, if I can figure out who this spirit is, maybe I can find the real killer. And, if I'm right and the *Lwa* is driving the individual to commit the crimes…well…I don't know. I'll have to cross that bridge when I get there. But, the truth is, if she knows the nature of the *Lwa*, and she keeps inviting it in, then she's just as guilty."

"But, the police are convinced that it is your wife who is the culprit, yes?"

"I'm afraid so."

"If you don't mind my asking, why? Do they have some compelling reason to think such a thing?"

"They say they have evidence placing her at the two crime scenes here in Saint Louis, as well as the one in Myrtle Beach."

"That's not good. What about the one in New York?"

"Honestly, I don't know. The first I heard about New York was when you mentioned it earlier. However, the rumor is that they have seven other unsolved homicides throughout the United States with similar characteristics to these, so I suspect that is one of them."

"Seven?!"

"That's what I was told."

"How long has this been going on?"

"A few years, apparently. Since two-thousand three at least."

"And you were oblivious to it?"

"Of course I was," I returned sharply. "Why wouldn't I be? It wasn't Felicity doing it."

"Sorry, and I hate to say it, but, if the police have evidence…"

"Well, that's where it starts moving beyond simply adding two and two," I interrupted. "I don't think their evidence is legitimate."

"Why not? What is it?"

"Well…" I knew what her reaction was going to be, but I couldn't lie because if she found out, it would do nothing but destroy the re-establishment of trust I'd started to develop with her. "They say they have DNA linking her to the crimes."

"Remember when I asked about a 'compelling reason', Mister Gant? I'd say DNA evidence definitely qualifies as one of those."

"I realize that, but I have cause to believe it's bogus."

"You mean a lab error? Did they re-run it?"

"Three times, actually. But, my contention is that it was planted or purposely tampered with. Long story short, I have enemies who would like nothing better than to discredit me in any way possible. I sincerely believe that they wouldn't stop at framing my wife for murder in order to get to me, especially given that both of us are, or were, involved in the investigation. This is a perfect opportunity for something like that."

"You mean you have enemies within the police department?"

"Unfortunately, yes."

"So you think it's a conspiracy? I'm sorry, but now you're sounding like a television show."

"Trust me, I know that. And, if it wasn't happening to me, I'm sure I would say the same thing. But, given some of the events that have taken place in my life over the past few years, it's actually nowhere near as crazy as it sounds. Besides, it's the only logical explanation I can imagine right now because I know for certain that my wife isn't a killer."

"How can you be so sure?"

"She's my wife, Doctor Rieth."

"No offense, Mister Gant, but I assume you are familiar with the BTK killer?"

Of course I was. How could I not be? The only way anyone could have remained oblivious to Dennis Rader, self-dubbed BTK for his threefold methodology of binding, torturing, and then killing his victims, would be if they had been living in a total information vacuum. The history of his brutal crimes, his eventual capture and remorseless courtroom confession had held the attention of the nation, off and on, for the better part of the year. But, I knew that his sadistic legacy wasn't her point. What she was driving at was the fact that in everyday life the man had been a pillar of the community, and that his unthinkable activities had been hidden from his family for nearly two decades.

"Since you mentioned it, let's not stop there, Doctor Rieth," I replied. "It's not at all uncommon for the families of serial offenders to be clueless about the secret life their loved one is leading. You can lump John Wayne Gacy and a whole host of others right in with Rader.

"But, the fact remains that I am not a typical spouse wallowing in denial and disbelief as statistics would lead you to believe. Felicity is innocent, and I'll do whatever it takes to prove it."

She paused thoughtfully, but this time the silence didn't have the same hollow feeling as before.

"I guess right about now you're having trouble finding anyone to believe you," she finally said.

"You have no idea," I answered. "There are a couple of people in our corner, but at the moment it's pretty lonely where I'm standing."

"Okay then, so your wife is innocent, and it's up to you to prove it. I suppose we should get back to the part about the *Lwa*..." she verbally returned us to the impetus for the conversation. "You mentioned that your wife exhibited odd behavior, and this is what leads you to believe she was being ridden. Tell me about it."

Doctor Rieth listened attentively while I relayed the story of Felicity's out-of-character actions, including her missing memories and assault on agent Mandalay as well as her violent tryst with the man she had picked up in the fetish club. It occurred to me as I went over the events for what seemed like the thousandth time, just exactly how insane it all really sounded. Of course, I had assumed from the beginning that it probably came off as ludicrous to outsiders unfamiliar with the true nature of the supernatural. But, as for me, I had been there. I had seen it first hand and knew what was happening. The problem was that, even given my own knowledge and experiences, the whole thing was now starting to sound ludicrous to me too.

When I reached the end of the tale, I simply stopped. I had to admit, given my own wavering faith in the story I'd just told, I was fully expecting to hear little more than silence followed by a dull click as the phone was hung up in my ear. However, what greeted me couldn't have been much further from that if it had tried.

"Just for my own edification, your wife doesn't suffer from D-I-D, does she?"

"D-I-D?"

"Dissociative Identity Disorder. They used to call it Multiple Personality Disorder."

"No, she doesn't."

"Has she ever displayed odd changes in personality before this recent incident. Most especially childlike tendencies?"

"No," I said again. "No offense, Doctor, but I thought you were a sociologist who specialized in world religions, not a shrink."

"I am a sociologist, but as it happens I once had a teaching assistant with D-I-D, so I ended up learning quite a bit about it. I'm simply trying to cover all the possible explanations for your wife's behavior."

Her queries reminded me that Ben had used that very ailment as an excuse to defuse a situation with one of the local police departments when Felicity had first fallen under the influence of the *Lwa*. That was before we knew what was going on, and it had seemed like a reasonable course of action at the time. However, now I feared it was going to become ammunition for the other side even though it was entirely untrue.

"She's not a multiple."

"It's nothing to be ashamed of," she prodded.

"I understand, and I agree, but I assure you we can rule it out," I told her.

"Well then, if we assume that she was truly being ridden, the way I see it is that there has to be some kind of latent connection between your wife and the *Lwa*. Or, maybe even her and the killer."

Doctor Rieth's reply was immediate and succinct. In fact, she hadn't even paused before offering the analysis.

"So, you don't think this all sounds crazy?" I asked.

"Oh yes, it sounds crazy all right, but that's not the point," she answered. "Remember, many of the things I've written about in my book sound crazy to the uninitiated."

"Yeah, I guess they do."

"So, if we are to assume that your theory about the *Lwa* is correct, then we have to find the reason it chose your wife as a *horse*, especially given your contention that it already had one with a far stronger, and completely willing, connection. Knowing that may well provide a clue that will lead back to either the identity of the *Lwa* or even the original *horse*, which is the ultimate goal. Correct?"

"Correct. Any ideas on that front?"

"Like I said, it has to be a latent connection that superseded the connection with the other practitioner."

"Okay, but what could that be? Felicity doesn't practice Voodoo."

"She doesn't? I'm sorry. I just assumed she must because this would all make more sense if she did."

"I'm sure, but that's why I called you."

"Well, then that's the big question, isn't it?" she replied with a healthy sigh. "Still, there must be something connecting the two, and it could be almost anything. For instance, does your wife own any antique jewelry she purchased second hand? Especially recently? Something she might have been wearing at the time of the possession?"

"I'm sure she does. Own jewelry like that, I mean. But, I don't recall her making any recent purchases. I also don't remember her wearing any of it at the time, although I could be wrong," I said and then added, "At the point when she had the guy in the motel room, she wasn't wearing much at all, actually."

"Second hand clothing that may have belonged to the killer, perhaps?"

"Maybe. She's been known to visit resale shops. Aga be certain."

"Okay, you said she doesn't practice *Vodoun*, but has any chance dabbled with it at all?"

"No. At least not that I am aware of, and I think th something she would tell me. She's a degreed Wiccan with som strong ties to British Traditional WitchCraft, but no real dealings in any of the Afro-Caribbean practices other than a passing knowledge of them."

"So, she's a Witch too?"

"Yes, but that wouldn't be it, would it?"

"Just speculating. That would definitely make her far more open than your average bystander. Magick begetting magick, maybe?"

"She would almost have needed to work magick that somehow related to Voodoo though, wouldn't she?"

"Maybe, maybe not. Like I said, I'm just speculating."

"So, should I assume by the direction this conversation has taken that you are willing to help me?"

"I suppose that's pretty much how it looks, isn't it, Mister Gant?"

"Well, if that's the case, you might want to start calling me Rowan, Doctor Rieth."

"Then you should probably start calling me, Velvet."

"Mind if I ask…"

"Burlesque performer. My mother thought it was pretty."

"I see."

"No wise cracks."

"Wouldn't dream of it."

.APTER 15:

1 he reflection staring back at me from the two-way mirror on the opposite wall didn't look much better than the one I'd seen at home. I'd actually taken a few minutes to shave before getting into the shower and then tried to at least make myself presentable. None of those things, however, could mask my exhaustion or my foul mood, and it showed.

I turned my face away from the mirror. I knew someone was watching; they'd told me they would be. I suppose it was better than having a stranger parked in the room with us, which was the normal procedure as I understood it. But even so, it was more than a little disconcerting. I tried to push it out of my mind because I needed to deal with what I had at hand and not unseen distractions. But, I still found it hard to keep the invasion of privacy out of my thoughts. Of course, within these walls, privacy was a luxury that simply didn't exist.

Shifting nervously in my seat, I returned my focus to the redhead on the other side of the table.

Small talk seemed to have become the order of the moment. Twenty minutes had passed, and thus far we'd been engaged in short bursts of trivial banter. Things of no real import, such as the weather, what bills might have shown up in the day's mail, or any number of other equally unimportant distractions. The whole of it was making me crazy, and I suppose it was for that reason my mouth began to blurt out something my brain knew would be best left unmentioned. I didn't do it out of spite. I just needed to get something other than a flat, one word response from my wife.

"I probably shouldn't even tell you this…" I started but then caught myself before continuing. Getting a response was one thing. Triggering it this way definitely wasn't a smart move, and I knew it. I shook my head as much out of chastising myself as anything said, "No…just forget it."

"What is it?" Felicity asked. "Tell me."

At least this time the reply was something besides, "Y "No", or "Fine", even if I hadn't followed through with the statement

Her voice was still emotionless but heavily saturated with her inherent Celtic lilt. The accent was an omnipresent feature but one that usually resided in the background, noticeable but not overwhelming. It always became more pronounced, however, when she was stressed, tired, or had spent more than a few hours with her family. In some instances, thick was even too weak a word to describe it.

It wasn't hard to guess that the first two factors were what were driving it at the moment, and they were driving it hard. In fact, if she became any more stressed than she was now, I might well have trouble understanding her; for the brogue would not only start to be peppered with Gaelic, it would become so deeply accented as to almost obscure any English she might continue to use. In other words, we had more or less already arrived at thick and were definitely on our way toward a stronger adjective.

I dismissed her question with only a cursory explanation. "It's not important. Not right now, anyway."

"So tell me then," she pressed. "If it's not important, it shouldn't matter."

I let out a heavy breath and shifted in my seat. Everything mattered, especially now. I knew that for a fact, even if she didn't. I looked down at the table then reached up to massage my temple. My headache was coming back, not that it had ever completely gone away, but the dull ache had been something I could live with. I definitely didn't need seriously stabbing pains on top of everything else right now.

Little more than three hours had passed since my conversation with Doctor Rieth. The thread of positive luck—if you could really call it that—which had begun during the phone call, had seemed to continue in its wake. For a little while at least, as only a few moments

...ad hung up, the phone began to ring again. That time it had ...ackie calling to let me know that she'd managed to arrange a ...-ordered visit with Felicity.

The fact was, under normal circumstances, prisoners detained ...the Saint Louis City Justice Center had to schedule visitors in advance, and each particular "dorm" had specific days set aside for those visits to take place. By obtaining an impromptu judicial order, our—or given the events of last evening I should say Felicity's—attorney had succeeded in circumventing the system, getting me in to see her early this afternoon.

What I was going to end up owing Jackie for this bit of legal sorcery, I had no idea, but the truth is I didn't really care. I had to see my wife. I needed to know that she was okay. Moreover, I needed her to know that I had not forsaken her. That I was going to do everything in my power to stop this from happening.

And, now, here I was, downtown and just around the corner from where I had been the night before while waiting to wake up from this nightmare. From the looks of things, it appeared I still hadn't accomplished that task.

At this particular moment, I couldn't even remember which floor of the building I was on. In fact, I was lucky that I could even recall that the address was on Tucker. All that really stood out in my mind right now is that we had gone *up* after being patted down, wanded, and generally scrutinized by uniformed corrections officers. However, I don't think it was the frisking that was responsible for my sudden attack of geographical amnesia. More than likely it was the initial shock of seeing Felicity in her present state.

Her red hair, which usually spiraled about her soft face with fiery brilliance, was dull and limp. Down, it would hang past her waist, but at the moment it was twisted, wrapped, and tucked—sitting in a lifeless pile atop her head. While it wasn't that unusual for her to wear it in a Gibson-girlish coif, I had to admit I was a bit surprised since she wasn't allowed anything with which to affix it in place. I suppose it was staying up only by the grace of some bit of woman magick men can never understand, let alone duplicate.

Her smooth ivory skin was blotchy and beyond any definition of pale that came to my mind. Even ashen was too delicate a word to describe the greyness that seemed to envelope her.

Jade green irises, normally bright, were no more than flat disks swimming in the centers of bloodshot whites. They both stood out in contrast to the dark rings encircling her sunken eyes.

She was totally devoid of makeup, and it showed. It wasn't as if she really ever wore that much to begin with, but right now, unlike any other time, its absence was beyond glaring.

Her petite frame was clad in a loose fitting, sherbet orange jumpsuit, which was standard issue for inmates at the facility. The unnaturally brilliant color did little to help her altogether stark and sickly appearance.

Everything about the way she looked, right down to the way she carried herself, told me she'd managed to get no more rest than I had eked out of the long night. She looked absolutely horrible, and I'm certain the expression on my face upon first seeing her had betrayed at least that much.

Even so, to me, she still couldn't be more beautiful.

Unfortunately, just sitting here looking at her wasn't going to help either of us. We didn't have all that much time, and even less to waste. Court order or not, it wasn't going to be long before I was sent on my way by the guard on the other side of the mirrored glass.

Jackie's arrangement had specified what was called a "contact visit", something that might have been otherwise impossible considering the severity of the charges against Felicity. And, of course, somehow she had also managed to get them to leave us more or less unchaperoned in the room. However, that was as far as the indulgences went. Contact or not, the court order wasn't going to buy us any more time together than normal inmate visits prescribed.

The charges themselves, although making the arrangements for our visit a bit tricky, were actually working to my wife's advantage.

For one thing, I had been told that she was alone in her cell, as they were segregating her from the rest of the "population" due to her alleged crimes. Basically, in order to keep the petty thieves and DWI detainees safe, they weren't about to put an accused serial killer in direct contact with them without close supervision. I was certainly glad of that, but for much the opposite reason.

I continued watching my wife in silence across the small table. I hadn't yet replied to her urging, and I wasn't sure I could get away with the reticence for much longer. Refusing to tell her now would only widen the unexplained rift that seemed to have formed between us. The problem was, right now my brain was just too sluggish to come up with a convincing lie considering how I had started the earlier sentence.

"So, are you going to tell me, then?" she asked again, pushing the silence aside.

Thus far, she'd had a tendency to stare into space whenever she spoke, and that hadn't changed. I also noticed that she was still absently rubbing her red, swollen wrists where the handcuffs had chafed and bruised them. I sincerely hoped those marks hadn't been left by Ben because if they had, he wouldn't need to invite the next punch.

I opened my mouth to speak, mumbled through a false start, then offered up what I thought was a logical excuse, as I tried one last shot at disentangling myself from the self-inflicted mess. "I shouldn't have said anything. I really don't want to upset you."

"Too late, Rowan," she replied. "Take a look around. The police beat you to it."

"You still don't need any more to worry about," I told her with a shake of my head.

"And, you do?"

"No..." I replied quietly. "Neither of us do."

"Aye."

"Yeah, but still..."

"Misery loves company. Go ahead. Tell me, then."

"You aren't miserable enough as it is?"

"I think this is about as miserable as it gets, Row."

"Yeah, I suppose it is."

"Go on, then. Quit avoiding the question. Share."

"Well…It's nothing really…I've had a few somewhat unpleasant conversations with your father since yesterday morning."

"Aye, I can't say that I'm surprised by that."

"By the way, speaking of that…any insight on the phrase 'an rabe something-or-other'?"

"*An riabhach*?" she repeated, filling in the blanks.

"Yeah, that sounds about right."

"Did he call you that?"

"That's the gist I got. A couple of times for sure. Of course, he'd already called me quite a few things I already knew how to translate."

"It's been bad, then?"

"It hasn't been pleasant. Although, he does have a fairly predictable cycle. He calls, blames me for this, calls me names, demands to know what I'm going to do to fix it but doesn't give me a chance to answer, then I hang up on him. Then he calls back…lather, rinse, repeat."

My attempt at levity didn't provoke a laugh, or even a smile. She simply sighed and slowly shook her head. "Well, that phrase means, *the evil one*."

I gave her a half shrug. "Go figure."

"Aye."

"So, I guess the fact that he blames me for this isn't any big surprise either."

"No, I don't suppose it is, given the tension between the two of you, then. But, you should just ignore him. He'll get over it."

"Trying to. I've been letting the machine grab the phone lately."

"Good…so, is that what you thought was going to upset me?"

"Yeah."

"Liar."

"Excuse me?"

"You're lying. I can tell."

I'd managed to bluff her in the past, but I guess my acting skills were diminished by my emotional state, or my exhaustion. Actually, it was probably due to both.

"Yeah," I sighed. "Okay, so there was something else."

"What?"

"Well, I guess I should consider it funny, truthfully. Or, I suppose it could be if it weren't so sad… Anyway, what I started to tell you is that once this is all over Shamus wants to have you deprogrammed." I made the statement as calmly as I could, considering that I was unable to find in it any of the humor I had just espoused.

"That's it?"

"That's not enough?"

"Aye, he's just wailing at whoever will listen," she said with a shake of her head. "My father has always done that whenever he feels helpless. It's just his way. You know it's not going to happen."

"Maybe, but I'm not so willing to rule out an attempt. I think he might be serious about this," I offered after a moment.

She shook her head again. "My mother will put an end to it, never you mind."

"I hope you're right."

"Don't you know by now, we O'Brien women are the dominant type?"

"Yes, I do, but under the circumstances I don't think you should joke about that right now."

"If I don't joke about it, Rowan, I'll just be crying, then."

"Yeah…" I mumbled.

"So," she said, giving her head a sideways nod toward my bruised knuckles without actually turning to look. "When are you going to tell me what happened to your hand?"

I wasn't sure she'd even noticed. She hadn't really looked at me since Jackie and I had arrived, at least, not that I had seen. But, I wasn't going to gripe about it just yet. We now had a dialogue going and that was an improvement.

"Nothing really. An irresistible force met an unmovable object."

"Aye, so you were venting aggression, then. Do we need a new door or just a patch job on a wall?"

"Neither. Ben's jaw was the object."

"Oh, *Caorthann*..." she muttered, using the Gaelic version of my name. It was the first time since she'd entered the room that she had seemed to show any real emotion at all.

"Don't worry about it. He asked for it. Literally."

"Don't blame him, Rowan. This isn't his fault."

"Yeah. He keeps saying the same thing."

"He's right."

"That remains to be seen."

"Aye, you don't believe he's responsible for this and you know it."

"Responsible or not, he's the one who led you out of the house in handcuffs, and I'm afraid that's going to take a lot of forgiving on my part."

"He was doing his job."

"Uh-huh."

"Rowan..."

"I have my reasons, honey," I cut her off. "Why don't we move on to something else?"

I didn't think it would be a good idea to let her in on the fact that Ben wasn't convinced of her innocence. However, if we stayed on this subject, I was probably going to screw up and tell her just that. For now, I felt it was better to let her keep on believing he was one of the good guys. Maybe with a little luck he would come around, and she'd never have to know about his doubts.

"All right, then. What would you like to talk about?"

She still wasn't making eye contact with me, and I knew that wasn't good. However, since she'd seemed to open up, I decided to push a little further.

"Your turn to share. Why don't you tell me what your problem is with me?"

"I don't know what you mean."

"Look at me."

"What?"

"Look at me, Felicity. You haven't looked me in the face since they brought you into the room."

She sucked in a deep breath and slowly turned her head the necessary fraction to meet my eyes, but only barely. We held one another's gaze for a long moment before I finally broke the thick silence.

"Would you like to tell me what's wrong? Besides the obvious I mean."

"Aye, what are you talking about then?"

"Felicity, something's going on here that I'm not being told. Jackie informed me last night that you don't want her discussing your case with me. Then, after she moved the world to get me in here to see you today, we're making small talk about nothing, and I can hardly even get you to look at me. What's going on? Why are you shutting me out?"

"I'm not."

"Yes, you are."

"No, I'm not."

"Give me a break, honey. Yes, you are. Hell, a blind, deaf mute can tell what's going on here. What I want to know is why?"

"Aye, I don't want to talk about it."

"Well, guess what? I do."

"Well I don't. Not now."

"Dammit, Felicity!" I barked the reply as I pushed back from the table and stood. "There isn't time for this. If I'm going to help you,

I have to know what's going on from all sides. Cutting me off like this isn't going to get either of us anywhere. Least of all you."

She didn't even flinch at my minor outburst. Her face remained stoic and eyes focused on where I had been sitting. She didn't even bring her gaze up to meet mine.

"Maybe there isn't anywhere for me to get to."

"What's that supposed to mean?"

"Maybe I'm already there."

"Felicity, I definitely don't like the sound of this," I said, a mix of confusion and anger in my voice. "What are you trying to say?"

She dropped her head forward and stared down at her wrists as she continued to gently rub them. Silence filled the short void between us, and I continued to watch as her shoulders seemed to droop even more than they had only moments ago.

Finally, without looking up, she said, "I spoke with Jackie about this last night. I was going to wait a bit, but since you're asking now...anyway...I'm...I'm thinking it might be a good idea for you to file for divorce."

CHAPTER 16:

I f ever there was a sentence that could qualify as a sucker punch, there it was, and the fact that Felicity had just delivered it stunned me speechless. The force behind the meaning of the word landed square in my gut, and then just for good measure it backhanded me across the face. Of anything my wife could have said to me, that was absolutely the last thing I ever imagined. In fact, I hadn't imagined it at all, that's how far off the chart it truly was.

I honestly didn't know whether the air had just evacuated from my lungs of its own accord or if I had simply forgotten to breathe. What I did know was that my ears were ringing, and the wearisome headache was ramping up a little more with each and every heartbeat.

The cold hollowness that was drilling into the pit of my stomach started to extend its fingers outward through my body, and I felt like I wanted to vomit. All I could do was stare back at her with what I am sure was a mix of incredulity and utter shock on my face. The mask of confused emotions was entirely lost on her though because she was still staring at the table, not me.

I swallowed hard and forced myself to wheeze in a deep breath as stars started to dance in front of my eyes. My brain ran up and down the scale of emotions, randomly choosing one, trying it on for size, and then discarding it for another. Happiness wasn't one that ever made it into that mix. Finally, after the fifth or sixth emotional costume change, I found myself fitting comfortably into anger and I remained there.

"File for…" I blurted, unable to complete the sentence for fear of actually manifesting the act if I dared speak the word aloud. "What the hell are you talking about?! Have you lost your mind?!"

Felicity had yet to raise her eyes from the table, and even that jibe didn't force her to do so.

She muttered quietly, "You could probably use that when you file."

"Use it my ass!" I snapped. "And, I'm not going to file for a goddammed…you know…one of those things."

"Divorce."

"Don't say it!"

"Calm down, Rowan. It's just a word."

"Maybe so, but words and magick go hand in hand, especially with you…either way, I'm not going there."

"But…"

I cut her off. "But nothing. Who told you to do this anyway? Have you been talking to your father or something?"

"No."

"Was it Jackie? Because if it was, she's fired. I'll get you a different attorney."

"No," she returned, shaking her head but still not looking up. "No one told me to do this. It's my idea."

"Your idea?"

"Aye."

"Your idea. No outside influence. Just poof, you want a divorce."

"I already said yes."

"So, are you trying to tell me you really and truly want one of those?"

She paused then nodded her head slightly.

"No," I admonished. "You need to say it."

"Yes." There was no mistaking the marked hesitation that came before she choked out the word.

"Yeah, right. You'll excuse me if I don't believe you."

"Well, I do."

"Okay, if you want it so bad then why don't you file for it yourself?"

"I'm a little busy in case you haven't noticed."

"Trust me, I've noticed," I quipped. "So you came up with this idea all by yourself?"

"Aye. I've already told you that."

"Okay. How about you fill me in on the particulars, like, oh, I don't know, *why*?"

"It's the right thing to do."

"The *right* thing to do? Honey, this isn't like leaving a note on someone's windshield after you accidentally ding their car door on the supermarket parking lot."

"Do you really think I don't know that?"

"If you do, then get serious and tell me why? Have you suddenly stopped loving me?"

"I didn't say that."

"Well, it has to be something. As far as I can recall, I'm not abusive...or a deadbeat...I'm not unfaithful, and I'm certain you know that. You'll tell me when I start getting warm, right?"

She expelled a frustrated breath and shot back, "Look, I just want a divorce. That's all."

I know for a fact I visibly cringed at the word. The pain in my over-tightened muscles broadcast it loud and clear.

"Not good enough," I replied. "You're going to have to tell me the real why."

"I just did."

"Guess again, sweetheart. It's not going to fly. Give me one good reason for you suddenly wanting this. Did you find someone else?"

"NO! Of course not."

Felicity was a Taurus, through and through, and she manifested the stereotypical characteristics of the star sign often. However, out of all those idiosyncrasies, the aptly attributed bull-headedness was her most omnipresent. She had out-stubborned me on more than one occasion, and I truly feared she would do everything in her power to accomplish that now.

However, as pragmatic and obstinate as she could be, I wasn't going to allow her to win. I had emotion on my side, and I was going to appeal to it in every sense, no matter what. I knew this wasn't something she truly desired; I just had to get her to admit it.

"Then give me a reason."

"I don't have to."

"Yes, you do."

"Rowan…"

"Felicity…"

"Don't push me on this, then. Just take my word for it."

"Not happening."

"I'm not going to talk about it."

"Yes, you are."

"Damn your eyes, Rowan Gant!"

"Don't damn something you don't even have the guts to look at," I returned harshly.

"Don't do this, Rowan."

"After what you just asked me to do? Don't ask me for favors. You don't deserve any."

I hated playing the bad guy. I hated pulling her strings by offering up such a callous remark. And, I hated the cruelty of what I might be forced to say if she didn't give in soon. But, more than any of those things, I hated that she had put me in this position as she was trying to stonewall her way through it. So, I gave in and played the wild card. I would push her as hard as my churning stomach would let me and hope that it would be enough.

Fortunately, her own emotional resistance was down to nil, just like mine, and that last verbal shove was all it took.

"*Damnú ort!* It's for you!" she suddenly shrieked, finally looking up as she slammed the heels of her fists hard enough against the table to make it shudder. "All right? It's for you!"

I had only a brief moment to catch the anguish on my wife's face. Almost immediately following the loud report of her hands against the pressboard, I heard the dull metallic clunk of a deadbolt being thrown. Less than a second later the door swung open. Embarrassment added itself to Felicity's pained features and she turned away.

I twisted my own head toward the new sound just as the corrections officer who had been watching us filled the opening. She was alert, eyes fixed on my wife, with one hand riding on a holstered container of pepper spray at her hip.

"I think we might need to cut this visit short," she announced.

"No. Everything's fine," I told her.

"It didn't look fine to me."

"Really, it is," I replied. "Just a little emotional is all."

"That's exactly the problem, sir."

"Look, it's no big deal. And, I really need to finish talking to my wife."

She'd glanced over to me a few times, but still kept a close watch on Felicity. "How about it, O'Brien? Are we going to have any problems?"

Felicity gave her head a shake without looking toward her.

"Words, O'Brien," the officer pressed. "I need to hear you say it."

"No," Felicity muttered just loud enough to be heard. "No problems."

The corrections officer waited a moment then glanced toward me. "Okay, time's almost up anyway."

"Fifteen minutes, okay?" I asked.

"Five," she replied.

"Ten?" I bargained.

"Five," she repeated.

"Then go away," I remarked as calmly as I could, which wasn't very. "You're using up *my* time."

She didn't perpetuate the argument. She simply swung the door shut and threw the lock.

I knew I wasn't endearing myself to the establishment, but that was a sacrifice I was going to have to live with because if it meant saving my wife, it was more than worth it.

I turned back to Felicity and discovered that she'd again focused her stare on the surface of the table.

"Honey, look at me," I urged.

It seemed that her stubbornness had fled for the time being, and she slowly lifted her gaze back up to mine. I studied her face quietly and felt my heart rend at the very sight. What I hadn't noticed in that split second before the corrections officer interrupted was that her cheeks were wet and her already bloodshot eyes were starting to swell even more. As was her way, the reason she had been keeping her face hidden was that she'd been silently crying this entire time. I should have known, and I mutely cursed myself for not realizing it sooner.

I gave her a moment to gather herself then lowered my frame back into the chair and stared across the table at her. She was still avoiding direct eye contact, but I wasn't going to let that stop me.

"For me?" I finally said. "You know, that's funny, because I don't recall having a divorce on my wish list."

"Don't be glib, Rowan," she sniffed. "This is serious."

"Oh, trust me, I know that."

"Then don't make jokes."

"Aren't you the one who just said a few minutes ago that if you didn't joke about it you'd cry?"

"Aye, and it mustn't work, because crying is obviously what I've been doing then, isn't it?" she chided.

"Yes, it is. I'm just trying not to join you."

"Come on in," she offered. "The more the merrier."

"Who's making jokes now?"

She simply shrugged in reply.

"Uh-huh, well, I think I'll pass. It's not really my kind of merry. So, you've been sitting here trying to convince me you want a divorce, which we both know is a lie. And now you're telling me that it's a gift for me. Well, here's a news flash. I'm returning it because I don't want it."

"Rowan…this is serious."

"No kidding…Look, honey…I don't know where this is coming from, but it needs to stop. I feel like all I've done since yesterday morning is argue with everyone in my path. With some of them, it's been for good reason, and others…Well, as much as I hate to admit it, it's just been because I'm mad at the world right now.

"All I can tell you is that you are the one person I don't want to argue with…especially not now…so, the truth is if I don't treat this like a joke and laugh at it, my brain is going to seize up because I'm all out of tears right now."

"But, Rowan…"

"But what?"

"A divorce would be in your best interest, then."

My headache was still gaining ground. I took off my glasses and laid them aside while I took a moment to rub my eyes. After slipping the spectacles back onto my face, I folded my hands in front of me and regarded her quietly.

After what seemed a long pause, I said, "Okay, I'm afraid you're going to have to explain that one."

"Do you really want to visit me in prison?" she appealed.

"No. But that's a moot point because you aren't going to prison."

"Be realistic."

"I am."

"Rowan…think about it…look at the evidence they have."

"I haven't exactly been privy to much," I told her. "Especially since your lawyer won't talk to me about it."

"Sorry," she apologized. "I'll tell Jackie to get you back into the loop then."

"That would be appreciated."

"Well, either way, certainly by now you know about the DNA evidence they have. Right?"

I nodded. "Yeah, it was mentioned."

"Well, the way I understand it, that's pretty bad."

"I never said it wasn't."

"So, think about it. I must have done it. I must have killed them."

I shook my head at her. "You see, now I know I didn't just hear you say you killed those men."

"I don't know! I just don't know," she snipped, finally looking me in the eyes. Then, as she lowered her face once again, her voice became choked and almost whimpering. "I can't remember...I can't..."

Fear suddenly thrust icy fingers into my chest and took hold of my heart for a pair of beats.

"Felicity... Gods... Please tell me you didn't confess to these murders."

"No, I didn't," she whispered.

"Then just what did you tell the police?"

"Nothing really. Jackie has been handling it."

"Good." I let out a relieved sigh. "Let her. That's what she's getting paid for."

"But, what if..."

"We've discussed this, Felicity. There is no what if."

"I know we've talked about it, but listen to me, Rowan. What if you're wrong?"

"I'm not."

"But..."

"Listen to me. You did *not* kill anyone."

"How can you be so sure, especially when I'm not?"

"I just am."

"Rowan..."

"Honey, just think about it. If you had done it, don't you think someone on the other side would be slapping me in the back of the head about now?"

"Aye, maybe they are and you're ignoring them," she replied, still sniffling. "You've got a headache. I can tell."

"It's not that kind of headache."

"Liar."

"You know, you're going to give me a complex. That's the second time you've called me a liar in the past half hour."

"Only because it's the second time you've lied to me in that same half hour."

"Must be losing my touch. You usually don't catch me."

"No, I almost always catch you. I just usually don't say anything."

"Yeah, well, maybe so, but that still doesn't change the fact that you're innocent."

"Aye, I wish I could be as certain of that as you are."

"Well, I'm going to have to ask you to work on that because I need you to believe it as well."

"I'll try."

"So…after all that, do you still want a divorce?"

"No. I didn't really want one to begin with."

"Didn't think so."

"But you might."

I gave my head a frustrated shake. "I thought we'd…"

"Just hear me out for a second," she interrupted.

"Fine," I surrendered. "But please let's not start this argument up all over again."

"It's about the evidence."

"Okay, what about it?"

"What evidence have you heard about?"

"So far, just the DNA and the hair. They took some of your clothes from the house. They also grabbed some books from my office, but those were mine…and the library's, so they don't count. Other than that, not much, really."

She sighed and glanced away then looked back to me with a renewed nervousness.

"I love you, Rowan Linden Gant," she abruptly announced.

"Right back at ya', Felicity Caitlin O'Brien," I answered. "But somehow I don't think that qualifies as evidence."

"No, but my overnight bag is a bit of a different story, then," she confessed. "And, you need to know that no matter what they imply to you, I have never…"

She didn't get a chance to finish the sentence before the guard outside opened the door once again then stepped in and announced, "Time's up."

"Just another minute or so," I appealed.

"No sir. I already let you go long as it is," she replied in a vindictive tone. "*Your time* is up. Now you're wasting *my time*."

CHAPTER 17:

I wasn't smiling when I walked out into the afternoon daylight. There wasn't even an expression remotely resembling good humor in close proximity to my face. I know the chorus of the once popular song said that after "fighting authority", I was supposed to come out "grinnin'", but it just wasn't going to happen.

I'd been locked in this me-versus-the-law free-for-all since Friday morning, and it was getting tiresome. Thus far I hadn't accomplished much of anything other than digging myself into a deeper hole because, also like the song says, the bastards did indeed keep coming out on top. There was, however, a point other than the "grinnin'" where the lyrics and I would again be diverging—and that was very simply the fact that I wasn't about to let them "always win".

As far as I was concerned, they were welcome to claim victory in all of the skirmishes they wanted. The truth was they already had, with their latest triumph being my unceremonious ejection from the interview room and immediate escort out the front doors of the Justice Center. However, when it came down to the fate of my wife, I was going to prevail, not them. They just didn't know it yet. However, the fact that the details of how I was going to accomplish this were still radically fuzzier than my crystal clear conviction was a moot point at the moment, because my mind was actually elsewhere.

It was still back upstairs with my wife.

I was certain that had I been a bit less surly—okay, a *lot* less surly—in my interaction with the corrections officer, I might have gotten the extra minute or two I had asked for. Instead, I was all but manhandled out of the room before Felicity could really begin her story, much less complete it. The fact that it had begun in such a cryptic, confession-like manner worried me. It wasn't that I didn't trust her because I did, that wasn't the issue at all. However, when you mix "overnight bag" and "whatever they imply, I didn't..." together, the result can be more than just a little disconcerting. Suffice it to say, since something about an overnight bag had the police taking particular notice, and with an opening like the one she'd provided, I couldn't help but have a few questions of my own.

Of course, as it stood now, I had probably done more damage than good with the authorities inside where my visitation rights were concerned. With that, and the fact that Jackie was still inside with Felicity, I wasn't sure when I would be getting my answers anytime soon. Yet another overt and undeniable chunk of evidence to support what everyone around me had been saying all along—that I needed to calm down. Unfortunately, it was much easier for them to say than it was for me to do.

I stopped mentally castigating myself for a moment and looked up to glance at the traffic cruising along Tucker before stepping off the curb on my way around to the driver's side of my truck. As it turned out, it was a good thing there weren't any moving vehicles nearby because the voice that suddenly came from behind gave me an alarming start.

"So, how's she doin'?"

I flinched involuntarily as the unexpected words caused me to lurch then immediately stumble headlong toward the street. At the same instant I felt myself pitching forward, someone clamped onto my upper arm and pulled me back. It should have been obvious that whoever had grabbed me was merely trying to help, but my paranoid mind took it in a completely different direction. I twisted around quickly, tensing as I tried to assume what I thought would be a defensive posture.

Ben took one look at my face then released my arm and held his hands out in a yielding gesture as he took a half step back. "Whoa, Kemosabe. Just a bit jumpy, ain't ya'?"

I allowed myself to relax once I realized who I was dealing with, but only slightly. My mood hadn't exactly been uplifted recently, and to be honest, I wasn't in a big hurry to talk to Ben. We had made some headway last evening, but it had really only taken the edge off my anger. While that was a start, it definitely hadn't repaired the schism by any stretch of the imagination.

As we stood there, I gave him a quick once-over. He really didn't look any better than I felt, so I suspected he was dealing with his own demons and sleepless nights. I couldn't say that I was sorry about that. I also noticed his jaw looked just about as bruised as my fist. Right or wrong, I took a modicum of satisfaction in that.

"Didn't see you," I finally replied, voice flat.

"Yeah…kinda got that from the 'I'm gonna kick your ass' look on your face."

"Uh-huh…well, as I recall you're the one who told me to be careful when I'm in the city."

"Yeah, but I meant the parts where ya' really need ta' be careful. I mean, look around. Ya' got coppers all over the place down here."

"All the more reason to watch my back, don't you think?" I just couldn't stop myself from uttering the choleric words.

"Yeah, uh-huh. So, obviously you're right back ta' bein' major pissed," he grunted. "Thought we'd patched things up a bit last night."

"Maybe a little, but this is going to take more than a little patching. I mean, look at what I'm dealing with here? Can you blame me for being pissed off?"

"Guess not," he assented with a shallow nod. "But ya' need ta' try and get over it 'cause we ain't the bad guys, Row."

"It's been my experience that the bad guys rarely think of themselves as such."

"Yeah, okay," he replied, holding up his hands again in surrender. "Not gonna go there with ya'. Don't wanna argue right now. You're pissed, that's fine. It's all good. We'll just hafta work around it."

"Thank you so much for your approval," I offered with heavy sarcasm overtly tagged to the words.

He just shook his head but didn't reply.

"So," I asked out of curiosity. "Are you following me now? Am I under surveillance? On the verge of being arrested as Felicity's accomplice or something?"

"Gimme a break," he grunted. "If you were under surveillance, you wouldn't know it unless we wanted ya' to. The real deal is I was gonna call ya', but I noticed your truck sittin' here when I pulled in a couple minutes ago. Thought I'd just come over and talk to ya' in person instead."

"Are you sure that's wise?"

He shrugged. "Maybe, maybe not. But I was seen talkin' to ya' last night, so if there's gonna be any fallout, the damage is already done…for me, anyway."

I didn't really understand what he meant with his addendum to the sentence, but it wasn't important. The fact was that his obvious conclusion about me being concerned for his career, while somewhat logical, was a misinterpretation of my query. I thought I should probably just let it go, but again my mouth was running out of sync with my brain.

"Actually, I was talking about your jaw," I corrected him. "You aren't afraid I might take a swing?"

"Uh-huh," he said with a raised eyebrow. "Yeah. Well, don't expect another free shot anytime soon, white man. Ain't gonna happen."

"I'll bear that in mind."

"Yeah, whatever," he said, still not pursuing the caustic tone of my replies. Instead, he peered back at me with questioning eyes then repeated his earlier question, "So, anyway, how's Firehair?"

"She's been better," I answered. "Of course, that stands to reason when you think about where she is."

"Yeah," he mumbled, inspecting the sidewalk for a moment before looking back to my face. "But, she's tough. She'll hold up."

"Yeah. I just hope she's tough enough."

"She is."

"Glad you're so confident."

"You ain't?"

"Let's just say I'm worried."

"Yeah, I can understand that..." he agreed with a nod.

"So," I asked. "This great confidence you have in her fortitude...is that recent revelation?"

"Just drawin' from what I know about 'er."

"Really? I thought you'd pretty much discounted all of that last night when the irrefutable evidence became the thing."

"I never said that."

"Not in those exact words."

He shook his head. "Ya'know, the only reason I'm resistin' the urge ta' kick your ass right now is that I know your head ain't on straight."

"Okay. Am I supposed to say thank you?"

"It'd be nice, but I'd settle for ya' tryin' ta' be a little more civil."

"This *is* me being civil, Ben."

"Yeah, right," he harrumphed. "It's more like you bein' an asshole."

"Live with it."

"It ain't helpin' your wife, Row."

"Coming from you, that sounds a bit empty."

"Look, I've been doin' some thinkin' about all this and askin' a few questions."

"Oh yeah? Did you come to any conclusions?"

"Yeah, actually, I did."

"Let me guess...you still think Felicity is guilty."

"Actually, considerin' some of the answers I've gotten, what I think is some shit don't add up."

"Okay, so, is that a yes or a no on the guilty part?"

"It's a 'I think some shit don't add up'," he replied and then added, "On both sides."

"So what you're saying is that now you're on the fence?"

"Shit, Rowan, I was climbin' the goddamned fence last night. Just wasn't quite sittin' on it yet."

"I couldn't tell."

"Wanna know why? 'Cause ya' were too friggin' busy bein' pissed off ta' listen to me."

I paused for a moment to weigh what he had just said. In truth he was probably correct. Much of the previous evening was a painful blur, with even more excruciating but still out of focus highlights. I'm sure my emotional state clouded much of it just as it had been doing all along.

I finally gave him a shallow nod and replied, "Maybe so."

"Yeah…so listen…you wanna go grab somethin' ta' eat this evening?"

Taking into account the events of the past day, the invitation seemed to come out of nowhere. While I was willing to make a concession about my stubbornness, I was still on a roller coaster ride where my feelings about Ben were concerned. I was willing to talk, but I wasn't so sure I wanted to sit down to dinner with him. On top of that, I had more than enough to deal with at the moment.

"No offense, Ben," I replied, begging off the invite. "But I'm not much in the mood for socializing right now. And, to be honest, I'm still not so sure about the company."

"Yeah, well in case ya' didn't notice, that last part was actually kinda offensive."

"Sorry about that. Just being honest."

"Okay, but ya' gotta eat."

"Trust me, if I get hungry I've got food at home."

He reached up and smoothed back his hair before dropping his hand back down. He started to say something then glanced almost furtively from side to side. I followed his gaze and noticed a fairly steady stream of people moving along the sidewalk.

Gesturing obliquely, he fixed me with an odd stare. As he spoke, he carefully enunciated the words. "Listen to me, Row. I *really* think you need to come to dinner with me."

For whatever reason, I wasn't getting his point, even with the out of character exactness of his speech. In fact, the only thing I was getting was annoyed. "Ben, I just said…"

"Fuckit," he muttered, cutting me off as he shook his head then gave me an even more wide-eyed stare. "Listen to me very carefully, willya'?" His next sentence was slow and deliberate with heavy emphasis on each individual word. "You… Need… To… Come… To… Dinner… With… Me."

It finally dawned on my overtaxed and under rested brain that what I was getting was not a social invitation but quite possibly an offer of information, or even help.

"Oh" was all I could think of to say.

"Yeah, oh," he echoed. "Say around six-thirty. Meet me over at that Mexican place there in the middle of Westview Plaza?"

"Yeah, I can do that," I said with a nod.

"Good. So, look, I gotta get back ta' work."

"Yeah, okay. Guess I'll see you around six-thirty then."

"Good."

As he started away I called after him, "Hey, Ben, just a second…"

"Yeah?"

"Is Constance going to be there?"

He gave his head a quick shake. "Nope. Just me."

I scrunched my brow and cocked my head to the side. Once again, without bothering to think first, I spoke. "I don't get it then…Why the cloak and dagger? I thought you just said you weren't worried…"

He shook his head again and looked confused. "I got no idea what you're talkin' about."

Before I could say anything else, he shrugged then turned and continued on toward the police headquarters building down the street.

I looked after him for several seconds, the furrows in my forehead deepening. Still puzzling over the conversation, I gave my own head a shake then turned and stepped off the curb. After waiting for a pair of vehicles to pass, I finally managed to get into my truck without being startled and falling into the street.

I had already turned onto Market and was three blocks away when my cell phone began to ring. I extracted it from the cup holder on the center console and peered quickly at the display. The number showing on the liquid crystal was completely unfamiliar to me. I considered ignoring it but went ahead and thumbed the answer button anyway.

"Rowan Gant," I said, trying to remain businesslike despite my mood.

"Did you take a goddamned stupid pill or somethin' this mornin'?" Ben's voice hissed into my ear.

"What?" I replied.

"Jeezus, I knew I shoulda just called you."

"What are you talking about?"

"What'd I tell ya' yesterday, Row?"

"I'm not sure I follow?"

"Jeezus…Constance is about half an inch from gettin' put on administrative leave, white man."

"Okay, so what's that got to do with…" I stopped mid sentence as my brain caught up with what I was being told.

"I'm thinkin' you just had an 'oh shit' moment, right?" Ben chided.

"So she *is* going to be there," I returned.

"Ding ding," he said. "I'd give ya' a fuckin' cigar, but right now it's my turn to be pissed, so I'd probably shove it down your goddamned throat."

"Sorry. I'm just not all here right now."

"No shit. Jeezus! Now, keep your mouth shut and go home an' take a friggin' nap, willya'?"

Ben had made an excellent point, and one that I actually agreed with for a change. Sleep was something I desperately needed; the problem was I just didn't think I had time for it.

Upon arriving home I went through the motions of everyday life, if for no other reason than to keep myself on an even keel. Things like letting the dogs out, making sure they had plenty of food and water, and carting the kitchen trash out to the waste can at the back of the house. While they were mundane activities at best, they felt very much like they were probably the sanest events in my life at the moment.

A quick listen to the answering machine revealed a fresh pair of insult barrages from Shamus, one of our ongoing mystery hang-ups, and several frantic messages from various members of our coven. I knew I needed to call all of them and fill them in, but I was tired of explaining at this point. As much as I hated to leave them hanging, they were just going to have to wait.

The final voice on the machine turned out to be calm as well as familiar. It was my mother-in-law, Maggie. While I knew she wasn't any more a fan of mine than Shamus, I couldn't accuse her of ever being anything but a class act. The message was concise and even apologetic to an extent, simply asking that I please call them as soon as I had any new information about what was happening. She even went so far as to offer to help in any way they could. My paranoia told me the offer was likely nothing more than a way for Shamus to try assuming control over the situation again; however, I tried not to think about that and left the statement to stand at face value.

Of note was the fact that according to the time stamps, all of the messages had been left during a relatively short period very soon after I had left the house earlier in the day. Following up by checking the caller ID, it became clear that Felicity had been on target with her comment about her mother taking care of Shamus, at least in the interim, because she had been the last caller. Out of a weird curiosity, I even picked up the handset and checked to make sure the phone hadn't suddenly stopped operating.

There was little left for me to do now. Until Jackie called or I heard from Doctor Rieth again, I was in a kind of limbo for a few hours. I looked around the room and gave consideration to starting in on the cleanup but couldn't muster the energy to do anything more than simply think about it. Picking my way around piles of books, I wandered over to the sofa and sat down, eventually leaning back and letting myself sink into the cushions.

Sometime after that my body switched to automatic pilot. The last thing I clearly recall was thinking I didn't really have time to be sitting here doing nothing. However, as exhausted as I was, not to mention emotionally hot-wired, neither my brain nor my body was particularly concerned with what I thought.

CHAPTER 18:

Sleep fell upon me.

And, when I say fell, I mean it was the safe and I was the stupid shmuck standing on the sidewalk beneath. However, there are times when it is better to simply stay put and get flattened rather than to step out of the way. I suppose, all things considered, this was one of them.

Of course, this was not to say it was the best nap I'd ever experienced, but it probably wasn't the worst either. I don't recall dreaming, but in one sense that was probably a good thing since any such subconscious imagery would most likely have taken the form of "the nightmare" anyway.

In the end, I awoke in much the same position I had been in before being set upon by unconsciousness. At least, I think I did. I couldn't really remember much of anything other than the fact that one minute I was awake and the next, I wasn't. Still, I found that I was upright, sitting on the couch, and I did actually have a faint memory of planting myself there at some point in the recent past. The only thing that seemed to have changed was the fact that I now had one cat across my lap, one next to me on the arm of the sofa, and finally a third sitting on the corner of the coffee table returning my bleary-eyed stare.

"What are you looking at?" I mumbled as I stretched, but the feline simply scrunched its eyes shut then reopened them and continued watching me.

I had no idea why I was suddenly awake or even how long I had been out to begin with. I did know that the pounding in my head hadn't subsided in the least, but that really didn't mean anything. I could have been asleep for ten minutes, or ten hours, where that was concerned. Ethereal migraines were happy to hang around for as long as it took to get their point across, and it was becoming obvious this one was here for the long haul.

I tried to look at my watch and found my wrist to be a mottled blur. Reaching up to rub my eyes, I quickly discovered the reason; my glasses had fallen from my face. I sent my hand searching for them and at the same moment heard a sound that served to kick-start my brain.

"Rowan?" Ben's voice issued from the speaker on the answering machine then briefly paused. "Goddammit, Rowan, if you're there, pick up the friggin' phone!"

I got the distinct impression from the exasperation in his voice that this might not be his first attempt at calling. If that was true, I was pretty sure I now knew what had roused me from my impromptu slumber.

I nudged Dickens from my lap and pushed myself up from the couch, sending my eyeglasses skittering across the floor as they fell from wherever they'd been hiding. Dancing through the mounds of one-time shelf contents, I snatched up the handset and pressed it against my ear.

"Yeah, Ben," I croaked groggily. "I'm here."

"Yeah? So why aren't you *here*?"

"What?"

"It's a quarter after seven, white man," he returned. "You were s'posed ta' meet us here at six-thirty, and you ain't one for bein' late."

"Damn," I mumbled, remembering the meeting we'd set up earlier. "Sorry. I accidentally took your advice and fell asleep."

"S'okay," he huffed, a note of understanding in his tone. "Ya' prob'ly needed it pretty bad."

"Yeah, I think so. Listen, I'll get cleaned up real quick, and I can be there in half an hour…maybe forty-five minutes."

"Don't worry 'bout it," Ben grunted. "Just gargle and put some coffee on. We'll come to you. You want some food?"

"Nah, I'm good." I shook my head for no one's benefit but my own. "I'm not really hungry."

"When'd you eat last?"

"It's not important."

"Yeah, it is. When?"

"I don't know," I replied, somewhat annoyed. "Yesterday I think."

"You gotta eat."

"Really, I'm good, Ben."

"You want burritos or tacos?"

"Ben, really…"

"Forget it. We'll just get ya' both," he continued, completely ignoring me. "We'll see ya' in twenty."

I started to object again, but he had already hung up. I dropped the handset back into the cradle then stifled a deep yawn. Turning around I located my glasses and scooped them up from beneath the coffee table, giving the lenses a quick swipe with the tail of my shirt before sliding them onto my face. Continuing on to the kitchen, I set about starting the coffee before I tried to make myself presentable.

I was already on my second cup when they arrived.

It seemed that the scant few hours of shuteye had left me with little more than a crick in my neck and a patent desire for more sleep. Well, that wasn't entirely true. I did have something a bit more worthwhile to show for it, and that was a noticeable semi-softening of my mood. While the respite certainly hadn't been a panacea, it did seem to have had a moderate analgesic effect on my anger. Therefore, by the time Ben and Constance made it to the house, I really didn't feel much like hitting him. Although, to be honest, I really wasn't sure if it was truly because the rest had calmed me down or if I was simply still too tired. Whatever the reason, in the grand scheme of things, the end result definitely qualified as a positive note on the day.

"Thought you weren't hungry," Ben said as he sat watching me toss down the last of an oversized burrito they had brought along from the restaurant.

I shrugged while I finished chewing then swallowed and washed it down with a swig of coffee before replying, "Guess I was wrong."

"Told ya'."

"Yeah, Ben, you're a stark raving genius."

"You've got to take care of yourself, Rowan," Constance interjected before he could retort.

My mood truly was better, but my mouth apparently hadn't caught up to it yet.

"I'll have time for that after I die," I quipped, mimicking Ben's penchant for clichés.

"You aren't going to be able to do Felicity any good if you make yourself sick," she pressed.

The petite FBI agent was standing in the doorway that led into the kitchen, her back pressed into the jamb. She was still clad in work attire, a fitted suit which certainly accented her figure but did little to hide the forty-caliber *Sig Sauer* parked on her right hip.

Though her shoulder-length brunette hair was neatly styled, it still exhibited an end of day droopiness that matched her slouched posture and sagging expression. Even though she was right at a decade younger than either Ben or me, the power of her youth was visibly running out of steam. Judging simply by the way she looked, it was obvious that she was wearing down just like us.

"You get used to it," I said, responding again to her attempt at mothering me. "After awhile it just doesn't matter. You do what you have to do and get sick later."

"You're sounding just like Storm," she countered.

"I probably got it from him," I agreed.

"I'm sure you could pick a better role model to emulate, Rowan."

Ben piped up. "Hey! Ya'know, I'm right here in the room."

"Uh-huh," I grunted. "You're kind of hard to miss. Besides, I think she's kidding."

"Yeah, well I wouldn't place any bets on that," he returned.

"A little sensitive tonight, are we?" Constance quipped in his direction.

"You'd like that, wouldn't ya'?"

"Can you two pick at each other later?" I sighed and then switched the subject. "So, anyway, what do I owe you for the dinner?"

"Depends. You gonna eat any more?"

"No, I'm done."

"Let's see then, you ate the burrito...," Ben mumbled as he reached out and grabbed the sack, inspected the contents, then stuck his hand in and extracted one of the tacos. He already had it unwrapped when he added, "Well, near as I can figure, looks like nothin'."

"You're sure?"

"Uhm-hmmm," he grunted with a nod, his mouth full.

"Thanks."

"Don't mention it," he said after swallowing. "Besides, the Feeb bought."

"Ben!" she snapped.

I shook my head, embarrassed by my chauvinistic assumption. "Sorry, Constance, I thought...Oh, hell, doesn't matter. What do I owe you?"

"Nothing, Rowan," she replied. "I didn't buy, he did. He's just yanking your chain."

"Great," I said, shooting him a disgusted look. "You've just got to pick at somebody, don't you? Did you forget I'm still kind of pissed even if you did bring me dinner?"

"Hey," he grumbled. "Ya' seemed like you were in a okay mood when we got here. You've even been halfway pleasant. Well, sorta. Anyway, I figured it couldn't hurt ta' lighten things up a bit more."

"Yeah, whatever," I dismissed the comment. "Light isn't my thing right now. I'm going to need a lot more sleep before we go there."

He simply shrugged and continued devouring the taco.

"You know," I finally said, looking back over to Ben after taking another swig of coffee. "I hate to be an ungracious host, but earlier today you made out like there was some big reason for us to be having a secret meeting. Or, was I just dreaming all that?"

"The skulking around was Storm's idea," Constance offered. "He's worried I'm going to get myself booted out of the Bureau."

"Well, dammit, at the rate you're goin' you are," he admonished, almost choking on his food before he could blurt the words.

"Don't be so melodramatic," she returned. "At worst I'll get a letter of censure. And that's only if I get caught."

"You just got one a' those for losin' your damn sidearm," he chided. "That'd make two in a row, and even I know that ain't good."

He was correct. One of the strings Constance had pulled when getting Felicity out of the assault charge against her was somehow talking her superior into recommending a letter of censure go in her own file. Effectively, she had taken the blame for the situation and glossed over a few damaging facts in order to get my wife off the hook. On paper, what my wife had done had somehow been turned into Constance being reprimanded for temporarily misplacing her government issued weapon. How she'd pulled that off was anyone's guess, but I suspected it was better if I didn't really have that answer.

"Well, no offense, Constance," I interjected. "Because, you know I appreciate everything you've done. I really do, and so does Felicity. But, right now I'm afraid I have to admit that she is way more important to me than your career, as harsh as that may seem. So, if there's something you know that might help..."

"Don't worry, Rowan, I understand," she replied with a nod. "Honestly, clearing Felicity is more important to me too."

"Okay, so why this secret confab? What is it you know?"

"I'm not entirely sure," she replied. "But I ran across something that sent up a flag...for me anyway...How much do you know about DNA, Rowan?"

"I know how to spell it," I replied.

"God, Storm really is rubbing off on you."

"Yeah, it does seem that way, doesn't it," I agreed.

"All right you two, who's doin' the pickin' now?" Ben grunted, but left it at that.

"Actually, I do know the basics," I spoke up again. "If I remember high school biology correctly, it stands for deoxyribonucleic acid. Everybody has it, and a lot of it is the same, but there's a part of it that's as unique as a fingerprint. When it comes to being used as evidence, it can be pretty damaging. Other than that, I know it's the reason my wife has been taken from me and charged with crimes she didn't commit."

"Yeah, well it might interest ya' ta' know that when it comes to evidence, there're a coupl'a different kinds of DNA," Ben added. "Mitochondrial and autosomal."

I turned my head, quickly shifting my gaze from Constance and fixing it back on him. His expression was enough to tell me that my own face was showing more than just a little wonderment.

"Don't look so goddamned surprised, Row. I'm not really as stupid as ya' seem ta' think I am. I just let everybody think so."

"Yeah, okay."

"Ben's right," Constance chimed in.

"Thanks," he chirped. "About time ya' stuck up for me."

"I meant the part about the DNA," she said.

"What? You think I'm stupid too?"

"Look, I never said you were stupid!" I interjected, a sharp note of exasperation sounding in my voice. "Now, I would really like to get back on subject here…Jail…Felicity…DNA…"

"Ben actually did hit on the point I'm trying to make," Constance volunteered. "Mitochondrial versus autosomal DNA."

"Okay, I'll admit to my own stupidity on this one. I've heard the term mitochondrial but that's about it. I don't really know what it means."

"Well, in basic terms, mitochondrial DNA comes from your mother," she explained. "Autosomal, however, is not gender specific and can come from either the mother or the father. When using DNA for identification, the preferred method is autosomal unless there is no other choice."

"Why?"

"Because it is where the true DNA profile actually resides. Mitochondrial is not as unique, and it just gets you into the ballpark. Let me give you an example. I inherited my mitochondrial DNA from my mother, she inherited hers from her mother, her mother's came from her mother, and so on. Since M-T-D-N-A doesn't change, if you were to compare samples from all of the women in that line, the mitochondrial DNA strand would be identical. No way to distinguish between us."

"So, you're telling me the DNA used to ID Felicity is mitochondrial?"

"Yes and no," she answered. "The problem is that's the only kind of DNA that can be found in the shaft of hair. While it can be used as evidence in a crime, usually to narrow the field of suspects, it isn't an absolute identification of an individual since it will be prevalent throughout a maternal family tree."

"Okay," I struggled to contain my impatience. "So what about the yes and no thing? Which is it?"

"I'm getting to that. As you know, the DNA samples we are working with came from hair. Autosomal DNA, the kind used for positive identification can be extracted from the actual follicles or roots. Using something called polymerase chain reaction, or PCR, the DNA is replicated—or what they call amplified—then separated and compared.

"What they look for are matching alleles at given points in the strand, called loci. The standard for CODIS, the Bureau's Combined DNA Index System, in order to guarantee the match is thirteen loci. Unfortunately, when dealing with degraded samples, the result they can get is sometimes eight or nine."

"Not that I don't appreciate the biology lesson," I remarked. "But, you still haven't answered my question."

"I just want you to understand how this works, Rowan," she explained. "In Felicity's case, the samples taken directly from her match exactly on the mitochondrial DNA with all the others. However, of the samples taken from the three crime scenes, there is a variance on the autosomal profile. On one of them there was a full match of the thirteen core markers..."

"Tell me that was the Wentworth homicide," I said.

She nodded. "Yes, it was."

"That makes sense," I offered. "She was actually present at the scene, and it's entirely possible for her to have lost a hair or two while shooting the photos, especially the way she had to contort herself to get a couple of the shots."

"Agreed. However, she did have an autosomal match with the sample from the Hobbes crime scene. But, it was only partial and that's where the variance comes in. On that sample they hit on seven markers. Not all thirteen. The Myrtle Beach sample was only a mitochondrial match, but that was simply because all they had was a small sample of a hair shaft, and no root."

"Well, then doesn't that prove it isn't her?" I asked hopefully.

Constance shook her head. "Not necessarily. Remember, I said this sometimes happens with degraded samples, and that's what they were dealing with. While it definitely does cast some doubt on a positive match, given the state of the samples, it's enough for a prosecutor to take to court if there is other supporting evidence."

"So this is the big secret?" I asked. "Isn't this something our attorney would be privy to anyway?"

"Eventually, yes. But they are keeping the details under wraps for the moment, at least until they see if there are matching DNA profiles from any of the other scenes that were kicked out by NCIC. In fact, I only found all this out by accident."

"Accident?"

"Yes. I accidentally saw the results from the lab in DC."

"Why am I thinking your use of the word accident may be a bit facetious?"

"It's not my fault the door was unlocked, and the folder was right there on the desk."

"See what I'm sayin' about hot water, Row?" Ben chimed, gesturing toward her.

"Yeah," I replied. "But you would have done the same and you know it."

"That's different."

"Different how?" Constance demanded.

"I dunno, it just is."

"So, are there actually more DNA profiles?" I queried, pushing the conversation back on subject.

"That's what we're hearin'," he said. "But, truth is we're both bein' kept outta the loop a bit."

"Of course, that's to be expected," Constance added. "Given our personal relationships with both you and Felicity."

"So they'll use that to their advantage when it *is* an advantage, but when it's not..." I said, leaving the rest of the sentence unspoken. I knew Constance would pick up on my inference about her recently being asked to use her friendship with us in an attempt to get information during a jurisdictional turf war between the FBI and local law enforcement.

"Pretty much," she agreed, without missing a beat.

"Okay, well, this is all well and fine," I cast my glance back and forth between the two of them. "And, while I appreciate the help, all you've really told me is that they have what they consider a smoking gun."

"Not really," Ben interjected again.

"Not really, how?"

"Like I said, the match is close, but not positive," Constance said with a shrug. "That opens things up for a world of doubt. The gun might be warm, but it's not smoking."

"Well, I've been saying that all along," I returned. "So, out of curiosity, do you think the samples may have been tampered with?"

"I doubt it," she said, shaking her head. "Ben told me that was your theory, and while I won't discount it entirely, I really don't think it's likely. Mainly because the easiest way to do that would have been to substitute her hair for the original samples from the unsubs, which would have given a full positive match across the board."

"Doing that would have been a bit obvious, wouldn't it?"

"Not really. And, besides, if you're going to tamper with evidence, you sure don't want to get too complicated. The KISS principle is usually the best way to keep from getting caught."

"Okay, but let me ask this. You're telling me the mitochondrial DNA actually was a full match across the board. I understand it won't work for positive identification, but isn't it pretty damning?"

"All it really means is that the killer and Felicity share a maternal link somewhere in their ancestry. That's not actually as uncommon as you might think, especially when you consider ethnic origin and those sorts of factors. Still, you could be talking about a relative, close or distant."

I let out a frustrated breath and sat back in my chair. "I'm really afraid all this conversation has done is…"

I wasn't allowed to finish the sentence. The angry pounding that suddenly issued from my front door didn't let me.

CHAPTER 19:

The dogs began barking immediately; vociferously defending their territory against the mysterious would be intruder. However, my gut suspicion was that they could bark until they were hoarse, and it wasn't going to scare away the person on the other side of the door.

"That don't sound like a very happy knock," Ben ventured. "You expectin' company, or did ya' just piss somebody off?"

Now it was my turn to give an ambiguous answer. "Yes and no."

"Yeah, and that means?" he prodded.

I was already getting up from my seat. "It means no, I wasn't actually expecting anyone. Well, not that I invited, anyway. But, yes, I'd say it's a good bet he's angry with me."

"Sounds like you think ya' know who it is."

"Judging from the knock, I'd say it's probably my father-in-law."

"I'll bite. Why's he pissed at you?"

"Other than the fact that he just generally hates me? At the moment, he blames me for Felicity being in jail."

Constance gave her head a confused shake. "He blames you for this? Why?"

"It's a long story."

"Well, if you'd rather not deal with it, I'll be happy to get the door for you," she offered.

"No, better let me," I replied. "If it's him, there's no reason for you to be stuck in the middle of a family squabble. I know how you law enforcement types feel about those things, and I don't blame you."

The hammering echoed through the house once again, coupled with a muffled shout that sounded something like my name. The dogs had quieted momentarily during the brief lull but now renewed their bid to repel the noise with some of their own.

Giving my head a shake that was the obvious product of embarrassment, I strode out of the kitchen and through the dining room. Both Ben and Constance followed along a few paces behind. I guess if I took into account the concern they'd shown for whether or not I'd been eating, their watchful attitudes in this situation were to be expected.

Shushing the canines as I waded between them, I reached for the lock. Out of habit, before turning the deadbolt I put my eye to the peephole even though I was certain I knew whom it was I would see. However, the distorted countenance on the other side of the fisheye came as a total shock. Instead of finding my father-in-law as I had expected, there was someone else entirely standing on my front porch, pummeling my door.

"What the..." I mumbled.

"What's wrong, Row?" Ben asked.

"Well, apparently I was wrong," I replied. "It's not Shamus; it's Austin."

"Who's Austin?"

"My brother-in-law."

"That a good thing or a bad thing?"

"Actually, besides Felicity, he's the one member of that family who doesn't seem to hate me," I said with a shrug.

Under the circumstances, I don't suppose Austin's presence really should have come as that big a surprise. He was, after all, Felicity's older brother, and he had a habit of being very overprotective of his "kid sister."

However, there was also the glaring fact that he made his home almost four thousand miles away in Ireland. I remembered Felicity having made mention that he was planning his vacation around the Thanksgiving holiday in order to visit with family, but I also seemed to recall he was supposed to be arriving late in the coming week. Friday, I thought.

Of course, I suppose it was a good bet he had received a call from Maggie or Shamus telling him of his sister's current plight, and that may have prompted him to re-arrange his travel plan. Something he would have had to do in a huge rush, but that wasn't something I would put past him. Whatever the reason however, obviously he was here sooner rather than later.

Rather than stand there trying to reason out the logistics that now brought him to my doorstep, I twisted the lock and unlatched the door then pulled it open wide. In retrospect, I probably should have taken the time to do some of the pondering I had so quickly dismissed.

Just as I had told Ben, Austin and I had always gotten along famously. Other than my wife, he really was the only member of the O'Brien family who accepted me for who I was and didn't pass judgment on my religious path or lifestyle. In fact, he had even gone toe to toe with his father in my defense on more than one occasion. Therefore, I can honestly say his fist racing toward my jaw was absolutely the last thing I ever imagined would happen. Of course, my imagination had been running incredibly rampant as of late, so possibilities that would have been obvious to others simply didn't fit within its outlandish scope.

An almost sickeningly strong smell of whisky flowed in on the wake of the opening door and thrown hand. The odor served as a good indicator of how Austin had come by the mood he was presently wearing. Truth is, he tended at times to fall into the negative stereotype of the drunken Irishman who was happiest when in the middle of a bar room brawl. Not that he spent all that much time drunk, mind you, but whenever he did set about imbibing alcohol, he wasn't one for temperance. And, unfortunately, violence often ensued.

My ears detected something that may or may not have been a curse echoing through the room, but at this point whatever he was actually saying was completely obscured by the alcohol slur that permeated his speech. The intent in his tone, however, was unmistakable, so I didn't waste time trying to figure out the actual verbiage.

A strong sense of déjà vu invaded my brain as my brother-in-law's fist arced through the air between us; however, in this instance I could actually explain why I felt like this had happened before— because it had.

Ben had done exactly the same thing only a couple of years back, also while in a similarly inebriated state. In his case, while the punch landed with far more force than he'd intended, there had been no malice attached. I was reasonably certain I couldn't say the same for Austin.

Unfortunately, my brother-in-law's speech seemed to be the only thing impaired by the whisky. Both his coordination and depth perception appeared to be perfectly sober. Of course, I suppose it could have been that his aim was off to begin with, and I simply chose the wrong direction to dodge. In any event, his incoming knuckles glanced across my jaw, and my head snapped back as an altogether new pain inflicted itself on the lower half of my face. Literally reeling with the force of the blow, for the second time in the past two days I staggered backward across my living room.

Rattled though I was, I managed to catch the fact that Austin was quickly following the punch through the door and had already cocked his left arm in preparation to launch another fist. Of course, with his anger focused so intently upon me, the thing that was escaping his attention was the fact that I was more or less flanked by a cop and an FBI agent who had already demonstrated that they were more than just a little concerned about my continued well-being.

I don't know which one of them was the first to move, Ben or Constance. I wasn't really in a position to see, and the chaotic tableau was made even more disconcerting by the dogs as they growled and yelped in response to the unexpected attack. I'm sure they were just as confused as me, given that they were familiar with Austin as a friendly face but were now witnessing him as an aggressor. They didn't seem to know whether they should go after him, or run and hide, so they chose the middle ground of positioning themselves between the two of us and assuming a loud and menacing posture.

Even with all that, I did manage to catch quite a bit of blurred movement on either side of me before my brother-in-law's second punch even began its trajectory. As I was falling, I felt Ben's hand clamp onto my arm then physically yank me up and to the side, pulling me out of harm's way.

Had I blinked, I probably would have missed the entire episode, but I somehow remained focused on the flash of motion before me. Constance immediately filled the void from the other side, snatching Austin's wrist then twisting as she thrust one foot out in his path. In one easy swipe, she took his legs from beneath him, and he crashed face first onto the floor.

While I'm certain his lack of balance from the alcohol made her task somewhat easier, there was no doubt in my mind she would have been able to subdue him had he been cold sober, ten years younger, and a foot taller. In the end, Austin wound up kissing the hardwood, with his shoulder straining in its socket as the petite FBI agent wrenched his arm upward and held him in place with one knee in his back. She had already filled her hand with a pair of handcuffs and was beginning to apply them when my sluggish brain caught up to the action transpiring around me.

The dogs had stopped barking but remained stationed between us, an occasional low growl emitting from one or the other as they nervously danced in place.

"Aye, get the hell off me ya' goddammed *saigh!*" my brother-in-law bellowed, his voice reflecting upward from the hard surface of the floor.

"You need to calm down and cooperate, sir," Constance instructed, slapping the stainless steel around his wrist and ratcheting it tight. "I think I should also warn you that calling me a bitch isn't a very good start in that direction."

Constance had heard Felicity use that very same expression more than once and knew all too well what it meant. In fact, considering the young woman's seemingly photographic memory, it was very likely she remembered any and all Gaelic she'd ever heard my wife utter then explain.

At this particular moment, I was guessing that Austin was using the foreign language simply out of habit, as did most everyone in his family. I suppose it could have been done in a calculated attempt to get one over on Mandalay, but I doubted that. Whichever was the case, however, I was sure the result he was getting definitely wasn't the one he was after.

I absently touched my hand to my stinging face, causing myself to flinch. When I pulled it away, there was a healthy swath of blood on my fingers and palm. Judging from that, and the way my mouth felt, I was guessing I had a split lip. Either that or a missing tooth my tongue just hadn't noticed yet.

As annoyed, and even downright angry as all this made me, I heard myself say, "Please don't hurt him, Constance."

"That's up to him," she returned without looking up.

"Jay-zuss! Get off me, damn you!"

"Sir," she instructed again, switching on her official voice. "I'm telling you again to calm down. I am a federal officer and I expect you to cooperate. Now, give me your other hand."

"Not on your life."

"I'm not going to ask you again, sir. Let's not do this the hard way."

"*Fek tú!*"

"Not on your best day, asshole," she returned sharply, shifting out of official speak for a moment, then she leaned forward hard on her carefully positioned knee.

He groaned heavily as she pressed her weight into his lower back, not that she was endowed with that much, petite as she was; but obviously she knew how to use what she had to make her point. With a practiced motion, she took hold of his other wrist and brought it behind his back then quickly applied the other cuff. Once he was secured, she backed off the pressure on his spine and stood up then stepped over him.

"Are you okay, Rowan?" she asked.

"I'll live," I replied with a nod.

The space between us was no longer blocked, as the dogs were preoccupied with sniffing at the prone man on the floor, seeing him now as a curiosity rather than a threat.

"Let me see," she demanded, moving forward and gently taking my chin in her fingers.

I brushed her hand away and twisted my head, pulling back. "I'm fine."

"You need to put some ice on that," she pressed.

"I said, I'll be fine."

"Storm," she said, shooting him a glance then cocking her head toward Austin.

"Yeah, I got 'im," he replied with a nod. "You get Row some ice."

"Isn't anybody listening to me?" I objected, voice filled with a mix of anger and exasperation, but the words came too late to matter. Constance was already halfway to the kitchen, and she wasn't slowing down.

Ben stooped over and dragged my brother-in-law onto his knees by his upper arm, "Come on. Get up."

"Jay-zuss, ya' bastard!" he yelped. "You're breakin' me goddamned arm then!"

"You just don't know when ta' shut up, do ya'?" Ben snapped as he finished pulling him up to his feet. "Now, I know I heard Mandalay tell ya' ta' calm down. You got some kinda hearin' problem or somethin'?"

"Aye, it's best you stay out of this," my brother-in-law spat. "It's personal. It's not your problem, then."

"Yeah, well, trust me, I know all about personal," Ben replied, shoving him into the dining room and planting him in a chair. "And, maybe this is, I dunno. But, the thing ya' gotta be aware of is you made it my problem when ya' attacked an innocent citizen right in front of me and then resisted arrest."

"Innocent my arse!"

Ben looked over in my direction but kept himself positioned between the two of us. "Jeezus, Row. I thought you said this is the guy that liked ya'?"

"I guess he changed his mind," I replied with a shake of my head.

Halfway through the motion I stopped, closed my eyes, and groaned. The rattling in my skull still hadn't subsided, and now that it joined forces with the fresh ache in my jaw, moving just made it that much worse. When I allowed my eyes to flutter open once again, I saw that Mandalay was already heading back through the dining room with a dishtowel in her hand.

"What've you done to my sister, ya' bastard?!" Austin shouted, lifting up and leaning to the side to look around Ben's frame.

Before I could answer, Ben snapped, "Can it!" Then, pushing him back down into the seat he added, "Now, I'm not gonna tell ya' ta' calm down again, got me?!"

I was determined that someone was going to listen to me, so I shot back with, "I haven't done anything to her, Austin!"

My own voice rose in volume as I expelled the words, and that didn't help my head either. However, the sudden rush of anger was enough to at least blunt the pain.

"Liar!"

"Goddammit, Austin, I…"

"You too!" Ben returned, cutting me off while stabbing a finger at me. "Not another word outta either of ya'. Hear me?!"

Constance interjected her voice into the auditory fray as she came to a halt in front of me. "Stand still, this might sting a bit."

With only that comment as warning, she began dabbing at the lower half of my face and lip with a damp towel. I immediately winced and pulled away, reaching for her wrist out of reflex.

"A bit?" I yelped.

She slapped my hand away and continued undaunted, quickly adding, "I said, stand still."

"Dammit, Constance," I muttered. "You aren't my mother."

"I'm not your wife either, thank God," she quipped softly. "But, someone has to look after you, and until we clear Felicity, it looks like I got the job whether I want it or not. Now, hold still."

"Bastard!" Austin snipped.

"I thought I told ya' ta' shut up!" Ben snarled at him.

"I'll be fine," I reiterated to Mandalay.

"Come over this way," she instructed, tugging on my arm. "I need more light."

"Constance…"

"Jeezus, Row," Ben urged with a healthy measure of exasperation in his voice. "She ain't gonna take no for an answer, so will ya' just let 'er look at it and get it over with?"

I didn't say another word, but I did let out a heavy sigh before following her a few steps over to the floor lamp. Then, giving in to yet another of her demands, I twisted my head so she could have a closer look.

"Mmhmm," she hummed. "It's not too bad. I don't think you'll need any stitches."

"Thanks, *Doctor* Mandalay," I returned, unable to keep the sarcasm from bleeding through.

She ignored the dig and instead simply produced a second dishtowel from her other hand then carefully pressed it against my lip. It was damp and cold where the fistful of ice it was wrapped around had begun to melt through.

"Here, hold this on it for a while."

"If I do, will you stop mothering me?"

"No."

Unfortunately, there wasn't much I could really say in response, so I sighed again and held the icepack against the lower half of my mouth as I mumbled, "Okay. Fine. If it makes you happy."

"Well isn't that just a pretty picture then," Austin grumbled. "Just couldn't wait, could you, ya' bastard?"

"Hey," Ben barked. "What did…"

"No, Ben," I snapped, cutting him off. "Let him say what's on his mind."

"Aye, I suspect you don't want to be hearin' that, now do you," my brother-in-law responded with an angry snort.

"Keep it civil," Ben instructed, taking a half step to the side, so we could see one another. "Both of ya'."

"Actually, yes. I do want to hear it, Austin," I replied. "Just what couldn't I wait for?"

"Her," he snipped. "Felicity's in jail, and you've already got yourself a *cailín* here in her house…"

"A what?"

"Are ya' daft?" he spat, thrusting his chin toward Constance. "Your girlfriend there."

"Gods, Austin, get a clue. She's an FBI agent," I returned incredulously. "She's not my girlfriend."

Constance slipped out her badge case and flipped it open as she stepped toward him. "I've already identified myself as a federal officer, here's my ID," she told him coolly. "And, he's telling the truth. I'm not his girlfriend."

He simply harrumphed in return, giving her credentials only a cursory glance.

"So, are you trying to tell me everything was just fine until you saw Constance standing there at the door, and that's why you decided to take a swing at me? Because, I hate to tell you this, but I have trouble believing that."

"Aye, I was planning to hit you anyway, that's a fact."

"Yeah, no shit. Want to give me a clue as to why?"

As an answer he simply repeated his earlier question. "What have you done to my sister?"

"I haven't done a thing. Just what the hell makes you think I did something to her?"

"She's in jail, ya' bastard."

"Dammit, Austin, you think I don't know that? I didn't put her there, you idiot, but I'm trying my damndest to get her out!"

"That's not what I've been told."

"By who? Shamus?"

"Aye."

"Yeah, well why am I not surprised by that? What does get me though is that you believed him."

"Well, you might as well get used to it, then."

"Really? So when did you all of a sudden start taking his side?"

"Does it matter?"

"Yeah, I think maybe it does. What the hell did he tell you, Austin?"

"The truth."

"*The* truth, or *his* truth? Because we both know they aren't the same thing."

"Says you."

"Gods," I muttered, worry filling my voice. "What the hell did he say to you, Austin?"

"He told me the things you've forced my sister to do."

"He what?"

"The devil worship. The sacrifices. Everything."

"Gods, Austin, give me a break, will you? You, of all people, know better than that. Hell, you've been one of the first to defend me when he's started in on that crap before."

"Aye, but that was before I knew the real truth."

My frustration was starting to get the better of me. "Real truth? What real truth? What are you talking about?"

"Stop lying, you bastard. He still has the letters."

The only thing keeping my irritation from reaching a volatile flashpoint was the sudden dousing of confusion applied by his words. "Letters? Dammit, Austin. Just spit it out. What the hell are you talking about?"

"The letters Felicity sent, begging him to help her escape you," he growled.

"The what?" I snapped back at him, incredulity tightly wrapped about the words. "Give me a break. He doesn't have any such thing and you know it."

"Aye, but I do. I've seen them. And, they're written in her own hand, by God."

CHAPTER 20:

The only thing I truly remember hearing on the heels of Austin's retort was Ben's voice as he all but spat the word "bullshit" into the room. If my brother-in-law responded to it verbally, either I didn't hear him, or his words simply weren't registering because I was no longer paying attention to his rhetoric.

In fact, I wasn't paying attention to anyone.

Of course, even if I had been able to blurt my own objection, once again there was no need, because Ben delivered the comment with enough disdain for the both of us. Besides that, the single word summed everything up in a neat and wholly unambiguous package. There was nothing for me to add.

It took a moment for me to notice that all normal sound had been replaced by a loud ringing as my blood raged through my body. My ears and face began to feel hot, and the room seemed to waver as an emotional claustrophobia swaddled me in an ever-tightening blanket of anguish. I couldn't even describe what I was feeling as blind anger, because it went so far beyond that.

It was a good thing Shamus wasn't the one in the chair because this was all simply too much. I'd finally had everything I could possibly take, and the fragile self-control I'd maintained thus far was a rapidly fading memory. I couldn't say for certain what I would have done had it actually been him sitting there, but it's a good bet that an ambulance and some manner of charges being filed against me would have been a big part of the aftermath.

I stood there, unmoving. I didn't even utter a sound as Austin's words replayed in my head. I simply stared back at him while every painful event in my recently shattered life joined together and came to a dangerous climax. Then, just as I felt myself pitching over that precipice toward a violent eruption, something far more frightening happened.

Calm swept over me in a comfortable shroud.

Cold, emotionless, calm, and with it came a strange sense of clarity. It was, however, a form of lucidity that I couldn't readily identify. I knew full well that while it could in fact be reality, it could just as easily be the edge of insanity. But, at this point, it simply didn't matter one way or the other.

Thoughts ricocheted around the inside of my skull, and I inspected them with mild interest, still remaining staunchly silent.

There wasn't even the most miniscule thread of doubt in my mind that what Austin had professed was exactly what Ben had said it was—pure, high-grade fertilizer. There could be absolutely no truth to it whatsoever, and that was simple fact. On top of that, it was fresh ordure. It simply stank too much not to be. But, unfortunately, I also knew that right now, Austin firmly believed every word of the steaming pile he had just shoveled.

Given the conversations I'd had with Shamus in the past twenty-four hours, it really didn't come as a shock that he would fabricate something to help prop up his plan to have Felicity deprogrammed. The simple fact that he claimed to have contacted an "exit counselor" was enough to tell me that much.

When it came right down to it, even though Felicity had said she was certain her mother would shut him down, in the back of my mind I had been just as certain that she couldn't. Not this time. I'd hoped that maybe I would be wrong, but the evidence at hand said otherwise.

Still, all I had truly expected from my father-in-law were a couple of fictional diatribes. A few easily discountable rants spewed forth by a man who wasn't willing to accept anything other than the narrow vision he stubbornly saw as truth. I hadn't begun to imagine that he would go as far as trying to produce some form of bogus documentation to lend credence to his accusations. Obviously, even with my belief that he wouldn't back down from his threat, I had still underestimated his conviction. It seemed that every time the man stepped over a line, he would just go find a new one to cross. This line, however, was final. There were none beyond it, not where I was concerned anyway.

The sad thing was, in reality, we were both heading toward the same end—that being the safety and sanctity of Felicity. He was just approaching from a diametrically opposed direction. Unfortunately, one of the important points on his roadmap called for sacrificing me in order to arrive at that final destination.

In a sense I suppose I couldn't blame him. I had to admit I was more than willing to fall upon my own sword if I believed it would help my wife in the least. But, it wouldn't and I knew that, especially not the way Shamus was trying to make it happen. In fact, if he kept this up, which was plainly his intention, I wasn't going to be his only victim. He was going to end up helping put away his daughter as well.

"Hey, Row?" Ben prodded. "You okay?"

The ringing in my ears had died away. When, I didn't know, but it had been replaced by the ambient noise of the room. I just still wasn't paying attention to that noise. Words being directed toward me, however, seemed to break that barrier.

Ben's query served to alert me to the fact that I must have been staring in silence for longer than I'd realized. It took a moment for his voice to register, but when it did I set aside the random thoughts which had been occupying my conscious brain and tried to focus on the world around me. I became suddenly aware that the side of my thigh was wet and cold where the makeshift icepack in my hand was resting against it. But, instead of moving the dripping object, I simply clung to it, trying to use the physical sensation to draw me out of the bizarre catatonia.

I felt a bit like a voyeur, as if I was standing before a window watching something transpire in front of me, all the while hidden from the players in the act. At the same time I felt like I was at the center of it all and that nothing could continue without me.

I began to wonder if what I was experiencing truly was calm, or if it was nothing more than confusion. Of course, blithering insanity was always an option as well, and I can't say that it was all that unattractive at the moment because this particular reality had been doing its best to kill me.

I briefly considered trying to find my voice; but after a half-hearted search, I decided it was hidden too well. My head didn't seem overly interested in moving either, so I was unable to even look toward my friend to acknowledge hearing his question. Of course, none of these things really mattered to me. Be it calm, confusion, or flat out insanity that had come over me, I was comfortable for the first time in two weeks, and right now I saw no compelling reason to disturb that feeling. Taking the easy way out, I simply remained focused on Austin.

With no response coming from me for several beats, my brother-in-law drew his own hasty conclusion and cast his eyes toward Ben as he proceeded to gloat. "Aye, the bastard's got nothing he can say to that."

It was obvious from the tone of his voice that he was clearly delighted with himself over what he saw as a victory. Since he was still cuffed, he glanced back in my direction and thrust his chin out sharply, directing his next comment to me personally. "Do you, then, Rowan?"

His belligerence had no effect. My tongue continued to lie dormant, and waited. But, it didn't matter because for some reason I didn't feel the need to respond. Not to him, anyway.

"Rowan?" Constance made her own attempt to return my attention to the room. Her words fell into the same scrap bucket as everyone else's, instantly disregarded even as they were heard. It wasn't until she reached out and laid her hand on my arm that my two worlds once again fully merged.

I suddenly found myself looking down at her hand, regarding the appendage with mild curiosity. As the seconds ticked by, I eventually brought my gaze back up to her face.

"Yeah," I finally said, finding my voice once again, though I'm certain it would have preferred to remain hidden.

"Don't listen to him," she offered.

"I'm not," I told her.

"You go *Twilight Zone*, white man?" Ben called out.

"I honestly don't know," I said.

Constance continued, "Rowan, I'm sure Felicity didn't write any such letters."

"She did!" Austin insisted.

"No, she didn't," I announced calmly, rotating my head to bring my unblinking eyes back to bear on him.

"I've seen them," he countered.

"Them," I repeated. "As in more than one?"

"Aye. I saw them with my own eyes."

"Yes, I'm sure you did," I replied with a nod, still keeping my voice even. "But, let me ask you a question. Are you just drunk, or did you suddenly get stupid too?"

"*Fek tú,*" he snipped bitterly.

"I'm serious, Austin," I said, ignoring his insult entirely. "You know your sister well enough to realize she isn't going to be forced into anything against her will."

"Aye, but if…"

"No," I cut him off. "There is no *but if.* They don't come any more stubborn than Felicity and you know it."

"That doesn't mean anything," he objected. "You found a way to coerce her."

"Row…" Ben interjected hesitantly. "Just drop it. You're just wastin' your breath on 'im."

"No," I replied. "He needs to understand that he's the only one being coerced here and that it's not being done by me."

"Talk all you want, Rowan," Austin huffed. "I won't be believin' your lies anymore."

I thought about that for a moment. Both of the men were probably correct. Everything I'd been saying was for all intents and purposes being wasted on someone who had already made up his mind that whatever came out of my mouth was one hundred-eighty degrees opposite of the truth.

Of course, I also knew that most of Austin's attitude, if not all of it, had to be the alcohol talking. He really was a level headed and logical man; right up until a bottle of whisky took hold of his senses. I could only surmise that Shamus had been firmly behind his state of inebriation, effectively putting him into the necessary frame of mind to sway him with the bogus letters. Whether or not it was my father-in-law's intention for him to come over here and attack me, well that was a matter for debate. While in one sense it wouldn't surprise me, in another I'm not so certain he would want his hand tipped in my direction just yet.

I finally shook my head and shrugged.

"Yeah, probably not," I agreed, then looked down and regarded the wet, blood stained towel in my hand. Tossing it onto an end table, I continued to look at my hand for a moment before looking back to my brother-in-law and continuing. "But, do me a favor, Austin. When you dry out, I've got a couple of things for you to think over. First, your parents are twenty minutes away. If Felicity really wanted to get away from me, why didn't she just call them? Or better yet, go over there? Why bother sending letters?"

"If she…"

"Shut up," I ordered, though my voice remained unruffled. "I'm not finished. You've said plenty. It's my turn." I paused, and when he didn't object again I continued. "Now, second, and believe me this is the big one. In fact, this right here is the huge fucking enigma that's been making my brain hurt ever since you said it. You're telling me that Felicity sent *several* letters. Correct?"

"Aye."

"And I'm guessing since there were several, Shamus got these over a period of time? Weeks? Months? I don't know, years?"

"Over some time, aye."

"Why did he wait until now to show them to you?"

He started to reply but didn't. I could see in his eyes that I'd already set his brain into motion, and what I'd just offered was only a minor point.

"Yeah. Makes you go 'huh', doesn't it?" I said. "In all the times you've stood up for me whenever he's started putting me down or berating me, don't you think maybe he would have pulled out those letters and proven to you what an evil bastard I am?"

He remained silent, but the look on his face told me I was getting through.

"But, you know, that's not even the real kicker. Give this one some serious thought and come up with an answer for me, because my evil, coercive brain just can't wrap itself around the concept. Why is it Shamus didn't haul his ass over here to rescue his daughter from me the minute he got that very first letter? Hell, from what you're saying, apparently she asked him to do just that. What was he waiting for?

"I know if I had a daughter, and I had proof that she was in danger, I really don't think there's all that much that could stop me from going to her. And, before you say anything, even if he didn't feel that he wanted a confrontation with me, why didn't he take the letters to the police? I mean, according to you 'sacrifices' were mentioned. Sounds like evidence of illegal activities to me."

"Yeah, me too," Ben agreed.

Austin opened his mouth as if to object but once again stuttered to a stop, never fully forming a single word. Now he was really starting to sober up, and while the passage of time and physical exertion had gone a good way toward that end, I knew my questions had played a large part in yanking him back into reality.

The peal of the telephone suddenly issued from across the room, filling the empty wake that had been left behind my words. While the ringer didn't physically sound any different than any other time, there somehow seemed to be a particular urgency about it that I just couldn't explain. Even so, I didn't bother to turn; I simply continued to stare at my brother-in-law. The second ring echoed through the room and still I didn't move.

"Do you want me to answer that, Rowan?" Constance asked.

My first inclination was to tell her to let the machine get it. After all, it could very well be Shamus, or even the mystery caller who liked hanging up as opposed to talking. However, that odd feeling of urgency tickled the back of my brain and set me wondering just who might be at the other end of the line.

"Yeah," I replied, never breaking my gaze.

She stepped around me, picking her way through the still trashed house as she headed for the bookshelves. At my back I heard her pick up the handset, cutting off the ringer in the middle of its clamor for attention.

Her voice replaced the bothersome noise a second later, "Gant-O'Brien residence."

There was expectant pause after her words, but it didn't last long at all. In fact, only a handful of heartbeats passed before her voice spilled into the room again.

"My God... Are you okay?" she said. "Where are you?"

I was still watching Austin, but I couldn't help noticing Ben perk up at the words. Turning his attention to look toward her, he asked, "What's wrong?"

I could only see his half of the silent exchange that went on between them, and what I was privy to turned out to be indecipherable. Finally, Ben furrowed his brow and gave his head a slight shake as if he didn't fully understand.

"Rowan..." Constance called my name.

Even in my disconnected state, I couldn't help but notice the strange reverberation woven through her tone. Still, even though I could easily sense it was there, I was unable to tell if the underlying emotion was excitement or fear.

"Yeah?" I answered.

It was then she shattered my newfound calm with the words, "Rowan...it's Felicity."

I turned to face her, a full-blown mask of confusion pinned to my features. "Felicity?"

"Felicity?!" Austin yelped.

"You shut up," Ben ordered him.

Mandalay nodded and held the handset out toward me. I didn't waste time repeating the question. Stepping around the mess and knocking over a pile of books in the process, I traversed the space between us and took the phone from her.

Placing it to my ear I spoke, "Felicity? What's wrong?"

"Aye," her exhausted voice flowed out of the handset. "Could you come pick me up?"

"Pick you up?"

"Aye."

"What do you…" I started the question then instantly stuttered to a stop as my overactive imagination began putting outlandish scenarios into motion. "Felicity, you didn't…"

"Didn't what?" she asked.

"You didn't break out of jail or something, did you?"

"No," she replied, her fatigue suddenly even more apparent. I imagined I could see her shaking her head as she made the matter of fact statement. Then, her voice quavered as repressed emotion started to encroach. "They turned me out, Rowan. They…they just let me go."

I didn't ask why. There would be time for that later.

"Where are you?"

"I'm in the lobby of the Justice Center."

"Don't move. I'm on my way."

I was through the door before the sound of the handset clattering into the base had even begun to fade.

I was only mildly aware that my name was being called. I heard the voices but wasn't interested in them. When I shot out the door, I took the stairs in twos, hitting the flagstone walk at a fast jog. It was right about that moment I began to notice that even this, the best thing to happen in the past two days, came fully equipped with obstacles.

The first hurdle that came to light was my congested driveway. The car Austin had driven to the house was angled haphazardly across the end of it, effectively blocking my exit.

It took less than a second for me to decide that something so minor wasn't going to stop me. The only thing that mattered at that moment was getting to Felicity and bringing her home before someone pinched me because I knew as soon as they did, I would wake up and be back in the nightmare. I also knew that such a fear was irrational, but right now I seemed to be living in a world where irrational was the norm, so I didn't discount anything. I simply wasn't going to hesitate and give anyone the chance to take this away. I was fully prepared to drive across the front lawn to get out if need be. It's not like it would have been the first time. I'd done that very thing once before.

Problem solved, or so I thought.

Roadblock number two turned out to be my keys because when I reached into my pocket, they weren't there. In my single-minded haste, I had run from the house without them. This one wasn't going to be quite as easy to make disappear. The only way I was going to overcome it was to go back inside; something I really didn't want to do because in my mind that constituted a chance for someone to burst this bubble. Unfortunately, there was no way around it.

Of course, this was when I slammed face first into number three, which happened to be Ben and Constance, both of whom had been less than two steps behind me the entire time. And, when I say I slammed into it face first, I mean literally, for when I suddenly turned to go back into the house, the three of us collided.

Now, I had no choice but to pay attention to them.

I don't know if there was a physical manifestation, but on the inside I know I cringed, fully expecting a horrific reality to descend upon me once again. Fortunately, it didn't, and the bubble held.

It didn't take long to become apparent that my plan didn't fit with the one the two of them had devised between themselves. Since it was two against one, I didn't have much hope for winning. Besides, I was lucid enough to realize that standing here arguing would just waste even more time, and that was the last thing I wanted to do. So, rather than perpetuate the disagreement in tactics, I quickly gave in, surrendering to their scenario.

Ben volunteered to stay behind and handle the situation with my brother-in-law. Constance drew the duty of taking me to pick up Felicity. Since they had come in her vehicle, and it was currently parked on the street in front of the house, we were unencumbered by both obstacles number one and two. Since they, themselves, were number three, all barriers were now rendered moot.

Before we left, both of them offered to give statements to the local police if I wanted to press charges against Austin. I pondered the idea then decided against it. I suppose in the end I made the choice for Felicity's sake. Given all that she'd been through, having her husband swearing out a complaint against her brother probably wasn't something she needed thrown on the pyre right now. I will admit, though, I seriously considered it, even if only for a moment.

What I did tell Ben was that I wanted the man out of my house before I returned. He may well have been on his way to coming around since my posing the questions to him, but I wasn't interested in taking chances right now. As I was climbing into the passenger side of Constance's sedan, my friend guaranteed me that he would see to my wish, admitting that it was likely to mean a call to the local police for a patrol car, a Breathalyzer, and a tow truck.

To be honest, that solution suited me just fine.

CHAPTER 21:

"I just don't get this," I said aloud as I shifted uncontrollably in the passenger seat. It seemed as though I was infused with enough nervous energy to power a small city, and I just couldn't get comfortable. I settled back and tried to stop myself from fidgeting then added, "I don't understand what's going on."

The verbal lament wasn't actually a question; it was really nothing more than an observation born of frustration so intense that my brain was no longer willing to keep the thought to itself. Even so, it was the truth. While I was all about serendipity, especially in this case, Felicity suddenly being released without some type of advance notice just didn't make sense. I was honestly perplexed by what was happening, and I really did want to understand.

Of course, the fact that I was less than a step shy of being officially overwrought certainly wasn't helping. I guess my tone conveyed that sense of confusion in spades because Mandalay took it as a cue to provide a simplistic explanation.

"Something must have happened," she stated without embellishment.

I'll admit I was confused, but I also hadn't gone totally dense. Without thinking I fired back a retort, and this time the unfiltered response was even more heavily rimmed with the emotional overload. Unfortunately, the bite in my voice was not only obvious, but also exceptionally unpleasant. "Well, hell Constance, I think maybe I kind of figured that part out on my own! The question is *what*?"

She glanced over at me as she eased the speeding sedan across the full breadth of Highway Forty and settled into the left lane. Reflected splashes of radiance from a self-contained deck strobe, which was resting on the dash, cast her face in a chaotic flicker of red and blue. It allowed me to see that she was frowning, but it also made her expression seem terribly harsh. I couldn't truly be sure if the look she was wearing was one of anger or merely pity.

I doubt anyone else, least of all the police, would feel our mission warranted the use of the pulsating emergency lights, but they had been Constance's idea, and not mine. Well, that wasn't entirely true. She had just managed to pre-empt me before I made the suggestion myself. In fact, the idea was about to tumble out of my mouth when I noticed her suction cupping the device into place.

"Calm down," she said, shaking her head as she aimed her eyes back toward the road. Her voice was stern, but there was no real anger to speak of within the words, just annoyance. I'm sure she was experiencing her own attack of frustration, both with the situation and with me. "I'm saying something has to have happened that seriously undermined their case against her."

"Sorry," I apologized quickly then tried to offer an explanation for my comments. "Look, I'm not complaining, believe me. They never should have arrested her in the first place. I'm just trying to understand what's going on."

"I know, Rowan, but..." she stopped her sentence short, again focusing her attention completely on the road.

Lightly tapping the brakes, she canted the steering wheel slightly and veered onto the Eleventh Street-Stadium exit ramp then headed into the sharp curve. I was pressed against the door from the outward force as she eschewed further use of the brake and immediately gunned the engine, accelerating through the turn, shooting down the ramp, and off onto Eleventh Street. It was a good thing nothing was scheduled at the nearby indoor sports complex because that meant traffic was light, and there was no one to get in her way. As she merged onto the northbound street, she continued speaking where she had so abruptly left off, "What I'm trying to tell you is that you can bet whatever it is that happened, it cleared Felicity hands down."

"Why? I mean, that's great and all, but why?"

"Because, it's Saturday night. The prosecutor had to suck it up and interrupt a judge's evening. Who knows, maybe he even had to get a judge out of bed in order to get her released right now."

"Okay, I admit I was wondering about that," I replied with a nod. "Our attorney said it's almost impossible to get a bail hearing on a weekend. She had to pull some serious strings just to get me in to see her today."

"Your attorney is correct, but that's just it. This isn't bail; this is release. As of this morning she was being charged with murder, but now she's walking. That means the charges got dropped almost as soon as they got filed. For the prosecutor to go to a judge, hat in hand, on a Saturday evening to get charges dropped means they're painfully aware that they screwed up royally.

"What it basically says is that either there was gross incompetence that they knew was going to bite them in the ass, or something happened that screwed up their case. Either way, it's not something that looks good on a résumé at all. Given the track record of the prosecutor, I'm betting it wasn't incompetence on his part. Maybe someone else, but not him. Either way, something happened. Something big."

"Big how?"

"I can think of several things," she replied. "New evidence, mishandling of existing evidence, or even another murder while she was in custody.

"No matter what it is, though, there's one thing you can be sure of—a lot of embarrassment is being dished up right now, and someone's ass is going to be in a sling. Count on it. The fact that they are letting her out in such a hurry is evidence enough of that."

"Why?"

"Easy. They want her free before the press can get hold of it."

"Won't they still?"

"Sure, they always do, but it won't make anywhere near as big a splash as it would if they had video of her walking out the doors after all the hoopla that got made over her arrest. I'm actually surprised they didn't wait until later tonight to spring her. More like midnight or one in the morning."

"One in the morning?" I repeated in disbelief.

"Yes, one in the morning," she replied. "I know it sounds insane, but it's not as off the wall as you might think. It's been done before, more than once, actually. All in order to sneak it by the press. What's unfortunate is that this sort of thing happens more than you'd care to know."

We had already blown through a stoplight at Spruce and were now approaching Clark Avenue. Constance began slowing the vehicle as cross traffic loomed in the headlights.

"You're kidding, right?" I asked, reaching for the dash as the brakes took hold, then instantly released, causing me to pitch forward against my shoulder harness.

Constance pulled around the car ahead of us and continued forward, cautiously nosing her way into the intersection. Once everyone stopped to allow her through, she whipped immediately into a left turn from the center lane and punched the accelerator.

"I wish I were, Row," she finally responded in an absent tone. "I mean, don't get me wrong, it's not like it's a daily occurrence. But, the truth is, Felicity definitely isn't the first person this sort of thing has happened to."

"No offense, but for me that doesn't inspire a lot of confidence in our legal system."

"I know, Rowan," she sighed. "Trust me, I know. Sometimes I wonder about the system myself and I'm part of it."

As the buildings along the block slipped past the windows, and the distance closed on the next intersection, she again tapped the brakes to slow the sedan. If ever we were going to attract attention to ourselves, now would probably be the time because city police headquarters was almost directly ahead of us on the left, just across Tucker Boulevard. Given our speed and the flashing lights, it was almost a given that we would gain ourselves an entourage.

Constance shot a quick glance in both directions and finding it clear, she barreled on through the traffic signal. Cranking the wheel hard and mashing on the accelerator, she instantly made a sharp right onto the main thoroughfare and punched forward. Just over ten seconds later, she was bringing the car to a skidding halt next to the curb.

I was out of my seatbelt before she had even begun braking, and I'm almost certain we were still in motion when I popped the door and started to jump out. At least, that's the only way I can think of to explain why my feet scraped horizontally along the sidewalk.

It took everything I had not to break into a dead run the minute I was fully out of the vehicle. In fact, I didn't even bother to close the door as I started toward the stairs at something between a fast walk and a jog. As I had suspected, a pair of patrol cars with light bars fully ignited were sliding to a halt behind the sedan before I'd made it five steps. I didn't bother to stop. Constance could take care of them. Continuing forward and looking up at the entrance, I immediately spotted a slight figure moving quickly in my direction.

Felicity shot down the stairs without restraint to meet me at the bottom, her petite frame slamming into me so hard my breath escaped in a perfunctory huff. She threw her arms around my neck and buried her face against my shoulder as she started to sob quietly. I instantly wrapped my own arms about her and held her tightly, lifting her from the bottom step and slowly turning in place before finally settling her back onto the sidewalk. Still, I didn't let go and neither did she. If anything, we both gripped one another even tighter.

As we stood there tangled in an emotional embrace, a cold November wind whipped around us on its trek through the downtown streets. But, even though I wasn't wearing a coat, the chill didn't faze me. I had something far more important occupying my attention, and keeping me warm.

After a moment, however, I did notice that I hadn't yet bothered to take a breath ever since the wind had been knocked from my lungs. But, that was okay. There would be plenty of time for breathing later.

"All they said was 'Sorry for the inconvenience, Miz O'Brien, you're free to go,'" Felicity announced softly. She paused before repeating a particular word from the sentence, her voice falling into an annoyed whisper, "Inconvenience."

I didn't have an answer for that. There was nothing I could possibly say that was going to make it better or make either of us understand. Right now it didn't matter, though, because I knew all she wanted was for someone to listen. That was a task I was more than happy to perform, if for no other reason than to hear her voice once again inside the walls of our home.

She continued, slightly louder, but still subdued. "I wasn't even sure if they were going to let me use the phone. The first person I asked said no. I guess I just got lucky when I asked someone else. I suppose I should be grateful for that."

"Did you say thank you?" I asked facetiously, my voice low.

"No. I think I was still too stunned."

"I wouldn't worry. They'll get over it."

True to his word, Ben had seen to the removal of Austin. He surreptitiously pulled me aside once we had returned home to let me know that my brother-in-law was being held overnight by the Briarwood police for violating a public intoxication ordinance and that he would most likely be cut loose in the morning. I sincerely appreciated his tact where that situation was concerned because it was something Felicity didn't need to worry about at this moment. Hopefully, once Austin was fully sober, he would give some more thought to the points I had tried to make. Then, maybe we could have a truly productive discourse.

After that, Ben and Constance didn't stay long. Once they were certain we were settled in, they said their goodnights and left us alone.

I had offered to put on a fresh pot of coffee, but they immediately declined. It seemed the elation of having my wife home had nullified any of the remaining anger I was feeling toward Ben—at least, for the time being. While it would be impossible to forget everything that had transpired, I hoped that our friendship was on the mend. Of course, that was really up to me, not him. He had remained loyal throughout it all, even if my rampant emotions hadn't allowed me to see it.

In any case, it was obvious that even though we had several questions, they were just as in the dark about the situation as us. They both definitely planned to find out what they could, but for the moment the mystery behind my wife's sudden release was going to remain just that. Besides, and perhaps even more important than solving that riddle, they also knew what Felicity and I really needed in the wake of all this was some time alone. In the end, that was a bit of wisdom with which I couldn't disagree.

"You're sure you don't want something to eat?" I asked after what seemed like several minutes of silence.

I was sitting on the floor of the master bathroom, my back against the cool tiled wall. Felicity was in the tub, up to her neck in warm water and lavender scented bubbles. I had offered to make her something to eat earlier when we had first arrived home. Ben had even offered her the left over tacos he hadn't gotten around to devouring, but she didn't seem to have an appetite. All she wanted to do, she said, was soak in a hot bath. That was a desire I found easy to help her fulfill.

"I'm sure," she told me softly.

"A drink? I think we still have a bottle of *Bushmills* in the cabinet. There might even be some *Black Bush* in there too."

"No...well, maybe...but, not just yet."

"Okay. Just let me know."

There was a quiet splash of water as she shifted then sighed with what sounded like reserved contentment. She stayed silent for a moment and then finally said, "You don't have to wait on me hand and foot, then, Rowan."

"I thought you were into that sort of thing."

"Well...yes...I am...but, that's...I mean...not right now...I just..."

I replied without looking up, rescuing her from the incoherent stammer. "It's okay. I know what you're trying to say. And, don't worry about it. I don't mind."

"Aye, I love you, you know."

"Yeah. I do. Same here."

Another quiet interlude fell in behind our words. Eventually it was pushed aside by the sound of movement, but this time it was me who shifted, seeking a somewhat more comfortable position.

Reaching to the side, I picked up one of the towels that had been carelessly tossed to the floor during the search. Leaning forward a bit, I shoved it behind myself then settled back with an involuntary groan.

"You don't have to stay in here with me," Felicity said. "You can't possibly be comfortable."

"Do you want to be alone?" I asked. "I can go do something else."

I was sincere in my offer to give her solitude, but inside I hoped she wouldn't take me up on it.

"No...not really...but..."

"But nothing," I cut her off gently, feeling a sense of relief. "I'm with you, which is right where I want to be."

She whispered, "Thank you."

"You're welcome."

In keeping with the sporadic, up and down trend of the conversation, a period of quiet settled in between us. After a few moments we heard the metallic rattle of dog tags, followed by the click of canine toenails on hardwood. The sound came closer and finally our English setter poked his head in through the doorway. He looked at us curiously and then huffed out a low "woof". I knew from experience, he was beckoning us to come to bed. It was readily apparent that, as far as he was concerned, his routine had been upset more than enough, and it was time for things to return to his concept of normal.

"We'll be there soon," I told him. "Go on back to bed."

He looked at me as if he understood, woofed softly once again then turned and padded away, presumably back to his overstuffed pillow.

"Been rough on the kids," I offered.

"Aye, I'm sure," my wife replied. "And, you too."

"Yeah, in more ways than you know. But it was a lot worse for you."

"I'm not so sure," she began, seizing on the opening I'd unconsciously given her. "When are you going to tell me what happened to your lip?"

I had all but forgotten about the wound that graced the lower half of my face courtesy of her brother. Her mention of it reminded me that it was still throbbing and soreness was setting in. Still, it was a subject I didn't want to get into right now.

"I cut myself shaving," I replied.

"Rowan…"

"It's nothing."

"Don't tell me you and Ben got into it again?"

"No," I answered, shaking my head out of reflex but stopping quickly when all it did was further enhance my pains. "I think I would have ended up with more than just a split lip if I had."

"What happened then?"

"I'll tell you tomorrow."

"Row…"

"Really, I will," I told her, overt sincerity in my voice. "I promise…Right now, let's just pretend for a while."

She paused for a long moment, and then with a thread of disquiet accenting her voice, she whispered, "Pretend what?"

"Pretend that this is all over."

Another weighty interval of quiet filled the room. I closed my eyes and tried to relax but didn't meet with much luck.

"It really isn't, is it?" she asked, her voice a faint whisper.

We were going to have more than enough to deal with where Shamus was concerned, but that wasn't what worried me right now. I reached up to rub my temple even though I knew it was a lost cause. I had hoped that Felicity's freedom would make the agonizing throb inside my skull subside, but it hadn't. In fact, the pounding had only grown worse since we'd arrived home, and I couldn't keep denying what it truly meant.

"No," I finally said. "Not yet."

CHAPTER 22:

"Well, on a positive note this gives us an opportunity to reorganize the shelves," I said as I began sorting through the piles of books on the floor.

We had gone to bed almost as soon as Felicity was finished with her soak in the tub even though it was still relatively early in the evening for a Saturday. Of course, we were both exhausted, physically and mentally; and, on top of that my quick nap earlier had served only to whet my appetite for more shuteye. With my wife safely home, the autonomic portion of my brain took it upon itself to have a clandestine meeting with the rest of my body. The immediate consensus was that the crisis was over for the time being, and ethereally driven headache or not, it was time for me to rest.

And, so it was decreed. Without warning, the flow of adrenalin that had kept me going for the past two days came to an immediate halt, and I was left with no other choice than to give myself over to the dire need for sleep. Even with that, Felicity had been a half step ahead of me and was already drifting in a quiet slumber by the time I slipped beneath the blanket.

"I suppose that's one way to look at it," my wife replied as she surveyed the mess. Her voice, however, was devoid of anything resembling good humor. "I mean, was all this really necessary?"

"Depends on your point of view, I guess," I told her. "Apparently they felt it was."

She let out a heavy sigh and knelt to the floor, starting in on the pile nearest her.

While the evening had been an early one for us, so had the morning. Even with my gut feeling that more strife was barreling toward us with no intention of slowing down, I wanted to at least make an attempt at returning our lives to something near normal, so I started in on the cleanup project with minimal delay. Actually, we both did.

I had rolled out of the bed well before the dawn, my body immediately complaining that it wasn't quite finished with its hiatus from the land of the conscious. But, I pressed on; there was way too much work to do. I barely had the coffee started when Felicity joined me in the kitchen, wordlessly slipping her arms around me from behind and resting her cheek against my back as she squeezed for all she was worth. The carafe had been full, with the java maker sputtering its way through one last steamy gurgle before she finally let go.

"I'm putting fiction here and non-fiction over here, for the moment," I offered, nodding toward the two separate stacks as I quickly shuffled a pair of books between them. "So...I'm almost afraid to ask, but I guess I should—how much laundry do we have to do?"

"I'm not sure I even want to think about it," Felicity replied then shook her head and continued anyway. "I'd say four loads at least, probably more. I think the cats made themselves a nest in there. One of my formal gowns is snagged so badly it's completely ruined. Several of them are covered with hair, and one of your suits as well. I'll need to run a lint brush over those then take them to the dry cleaners."

"Sorry about that. I guess I should have moved everything, or at least thrown something over the pile."

"Like you didn't have enough to worry about?" she quipped. "I'm not upset with you. I blame them."

"The cats?"

"No, the police. I should send the bastards a bill. That was a four-hundred-dollar dress."

"Well, at least tell me it wasn't the shiny black one with..." I waved my hands about in a failed attempt at gesturing my way through the description.

"Aye, if you mean the black satin off the shoulder, with the full skirt and basque waist. Yes."

"Yeah...okay...whatever all that means..." I replied. "But what I really want to know is if it's the one that really shows off your back and legs and has that design on the front with all the sparkly things?"

"Yes."

"Damn," I mumbled. "You looked really hot in that one."

"I know," she replied not even attempting to feign humility. "That's exactly why I bought it. And, it's still in style, too, dammit."

I chuckled lightly. Even though my head still hurt for reasons beyond the natural, there was something very restorative about this conversation. In fact, it was comforting enough to allow me to forget about the pain for a while.

"It's not funny, Rowan. The dress is ruined."

"I wasn't laughing at that, honey. It's just…never mind. It's not important. I'm just happy you're home."

"Me too."

"So, ruined, huh?"

"Yes, ruined. Remember, they got hold of one of your suits as well. Fortunately, it just looks like it's only covered with hair. No damage that I could see."

"Well, save some money on that one. You can just hit it with a lint brush and give it to charity," I said, half-joking. "It's not like I wear suits that often."

"Aye, I think not," she replied as she looked toward me. The corners of her mouth turned up in what might have been a slight smile. "It's the charcoal grey suit you just bought, and I think it makes you look very handsome. You'll be keeping it."

"Can't blame a guy for trying."

"Sure I can," she returned in a light tone that was suddenly replaced by anger as she sputtered, "Dammit! Dammit!"

"What's wrong?"

"Look at this!" she exclaimed, holding up a tome that bore a severely bent corner and a large rip traversing three-fourths of the cover. "This is my autographed first edition of *Lucinda's Web. Damnnú iad*! Where does it end?!"

"Calm down, honey," I soothed. "I'll get you another dress, and I'll get you another book."

"That's not the point," she grumbled then hung her head, carefully caressing the damaged novel. Eventually, she sniffled and then whispered, "After everything we've done for them...after everything *you've* done for them, and what you've been through...why? Why did they do this to us, Rowan?"

After everything...

That preface was running through both our minds but from somewhat different points of view, as my thoughts were wallowing in the land of after everything *they've done to us,* why do I still feel compelled to help them. It was a quandary I wasn't sure I'd ever work out.

Still, I couldn't blame my wife for her reaction to the situation. The damaged book was yet another act of disrespect heaped upon a towering mound of contempt, with us at the bottom. My own feelings had been a mirror image of hers just a day before. I'd just had more time to come to terms with it than her.

I replied softly, avoiding the obvious slur against Albright that was lacerating the tip of my tongue and told her instead, "I don't know, honey. I wish I did, but I just don't know."

"Why can't we just be normal?" she lamented.

I took in a deep breath then sighed. "Believe me, sweetheart. That's one I've been asking myself for a long time now, and I don't have an answer for it either."

The ding of the doorbell joined together with the sound of shuffling footsteps on the front porch and was instantly followed by a quick round of yaps from the dogs, effectively bringing our moment to an end. I started up from the floor, but Felicity was already on her feet, quickly brushing her dampened cheeks with the back of her hand.

"I'll get it," she mumbled. "I'm closer."

I stood up anyway and immediately began stepping around the semi-sorted piles to close the gap between us. My protective attitude regarding her was still set to high, and I wasn't overly excited about her being the one to answer the door. At this stage of the game, it wasn't out of the question for whoever was standing on the other side of it to be determined to snatch her away from me once again.

Reaching the door, she stood on tiptoe and put her eye to the peephole. Almost instantly, however, she pulled back and began quickly fumbling with the lock.

"Who is it?" I asked.

"Austin!" she almost shrieked.

"Felicity, no!" I yelped, but I was too late. She had already pulled the door open wide and was rushing forward into an embrace with her brother.

"Austin!" she yelped his name again. "Gods! I thought you weren't coming until the end of the week?"

I covered the remaining distance in a pair of steps, coming immediately behind my wife, my face wearing what had to be a mix of anger and fear.

"*Máthair* called me, so I changed my flight and got here yesterday," he said to her as an explanation. "Are you okay, then?"

"I'm fine," she replied. "I'm fine. Even better now."

I hated to break up the reunion, but as far as I was concerned, my brother-in-law's motives were still suspect. I started to reach for Felicity, but as I did Austin met my eyes with his own and spoke.

"Aye, Rowan," he said almost apologetically. "It's all right, then. You needn't worry, I'm sober. And, I'm only here to talk this time."

"What?" Felicity asked, pulling back and casting her puzzled glance back and forth between us. "What do you mean this time? What are you talking about?"

"Austin and I visited with one another last night before you called," I answered, my voice flat.

She looked back at me with a puzzled frown. "What? You knew he was already here, and you didn't tell me?"

"Given how it went, it wasn't exactly high on my priority list."

"Don't blame him, Felicity, it's understandable," Austin interjected. "Like Rowan said, it wasn't what you would call a pleasant meeting." He gave her a meek shrug then nodded toward me. "I'm afraid I'm the one responsible for marking up his face."

My wife instantly turned a heated glare back at her brother and snapped, "You hit him?"

"Aye, I hate to…"

The rest of his sentence was cut short by the sound of Felicity's open palm connecting firmly with his cheek.

"I can't believe you would let our father get to you that way, Austin," my wife admonished her brother as she placed a cup of coffee in front of him then scooted into a seat on the opposite side of the breakfast nook.

Between the two of us, we had given her a rough sketch of the events that had transpired the previous evening before I received her call. Austin volunteered the fact that he had spent the night only a few miles away in a cell at the Briarwood police station. Fortunately, he didn't seem to be holding a grudge against me in that regard. Of course, Ben may not have told him that I had sanctioned the idea, and right now wasn't the time for me to be making confessions.

"Well, remember, I was drinking," he offered as an explanation.

"Obviously," she shot back. "But, even then you should know better."

"Maybe you're right. I don't know for sure," he half-agreed. "I'll be honest, I didn't believe him, not at first. Not until he showed me the letters. Then I had to start wondering if maybe he was telling the truth."

"Letters?" she asked. "What letters?"

"That's a little detail that got left out earlier," I offered.

"Go on, then," she urged. "One of you add it back in."

"He has letters, Felicity," Austin began. "From you. Letters written in your own hand begging him to help you get away from Rowan and his cult."

"*Cac capaill!*" she spat, screwing up her face and shaking her head adamantly. "He does not."

"Aye, he does. He showed them to me."

"Are you sure you didn't imagine all of this, Austin? Just how much did you drink last night?"

"I didn't imagine them, Felicity."

She shook her head again. "I know he's got his problems with Rowan and our religious path, but that's just insane."

"You're not going to get any argument from me there," I interjected.

"Maybe it is, maybe it isn't. Can you explain them?" Austin asked.

"Yes. Like I said, you were imagining things."

"Hand to God, dear sister, I saw them with my own eyes."

"And, were you already seeing double?"

He shook his head and objected. "I may have been drinking, but I was sober enough to know what I saw."

"I can't imagine why *daid* would make up something like that, but all I can tell you is that they aren't real."

"Are you certain?" he pressed.

"Aye, do you think I'm daft? Don't you think I would know if I had written them?"

I watched as Austin hemmed and hawed for a moment then made a shallow nod in my direction. I'm sure he thought he was doing it on the sly, but I caught it easily, and the significance of the motion wasn't lost on me.

"What?" Felicity asked, shaking her head. "Spit it out."

"He's trying to tell you he thinks you might be lying because you're under duress since I'm sitting right here," I offered.

"That's ridiculous!" she sputtered.

"I can go in the other room if it would make you feel better, Austin," I offered flatly, starting to rise from my chair.

"You, stay put," Felicity ordered, then she turned back to her brother. "Austin, are you still drunk? Do I look to you like I'm afraid of my husband?"

"No, but the letters were written in your own hand, Felicity," he appealed. "How can you explain that?"

"How can you be so sure?" she countered. "When did you become an expert on handwriting analysis? And, besides that, when did you last see anything I'd written by hand?"

"He showed me some old letters you sent home from university," Austin explained. "I checked and the handwriting looked the same to me."

"Well, I'm telling you…" she started then immediately stopped herself and cocked her head to the side thoughtfully. After a moment she resumed speaking. "Wait a minute. He had the letters I'd sent home from school?"

"Aye, that's what I said."

"Did you *ask* to see those?"

"No, he just offered."

"That's it then."

"What's it?"

"Remember when we were kids, how *daidí* used to have people write down their names, and then after looking at the signature for a minute, he would make a copy with his own hand?"

"Aye," Austin replied with a slow nod. "I do remember that."

"Shamus was into forgery?" I queried.

"No." Felicity shot me a glance and gave a quick shake of her head. "It was just a trick he could do, a bizarre talent. He used to entertain everyone by doing it. Of course, they weren't perfect, but they were close enough."

"So you're thinking he forged the letters he showed Austin, using your old correspondences from college to work from?" I asked.

"That's the only explanation I can think of," she replied. "Because I damn sure didn't write them."

"Aye, and I suppose if anyone could do it, Shamus O'Brien would be the one," Austin agreed.

"That would also explain why he made it a point to show you the old college letters," I added, directing myself to Austin. "It gave you something to compare them to. It was his way to prove to you that the forged letters were legitimate. But, given what you two just said, I think that move might have just backfired on him and tipped his hand."

"But why?" Felicity asked. "Why forge letters like that? I still don't understand why he would do something so mean."

"Because he doesn't see it as mean," I offered. "He's doing it out of love for his daughter."

"You're defending him?" she asked, raising an eyebrow.

"Not so much defending as understanding," I replied. "Believe me, over the past two days I've had my fill of your father. But, like I said to Austin last night when I was trying to convince him that you couldn't possibly have written the letters—if I had a daughter, and I had any inkling at all that she could be in danger, I would do anything in my power to help her. Even if she didn't want my help. I can see where that would include forging some type of evidence to help me effect that rescue."

"But I'm not. Not from you, anyway."

"Agreed, but that's not how he sees it. I'm not saying he isn't misguided, and I'm also not saying that I don't want to wring his neck because I do. But, stepping away and looking at it from a different viewpoint, I can understand how his skewed logic is driving him to do it."

"But all he's doing is creating a bigger rift," she replied.

I nodded. "I know. But, remember, he told me himself that he has already contacted someone about having you deprogrammed."

"He'd best forget that idea right now," my wife spat.

"I agree, but I don't think he's going to. I think the fact that he went to the trouble of forging those letters is evidence enough of that."

"I'm afraid Rowan might be right, Felicity," Austin agreed. "He was talking of it yesterday when he showed them to me."

"What did *máthair* say about it then?"

"She wasn't happy about it at all." He let out a small huff. "In fact, when I left the house they weren't speaking. She had gone upstairs, slamming doors all the way."

"So that's where you got it," I commented, but my observation was met only by Felicity frowning and rolling her eyes at me.

"Well, maybe she's talked some sense into him by now," she mused.

A moment of sullen quiet fell over all of us as we sat and sipped our coffee. Finally, Austin cleared his throat.

"Aye, well how did he sound when you told him they let you go?" he asked.

"I haven't called yet," Felicity returned coldly. "And, now I'm not so sure that I'm going to."

Her comment wasn't an idle threat. As it turned out, she never actually made the call herself. It was the other way around, for Shamus began calling us as soon as her release was reported on the midday news. At last count he had managed to leave six messages. How many attempts it took for him to accomplish that feat was a mystery, however, because the phone itself was ringing non-stop before Austin ever left. Reporters from every television and radio station, as well as newspaper, in the area were looking for an interview—or at the very least a comment from the newly freed and wrongly accused Witch. Felicity ignored those as well, leaving them to me. But, after I doled out more "no comments" than I could tally in my head, I gave up on the annoyances myself and started allowing the machine to get the calls.

The first two messages from my father-in-law were relatively calm, though they were definitely replete with general concern and a note of relief. But, by the time the total reached the half-dozen mark, he was right back at verbally berating me, this time for keeping Felicity from talking to him, as he was sure that was the case. I suspect Austin and Maggie were all that was keeping him from actually showing up on our doorstep by that point.

I found myself in a bit of a quandary about the outbursts. On the one hand, I was glad Felicity was hearing him so that she could understand why I felt this was more than just his usual disdain for me. But, on the other, I hated for her to be subjected to listening to his tirades. It was never my aim to alienate her from her family, even if at least one of them thought so. I even started to pick up during one of the rants if for no other reason than to bring it to an end. However, when I reached for the handset, I suddenly found her hand pressing down on the back of mine as she muttered in a cold voice, "Leave it be."

It was almost eight p.m. when my wife finally elected to step over to the phone as it once again began to peal. The angry stream of Gaelic which spewed from her mouth the moment she had the device in hand was enough to tell me who was at the other end.

I decided then that it was a good time for me to work on straightening up the office upstairs.

CHAPTER 23:

"**G**ood mornin'," Ben said as soon as I swung open the front door.

"It is Monday, isn't it?" I asked in reply.

"Last time I checked."

"Then shouldn't you be at work?"

"I am. Sorta. Here." He shoved a fold of paper into my hand as he invited himself in. "You got anything ta' eat?"

He wasn't even completely through the door when he handed me the envelope and just kept going toward the kitchen. I looked at it, slightly puzzled at first then suddenly fearful. Felicity's name was typed across its face, and the return address of the prosecutor's office was imprinted in the upper corner.

"This damn well better not be another warrant," I snapped.

"It ain't."

"Okay, then what is it?"

"Look at it."

"Let's not start that again," I replied, swinging the door shut then following along behind him.

"Don't worry, it ain't anything bad."

"Famous last words. So, what is it?"

"You got coffee on," he asked, completely bypassing the query.

"Yeah, actually Felicity just made a fresh pot a few minutes ago," I replied. "And, you know where the cups are. Now are you going to answer my question or not?"

"Jeezus, calm down and just open the damn envelope," he replied as he snagged a mug from the cabinet and began filling it over the sink. "It's a property release. Ran into the prosecutor, and I offered to save the city some postage."

"You just happened to run into the prosecutor?" I echoed, interrupting him. "Isn't that a little out of the ordinary, even for you?"

"Yeah, well, kinda." He shrugged. "I'll admit it was accidentally on purpose 'cause I was doin' some diggin' and happened ta' be standin' in his office, but that don't matter right now." He paused to take a swig of the coffee then topped off the cup before sliding the carafe back into the base. "Anyhow, all ya' gotta do is take that an' your copy of the property voucher the crime scene guys had ya' sign then go downtown and ask to see the properties officer. Give 'em those, show 'em your ID, coupla' signatures, and ya' can pick up everything they took during the search."

"Really?"

"Uh-huh. That's pretty much how it works."

"No...I mean, yeah, I know that...I'm just saying that this was awfully fast." I hmmphed thoughtfully. "I mean, I just talked to Jackie yesterday afternoon about what we needed to do to get our stuff back."

"Well, yeah, it's not unusual ta' hafta get your attorney involved, but I don't think ya' can give 'er credit for this one. They're kinda in a hurry ta' get past all this."

"Any idea why?"

"Yeah, 'cause they fucked up."

"Obviously," I said with an animated nod. "But what I mean is did you manage to get any details about what finally brought that fact to their attention?"

He looked around. "Where's Firehair?"

"Downstairs starting another load of laundry; she'll be up in a minute. Why?"

"I'll tell ya' when she's here too, that way I only gotta say it once. So, look, ya' got any sandwich stuff or anything? I skipped breakfast."

"What happened?" I quipped. "Did coming here cause you to miss out on your donut fix this morning?"

"There ya' go with the donut jokes again. Ya'know, ya' better be careful. Not all coppers got as good a sense of humor as me."

"I'll keep that in mind."

"Sandwich?"

I shook my head. "There's stuff in the fridge. Help yourself, but seriously, Ben, don't you ever buy groceries?"

He was already rooting through the shelves of the refrigerator, loading the crook of his arm with whatever happened to strike his fancy.

"Yeah," he replied over his shoulder. "But yours are better."

"Why? Because they're free?"

"Well, yeah, that's part of it," he chuckled.

"You *are* going to put all that away when you're done, aren't you?" Felicity's voice rang out from the doorway. "We've been cleaning since yesterday, and I don't need you making a mess in here."

"And how are you?" Ben asked without turning.

"I'm just fine, as long as you don't wreck my house again."

He turned toward her and held up his hands. "Hey, it wasn't me that trashed the place."

"Rowan tells me they had badges, so that means they were part of your little fraternity."

"Ouch," he feigned a wince. "Row's got you hatin' cops now too, eh?"

"I have a good reason of my own."

"Yeah, I suppose you do."

"And, destroying my belongings didn't help," she added.

"Again, not me."

"There is the whole guilt by association concept."

"Is there any way I'm gonna get outta this?" he asked, looking over at me.

"Probably not," I replied. "You're convenient right now, and there was definitely some damage done during the search. She's not happy, as I'm sure you've noticed."

"I'm pissed off is what I am," she interjected.

"Shit," he huffed. "A lot of damage?"

"Enough," Felicity spat. "Besides, any at all is too much."

He turned back to the pile of foodstuffs and began untwisting the tie on a loaf of bread. "Bag it, tag it, and make a list, then give it all ta' your lawyer and tell 'er what happened."

"What good will that do?"

"Depends," he replied. "Did ya' take pictures of the place before ya' started cleanin' up?"

"No." I shook my head even though he wasn't looking my way. "I guess we should have."

"Woulda' been a good idea."

"Well, it just didn't cross my mind given everything that's been going on."

"Yeah, I can understand that. Either way, ya' still need ta' give the stuff to your mouthpiece. She might be able ta' get ya' a coupla' bucks if the damage can be deemed unnecessary."

"Aye, it was damned unnecessary," Felicity spoke up again, her temper starting to flare. "I can tell you that right now."

"Why don't we change the subject." I endeavored to shift the conversation away from re-lighting her fuse. "You had something to tell us, Ben?"

"What? Oh yeah..." He finished mounding deli meat and cheese on a slice of bread and then started twisting the lid from the jar of mayonnaise. "So, Firehair, you got a sister you been hidin'?"

"No," she replied flatly, scrunching her brow. "And just where the hell did that question come from anyway?"

"The DNA tests."

"What do you mean?" I asked.

"Seems the DNA what hung ya', sprung ya'."

"Cute, but don't quit your day job," Felicity quipped. "Would you mind explaining just exactly what you're talking about?"

Ben looked over to me. "Remember what Mandalay and I were tellin' ya' about the DNA last night?"

"No. I wasn't here if you recall," my wife chimed in an annoyed tone.

"I was talkin' ta' Rowan."

"Well talk to me. It's my DNA you're babbling about."

"Jeezus H. Christ, if it ain't one of ya', it's the other. You wanna take a swing at me too?"

"If you don't get to the point, aye, maybe I will."

"Felicity," I interjected. "Give him a chance to talk, okay?"

She let out a hard breath, and her shoulders drooped in unison with it. "I'm sorry, Ben," she offered. "I've had better weekends if you know what I mean."

"S'okay. It's understandable," he answered as he placed the dressed slice of bread atop the mound on the counter and mashed it down to a manageable thickness. "So anyway, we were explainin' to Row about how DNA is used as evidence. The long and short of it is, what they got on you was a partial match. Thing is, it was such a close partial, and since the samples were degraded, it looked like enough ta' go after ya'."

"But it wasn't?" she asked.

"Well, as it stood, yeah, it kinda was. Up until Saturday afternoon."

I asked, "So what happened Saturday afternoon to change it?"

"Gettin' ta' that," he said then grabbed the sandwich in one hand, took a huge bite and began to chew as he started putting away the makings.

Felicity watched him as he started placing things back into the refrigerator but by the third item was shouldering her way in front of him.

"Go sit down and eat," she instructed, grabbing the mayonnaise from the center of the top shelf and placing it in the door where it belonged. "It'll be easier if you just let me do this."

"I promised I'd do it," he mumbled as he chewed.

"No, actually you didn't," she replied then pointing in the direction of the breakfast nook ordered, "Now, sit, swallow, talk."

"Okay," he grunted as he choked down the mouthful then picked up his coffee and headed for the table, adding in a much clearer voice, "Whatever you say."

"Careful, she likes obedient men," I joked.

My wife snipped, "He'd take some serious training before I'd call him obedient."

"Jeez, let's don't even go there, you two, okay?" he moaned.

"Then finish what you were telling us," she urged.

He hastily complied. "So anyway, got some info in from some of the other homicides the NCIC had linked with the two here. Most of 'em had squat, but turns out a couple of 'em had even better samples to work with than us. Because of that they had complete DNA profiles."

"So are you saying they didn't match with me?" Felicity asked.

"Yes and no."

"Make sense, Ben," she said.

"That's the thing. They cleared you because the full profile was different enough from yours. But, it was still damned close, and dead on with the partial from the other scenes."

"So that's why the crack about a sister," I observed.

"'Zactly," he said with a nod. "Lab guy said the profiles are close enough they pretty much have to be siblings. Uncanny kinda close he said. If they had some of your father's DNA for comparison that'd probably clinch it."

"Good luck," I offered. "I doubt Shamus would give it willingly."

Felicity gave her head a confused shake. "Well, if they didn't have the results in from the other murders, and they didn't have an exact match, weren't they a little premature in arresting me?"

"Yeah, well that's another yes and no."

"How is that?"

"Well, yeah, they were jumpin' the gun a bit, but believe me, when ya' got a dead federal judge and a dead cop, there's a ton of pressure on."

"So much that they were willing to do this to me even though they weren't sure?"

"I'm afraid that's the way it works, Felicity," Ben replied. "Arrests don't always come with a hundred percent guarantee that ya' got the right person. You go based on evidence and reasonable suspicion."

"But it sounds like the evidence wasn't all in yet."

"No, but sometimes you go with what you got, and if there's a pile of circumstantial that fills in the holes, it starts makin' for a case."

"What other evidence did they have against me? Surely nothing they found here. Unless..."

"Unless what?" I asked, perking up at her tone.

"It's nothing," she replied quickly and with little conviction.

I had a suspicion about what the "nothing" actually was, and the look on Ben's face told me he was debating about what he should say which meant he probably knew for certain. I considered turning to him for the answer, but given the situation I decided it would be better to let it go for the time being.

"Yeah," Ben finally offered after an uncomfortable pause. "Well...Yeah, there was definitely some stuff that they dragged outta here they were gonna toss on the pile just for the sake of havin' it, but they definitely had some other shit they thought was even more incriminating."

"What?"

"It's pretty obvious actually. How do ya' know an elephant's been in your refrigerator?"

"Excuse me?"

"How do ya'..."

"I heard the question, Ben," she returned. "I just don't understand what a silly children's riddle has to do with what I just asked you."

"The footprints in the butter," I chimed in, going ahead and answering the old joke for him because I knew exactly where he was headed with the reference.

"Ding-ding," he said, then looked over to my wife. "In this case, actually it was your shoe prints all over that fruitloop you picked up in the nightclub."

"But I thought he wasn't pressing charges," she replied. "In fact I know he isn't. Or at least he wasn't as of last week."

"He still ain't that I know of," Ben shook his head. "But that didn't stop the crime scene guys from gettin' pictures and more than just a little of his blood off your shoes."

"But I didn't..."

Ben held up his hand. "I know what you're gonna say...You didn't kill 'im. They know that too, but it ain't the point. Ya' did shit to 'im consistent with the killer's M.O., and on top of that ya' drew them freaky ass symbols all over the mirror in the motel room."

"What symbols?

I perked up once again. This was the first I'd heard about her having drawn anything in the room, and I hadn't been inside it myself to see. At the time, investigating a crime scene hadn't been at the top of my list, protecting my wife had.

"Yeah, what symbols?" I asked.

"The one's you said were all about that Voodoo stuff."

"The *veve*?"

"Yeah." He nodded then finished off the sandwich in a single bite before adding, "Those things. Right there on the mirror in bright red lipstick."

Felicity frowned. "I don't remember that."

"Why didn't you say anything about this before?" I asked.

"I couldn't," he replied. "I think I 'splained that to ya' about forty times in the last few days."

"Okay, not that I'm wanting to help the prosecutor build a case or anything, but isn't that pretty incriminating in and of itself?"

"Well, yeah, but it's still circumstantial, and there's no actual proof that Firehair drew 'em. I mean, I think we can all be pretty sure she did, but there were people in and out of that room before she got there." He looked over to my wife. "Not to mention the lipstick in your purse didn't match, and they never found any in the room that did. So, by itself, not so solid.

"But when they got the DNA, that just became some more circumstantial filler. Then, after the DNA went south, it was back to bein' nothin' but suspicion. Now ya' got reasonable doubt and nothin' ta' counter it with."

"So Felicity is still under suspicion?"

"Some people still got some questions, but like I said, the DNA pretty much cleared 'er even if it was freaky close. Although, because of that, there's a new prevailing theory that she might still be in on it and is just coverin' up for a sibling."

"That's ridiculous!" Felicity snapped.

"Hey, it's not my theory."

"Well, as far as that goes," she continued, "I don't know what to tell you. Unless my brother is running around in drag doing this, it's got to be some kind of bizarre fluke."

"Well, it's definitely female DNA," Ben added. "So I think your brother is safe on this one. Speakin' of him, everything okay there?"

"Yeah," I said with a nod. "With him, anyway. Can't vouch for the rest of the family."

"Aye, I'd rather not get into that," Felicity interjected coldly.

"Yeah, me either."

"So, you're absolutely sure ya' don't have a sister?" Ben tossed the question out again.

"I already said so, didn't I?"

"Yeah, but are ya' sure is what I'm askin'."

"Look, Ben, when I was a child, like most little girls, I wanted a sister, yes," she replied with an annoyed sigh. "But I sure as hell didn't manifest one. So, yes, I'm sure I don't have a sister. Only a brother."

"Well, I know ya' didn't wanna talk family," he pressed. "But ya' might wanna open a coupla' closets 'cause the lab guy says he'd bet hard money you do."

"So...is this it?" I asked, looking across the table at my wife. "The 'nothing'?"

"The what?" Felicity returned her own query, only briefly glancing up from the box she was unpacking.

"This," I said, pulling a dark purple bag from a cardboard box and hefting it up in front of her. "When I saw you on Saturday you tried to tell me something about an overnight bag, but we got interrupted. So, I just kind of assumed it was something the police had in their possession.

"Then today when we were talking to Ben, something about evidence taken from the house had you a bit on edge, and when I asked you about it..."

"I said, it was nothing." She finished the sentence for me.

True to what Ben had told us, the recovery of our seized property was far easier than I had expected it to be. In fact, the drive downtown and back took longer than the actual paperwork. The only requirement over and above that which he had detailed for us was that I also needed to show my handgun permit in order to get my confiscated revolver returned to me. Fortunately, I had anticipated such and had it in my wallet.

While there, Felicity had quickly inventoried the items against the voucher and everything appeared to be intact. Everything that was on the official list, anyway, because at the time of seizure, I had angrily signed the piece of paper they presented with little more than a quick glance. All I had wanted right at that moment was to get them out of my house, so I wasn't using the best judgment. The truth was, they could have walked out with things they didn't bother to list, but there wasn't much I could do about that at this point. I was going to have to take them at their word.

We had only just returned home and unloaded the trio of boxes from the back of my wife's Jeep. Immediately emptying them of their contents and putting things back where they belonged seemed like the best thing to do, rather than have them sit around as a reminder of the legally sanctioned violation of our lives. So, that task became the undertaking of the moment.

The overnight bag just happened to be at the top of the pile in the first box I opened.

"Umm...yes," she spoke again after a long pause then repeated while still staring at the bag, "Yes, that's it. I'd actually almost forgotten about it until this morning...actually, you weren't supposed to get that box...I must have mixed them up."

"Okay," I said with a shrug then placed the weighty carryall on the seat of the dining room chair between us. "Then I'll forget about it too."

I was lying. I wasn't going to forget about it. There was really no way that I could. The urgency in her voice when she had first mentioned the overnight bag back at the Justice Center still hadn't left me. Then, there was the "nothing" comment on top of it. Obviously something about it concerned her greatly. Even more so, what my impression of it, or something inside it, would be. Therefore, although my mind had placed the snippet of conversation in a holding pattern for the past few days, it was still there. Seeing the bag now had simply returned it to the forefront.

My curiosity, however, was going to need to remain unquenched. Whatever the mysterious purple bag held was apparently deeply personal for Felicity, otherwise I would have known of it before now. Violating its sanctity would make me no different than those who had already crossed that boundary, and pressing her to talk about it would only demonstrate distrust on my part.

I delved back into the box before me and began extracting the stack of books lined in the bottom. I was going to need to sort them out and return a few to the library sometime this week. I was on my third handful of the tomes when Felicity spoke.

"You want to know what's in it, don't you." She wasn't asking a question, she was making an observation.

I looked up at her and shrugged again. "No. It's not important."

"You're lying."

"Yeah, so?"

"It's just…I mean…It's…"

"Honey, don't worry about it."

"I can't not," she appealed. "I don't want you to distrust me."

"Why would I distrust you?"

"For keeping something from you." She motioned toward the bag and added, "For keeping *this* from you."

I stopped what I was doing and slowly let out a thoughtful breath. I couldn't be sure if she was opening the door and inviting me in or if it was only cracked enough to pull the safety chain taut, affording her the ability to slam it in my face if I misspoke.

I took in a fresh breath and smiled. "Not long ago, a dear and very wise friend told me that we all keep secrets, even from those we love. And, that sometimes we do so for that very reason. Out of love."

She cast a glance toward the bag and fidgeted nervously for a moment then looked back to my face. "Helen."

"Yes. Helen."

"What else did she tell you?"

"Nothing I didn't already know."

She remained silent in the wake of my answer, so I continued. "Felicity, Gods know I've kept things from you over the past few years. Things about cases I've helped work, things about visions I've had. Believe me, there are still some things locked away in my head that I haven't told anyone, especially you, all purely out of love and my desire to keep you safe. So, you see, it's a two-way street."

"But, that's different," she objected.

I shook my head. "Not really. Obviously whatever is in that bag is something you think may hurt me or change the way I feel about you. Correct?"

"Aye."

"Then it's no different, and there's nothing to worry about."

"Are you certain?" she asked tentatively.

"Yes."

"I just want to be sure," she said. "I need to know that you trust me."

"I do."

"Even with this between us?" She nodded toward the bag.

"Let me ask you this. Do you want to show me what's in there?"

Again she cast a furtive glance at the duffle, dwelled there for a moment, and then looked back to me. "I don't know yet."

"Okay, then, you don't have to. I trust you. And, I trust that if you ever decide you want me to know this particular secret, you'll share it."

"How can you be so sure, when I'm not?"

"Easy. You sat in our kitchen around two weeks ago and announced that you had a fairly rich history with the bondage sub-culture. That was something new to me."

"Yes, but that just sort of came out. I think it might have been the circumstances, the investigation and such because I even surprised myself by saying it. I wasn't really thinking."

"I'm sure it probably was the situation, and actually you really were thinking, sweetheart. You knew you could shed some light on a minor mystery and you did. Admitting *how* you knew the things you did was merely a natural progression from there."

"At the time it seemed okay," she replied. "But, after the fact, I was afraid I'd made a very bad mistake in telling you."

"Honey, I may not have known about the history, but I can't say I was surprised. You've got the personality. I even told you that."

She let out a nervous laugh. "Aye, I know I do."

"And, there you have the answer to your question. The reason I can be sure is because I am fully aware that if and when it comes time for me to know, you'll tell me."

The trepidation faded from her face, and she finally managed a tentative smile. "Have I told you today that I love you, Rowan Linden Gant?"

"A couple of times, but I can stand hearing it again."

Wednesday, November 23
11:04 P.M.
Baton Rouge, Louisiana

CHAPTER 24:

The hunger was coming upon her again.

Only a little more than two weeks had passed since Saint Louis, and here it was creeping into her again. This was too soon.

It was like a drug. An addiction she just couldn't shake, and there were no steps to help her cope. Homicidal Sadists Anonymous simply didn't exist, not in any phone book she had seen.

She was coming.

And, *She* wasn't going to take no for an answer. *She* never did no matter how much she begged.

"Where had it all gone wrong?" she wondered. "When had it taken this turn down a dark and dead-end path?"

She couldn't remember. Or, maybe it wasn't that she couldn't. Perhaps it was that she didn't want to. The pleasure was her reward, and the reward was sweet.

There was a time she knew she should have heeded the warnings. Seen the signs. Run when she had the chance. But that was all in the past. Now she belonged to *Her*, and there was no escape, even if she wanted it.

And, sometimes she did, though she wasn't sure why.

She rolled over in the bed and lifted her arm to her face, inspecting it in the dim light. Softly, she caressed the scar where she had once sliced into her own wrist in a bid for escape. She wondered if perhaps she should try again before *She* arrived. That was the only thing that had saved her then. *She* had made her call 9-1-1, and the paramedics had arrived just in time.

No, if she tried to kill herself, *She* would just save her again. Besides, this feeling of dread always came just before *She* arrived, and it always passed.

No. She would simply wait it out. The bad feelings would be gone soon, and the pleasure would come in their place.

It's not that she didn't enjoy the things she did whenever *She* was with her. She always enjoyed herself. She always had. Even before *She* came along, sex had never been satisfying unless she was in complete control, and even then it was mediocre. Often, even disappointing.

But, dark thoughts sometimes become dark actions, and with those actions come discovery. Her revelation had come so many years ago it seemed like forever. And, yet it seemed like yesterday.

She bent her knees and kicked then grasped the sheet in her hand and whipped it back in the darkness. Just thinking about it made an unreachable itch begin down below. She was already getting hot, and the cool air in the room felt refreshing against her warm skin. Staring at the ceiling, she wondered about the boy and what he was doing now. She couldn't even remember his name.

Mike...

Joe...

Kevin...

It didn't matter. There had been so many since him, and she couldn't remember their names either. But, they say you never forget your first, and she hadn't.

Even if she couldn't remember his name, she could remember the details...

She was a college freshman, and he was an upperclassman. While he certainly wasn't innocent, she was as far removed from virtuous as anyone could be, even if no one was the wiser. He'd been begging her for a date for more than a month, and it amused her. So much so, that it had set her mind to work.

When she finally agreed, it was on her terms, as always. She strung him along for two weeks, promising everything and giving nothing, just as she would do with any other boy. But, for this one, she had bigger plans. When she was certain he was primed and ready, she gave in, or so she led him to believe.

The room had been dank and dingy. The décor was so far out of date as to not even have a recognizable style. She was certain that it had been cheap, but for her purposes she didn't care. Besides, she was the one who picked out the fleabag motel in the first place.

It was private, sitting along a secluded stretch of blacktop just outside of town. It was a place where no one asked questions about what went on behind the red, chipped paint of the scuffed doors. It was perfect.

Had it been up to him, they would have just made it in his room at the fraternity house, but·she had needed the privacy for her plans. She had insisted that he get the room, and by that point she was sure his family jewels were probably navy blue, so it wasn't hard to get him to shell out the cash.

Just like it wasn't hard to get him to strip naked almost as soon as they arrived.

Just like it wasn't hard to get him to go for something a little "different" when she pulled the cotton clothesline out of her purse.

Once he had let her tie him to the bed, it was all over. She'd had to reassure him several times when he complained of it being too tight, asking if she was certain she knew what she was doing, but by that point, for him, it was too late. She'd made certain that he couldn't move, and the cotton panties in his mouth with the duct tape over his lips made certain no one would hear. Getting those into his mouth had been the hardest part, and she was sure he was going to scream before she could get it done. But, somehow, she had managed to do it, and then she wound the duct tape around his head to secure it.

The struggle itself had aroused her, just as had the anticipation.

Then, she had sat astride him on the bed for several minutes, not quite sure where to start. She had fantasized about this for as long as he had pursued her, working out the details of how to get him to this point. But, now that she was here, she didn't know how to begin.

After several moments, she simply slapped him hard across the face. The tickle that had been welling in her belly now became an itch, and she liked it. She slapped him again, harder this time, and felt him squirm beneath her as he struggled against the bonds. The itch grew stronger.

She remembered feeling herself smile.

She perpetuated the feeling with various mild cruelties. More slapping. Scratching him with her painted nails. Pulling his hair. But, her first true orgasm had come at the exact instant she twisted a burning cigarette against his bare chest. As he writhed and squealed against the gag, she felt the itch explode. The intensity of the feeling had taken her by surprise, making her fall back across the bed, gasping for breath. The ripple had then driven through her, and it was unlike anything she had ever experienced before. When it had finally died away, the only thing she could think about was having that feeling once again.

She remembered climbing back on top of him and looking down at his frightened eyes as she lit another cigarette...

She had untied him before she left. He was unconscious, passed out from the pain, she assumed.

She was spent.

He'd had enough money in his wallet to cover the cab fare back to campus, and she had gladly taken it. That was also when she had taken her first souvenir. His class ring. She wasn't sure why she had taken it back then, but it all became obvious years later when she met *Her*.

In fact, the ring was still on her altar.

Of course, that was then, and it had been wonderful. But after that night, as good as it was, she could never recapture the intensity of the feelings she had experienced.

That was until *She* came into her life...

Now, even the fond memory of the night paled by comparison to the depth of pleasure *She* had shown her. Not only was it better, it was better than she could have imagined. At times, the mere anticipation of the pleasure was almost as good as the reward itself.

Of course, *She* took it farther than she was ever willing to go before. Then, it was play. Now, it was so much more...

For them both...

As the memory began to fade, she rolled and sat up on the edge of the bed in one fluid motion. Reaching out, she twisted the switch on the bedside lamp, bringing luminance into the room. Sliding her thumbs along her jaw line, she gathered her long red hair and tossed it over her shoulders to cascade down her bare ivory back.

The tickle was now a burning itch.

She was here.

It was time.

Thursday, November 24
2:13 A.M.
Saint Louis, Missouri

Thursday, November 24
2:13 A.M.
Saint Louis, Missouri

———

CHAPTER 25:

I can hear the footsteps coming.

They thump hard against the wooden stairs below, but I know that is not where they will stay. They are already getting closer.

Each footfall comes louder...

Faster...

As if driven by sheer excitement, they move upward, coming for someone. I pray that this time it will not be me.

I can hear the wails of the others. They, too, know she is coming. Nearby, someone is sobbing. I think it is a woman but I can't be sure. It has been so long now that they have all begun to sound alike.

They are genderless...

Pitiful moans...

Terrified screams...

Barely even human...

They have become nothing less than a cacophony of anguished noise...

But, no matter how loud it becomes, even it cannot drown out the cruel sound of her feet against the stairs.

I listen in the darkness.

The footsteps are near now, just outside the door.

I wait.

I listen.

And, I wait.

But, the telltale creak of the hinges never comes.

Then I hear her feet shuffle, and the hard noise begins again.

The cruelty is there, but the excitement is gone. It is, instead replaced by annoyance.

This time they fade, growing more distant with each step.

Until, finally, they are no more than a fresh memory of an endless nightmare.

I rolled over in the bed and opened my eyes but found myself staring at nothing. I pondered this for a moment in my groggy state as I listened to my heart thumping. It was beating faster than it should for someone at rest, or so it seemed. But, it was quickly slowing, and with the afterimages of the nightmare still lingering in my head, I thought maybe that was a good sign.

This was the first time the terror had invaded my sleep since the night before Felicity's arrest. My ongoing headache had actually lessened to a dull throb over the past few days, and with the advent of several decent nights sleep in a row, I was beginning to think that maybe, just maybe, I had been wrong. That perhaps by some miracle of the Gods, this was going to all fade away for a change and leave us alone.

Of course, I knew better, but I could always hope.

The stab in the back of my head was working its way forward, but for the moment it was bearable. I was sure that I couldn't count on that lasting for long. I sighed and went back to considering my lack of visual input. I knew I was awake, so it wasn't part of the nightmare. As my eyes worked at focusing, it became apparent that the nothing I was seeing was actually a dark pattern. I shifted slightly and the pattern moved, brushing softly against my cheek.

Raising my arm, I pushed the pattern away and found that it was the comforter, which at some point I had pulled over my head. Blinking, I now found myself face to face with a pillow on the opposite side of the bed. The only problem my brain found with that picture was that my wife's head wasn't on it.

I pushed myself up on one elbow, eyes drowsily searching the room. Before any unwarranted panic managed to set in, however, my ears caught the sound of rushing water and a porcelain throated burp as the toilet was flushed.

Dropping my head back onto the pillow, I mentally chastised myself for letting my fears get the better of me and then rolled over to face the wall. I was tired, and it obviously wasn't morning yet, so I closed my eyes.

The nightmare hadn't been so bad this go around. Maybe it really was just a product of my overactive subconscious.

This time.

The reprieve had been too short, but then they always were. It's just that this one was even shorter.

Footsteps advanced once again up the stairs, pausing only for a moment, then proceeding, coming closer with each hard strike against the wooden planks. The sobbing filled in the short voids between them.

But, there was something different about their sound.

They were still excited.

They were still cruel.

But there was something acute about their tone. No longer the familiar thud, they had become a sharp clack. However, different as they were, I knew they belonged to the same monster.

And, the fear they brought with them bit deep into my soul, for this time I knew they were coming for me. How I knew, I couldn't say. But, there was no doubt that I was to be her chosen victim, and there was no escape.

I began to pray, but my request had changed drastically from what it had once been. Instead of asking to be spared as I had countless times before, now I prayed to die quickly and not linger, suffering for days—even weeks—like some of the others. I could hear myself whispering in the darkness, even above the growing cries and awful footfalls.

When they stopped outside the door, I was more than just simply aware my time had come. I could feel it deep within every inch of my body, and that just made the panic grow.

The door creaked on un-oiled hinges, allowing a swath of dim light to fall across the room. I couldn't keep myself from trying to raise my head, but try was all my weakened muscles could manage.

Terror made me strain and pull, trying to escape, even though I knew I was held fast. The flight reflex made me try yet again, but my wrists and ankles screamed with pain as something bit sharply into my flesh. I was left with no choice but to give in to my fate, horrific, as I knew it was to be.

The door creaked again as it swung wider, then the steps clacked closer, stopping near my head, just out of my sight. I felt my stomach tighten, then heave, as it tried to expel contents it didn't have. The bile rose in my throat, burning and making me gag. But even through that, I continued to pray.

There was a shuffle, and then the steps continued, clacking away across the room. But, I knew they would be back.

The moans of the others hummed in my ears, punctuated by animalistic wails that were born from the bowels of hell.

A sudden, loud clunk sounded in my ears, and bright light flooded into my eyes. I had been in darkness for so long that the luminance brought only pain. A searing pain that made me squeeze my eyelids tightly shut.

The footfalls came again as they moved across the plank floor, returning to their station at my head. I continued to hold my eyes shut and struggled through a gasping breath as I began to sob with the others.

Now, instead of the acrid stench of rot and excrement to which I had grown so accustomed, the sweet smell of perfume burrowed deeply into my nostrils. Its thickness caused me to gag again, and my chest began to tighten.

Another shuffle and pair of excited steps met my ears. A moment later a pressure settled across my belly making it even harder for me to breathe.

I began to beg. God wasn't listening to my prayers, so I had no other choice.

As the mumbled words started tumbling from my mouth, a sharp sting lashed across my cheek, and a feminine voice, dripping with false sweetness drawled, "Wake up..."

I was jolted awake by the intense feeling that someone, or something, had just struck me hard in the face. My heart was pounding and my chest was tight. I felt as if a weight were resting on my stomach, causing me to labor for each breath. My head was throbbing with unnatural pain, and I was beginning to feel sick to my stomach.

The nightmare had returned, and this time the abject terror was fully intact. I started upward as I had done countless times before when awaking from this horrific vision, but got nowhere. In fact, not only did it feel as though something was pressing me back downward, an odd sensation bit into my wrists and arms. Confusion joined the pain in my grey matter as I fought to reason out what was happening. I was almost certain I was awake. I didn't have the odd feeling of disconnection that so often came with channeling a spirit. And, I had the headache. That was a pain that always remained within the boundaries of my wakefulness. Light was streaming in through the thinness of my eyelids, blood red and far too bright for comfort. I found that I was still holding them tightly shut, an artifact of the nightmare I assumed, but one I didn't mind. Since it appeared that light was now also invading my corporeal world, I knew its sudden influx would only serve to make the headache even worse.

Still, something was definitely off kilter, and I needed to know what it was. I was just about to take the plunge and open my eyes at least enough to get my bearings when another lacerating sting tore into my cheek.

This time I knew it was real.

"I said, time to wake up, little man." The nightmare woman's voice rolled into my ears, heavy with a sugary Southern drawl.

My eyes flickered open, and as I suspected, the glare of the overhead light acted as an accelerant on the ache in my skull. Blinking my way toward some semblance of focus, I looked upward toward the direction of the voice. Staring back at me was a visage that would have been comfortingly familiar had it not been for the frightening expression it wore.

My wife was straddling me in the bed, looking back down at me with an imperious gaze. No longer wearing her pajamas, she was now scantily clad in something black that appeared to be composed of tight-fitting leather and a touch of lace. It was something I didn't recall ever having seen in her wardrobe before, and that told me that perhaps I was now getting a glimpse of the contents from the overnight bag, up close and personal.

Her face had obviously been in recent contact with more than just a touch of makeup and was accented in such a way to enhance the severe expression lining her features. She continued looking down at me, and I started trying to convince myself that I wasn't really awake.

After a long pause she gave her head a toss then giggled and said, "That's better."

Even though the sentence was no more than two words, the uncharacteristic geographical drawl was obvious and intact.

Following the utterance, she placed a cigarette between glossy red lips and drew on it hard. The end grew bright, sizzling audibly as I watched the paper and tobacco slowly burn a full one-half inch down the length right before my eyes. In a fluid motion, she pulled the cigarette from her mouth, flicked the spent ash at my face, then pursed her lips and blew out a long stream of smoke.

Never once had she taken her eyes from mine, and now her mouth spread into a contented smile. I started upward again; knowing suddenly that telling myself this was a nightmare simply wasn't going to make it so. Fear was definitely starting to work its way into my spine.

Again I found myself unable to go far and realized that my arms were outstretched to the sides and above my head. I cast a quick glance to the right and saw my wrist encompassed by a wide, leather-looking cuff that was securely fastened to the bedpost. I didn't have to look to the left to know it too was similarly bound. I didn't feel anything around my ankles so I tried to move my legs, only to find they were bound in some unseen way.

I instantly regretted being a heavy sleeper.

"What's wrong, little man?" my wife asked.

Actually, it was the voice asking the question. It just happened to be coming out of my wife's mouth.

"Felicity?" I questioned out of reflex.

I didn't catch the blur of motion, but I definitely felt the sting of her palm against my cheek as she slapped me hard enough to crank my head to the side.

"And, who, pray tell, is Felicity, little man?" she asked.

"You are," I replied with a groan as I turned my face back to her.

Judging from the force of yet another slap that immediately followed my reply, apparently, it was the wrong thing to say.

"You will call me, Mistress Miranda, little man," she commanded.

What I had earlier thought to be fear was just a trial run of the emotion. In the grand scheme of things, it had been nothing more than a shot of anxiety with a confusion chaser just to get the ball rolling. Hearing the sentence just spoken by the evil inhabiting my wife's body was the catalyst, and now true horror set in.

At this stage of the game, I wasn't sure what this *Lwa* feasted on, but it was a good bet that pain played into that picture, and I suspected fear was at the very least an appetizer. If that was true, judging by her satisfied grin, I was apparently serving up the first course at this very moment.

"Oh, what's wrong?" she asked, feigning concern. "Am I scaring you?"

"No," I returned.

"Liar."

"Guess it's your word against mine," I said, mustering whatever semblance of calm bravado I could.

She sat back and regarded me coolly. Felicity truly didn't weigh much more than one hundred pounds, but with the panic starting to well in the pit of my stomach, even that amount of weight on top of me was making it hard to breathe.

After taking another long drag on the cigarette, she pulled it slowly from her mouth and smiled then let the smoke out in a thin stream.

There was no way I could read what was going on behind the still pretty, but frighteningly severe, mask her face had become. In retrospect, given what I knew from the crime scenes, I should have been able to at least predict what she was going to do. Unfortunately, a by-product of terror is that one doesn't always think straight.

I suppose that's why it came as such a complete shock to me when, without a word her smile grew even wider, and she began to slowly grind out the burning cigarette against my bare chest.

CHAPTER 26:

Something kept me from screaming out in response to the pain. I wanted to in the worst way, and in fact, I even tried. However, the yelp instantly caught in my throat and remained there, emitting little more sound than a soft groan. The only reason I could imagine for the abrupt stifling was that I knew the spirit was feeding on my pain and fear, and I supposed it was just my subconscious attempting to deny it the meal. Of course, whether or not I screamed probably was a moot point. It knew I was afraid, there was no doubt of that, and my body definitely betrayed me in the pain department.

I tensed in reflex even as the sound stuck in my windpipe, gurgling quietly through my clenched teeth. As she continued to grind the burning ember into my flesh, I sucked in a quick breath, steeling myself against whatever might be yet to come. I couldn't help but notice the odor of singed hair and skin. If that wasn't bad enough, it had joined the spicy scent of her perfume, mixing on the air to become a peculiar, sweet funk that did little for my already queasy stomach.

Even though I was fighting to deny anything to the evil that had invaded our home, the look on my wife's face told me I was losing the battle before I had even started fighting back. No longer was she wearing the wide, mischievous grin. She had gone far beyond that. Now, her face was molded into an expression of near ecstasy. Her eyes were closed; and her lips were slightly parted as she slowly tilted her face upward. She began to pant, and suddenly a bizarre moan filled the room. It was something I could only describe as a poorly synchronized disharmony of sound, both human and inhuman. The worst part was that I knew they were both coming from deep within Felicity. One of them the product of her own hijacked voice, the other from somewhere on the other side of the veil, dwelling in an inky darkness that was blacker than I ever wanted to imagine.

She arched her back as the sigh of pleasure grew louder, and its jarring duality grew even stronger. Her posture served only to make her look like a player in an adult movie acting out the generally accepted portrait of an earth shattering orgasm for an unseen camera.

Unfortunately, I knew all too well that this wasn't acting.

This was for real.

My wife began to sink as she literally allowed herself to slump backward. Her breathing grew shallow, coming in rapid pants as the unearthly sound continued trilling through the room, joined by a rapturous whimper of corporeal origin.

The initial shock of the lit cigarette against my chest had now faded to a dull burn that took up residence in the background, hiding behind my many other ignored pains. Lifting my head, I watched as Felicity tensed and twisted, all but writhing in unfathomable ecstasy. She was still straddling me but was pitched backward at an angle, bracing herself with one hand on the edge of the bed while the other roamed her body of its own accord. Had I not been fully aware of the why and how this was happening to her, it would have been an immensely humbling sight, being that I wasn't responsible for it. However, my prowess in regard to pleasing my wife was the furthest thing from my thoughts at the moment. What lived in the forefront was the horror of knowing that by succumbing to the ethereally dispensed pleasure, Felicity was only cementing her bond with the *Lwa*.

Of course, her ability to resist had been negated the moment the spirit had assumed control, and even in my present state, I recognized the power of what I was witnessing. Though I had no doubt that my wife had not initially given herself over to the *Lwa* willingly, I almost wouldn't have been able to blame her if she had. The apparent reward she had just received in return for what was, in the grand scheme of things, a fairly mild act of cruelty, was one that could not be easily refused.

I dropped my head back down and twisted it to the right, looking toward my hand. Without my glasses I couldn't see much detail, but the leather-looking cuff appeared to have a metal buckle and

D-ring type of hardware securing it both to my wrist and then to the bedpost by a short strap. I twisted my arm slowly and found that the restraint was loose enough to allow movement within it. I glanced back quickly and saw that Felicity was still in the throes of her experience and paying little or no attention to me for the moment.

Rolling my head back to the side, I rotated my arm once again, this time pulling as well. The heel of my palm slipped down into the cuff and stopped cold, the hard edge of the restraint bit sharply into the back of my hand, and I could feel it abrading the skin as I kept applying the downward pressure.

Casting my glance to the left, I tried the same tactic on the other arm, gaining the same fruitless results. Still, I didn't give up until I heard my wife's breathing begin to come under control and then felt her weight shifting back fully onto my stomach as she pushed herself up and forward.

She was wearing an expression of pure contentment, with her eyelids drooping heavily and a pouting smile caressing her lips. But, simply the way she was breathing told me she wasn't going to roll over and go to sleep—nor did she have plans for cuddling.

No, *Miranda* was just getting started.

"Hmmmmmm," she purred. "That was good."

"Glad you enjoyed it," I quipped, unable to contain my disdain for the spirit inhabiting my wife.

She giggled, almost musically, looking down at me with a wicked smile.

"I did," she replied. "Didn't you?"

"Not particularly."

"Hmmmmm…" she purred again, a thoughtful tone underscoring the hum.

She rocked to the side, lifting up and planting her stocking clad knee in the center of my chest, then pitched forward and placed her weight on it. I grunted as the air was forced out of my lungs, and I felt my ribcage flex inward. I heard her quickly shuffle something off to the left of my head, then she rocked back and slid her knee down as she dropped herself hard onto my stomach, forcing me to huff out the breath I'd only just managed to suck in.

Settling herself in, she slipped the wrapper from a cigar and then nipped the end of it with my guillotine cutter. I recognized the stogie as one of the real-deal Cuban smokes a friend had recently brought back for me from a trip to the Caribbean. How he had gotten them back into the country I hadn't asked—not that it mattered now.

She was watching me watch her, and she seemed to find it amusing. After a moment of fiddling about with the dark brown roll of tobacco, she waved it in front of my face.

"You don't mind, do you?" she drawled in a mocking tone. "I helped myself."

"Go ahead," I returned. "Tell him it's with my compliments."

"Him?" she asked, cocking her head to the side.

"*Papa Legba*," I replied.

"What makes you think it's for Papa?"

"Educated guess."

"Hmmmmm," she purred once again.

Without another word she double-clicked a lighter then brought the long stream of flame against the foot of the cigar, rolling it slowly. Then, she carefully placed the tight roll of tobacco between her lips and proceeded to set the end alight, twisting it slowly and puffing hard. A cloud of blue-white smoke billowed around her, and she didn't even flinch. Just one more sign that my wife was no longer my wife, as she would have gone into a sneezing fit immediately.

My hands were already starting to throb where I had pulled them down into the restraints. I knew that the scrapes were going to start getting inflamed, and swelling would be quick to follow. I wasn't even sure that I would be able to extract my hands as they were now, but if they became swollen, there wouldn't even be a thread of a chance. Of course, I also knew it was going to take more than a mere second or two and some obvious strain to accomplish, if at all. Therefore trying to make it happen while her attention was actually focused on me was out of the question. That would only prompt her to tighten them more or do something even worse. What, I didn't even want to imagine.

"So," she finally said, still regarding me as she puffed gently on the Cuban stogie. "How do you know about Papa?"

"I read a lot."

She didn't reply. Instead she hooked her dainty finger around the cigar and pulled it from between her lips. With a quick flick she knocked ash from the end, aiming it directly at my face as she had done earlier with the cigarette. Then, pursing her lips, she blew gently on the burning end of the roll, making the ember glow bright reddish-orange. Turning it in her hand, she then carefully placed the lit end into her mouth and closed her lips tightly around it.

Once again a billow of smoke began to encircle her head as she blew out through the cigar. Just as I knew from my research, that the cigar was intended for *Papa Legba*, I also knew that what she was now doing was, in effect, smoking it for him.

After a few moments, she extracted the cigar from her mouth and grinned at me. Once again, without warning she set about her regimen of torture. Reaching forward to my chest, she took my left nipple between her thumb and forefinger, squeezed hard, and then twisted.

This time my subconscious didn't intervene. I immediately yelped as the pain shot through the sensitive nerve cluster then grimaced as she continued to pinch and twist.

"How..." she began.

Even through my pain, I could tell that she had caught her breath before she could get the sentence out of her mouth, and that could only mean one thing. She was getting aroused all over again.

"How does that feel?" she finally said, managing to get out the entire sentence before she began to pant as she had done before.

The throb in my skull ramped up and seemed to pulsate in unison with her oncoming orgasm. I fought to concentrate through both it and the pain she was inflicting on my chest. I knew an opportunity was soon going to present itself; I just had to be able to take advantage of it. Unfortunately, whether or not that would happen was going to be directly connected to how much pain I was going to be able to endure and still remain conscious.

She let go of the sensitive skin then slowly raked her nails across my chest, digging hard at the earlier burn as she continued watching my face.

The influx of pleasure that was overtaking her seemed to be coming faster—and even more intensely than it had the first time. If this was the normal pattern then it had to be like a drug. Something akin to the neuro-psychology experiment where a rat was wired to be able to self-stimulate the pleasure centers of its own brain with the press of a bar in its cage; which it did with relish, foregoing food, water, and sleep, until it simply expired. Only, this wasn't an electrode-wearing rat in a lab. This was my wife's body, and a malevolent spirit was using her as a vehicle in order to experience the same repetitive rush.

Given what I was seeing now, it wasn't hard to extrapolate what had occurred at the various crime scenes. If progressively intensifying sexual climaxes in return for increasingly cruel tortures were how this *Lwa* worked, I couldn't even begin to imagine what level of rapture the actual kill would trigger. I looked back up at her and watched as she carefully regarded the burning end of the cigar, flicking her gaze between it and me. It didn't take a genius to see what was coming, and I wasn't entirely sure I was prepared for it, even with the advance knowledge.

Still, the last climax had kept her occupied for a few minutes. If this was going to be even more intense, I just might have enough time to get free. What I was going to do after that was anyone's guess, but at least I would actually be in a position to do something other than die. I decided quickly that as insane as it seemed, antagonizing her into the next phase of cruelty was my best course of action. Judging from her present state, it wasn't going to take much to set her off.

She started to grin then pursed her lips and blew on the end of the cigar again, brightening the ember and creating a thin stream of smoke.

"Just what is your kink, little man?" she finally asked. "You males all have one. What does it for you?"

"You haven't found it yet," I croaked, my voice slightly strained from the earlier cry of pain.

"But, I will," she replied breathily.

She was starting to undulate her hips against me, and her chest would occasionally swell each time she would draw in a deep breath between the ongoing shallow pants. The ethereal moan was starting low within her, and her own voice was adding a nasal whimper of pleasure to the mix.

"We'll see," I returned.

"You don't think so?"

"You haven't impressed me yet."

She took hold of the tender nipple once again and twisted hard. I held my breath as I grimaced and clenched my teeth, struggling to keep from screaming. When she finally let go, I let the heated contents of my lungs spill slowly out then calmly as possible took a fresh breath.

After a moment I said, "Is that all you've got?"

She smiled back down at me, seeming to take great joy in my defiance.

"Tell me that you love me," she ordered.

"Go fuck yourself."

"Mmmm-hmmmm, that's the idea," she whispered.

I closed my eyes the minute she started to lean forward. I felt her touch the business end of the stogie to the nipple she had just tortured moments ago and then begin to twist it slowly. I could tell by the amount of pressure applied that she was purposely maintaining enough air space between the ember and my skin to keep it lit and hot, so I knew this wasn't going to be quick.

On top of that, this time she not only had more fire, she had picked an even more sensitive spot on my body to attack. Once again my subconscious kept out of the way, not just because I wanted it to, but also because I could no longer contain myself in the face of the agony. I screamed out, giving her possessor auditory evidence that she was causing me excruciating pain. I felt her thighs tighten against my sides as she tensed, the first real wave of pleasure hitting her hard. She continued to press the cigar into my blistering flesh, moaning and whimpering in delight with each deliberately languid twist.

My own body tensed out of reflex, and my arms pulled inward, tugging hard against my bonds as I squirmed beneath her, wailing like a wounded animal. As I did so, I actually felt my hand slip deeper into the cuff and at the same time, the cuff bite deeper into its flesh.

Suddenly, the pressure that had once been firmly positioned on my stomach lifted. I twisted my face upward and squinted my watering eyes toward her, seeing that she was arched back once again, literally squealing with ecstasy as she struggled to catch her own breath.

The cigar had been forgotten and was now lying on my chest, smoldering as it singed hairs and blistered a new spot. Even though I suspected I would have longer than I had the last time, there was no guarantee, and I had to make my bid for escape now. Things were only going to get worse, and though I had repeatedly experienced death and torture on an ethereal level, I was now coming to the conclusion that facing it in this realm was just as bad, if not worse.

Pressing my thumbs in tightly against my palms, I gathered my fingers into a point, trying desperately to almost fold my hands. I continued to pull hard, feeling the leather cuffs raking my flesh and tearing my skin. I'm not sure if it was sweat or blood, but my hands were starting to feel slippery. I didn't take the time to look. My attentions remained focused on my possessed wife as she tossed her head back and emitted what sounded to be a mixture of both a groan and a delighted giggle.

I felt my left hand move slightly, and a sharp pain instantly radiated up my arm. I grimaced through it and continued to pull with renewed fervor, and a split second later it popped free of the cuff. Giving the right a hard tug, it too came loose, minus several layers of skin across the back and knuckles.

My hands were free, but my legs were a different issue. I wasn't quite sure what to do, but at this point I was committed. Once she settled down she would be ready to start again, and the fact that my hands were no longer bound would be plainly obvious.

Knowing I had no choice but to act, I sat up quickly and pushed Felicity off of me, using her somewhat prone position against her. A quick glance showed me that the restraint for my legs took the form of a mummy-like wrap of the bed sheets. Tearing at them with my raw hands, I rolled in the opposite direction of my preoccupied wife. In my haste I fell completely out of the bed, as I fought to disentangle myself from the twist of fabric, and crashed onto the floor. I heard Felicity and the spirit moaning in unison. I kicked and tore at the sheet, pulling one leg free then the other, partially. I scrambled up to my feet, tripping over the wound fabric as it fought to cling to me, managed to catch myself before hitting the floor yet again, then aimed for the bedroom door. As I barreled forward, I cast a quick glance over my shoulder and saw my wife reaching for me even as her body was being racked by an ethereal orgasm.

Just as I pulled open the door, the displaced Southern voice was screaming from her throat. But, even in my panicked haste, I easily made out the words "No! Stop!"

I didn't bother to pay them any heed.

CHAPTER 27:

With everything that had been happening in that room, my attentions were obviously occupied. Even so, given the amount of noise I had made along with the various sounds emitting from my wife, it was a wonder the dogs hadn't been trying to tear down the door. That was something I would have had no choice but to notice, preoccupied or not. But now, in a sudden flash of gut-churning retrospect, their presence was something I realized had been conspicuously absent. Still, due to the circumstances, it hadn't even dawned on me that they were nowhere around until that very moment.

As if I wasn't biting back enough fear to begin with, a new one added itself to my list. Even though there was no doubt in my mind that unless I could bring an end to this possession, my wife was going to do everything in her power to kill me, a fresh concern took to rampantly overtaking my mind: What had she done to the dogs?

I quickly twisted through the opening and slammed the bedroom door shut behind me, but the lock was on the other side, and I had no way to barricade it. I knew it wasn't going to stop her if she came after me, which I was betting she would, but I hoped that it would at least slow her down. I immediately spun and lurched down the hallway as I was plunged into darkness, my eyes fighting to adjust as I bounced from the walls and tripped over my own panic-stricken feet. I wasn't hearing any movement behind me—yet. However, I was certain it would be coming at any moment.

For some reason I still couldn't stop thinking about the dogs. I suppose it was more comforting to be concerned for another being's life instead of my own. Whatever the motive, it bounced between the forefront of my brain and the pit of my stomach. I didn't know to exactly what extent *Miranda*'s cruelty reached, except with regard to human beings of the male gender. Since killing animals is sometimes a part of a serial killer profile, I certainly wasn't going to put it past her.

All I could really do, however, was hope that I was getting ahead of myself.

As callous as it felt, I fought to put the fear out of my mind because right now my brain had no business doing anything other than figuring out a way for both Felicity and me to survive this nightmare.

My wife's commandeered voice, still thick with the Southern accent and now filled with anger, was bellowing from the other side of the door, demanding that I stop. I wasn't about to pay it heed. Of course, at this particular moment that was just about the only thing I knew for a fact that I was or wasn't going to do. My next move was still a mystery, even to me. Her demand was followed by a shriek and a small crash, as if something had just been launched at the wall. I just kept moving.

The fresh blisters on my chest were still burning, sending hot pains inward through my flesh to join every other ache that was plaguing me. My hands were stinging and had grown sticky with the blood I already knew was seeping from the abrasions. The muscles in my arms throbbed from being stretched and overworked during my escape from the bonds. Tying it all together was the almost blinding pain in my skull. In the back of my mind, I knew grounding and centering would probably go a long way toward at least dulling that last angry stab, but I wasn't exactly in a position for such an exercise.

Exiting the hallway, I immediately slammed into the corner of a chair, catching it with my hip and yelping as I careened from it before stumbling out into the living room. Going from the lighted bedroom straight to the darkness of the rest of the house was playing havoc with my sight, not to mention that my eyes were still blurred and watering from the torture I'd just endured. If that weren't enough, my glasses were still on the nightstand.

I suddenly noticed that the atmosphere in the house actually felt warm against my skin. Since it was still dark, I knew the offset on the thermostat shouldn't have caused the temperature to rise just yet. It was then I realized that the warmth was relative. The bedroom had simply been colder than the rest of the house as a side effect of its unwanted ethereal occupant.

I aimed myself to the right, heading through the dining room and crashing against the table then stubbing my toe on a chair leg. I knew it wasn't only the darkness causing me to keep falling over myself; it was the rampant fear as well.

Quite the opposite of what Helen Storm had assured me when I had relayed my suspicions about my dream, I truly was afraid of my wife. Not just *of* her, but *for* her as well. Of all the horrors I had so far experienced in my life, and they were countless, this combination was the worst of them. So much so, that even my body had stopped responding to the signals from my brain.

I tried to wipe my eyes with the back of my hand and managed only to foul them somewhat with the blood. I pressed forward, trying to control my wild frenzy and blinking hard as my eyes continued adjusting to the dimness. There was a dull light coming from the kitchen, so I headed for it, still totally unsure what my plan of action was to be other than putting distance between the two of us.

For a split second, I thought of simply bolting out the back door, climbing into my truck and leaving. That would certainly get me out of harm's way. Of course, it would also mean turning around and getting my keys, but that wasn't the worst of it. If I left, it would mean Felicity would then be alone, except for the *Lwa* inhabiting her. I knew from experience that wasn't a stellar idea. The last time it had happened, she disappeared, and it had taken several hours to find her and almost cost a man his life. In reality, even finding her then had only been accomplished by the grace of pure luck.

My only option was to stay and face her down. Even with what she had done to me, I was still stronger than her and had both a height and weight advantage. Of course, the last time I had taken that particular path, she had fought back hard, and as much as I hated to admit it, she won. The simple fact that gave her the upper hand was that she had been perfectly willing to inflict damage. I, however, was not.

It was no different this time around. It didn't matter what she had done to me so far, or would do in the coming minutes, because I knew it really wasn't her. I simply couldn't bring myself to harm the vessel I knew as my wife, no matter what the consequences for myself.

I half fell through the doorway of the kitchen, grabbing the frame and swinging myself around behind the wall where I finally stopped and waited. Listening intently, at first all I could pick up was my own pounding heart and heaving breaths. I reached for my chest and flinched as my fingers brushed the blistering burns. Then I continued to hug the wall as I strained to hear anything more than the sounds made by my own body.

I furtively glanced up toward the microwave and saw the large, luminous numbers on the digital clock. They read 3:47. Turning my head back toward the doorway, I pressed myself against the cool wall and watched the darkness as my breathing began to slow and my heart rate shifted down from overdrive and into the lower gears of panic. I kept listening, but still, I heard nothing.

My fear was still fully intact, but it had become a manageable burden as I concentrated on picking up auditory cues. However, as I stood there, a new hollowness filled the pit of my stomach. My revolver was loaded and resting in my sock drawer back in the bedroom. Felicity knew right where it was, and that meant so did the *Lwa*. While I suspected she wasn't through torturing me for her pleasure just yet, she had also demonstrated a definite instinct for survival. I could easily conceive of a bullet shattering my future, and Felicity's as well.

Still hearing nothing out of the ordinary, my mind started to race. If she actually had the gun in hand, she was liable to take one of two different paths. Either she would come around the corner at any moment and splatter me across the front of the refrigerator, or she would simply sit and wait for me to come to her. I suppose it all depended on whether or not she was afraid I would actually leave.

Either way, simply sitting here waiting wasn't accomplishing anything.

"Think, Rowan, think!" I admonished myself in a low whisper.

Unfortunately, ridding oneself of malevolent spirits wasn't as easy as it was made to look on television. Three drop-dead gorgeous sisters, clad in the latest fashions, whipping up a "potion" from ingredients they had lying about the attic, then vanquishing evil without mussing their hair or smudging their makeup was undeniably a spectacular visual. But, it was also flat out Hollywood fiction.

I knew there wasn't much of anything in this kitchen that was going to help me in that respect. Or, was there? I quickly flashed on the last time Felicity had been inhabited by the *Lwa* when we were in her Jeep. My remedy that time had a stolen bit of spellwork, and I had attempted to force her to drink salt water. The basis was sound. Salt would purify and protect. The water as well, while also acting as a rapid delivery system. I hadn't succeeded that time, so I had no idea if it would really work. However, I couldn't help but remember how agitated the *Lwa* had been when she became aware of what I was trying to do, so apparently I had been on to something.

I looked over at the clock on the microwave and saw that it read 3:54. Seven minutes had passed while I stood there pondering a solution, and still nothing had happened. Shooting another glance at the dark doorway, I inched away from the wall and padded slowly toward the sink, keeping a nervous eye focused over my shoulder. It wasn't until I was actually up against the counter and reaching for the cabinet that I took my gaze away, and then it was only for a second.

Rummaging about, quietly as I could manage, I wrapped my hand around a sport bottle bearing the logo of a local computer repair company. A promotional giveaway I had picked up at a convention some time ago. Unscrewing the top while shooting random glances toward the doorway, I began to fill the container with water.

The bottle had reached almost half full when I cast my eyes to the end of the room yet again. Finding it clear, I looked back to the faucet. A heartbeat later the sound of a soft thump hit my ears, coming from directly behind me. My heart instantly fluttered, jumping into my throat and staying there as my knees went weak, and the pit of my stomach tightened into a knot. My grip automatically went limp, sending the bottle to clunk down into the sink and begin spilling its contents. Whether out of reflex, fear, or my knees just stopped working, I cannot say, but I fell to the floor and stayed there.

I listened, waiting for the telltale click of the hammer on the revolver but none came. Finally, after a frightful pause, I heard a soft meow. Slowly rolling to the side and looking up, I saw Emily, our calico, perched on the edge of the island and looking down at me with feline curiosity in her expressive face. I focused my gaze on the door and saw nothing but darkness.

Under any other circumstances, I would have laughed at my own jumpiness. Right now, however, I didn't find it amusing.

I dragged myself up from the floor and fished the sport bottle back out of the sink and started the process of filling it once again. This time, I managed to get it to three-quarters full, which is what I was after. Shutting off the water, I shuffled quickly over to the stove and grabbed the saltshaker. I gave the lid a twist then dumped the contents into the sport bottle. Replacing the top on the drink container, I made sure the spout was closed and began shaking it as I slowly made my way back toward the doorway to the dining room.

It was now just after four a.m., and she still hadn't come after me which could only mean she was waiting for me to come to her. As much as I didn't want to do it, I was going to oblige. It just wasn't going to be on her terms, or so I hoped.

Still remaining cautious, I peeked carefully around the corner and saw nothing but dimness and furniture. I slipped quickly around the doorframe and kept close to the wall, skirting around the buffet and inching up to the archway that led into the living room. Another quick glance around the wall, and I stepped through and started into the hallway.

My heart was already climbing back up the scale, adding beats with each passing second. I was straining to listen for any noise out of the ordinary but still heard none. I took a pair of steps and waited then advanced once again, creeping slowly up to the bedroom door.

Stepping quickly past it, I took up a station against the wall next to it. I was positioned such that if she opened the door, I would be in her blind spot.

I waited for what seemed like several minutes, desperately trying to work up the courage to do something other than stand here in the shadows. I still hadn't heard a thing, and I was sure that another several minutes had passed by now. Taking in a deep breath, I forced myself to reach to the side and grasp the door latch with my left hand. Pressing it down slowly, I heard the gentle click and then pushed the door open before quickly yanking my hand back.

Light from the bedroom flooded into the hall, and I continued standing there, cocked and ready to jump while I allowed my eyes to readjust to the new influx of luminance. Letting out a quiet sigh, I dropped my head down and swallowed hard. I blinked as I grew accustomed to the oblique shaft of light spilling from the opening, and now, with my gaze angled downward, for the first time realized that I was stark naked. Yet another ridiculous moment that was less than amusing to me under the circumstances.

After several heartbeats with nothing happening, I shrugged into my thin cloak of bravado.

"Miranda?" I called out.

I waited for several seconds and heard nothing.

"Miranda?" I called louder.

Now, my ears picked up a thin whimper, but it sounded nothing like the distorted whines of pleasure I had heard from my wife earlier. On the heels of the whimper came a soft sob.

"Felicity?" I called out.

My ears were met only with a renewed combination of the whimper and sob.

Part of my brain kept telling me that this could very well be a trap. That I was going to step out from the wall, round the corner, and catch a very fast moving hunk of lead right about chest level. Another part, however, told me that the *Lwa* was gone and that Felicity needed me. As the two sides argued, I flashed on the fact that while my headache was still intact it was nowhere near what it had been earlier.

I decided to believe the hunk of grey matter that kept saying it was Felicity who was waiting for me, and not Miranda. Still, I slowly and cautiously peeked in around the doorframe before fully coming out of my hiding space.

"Felicity?" I called once again as I carefully stepped into the room.

A harder sob met my ears, followed by a blubbered pair of syllables that sounded remotely like my name.

The twist of sheets were still lying on the floor and were streaked with blood from my hands where I had fought to disentangle myself. There was a smear or two marring the sheets that remained on the bed as well. The cuffs were still dangling from the bedposts by their straps, and while my uncorrected vision couldn't be sure, I was betting some of my skin was still attached to them.

I advanced farther into the room and worked slowly around the obstacles on the floor. After a few steps, I finally caught a glimpse of fiery auburn hair. The back of the top of my wife's head was barely peeking over the footboard of the bed. Still cautious, I moved slowly toward her until I could see fully over the edge of the blonde wood.

There she was, huddled on the floor, hugging her knees to her chest and rocking as she cried. In one hand was the framed picture that had been sitting on the headboard, the very photo that several days before had sent me waxing nostalgic about our trust in one another.

I knelt next to her and gently placed my hand on her shoulder as I softly called her name.

She started, looking up at me as if she hadn't realized I was there until just now. Her jade green eyes welled with even more tears while she quietly looked at my face and then my blistered chest.

"Oh Gods..." she whimpered, her voice thick with her Celtic lilt. It was a welcome sound.

"Shhhhh," I soothed.

"I didn't know..." she blubbered as the tears streamed down her face. "I saw the blood...I didn't know...I can't remember..."

"It's okay..." I whispered.

She reached out with a trembling hand and gingerly touched my chest near the charred flesh and growing blisters. I winced as her fingers brushed the area.

"God..." she mewled. "Did...Did I do that to you?"

"No," I reassured her, shaking my head. "Miranda did."

"She was in me, wasn't she?" she asked.

I didn't answer.

She started shaking again as my silence filled in the blank.

I looked down and remembered the sport bottle in my hand. I pondered it for a moment then handed it to my sobbing wife.

"Here," I said. "Take a drink of this."

As she accepted the bottle she managed to choke out, "What is it?"

"Just humor me," I replied.

She fingered the spout, unable to open it with her shaking hands. I popped it up for her then gently guided her hands, supporting the bottle as she placed it to her lips and took a swig. I gave it a light squeeze, and she swallowed a mouthful quickly, before sputtering and pushing it away. It didn't matter though; one drink was enough.

"Salt water?" she asked between choked sobs.

"Yeah. Sorry. I just want to make sure you stay Felicity for a while."

Thursday, November 24
Thanksgiving Day
9:53 A.M.
Saint Louis, Missouri

CHAPTER 28:

I looked at my watch and glared, giving the digits on its face an impatient scowl before twisting my wrist back down and sliding my hand into my coat pocket.

For lack of anything better to do, I pulled it back out and stuck the fresh cigarette it now held between my lips. Digging out my lighter, I lit it and took a deep drag. I had commandeered the pack of smokes from the nightstand in our bedroom. They were the ones that Felicity—or should I say *Miranda*—was smoking only a few hours ago. Where my wife had come up with them, I wasn't sure. I suppose prior to trussing me up in my sleep, she could have made a run to the local quick-shop. She didn't remember, and I didn't press the point. It was obvious at first glance that emotionally she didn't need to be badgered about anything, much less such a trivial fact; and in truth, it wasn't really all that important.

Besides, just as I'd had the craving the day she was led out of the house in handcuffs, I had it again now. I'm sure I should have just ignored it, but anxiety isn't always very tolerant of getting the cold shoulder, and they were right there, so I gave in. Right now I needed something to calm my nerves, and it was too early in the day for me to start downing Scotch. This was my chosen alternative. If it ended up blossoming into a full-time habit, I'd just deal with it and quit later. It wouldn't be the first time the horrors of an investigation had forced me down this road.

I turned and looked out from the balcony of the office building. The sun was arcing along the clear, southern sky, but it was still cold. I vaguely recalled hearing the weather blurb on the radio saying something about the high for the day possibly making it into the upper forties. It definitely wasn't there just yet.

I hung my head as I leaned against the railing and exhaled a combination of smoke and steam then glanced at my watch again. The numbers hadn't really changed significantly, but then I hadn't given them much of a chance to do so. Hearing a noise, I cast a quick glance behind me, looking toward the door to see if anyone had come out here to the building's smoking lounge. Given that it was Thanksgiving Day and the place was deserted, it would have to be either Felicity or Helen, as they were the only other people here.

Helen had actually offered to come to our house when I called her, but even we weren't there. The only way I had been able to calm my wife was to remove her from the "scene of the crime," which she had all but begged me to do. As soon as she had changed and I had thrown on some clothes myself, I made it happen. We had been sitting in an all-night diner, drinking coffee and quietly staring at one another when Felicity finally took me up on my repeated offer to call Helen. As usual, she was more than accommodating. We met here on the parking lot of the building a short time later—all three of us looking as though we could use several more hours sleep.

Of course, that was a while ago. The two of them had now been sequestered in Helen's office for over an hour, and that wasn't even counting the sixty minutes or so spent prior to me being ejected from the impromptu emergency session.

It wasn't that I had caused a problem. In fact, I'd actually kept my mouth shut for a change. Felicity and Helen both just felt there were some things that needed discussing without my presence. I can't say that I was happy about it, but I kept my objections to myself and complied anyway because if it was going to help my wife, then I was all for it.

I started to turn my wrist and glance at the timepiece again then caught myself. The rampant impatience was only serving to fuel my anxiety, and looking at my watch every thirty seconds was more than just a symptom. It was aggravating the situation. I desperately needed to get a handle on it before I let it tear me any further apart than it already had. I turned and leaned back against the rail, shrugging my coat around me in response to a light breeze, then immediately winced. I leaned back forward then with extra care reached inside the folds and gingerly adjusted my shirt where it was rubbing against the blisters on my chest. After taking another long drag on the cigarette, I let out a heavy sigh and tried to think about something else.

The first thought that came to mind was the dogs.

To my relief I had found them, alive and well, in the garage without so much as a scratch. They were nonplussed and maybe a bit chilled, but fine. They did, however, seem happy to be released from their temporary prison.

"There," I told myself aloud. "Happy ending, next subject."

Unfortunately, thinking about the canines just led me around in a big circle. The next subject simply turned into a continuation of the original that I had been trying fruitlessly to avoid.

I simply couldn't help but think about the fact that, in a sense, where I found the dogs told me something about Miranda. While control and dominance were the things she relished holding over her victims, there was obviously a thread of compassion somewhere within. She wanted the dogs out of the way, so she could proceed unhindered, but she hadn't physically harmed them. She was perfectly happy to do unspeakable things to a human male, but a different type of animal such as a dog or cat was apparently safe.

Felicity, on the other hand, hadn't seemed to fare quite as well as the canines. Physically she was fine, but emotionally she was a shattered mess. Apparently, the *Lwa* had exited rather quickly after I had made it out of the room, which explained why she hadn't chased me as I expected she would.

As it was, however, the only thing my wife truly remembered was going to bed the night before. After that she professed a complete blank until she found herself standing in our bedroom, decked out in one of her old dominatrix ensembles, feeling extremely disoriented, and highly aroused. I had no reason to doubt the truth of her story. That was pretty much the hallmark of a *Lwa*—pop in, pop out, leave 'em bewildered.

Of course, that was only the beginning of her mental collapse. Like anyone else would have, she had looked about the room trying to get her bearings as she fought off the confusion and began to realize where she was. While in this case the surroundings were familiar, what first met her eyes, unfortunately, were the remnants of the scene that had been playing out moments before. The bigger problem was that said tableau included my blood on the twisted sheets and me nowhere in sight. She was completely unaware of how the blood had come to be there, but considering what she had done during the last possession and how she now found herself attired, she immediately feared the worst.

She hadn't been able to summon the courage to go in search of me, primarily for fear of what she might find. Having taken that first set of crime scene photos herself, she knew first hand the sadism Miranda was capable of exhibiting. To her, the thought of finding me dead and most likely mutilated, especially if it was by her own hand, was more than she could bear to witness. Instead, she had simply stood there in a state of shock for several minutes. By the time I returned to the room and found her on the floor clinging to the photograph of the two of us, the psychological damage had been done.

I only came to find out an hour or so later that when she first heard my voice, she had automatically assumed it was inside her head and that I was calling to her from the other side of the darkened veil.

I sucked the remaining portion of the cigarette into my lungs and then dropped the smoldering butt into a sand-filled can nearby. Shaking my head as I huffed out the smoke, I muttered to no one but myself, "Oh well, so much for thinking about something else."

I pulled the pack from my pocket and gave it a glance. It had been around three-quarters full when I snagged it from the nightstand. Now it was down to four left. I fished one out, stuck it between my lips and tucked the pack away as I sent my other hand in search of the lighter.

"That does not look to me like your usual brand, Rowan." Helen's voice floated out from across the balcony, and I looked up to see her coming toward me, the glass door already levering shut on its hydraulic piston.

"Where's Felicity?" I asked as I pulled the cigarette from my mouth.

"She is in my office, resting. Don't worry."

"But, should she really be alone?"

"Don't worry, Rowan. As I said, she is resting."

"What did you do? Dope her up?"

"We usually frown on that terminology, but yes. I gave her a tranquilizer."

"I guess it pays to have both the sheepskins, huh?"

"I prefer to work patients through with analysis and therapy, but yes, being able to prescribe medication comes in handy, and is sometimes necessary."

"Okay," I finally sighed in resignation then looked at the smoke I was holding in my hand. I waved it absently and added, "It's just stress."

She shook her head, pulling a cigarette case from her own coat pocket. "You need not make excuses to me. I am not about to preach to you on the evils of smoking, you should know that."

I grunted acknowledgement and offered her my lighter, flicking it and cupping my hand around the flame. She set her smoke alight then gave me a nod as she sidled over to the railing a few steps away.

"So," I began after lighting my own. "How is she?"

"Disturbed," she replied succinctly.

"No offense, but I think I already had that nailed down," I replied. "The question is, how disturbed?"

"Enough to warrant concern, but not enough for you to get yourself overly worked up."

"You're being ambiguous, Helen."

"Yes, I know I am. Unfortunately, Rowan, I know of no other way to put it. Your wife is a very strong individual, however, for a period of time early this morning she truly believed that she had murdered you. The simple thought that she could be capable of such an act has affected her very deeply."

"She isn't," I objected. "Her body was being used by a spirit. Hell, she wasn't even in it."

"She is aware of that, Rowan," Helen explained. "However, our psyches are inextricably connected with our bodies. We are what we see and perceive ourselves to be. It is one of the things that sets us apart from other animals—the ability to look in a mirror and recognize ourselves. To be self-aware. In Felicity's mind, whether she was in control or not, it was her body that was inflicting the harm, and therefore it is she who is ultimately responsible."

"That's not how it works."

"For you, perhaps, but you must understand that even though you have been through your own tribulations, you have not directly experienced that which she faced. You might well think differently if you were to switch places with her."

I shook my head. "I don't know about that."

"Believe me, this is not something we need debate at this time. It is nothing more than speculation at best. The tables cannot be turned. The events simply are what they are. And, because of them, at this moment in time your wife is quite a bit more fragile than you are accustomed to seeing her."

"Okay, no debate. But, is she going to be okay?"

"Yes, eventually."

"Eventually?"

"The amount of healing she requires doesn't occur overnight, Rowan," she offered, then shifted slightly and cocked her head to the side in a thoughtful pose. After a moment she continued, "Now, I am certainly no expert on this possession phenomenon..."

"It really happened, Helen," I interrupted.

"I am not doubting that. Please, let me finish. As I said, I am no expert on the subject, however, I suspect from what you have told me about it that such an event, especially when it comes in such an unexpected manner, is truly at the root of the issue. When combined with the physical demands and the apparent literal separation of the Id from the individual, I can only surmise that the primary psychological fallout begins there. Her actions while possessed are rising to the surface as horrors for her, however, the trigger is the feeling of disassociation."

"Acting as a horse for a *Lwa* takes some getting used to, as I understand it," I said with a nod.

"I think that would be putting it mildly, Rowan."

"Yeah, well I suppose I'm trying not to think about it too hard right now."

"I can understand that, however, on top of the mild hysteria over knowing she severely harmed you, Felicity is exhibiting the classic symptoms of Post Traumatic Stress Disorder. Many of the emotions she described over the past hour when recounting this most recent event readily associate to the same feelings she experienced after the first possession."

"Okay," I shrugged. "That only stands to reason, right?"

"Yes, Rowan, however what I am trying to say is that in her case the effects are obviously cumulative, and I am not at all surprised. One either faces a severe stressor that triggers the PTSD, or the anxiety and negative experiences build up until the individual can no longer tolerate them. Felicity falls into that second category. Simply look at everything the woman has been through in the past few weeks. The fact is, I am truly amazed that she held up as well as she has."

I waited a moment then gave her a nod. "Yeah, well like you said. She's got one hell of a strong will."

"Fortunately, yes," she agreed. "For the both of you."

"Another issue that seems to be weighing on her heavily is something with regard to a sister. Are you able to shed any light on that?"

"Just that she doesn't have one that I know of."

"Yes, she said that she did not, but then she would always come back to an issue about a sister. She was never very clear on the point."

My brain kicked in and cut through the fog of the most recent events, bringing our conversation with Ben back around to the forefront.

"You know, I guess it might have something to do with the DNA tests," I said. "Your brother mentioned that when they got the samples that actually cleared her of the crime, the tests came out so close that the lab believes the actual killer to be a sibling."

"Interesting."

I nodded. "That's one word for it."

"Well, something about that has definitely struck a chord for her."

"Wish I could help you on that, but when Ben mentioned it she was adamant about not having a sister."

"I will take your word for it, however, I think a talk with her parents may be in order."

"I can give you their number, but as you know, I'm not high on their list, so you'll be on your own."

"I am sure I can appeal to them without bringing you into it."

A short lull fell between us as we both took a moment to digest the conversation.

"Okay, so what do I do now?" I asked, finally breaking the silence. "Do I bring her in to see you every day? Twice a day? Set up housekeeping for you in our guest room? Take her on a vacation in the Bahamas? What? Just tell me and it's done."

"That is part of what I came out here to speak with you about, Rowan," she replied, extracting a fresh cigarette and lighting it from the dying ember of her previous smoke.

"Okay, shoot."

She exhaled a thoughtful sigh as she stared out at the sparse wisps of clouds on the horizon. Her breath steamed on the crisp air, and the silence that fell between us was almost painful. I lit a fresh cigarette myself—using the task to fill the glaring void she was leaving. I could tell that for once, Helen wasn't simply taking time choosing her words; she seemed to be at a total loss for them.

Finally, I could wait no longer. "Helen?" I queried. "What is it?"

She gave in to my question and turned toward me. I took an immediate dislike to the expression she was wearing.

"I am afraid there is simply no other way to say this to you, Rowan," she finally said. "Felicity has elected to have herself voluntarily committed to a psychiatric hospital for evaluation."

"She what?" I stammered. "And you didn't try to talk her out of it?"

"No, Rowan," she replied with a shake of her head. "Actually, I am the one who suggested it."

CHAPTER 29:

"I'm still not sure how I feel about this, honey," I said as I switched off the truck's engine then sat back in my seat.

I left the keys dangling from the ignition. It was a conscious move, driven by a subconscious hope that my wife would change her mind, and I would be able to simply restart the vehicle and head for home.

Of course, I already knew I wasn't going to get my wish, but that wasn't going to stop me from trying. I tilted my head up and absently inspected the headliner because I knew looking at Felicity was just going to make my heart ache even more than it already did.

"I know," she replied, voice flat and soft. "But, it's for the best."

"I hope you're right," I answered, giving up and turning my face toward her. She didn't meet my gaze, instead leaving her eyes directed out the passenger side window. I exhaled heavily and added, "You know, you were just locked up in one institution, and now here you are going into another. I don't see how that's for the best."

"This is different," she replied. "I'm doing it voluntarily."

"Yeah, and that's what makes it even more disconcerting. You're walking out of one cell and right into another, all of your own accord."

"This is a hospital, Rowan, not a prison."

"Yeah, I know it is. But it's the kind with padded walls, locked doors, and grim-faced nurses named after hand tools."

My attempt at bringing levity to the situation fell flat, even for me.

After a moment she offered, "My insurance will cover part of…"

"Gods, Felicity!" I cut her off, shaking my head as my voice rose slightly. "That isn't my point! It's not the money, you know that. I'll spend whatever it takes."

She remained silent.

I closed my eyes and reached up to rub my forehead as I let out an embarrassed sigh. I hadn't exactly lashed out at her, but I knew my tone had been far less than patient.

"I'm sorry," I almost whispered.

"It's okay," she replied. "I know you're stressed out too."

"Yeah," I agreed. "Maybe I need to check in with you."

I looked at the clock on the dash, and it read a little past one in the afternoon.

"You know," I said. "Technically, you're supposed to be at your parent's house in less than an hour for Thanksgiving dinner. Your brother is in town for it and everything."

"Aye, *we* are supposed to be there. Not just me."

"Well, I figured after everything that's happened between your father and me..." I left the rest of the sentence unspoken.

She shook her head gently. "No. I spoke to my mother about that. You were expected too."

"Okay," I replied with a shrug. "Then what are we doing here now? Why don't we go get cleaned up and have dinner? Maybe you'll feel better after..."

"No, Rowan."

"You're going to miss Thanksgiving dinner? With the O'Brien clan all together under one roof for a change?"

"It's not all of them, you know that."

"Well, immediate family...and Austin is there. That's kind of a big deal unless I misunderstood."

"I know that, and yes it is. But, I've no choice in the matter."

"So, you're telling me you can't at least put this off until tomorrow?"

"No, I can't."

"Well, I don't get it."

"I don't expect you to."

"Honestly, I still don't understand why you just can't see Helen on a daily basis for a while."

"Because that won't do."

"So, how is seeing her here instead of at her office going to be any different?"

"The hospital will be safe."

"Her office isn't?"

"It's not her office I'm worried about."

"You don't feel safe with me?"

"Aye, I do," she whispered. "But you don't."

"What's that supposed to mean?"

"Nothing."

"Bullshit, honey, that wasn't a nothing sort of comment. What are you trying to say?"

She sighed. I knew she was tired and still feeling the effects of the tranquilizer Helen had given her a couple of hours before. I hated to press her, but she was talking in circles just like she had when she was being held at the Justice Center. I could tell the wheels were in motion beneath her fiery mane, I just didn't know what it was that had them spinning so fiercely.

"Think about what I did to you last night," she finally said.

"We've already established that you didn't…"

"Aye, I know," she interrupted. "Miranda did it, not me. You say that, but you also know Miranda was inside me. Controlling me. And, this wasn't the first time."

"Yeah, and your point?"

"You're afraid she could do it again. So am I."

"I wouldn't say I'm afraid…"

"You are. I can feel it."

"Okay, so maybe a little, but that's my problem."

"No, it's our problem."

"You know, I'm working really hard on making it not happen again."

"I know you are, but until we're certain it won't, you would be safer without me around."

"Dammit, Felicity, that's a load of crap and you know it."

"No, Rowan, it isn't, and *you* know it."

"Felicity…"

"No. Stop it. You know I'm right about this."

"So, what if you are? What am I supposed to do, honey? Come out here daily and play Parcheesi with you in the rec room?"

"You could," she said with a nod. Then, for the first time during the entire drive here, she looked over at me. "But, I'd much rather you do something more constructive with your time."

"And what's that?"

"Find her," she choked, her voice starting to crack as her eyes moistened with fresh tears. "Find Miranda and make her leave me alone."

"No, Maggie, just slow down for a minute and listen to me," I said into my cell phone, trying to stay calm while making my voice as stern as I could without losing control. "No one has been hurt. It's a psychiatric hospital."

Of course, I was lying about no one being hurt, but since it was only me, I doubt it would have mattered. Besides, that wasn't something she needed to know about anyway.

I had spent several minutes laying out the story in my head, selectively removing unnecessary details, before making the call to tell my wife's family we wouldn't be making it to the gala holiday dinner. I hadn't even been able to get half of it out yet, and we'd been on the phone for almost ten minutes.

I listened for a moment as she gibbered excitedly on the other end, asking a mouthful of questions while not bothering to stop long enough for me to answer even one. I had been slowly pacing along a six foot or so stretch of the waiting area during the call, just to work off the nervous energy, but now I was feeling tired all over again. I stopped mid-step and planted myself on a plastic chair, leaning forward and resting my elbows on my knees then I closed my eyes as I continued to listen.

When she finally stopped to take a breath I said, "Your daughter is not insane, Maggie, no one is saying that. Helen told me it looks like Post Traumatic Stress Disorder."

She immediately asked, "Who is Helen?"

"Her doctor," I replied. "Doctor Helen Storm. It just happens that she's also a good friend of ours, so I tend not to be overly formal."

I could hear Shamus in the background, cursing and making demands. He wasn't helping my mood at all, but at least it was Maggie doing the actual talking. She was a far cry from being a fan of mine herself, however, she always went out of her way to remain civil and try to tolerate the "damned and hell bound son-in-law", which was more than I could say for her husband. In my book, whether she hated me or not, she still showed me a graceful courtesy and I appreciated it.

"What is her room number, Rowan?" she asked.

"One twenty-one," I replied. "But she's not in there yet."

"Why not?"

"Paperwork and the like," I said, shrugging out of reflex. "They're supposed to get her settled in pretty soon though. They gave me a list of what she's allowed to have, so once she's in the room for a bit I'm going to run home and pack some things for her because we came straight here from Helen's office."

"Why? Why is this happening so suddenly?"

"It's a long story, Maggie. All I can…"

My sentence was interrupted by a click, and the phone suddenly adopted a hollow tone that told me an extension had just been taken off hook. Confirming my suspicion, a fresh and much less pleasant voice joined the conversation.

"Aye, what have you done to her now?!" Shamus barked.

"I'm not going to argue with you today, Shamus," I replied.

"Shamus William O'Brien!" Maggie barked, then her voice grew slightly distant as she pulled away from the mouthpiece on the phone. I could still make out enough of the one-sided conversation to discern the fact that she was calling for Austin to go occupy his father.

A moment or two later, some muted voices and a few curses filled the earpiece but were finally silenced by a second click as the extension was hung up.

"I apologize for that, Rowan," Maggie said. "Please understand that he is concerned for Felicity."

"Yeah, Maggie," I replied, surprising myself at being able to remain unruffled. "I know he is. So am I."

She paused for a moment then said, "I'll get Shamus calmed down, and we'll be there a little later. Is there anything we can bring her, or anything else we can do?"

I dropped my forehead into my hand and sighed. I really wasn't relishing the thought of dealing with the family face to face given this new turn of events. However, I couldn't very well tell them not to visit their daughter. Something like that would definitely give my father-in-law a fresh load of ammunition.

"I can't think of anything," I said. "But I'm sure she'd love to see you."

"What about you?" she asked.

"No, Maggie, I'm fine. As I can be under the circumstances, anyway."

"Have you eaten?" she pressed.

"Not yet, but I'll grab something later."

"Nonsense," she replied. "I'll bring you a plate."

"You don't have to do that, Maggie."

"I know I don't have to, Rowan. I want to."

I wasn't going to argue. My mother-in-law was a fantastic cook, and now that it had been mentioned, I took notice that my stomach was actually grumbling.

"Thanks," I said. "I appreciate it."

"Do you think they will let me bring a plate for Felicity as well, then?"

"I can ask, but I doubt it will be a problem. I've seen a few visitors bringing stuff in."

"Good," she replied then asked again, "Now, you're certain there's nothing else we can do?"

I answered her in a tired voice. "I suppose that when you get here, you could convince your daughter that she doesn't have a sister."

Why I said it was anybody's guess. I suppose it was just an aberration born of fatigue, concern, the situation, and everything that I'd been told over the past few hours. Either way, the words tumbled out at a nonchalant cadence, and even after I'd spoken them, I didn't pay the comment any serious regard.

I sat for a moment and realized that Maggie had not responded at all.

"Maggie? Are you still there?"

"Why did you say that, Rowan?" she finally asked, a thin tremor in her voice.

"What?"

"Why does Felicity think she has a sister?" she pressed, her tone still off key.

"It has something to do with the DNA tests the police did," I replied, intrigued by the trepidation I was detecting. "The sample from the killer matched so closely with hers, the lab says she must have a sister."

The charged silence continued on the other end.

I finally asked, "What's wrong, Maggie? Is there something we should know? Does Felicity actually have a sister?"

"I'll be leaving Austin and Shamus here, then," she replied slowly, the vocal tremor still in full force. "I should be there in thirty minutes or so. We need to talk."

CHAPTER 30:

"Fourteen days?" I asked, the tone of my voice betraying both my confusion and surprise.

"Yes, Rowan," Helen replied. "A seven to fourteen day observation is fairly standard. I would rather err on the side of caution, hence fourteen."

My mind had been churning ever since getting off the phone with Maggie, and I had once again been checking my watch far too often in anticipation of her arrival. I actually welcomed the fistful of mundane paperwork as a distraction when Helen presented it—right up until I read this most recent paragraph.

I shook my head and raised an eyebrow as I looked back at her. "So you're telling me that if I sign this, my wife is stuck here for a minimum of two weeks with no way out?"

"No," she replied. "I am saying that you are admitting her for fourteen days of therapy and observation within the confines of the hospital."

"You see it's that word 'confine' that's giving me the problem." I stroked my finger beneath a paragraph on the sheaf of papers. "And, then there's this legalese about not being able to leave the hospital grounds? Not to mention…Wait a minute, what do you mean *I'm* admitting her?"

"It is simply a legal formality for her own safety."

"Break it down for me," I urged, placing the pen carefully on top of the pages and folding my hands. "Because now I'm definitely not sure I care for the way it sounds."

"It is very simple, Rowan," she explained. "By admitting Felicity in this fashion, she will be unable to sign herself out of the hospital. That can only be done by you, or by me."

"Me alone or you alone. It doesn't take both of us?"

"No. Either one of us can sign her out individually; although I would prefer you speak to me before doing something rash."

"Uh-huh. So, she can be signed out at any time?"

"Yes, Rowan, at any time."

"Like, if I want her out of here tomorrow, I can come get her and we're done. Finished. No ambulance with men in white coats chasing after us?"

"I would not recommend that you do so, but yes, that is how it works. If you or I sign her out, she is free to leave. Rowan, stop being paranoid, this is not a prison, you know that."

"Yeah, I heard that somewhere before."

I stared back at her for a moment, not saying another word. I knew that she, of all people, wouldn't lie to me about something like this, but I felt like I was perched on a very unstable precipice right now. I didn't want Felicity to do this to begin with, but there was no talking her out of it. And, now it was somehow becoming my personal responsibility. The thing that kept going through my mind was that I was standing here committing my wife to an asylum. Though I knew that to be a somewhat archaic take on the situation, I guess I needed all of the assurances I could get.

With a heavy exhale, I finally picked up the pen and scrawled my name on the admitting form, effectively placing my wife in the hospital's hands for the next two weeks. I had a definite feeling that my notebook computer was going to be logging some serious hours because I was going to have work to do, but I also didn't plan on straying far from this place if I could help it.

"By the way," I offered as I slid the papers along the countertop toward her. "My mother-in-law should be here any minute."

"Do you feel like that is going to be a problem?" she asked.

"No, not necessarily. The reason I mentioned it, though, is that I was on the phone with her a little while ago, and she started acting weird when I brought up the sister issue. In fact, she is purposely coming down without the rest of the family and ended the conversation with something like 'we need to talk'."

"Really?" she asked, her tone thoughtful. "Do you think there might be some family history that Felicity has somehow repressed?"

"Maybe. I don't know," I said with a shake of my head. "Or maybe some she never knew about at all. All I can say is Maggie is a fairly unflappable type unless she thinks something dire has happened, but she started getting seriously flaky the minute I told her about the DNA tests. In fact, the sister thing was obviously what prompted that last ominous comment about needing to talk, so there's something that's been hidden away in a closet somewhere. I'm sure of that."

"So, is that all she said?"

"Yeah, I'm afraid it was."

"Well, even if there is some sort of revelation regarding a female sibling, I do not believe it will be a panacea for Felicity's mental state. She has been through far too much."

"It might help, though, right?"

"It might," she said with a nod. "But, then again, depending on what is divulged, it could be harmful instead."

"Not what I wanted to hear, Helen."

"You would prefer that I lie?"

"I didn't say that."

"Then stop complaining."

"Yeah, right, and you believe that miracle will happen when?"

She offered a thin smile. "Never."

"Uh-huh. Well, at any rate if we're talking about a living, adult sibling, then I'm sure the police would be interested too."

"Undoubtedly, given what you have told me."

"Either way, I thought maybe I would see if she'd be willing to talk to both of us when she arrives."

"That certainly would not hurt."

"To be honest, I'm not sure if she will, but I'm going to try to talk her into it. Just do me a favor?"

"What is that?"

"If she agrees, try not to mention anything about the *Lwa* possession or anything else that went on last night, okay? It probably wouldn't be a real good thing to lay on her."

She gave me a knowing nod. I knew that from my own sessions with her, at the very least, she was fully aware of the score when it came to my in-laws.

"I believe that information would be covered under doctor-patient confidentiality anyway, Rowan," she said. "You need not worry."

"I honestly hadn't ever expected to be having this conversation," Maggie said, shifting in her chair. She had calmed considerably since the phone call, but I could tell there was still a nervous streak underscoring her tone.

Looking at my mother-in-law, it was easy to see from which parent Felicity had inherited her looks. Maggie was slight, just like my wife, and sported a shoulder-length coif of chestnut hair, although it was rapidly giving itself over to grey. Still, it softly framed her smooth, delicate features and bright eyes to form a pleasing and deceptively youthful visage. In fact, discerning her true age simply by looking at her would be no easy task. A box of hair dye from the corner store would instantly shave off a dozen years. And, though she was still extremely pretty, she had been an absolutely stunning sight in her youth. In fact, I had seen hard evidence of it from old family photos.

"It's okay, Maggie," I replied. "I think that pretty much goes for both of us."

"Yes, I suppose that would be true, then," she agreed. "Although for different reasons, I'm sure."

"If it would make you more comfortable, I will be happy to leave you two alone to talk," Helen offered.

"No," Maggie replied hesitantly. "I think it may be important that you hear this."

"Yes, I will admit that any insight you can provide is most welcome, however, Rowan can fill me in later if you wish."

"No. You should hear it from me." My mother-in-law paused, and her tenuous composure faltered for a moment as she suddenly blurted, "Is my daughter going to be all right?"

"Yes," Helen replied. "She is going to be just fine. She has simply dealt with far too much strife in a very short period of time."

It was the truth. It was just missing all of the gory details.

"Maggie," I started. "I hate to sound impatient, but I'm really looking for answers here, and I got the feeling when we were on the phone that you just might have one or two."

"It's understandable, Rowan. You've dealt with more than your share of this, and we've given you little support where that is concerned."

"That's not important right now. I'm hanging in there."

She grew quiet and looked down at her hands where they were resting in her lap. Her right was absently fiddling with her wedding set, twisting the rings in a circle. Every now and then she would pull them up the length of her finger, almost to the tip, then slide them back on and begin twirling the interlocking gold bands yet again.

"I suppose I should give you a bit of background if this is to make any sense," she said as she looked up, casting her glance between Helen and me, though her fingers continued to toy with the jewelry of their own volition. "To begin with, and this you may already know, Rowan, I am an identical twin."

I nodded. "Felicity mentioned it, and I think I've seen a picture or two in the photo albums."

"Yes," she replied. "She may also have told you that, Caitlin, my twin, passed away many years ago. In fact, Felicity was very young."

I simply nodded.

"Actually, the story the children were told was that their aunt was killed in an accidental car crash, but, that is only partially true."

She stopped and stared off into space for a long moment then shot us both an embarrassed glance before lowering her eyes to her lap once again.

She continued. "That was nineteen seventy-two. One would think I could have come to terms with it by now."

"If you have been hiding painful details for all this time," Helen offered, "then it is unlikely you could actually come to terms with the event, as you have not allowed yourself to do so."

"Yes," Maggie replied without looking up. "I suppose you are correct. But it was necessary. We simply didn't feel a need to burden the children with the embarrassing truth."

"You said Felicity was very young. Austin isn't that much older," I observed. "Would they have even understood?"

"I don't know," she replied. "But they both adored Caitlin. Especially, Felicity. I believed then that our decision in sheltering them was correct, as I would now were it not for this turn of events."

I nodded then offered, "But, they aren't children any more, Maggie. They grew up."

She looked up at me with a soft smile that held a small hint of pity. "Yes, Rowan, they are still children. I know it sounds cliché, but they always will be, no matter what their ages. But, one must be a parent to truly understand that."

"I'll give you that," I replied.

Any other time I would have taken the comment as a diaphanously veiled reference to the fact that so far, neither Austin nor Felicity had produced a grandchild. Of course, I had a valid reason for the assessment because we had all heard the contentious remark several times in the past, though I'm certain they would prefer a set of genes in their pool that didn't belong to me. However, I could easily tell by her tone that this time she was sincere in what she had just said, and no goading or malice was intended.

After a pause I asked, "So, your sister wasn't killed in a car crash?"

She took in a deep breath and visibly gathered herself before continuing. "Yes, actually, she was. However, it wasn't an accident. She deliberately drove her car onto a railroad crossing, and waited."

"How can you know she did it on purpose?"

"Trust me, Rowan, she did."

"Was your sister being treated for depression?" Helen asked, obviously picking up on something in my mother-in-law's tone that I had missed.

Maggie nodded affirmation then added, "Not that it was doing any good, obviously. Her prescriptions more or less kept her from functioning normally. She couldn't think clearly, and all she ever wanted to do was sleep. She hated it. Caitlin just reached a point where she simply refused to take them."

"Given that it was nineteen seventy-two, they were most likely tranquilizers," Helen said as she jotted a note and then looked up. "Was she ever hospitalized?"

"Briefly. That made for its own embarrassment in the family."

"Mm-hmm," Helen hummed with a nod.

"Why would that be embarrassing?" I asked.

"The culture," she answered with a shrug. "Our generation, the way we were raised. Our parents were not particularly supportive of her for a number of reasons. They felt she had brought the depression on herself, and that she had disgraced the family."

"Because she suffered from depression?" I asked, unable to fathom such insensitivity from family.

"There were other reasons, Rowan."

Though I was still managing to keep my growing impatience at bay, I couldn't help but express my confusion. "Maggie, I'm very sorry to hear this, but I have to be honest, I'm a bit lost. I don't mean to sound callous myself, but I'm not sure what your sister committing suicide has to do with Felicity having a sister."

"Caitlin was dealing with a very specific type of depression, Rowan," she replied.

"Severe postpartum," Helen offered, already doing math that was escaping me.

"Yes," Maggie answered.

"And, your sister was unmarried," she added.

"Correct."

"Okay," I replied with a nod. "Maybe I'm just slow because I'm tired, but the way I remember the branches on a family tree, wouldn't her daughter be Felicity's cousin?"

She remained quiet and continued to fiddle with her rings. I watched as she repeatedly pulled the bands from her finger, silently inspected them, and then slowly slid them back on.

"Maggie?" I prodded.

She looked up at me and instantly apologized. "I'm sorry, what did you ask?"

"I said Caitlin's daughter would have been Felicity's cousin, not her sister."

"Yes, of course, you would be correct were it not for the fact that Shamus was the father."

CHAPTER 31:

"So, lemme get this straight," Ben replied. "Felicity's old man took a tumble with his sister-in-law and forgot to glove up, so nine months later, oops?"

"Yeah, trust me, Ben, I'm as floored as anyone," I said into my cell phone. "He's the last person I would have expected to do something like that."

"Yeah, well, it's always the holier 'n thou loudmouths that got somethin' ta' hide, Row."

"I suppose so."

I had already filled my friend in on where I was calling from and the highlights of the previous evening that had brought us here. He was already up to speed to some extent, as Helen had contacted him to cancel their plans for Thanksgiving dinner but had, of course, left it up to me to fill in some of the blanks as I saw fit. As it was, I had already managed to put a damper on the holiday for the both of them by calling Helen, and I was feeling a little guilty about it. Not so much so, however, that I was going to even think about hesitating to call Ben. At this point he was one of the few people I trusted, even though he wasn't actually assigned to the investigation. We would both just have to get over the intrusion.

After quietly mulling over the conversation thus far, he asked, "An' so you're sayin' the sis-in-law was your mother-in-law's identical twin?"

"It's not just me saying it, Ben. It's a fact."

"Fuck me."

"Yeah, I figured you'd say something like that."

"The lab guys are gonna love this 'cause identical twins got identical DNA."

"I figured they'd be close, but they're identical?"

"Yeah, definitely. Fraternal twins, no. Identical, oh yeah. Can't fuckin' tell 'em apart with a DNA test. You didn't know that?"

"No. Like I said the other night, genetics really isn't my forte."

"Damn, I know somethin' you don't. Gotta love that."

"Go ahead and write it on the calendar, Ben."

"I keep tellin' ya' I ain't stupid, white man. Besides, they teach us this crap so we can do cop type work. You know, catch bad guys and shit like that."

"Yeah, I figured as much."

"So," he continued his speculation. "With the identical DNA making it more or less the same mother from a genetics standpoint, and with exactly the same father, the match is gonna be close. Just like siblings."

"That was my thought."

"So Firehair's half-sister is prob'ly a serial killer. Man, that's fucked up."

"Uh-huh. I had that thought too."

He paused for a second then suddenly switched gears. "An' he's got the balls ta' jump in your shit and throw the Bible in your face after him screwin' around?"

"Yeah, well, we all have our dirty little secrets, don't we." I was commenting, not asking.

He was answering anyway. "Maybe so, but most of us try not ta' be hypocrites about 'em."

"I don't know about that, Ben."

"Yeah, well I ain't one."

"That's not really my point here," I returned with a mild note of exasperation.

"Yeah, well, it's a pet peeve."

"We all have those too. So, can we get back on track?"

"Yeah," he grunted. "So, Firehair know any of this yet?"

"Maggie is in there telling her the story right now," I replied. "Helen thought it might be a good idea under the circumstances."

"Why ain't you in there too?"

"Again, Helen. She thought it would be better for me to let them do this one-on-one."

"Well, sis knows what she's doing. If she says do it, do it. She'll take good care of the little woman."

"I know she will."

"So, anyway, like you said, back on track. What ended up happenin' with the kid?"

"That's the thing," I told him. "No one is sure where she ended up. Apparently, the family pressured Caitlin to give the baby up for adoption as soon as they found out she was pregnant. The way Maggie explained it, her sister told her she saw the child for all of fifteen minutes before she was taken away."

"Why'd they lay it all on her? Shouldn't your father-in-law have gotten the slap down too? I mean it takes two, and, well shit, he was married to their other daughter. He sure's hell wasn't lily white in all that."

"Nobody knew who the father was. Well, not the parents and the rest of the family at least. Just Maggie, her sister, and Shamus were privy to that."

"Bet ol' Mags was pissed."

"Yeah, and I get the feeling she still is to an extent. Or, harboring some resentment at the very least. But she stayed with him. I don't know why, and I didn't ask."

"Yeah, prob'ly a good idea ta' leave that one alone. So, anyway, why didn't the sister just get an abortion?"

"I asked the same thing and got a bit of a history lesson," I explained. "This all happened in nineteen seventy-two. *Roe v. Wade* wasn't decided until seventy-three, so it would have been a back alley deal. But, even so, her parents found out before she could make those arrangements, and they wouldn't allow it."

"Jeezus fuckin' christ, seventy-two..." He paused at the other end, and I heard him mumbling to himself. "Seventy-two...oh-five..." A moment later he directed himself back to me. "Shit, Row, wouldn't she have been in like 'er early twenties or somethin'? Couldn't she make 'er own goddamn decisions? I mean, the abortion thing maybe not such a good idea, but how could they force her to give up the kid?"

"Yes, she was in her twenties, but it was a different time, and her family was from a different culture, Ben. You'd be amazed at the power parents sometimes hold over their children."

"Yeah, well someone needs ta' tell that ta' mine, the little shit."

"Like I said, it was a different time."

"Yeah, 'pparently. So no one knows what happened to 'er? The kid I mean."

"All Maggie knew was what her sister told her. The baby was healthy and female."

"What about hospital records? Where'd she give birth?"

"She wasn't at a hospital. She gave birth at a convent or something of that sort, and the baby went straight into a Catholic orphanage. Her parents had made the arrangements and wouldn't give any information to the rest of the family."

"Pretty fuckin' cold if ya' ask me."

"I agree, but that doesn't help us now."

"Any idea which convent or orphanage?"

"No, only that it was out of state."

"Great. And, you said her sister is dead, so she can't even give us a clue."

"Yeah. She committed suicide something like eight months later."

"So can ya' like do a séance or somethin'? *Twilight Zone* out and have a chat with 'er?"

"You know it doesn't work like that."

"Well, I gotta ask."

"Yeah, I know. You always do."

"Shit!" he suddenly exclaimed. "So at least tell me the old farts are still alive, so we can go knock their heads together and see if the address falls out on the table."

"Unfortunately, her father died almost three years ago, and judging from what Maggie told me, he pretty much ruled the family, so

I'm sure he's the one who made the arrangements. Her mother is still alive, and she might know something of use, but getting to it is a different story. She's in a nursing facility suffering from severe dementia. According to Maggie, she doesn't even recognize her when she visits. She thinks she's an old playmate from school back in Ireland."

"Fuckin' wunnerful," he huffed. "We might have to give it a go anyway. So, any other line on where we could get some info?"

"Well, Maggie's mom didn't really end up completely losing it until about a year ago. According to her, they still have a lot of her stuff in storage, and she hasn't been through all of the paperwork her father had squirreled away quite yet. She's hoping there might be something in all of that."

"She's hopin'? So she's willin' to cooperate?"

"She is, but I don't know what Shamus's reaction is going to be."

"Well, ya'know I'm gonna have ta' take this to the lead investigator with the MCS since I'm not assigned. They might decide to jump on a warrant if they even think there's gonna be a problem with cooperation."

"Yeah, I know. Just try to make sure my wife's name isn't on it this time."

"Ouch. You ever gonna get off my ass about that, white man?"

"Eventually, Kemosabe. But not just yet. Maybe after this is all over. Just view it as an incentive."

"Yeah, fuckin' great. Just what I need, the Rowan Gant incentive program."

"Well, you know I'm not going to apologize. Right now I'm still feeling a bit desperate, and I'll do whatever it takes."

"Yeah, I understand, Row. Don't worry, we're gonna find 'er. I just don't know how yet."

"Do you think Constance could help? The FBI might have some more pull."

"Yeah, well she's already on 'er way here. We were gonna see what we could scrounge up since dinner got cancelled. Prob'ly gonna hit the Chinese place down on the corner. They never close."

"Sorry. I *will* apologize for screwing up your holiday."

"Don't worry about it. Helen's dressin' is always too dry anyway. But, don't tell 'er I said that."

"I'll keep it between us."

"So listen, I'll fill Constance in on everything and see what she says. But, if it's a convent, who the fuck knows? Might make it even harder gettin' what we need by havin' the feebs in the middle of it."

"Well, I'll leave that up to you."

"'Bout time. I been tryin' to get ya' ta' let us handle the shit for a while now."

"Well, you're in luck this time because I've got something else to take care of at this point."

"Yeah, your wife."

"Her too."

He was quiet for a moment as he digested my answer then finally said, "Row, what are you plannin'?"

"You don't want to know."

"Row…"

"Trust me, Ben," I said. "You worry about this side of the veil, I'll deal with the other."

"Jeezus…" he mumbled. "This got somethin' ta' do with that Voodoo stuff?"

"Like I said, you don't want to know."

"Dammit, Row, you also said 'trust me', and I learned a long time ago that when that's the first thing outta someone's mouth, then don't."

"Yeah, well I think you're going to have to make an exception to that rule this go around."

"Don't go doin' anything stupid, white man."

"You know me better than that."

"Yeah, I do, and that's 'zactly why I said it."

Tuesday, November 29
11:17 A.M.
Saint Louis, Missouri

CHAPTER 32:

"**G**ood morning, Judy," I called out as I came through the doors and started across the lobby toward the main desk at the hospital. I was trying to remain pleasant, which was a struggle considering where I was and why I was here.

"Good morning," she answered, giving me a wave.

Helen had quashed my original plan of more or less camping out and working from the hospital before it had even been put into action. I wasn't happy about it and had even argued with her for the better part of a day. In the end, however, she had convinced me that it would be in my wife's best interest if she could concentrate on herself and not fret about me worrying myself sick. After a bit of negotiation, we finally settled on a visiting schedule that worked out to one hour in the morning and two in the evening, each day.

The staff had quickly become accustomed to my face since I was in and out, twice daily, like clockwork, so it didn't take long before I was on a first name basis with most of them. Of course, I had my own ulterior motives for getting to know everyone here that I could. They were the people responsible for the care and well being of my wife during her stay. I needed to be sure that I trusted them with that task, so studying their faces, shaking their hands, and learning their names was just my way of convincing myself it would be all right.

I'm sure I was simply being paranoid, but I'd had plenty of things happen over the past month that had endeavored to make me that way.

"So, how was your evening?" I asked, drawing up to the desk and picking up an ink pen from the countertop. "Did you manage to get out of here on time for a change?"

I was just preparing to sign in on the visitor log when she reached out and put her hand over mine, stopping me from scrawling my name on the page.

"Just a second, Mister Gant," she said. "Doctor Storm asked to see you as soon as you arrived."

I was instantly alarmed. "Is something wrong?"

"Honestly, I don't know. She just left a message with the desk to call her as soon as you arrived and have you wait in the lobby for her."

I could tell she was lying, but making that accusation wasn't going to get me anywhere. However, she didn't seem to be trying to hide any excessive concern, so I struggled to swallow my sudden rush of panic and dropped the pen back onto the counter.

"Yeah, okay," I replied. "I guess you'd better let her know I'm here then."

"If you'd like to take a seat," she offered with a somewhat forced smile, pointing to the side of the lobby.

I nodded and trudged over to the waiting area, but I didn't sit. My initial reaction had been that something was wrong with Felicity, but I started trying to discount that because if it were true I would certainly have received a call. I quickly managed to talk myself into believing that rationalization then the next thing reached out and slapped me on the back of the head. It was entirely possible that Helen was going to try to convince me to lessen the frequency of my visits. She had grudgingly given in to the twice per day schedule as it was.

If that ended up being the case, I immediately decided that she was going to need an overabundance of evidence that could prove to me why I should listen. Of course, this entire line of thought easily replaced any lingering sense of trepidation with annoyance, not that trading one anxious emotion for another was any better. However, it didn't get a chance to grow much beyond that, as I only had to pace for a few moments before a ruffled looking Helen Storm rounded the corner, already shrugging into her coat.

"Let's talk outside if you don't mind, Rowan," she said, not even bothering to slow down as she strode past.

The first thing that struck me wasn't what she said, but how she said it. While her tone didn't seem completely off-key, it was harried. However, even more glaring was her choice of words. Helen was very exacting and deliberate in her speech. I had never known her to use two contractions in the same sentence if she could help it, so I instantly knew something had her rattled. Of course, that realization only served to shift me back to my original fear.

I hurried to follow, lagging several steps behind as she bolted out the automatic sliding doors and made a quick right onto the sidewalk. I didn't manage to catch up to her until she finally came to a halt beneath the tinted Plexiglas smokers' canopy forty or so yards from the entrance.

"Okay, so what's wrong?" I asked as I came beneath the overhang with her. "What happened? Is Felicity okay?"

"For the moment," she replied cryptically.

"What's that supposed to mean?"

She didn't answer me but instead set about lighting a cigarette before giving me a quick glance. After taking a healthy drag, she said, "Are you still smoking, Rowan?"

"Do I need to be?"

"Here," she replied, offering me her cigarette case and lighter.

I had actually been staying away from them since running out the day Felicity checked into this place. However, given Helen's apparent level of agitation, I took one and lit it then handed the case and lighter back to her.

"Now," I said. "I don't want to sound like an ass, but I asked you a question. Would you like to explain what you mean by 'for the moment'? Is Felicity okay?"

"I'm sorry, Rowan," she replied. "That was unprofessional of me, and I shouldn't have said it that way. Felicity is fine. She's resting right now."

"Okay, there you go again."

"There I go again what?"

"You just used three contractions, Helen," I pointed out. "For anyone else, no big deal. When you do it, it sets off bells and buzzers all over the place."

"I never noticed."

"You wouldn't."

"I apologize."

"Don't apologize, just tell me what's going on. You're not acting like yourself, and on top of that you're telling me Felicity is resting, and it's after eleven in the morning. What the hell happened?"

She regarded me quietly for a moment before replying. "Felicity experienced an episode with the spirit this morning."

"What?!" I yelped. "Why the hell didn't you call me?"

"We did, but all we got was your voice mail."

"Voice mail? But that's..." I pulled my cell phone from my pocket and immediately saw that it was switched off. Even so, I stabbed at the buttons with my thumb as if I could somehow change the fact that I had never turned it on this morning. Finally I muttered, "Dammit!"

"We tried both your lines at home as well, but there was no answer," she offered.

"Yeah, I had a breakfast meeting with a client, so I left early," I replied, waving my hand to dismiss the turn of the conversation. "But that's not important. What happened? Please tell me no one got hurt."

"No one got hurt, fortunately," she replied with a shake of her head. "We cannot be sure exactly when the episode started, however it could not have been too long before she was found. I was first alerted to it when the floor nurse went to check in on her and another patient because they had not come out for breakfast. She paged me as soon as she realized Felicity was not in her room."

"What do you mean she wasn't in her room?" I knew my voice held more than just a hint of agitation, but I couldn't help it.

"She was not considered psychotic or a threat to anyone, Rowan, therefore she was not housed in a locked ward."

"You said 'was'. I take it that has changed?"

"Yes, I am afraid so."

"Yeah, okay, but obviously you found her. Right?"

"Yes, we did, and fairly quickly. She was located down the hall in the other patient's room. She had somehow managed to get her hands on a set of restraints and was strapping him to the bed with them. Rather gleefully I might add."

"Gods," I mumbled, rubbing my forehead, and then I asked, "You mean he didn't try to get away from her?"

"No, he actually seemed to be enjoying it almost as much as she."

"I can guarantee you he wouldn't have if it had gone much further."

"Yes, I know."

"So then what happened?"

"We removed her from the situation, and she was brought to my office."

"There's more to it than that, Helen," I pressed. "You're too rattled, and that's just not you. What else happened?"

She finished her cigarette then immediately lit a fresh one from the pack. She offered me another, but I hadn't sucked down the first one as fast as she, so I declined.

"I think you are aware that excessive and unnecessary gore bothers me, yes?" she finally asked. "The truth is it makes me violently ill."

"I remember you mentioned that recently," I said, giving her a nod. "As a matter of fact I recall being a bit surprised by that, what with you having the MD as well."

"Yes, well, you do not see me working in an emergency room, now do you?"

"No, I don't. So tell me, what happened? You said no one was hurt."

"No one was. However, *Miranda* and I had a long talk."

"So, the *Lwa* didn't exit when you stopped her from tying up the other patient?"

"No, not at all," Helen replied, shaking her head emphatically. "*Miranda* stayed around for quite awhile."

"She didn't get violent?"

"No. In fact, her comment to me was something on the order of, 'I was wondering when you would show up'."

"As if she knew who you were?" I half asked, half stated.

"Yes."

"The *Lwa* has access to Felicity's memories, so in a way it makes sense. She knew where she was, and she knew someone would stop her."

"I think you are correct. She seemed far more interested in talking than anything else."

"So exactly what did you talk about?"

"Whatever she wanted, unfortunately."

"What do you mean?"

"As you may guess, her favorite topic is torture, Rowan."

"Yeah, again I'm not surprised."

"Oh, I think perhaps you would be."

"That bad?" I asked. "I mean I know what she did to Wentworth and Hobbes and that was…well, she…"

"Yes, that bad," she replied, saving me from my attempt to relay the harshness without actually giving her a description. "*Miranda* spent the better part of two hours regaling me with extremely graphic details about what she had done to several of her victims. Details that, I dare say, would turn the stomach of a horror movie fanatic."

"Okay, so that's what has you so nonplussed."

"Yes, she is actually a very eloquent speaker with an excellent command of the language. She paints intricate pictures with words, Rowan. They just are not very pretty to the rest of us."

"I can imagine."

"I doubt it," she huffed as she visibly shuddered. She was obviously still dealing with the imagery in her own head. "Of course, it did not help that the more violent or cruel the story she was telling, the more her eyes would light up. She was literally becoming aroused by reliving the horrors she had exacted upon those men. And, to make matters worse, she found my level of disgust amusing."

"Yeah, again I'm not surprised." I gave her a quick nod. "She really got to you, didn't she?"

"Yes. I hate to admit it, but yes. She did."

"That's not an easy task."

"I used to think so, but now I am not so sure."

"Well, remember Helen, you weren't just dealing with a disturbed individual. You were dealing with an incorporeal entity. They don't necessarily respond to the type of finesse you shrinks use."

"Perhaps you are correct, however, I would almost suspect that she has a background in psychology herself. She was quite adept at that 'finesse we shrinks use'. Unfortunately, it does not make this any less embarrassing for me."

"Anyone else know how you were affected?"

"No, not that I am aware."

"Then it stays between us. The whole patient-doctor confidentiality thing."

"I would say thank you if I did not suspect you were making a joke."

"Maybe just a little one," I replied. "So, anyway, do you believe me about the *Lwa* now?"

"I have never doubted you on that point, Rowan." She shook her head to punctuate the statement. "Another doctor, however, would most likely diagnose Felicity with an unidentified psychosis and more than likely, Disassociative Identity Disorder. To be truthful, if I did not know the things that I do, I would be inclined to agree with such an assessment."

"Then it's a good thing you're her doctor."

"That statement is more accurate than you know, Rowan. If the latent details she was giving me were accurate, what I listened to would easily qualify as a confession to several premeditated murders. It is a very good thing she did not do this while in police custody."

"Yeah," I mumbled, thinking exactly the same thing. "Okay, so then what? If she's resting now then Miranda must be gone."

"Yes, she is. She simply stopped speaking mid-sentence and a moment later Felicity was in her place. As soon as she realized what had happened, she began to cry hysterically and beg for you. I was left with no choice but to sedate her."

"But, she's okay?"

"Physically, she is fine. Emotionally, however, any progress we have made in the past few days is a complete wash."

I remained quiet, considering what she had just said.

Before I could form any sort of comment, she suddenly offered up a new subject. "I have not spoken to Benjamin lately. Do you know if they have had any luck locating the half-sister?"

I shook my head. "Not yet. Last I heard they were still sifting through the paperwork Maggie handed over, looking for leads."

"Well, they need to find her very soon. The last two episodes have taken a severe toll on Felicity. She is very strong willed, but she is beginning to break down."

"I agree that they need to find her, Helen," I replied. "But my worry is that even if they do, this isn't going to stop. The *Lwa* has obviously formed a bond with Felicity as well as Miranda, or whatever her name really is."

"How do you propose to address that?"

"Figure out who the *Lwa* is, and go at it from an ethereal angle."

"How will you find her?"

"I've been working on it with an expert on Voodoo. She's a college professor out of Baton Rouge who's written some fairly definitive books on the subject. She has some ideas."

"Anything promising?"

"Some, but nothing solid just yet. She's been running down some leads for me. In fact, I'm expecting a call from her today. The big problem is we're chasing after someone who's already dead. Sounds like it shouldn't be a big deal, but when you don't know who the dead person is, or even when they died, it gets a little tricky."

Helen lit her third fresh cigarette and again offered me another. This time I took it. Once she had taken a long drag and slowly exhaled the smoke, she turned her face to me. Her expression was hard and serious, which made the next words to come from her mouth even more of a contrast against her normally proper exterior.

"I would suggest that you chase faster, Rowan. This *Miranda* is a sick fucking bitch, and I do not like her."

CHAPTER 33:

"Hey there," I said, my voice soft.

The hard sound of a deadbolt snapping shut followed my words as the door behind me was locked. I had been warned that it would happen, as it was standard procedure for this section of the hospital. That didn't make the sound any less jarring. Of course, the entire feel of this floor was oppressive to begin with, so my nerves were feeling more than just a bit raw and exposed. Not to mention that since I wasn't hospital staff, I was violating policy by being in the room, but Helen had given the okay. Still, it all added up, and the sharp finality of the noise actually made me flinch.

Across the room, Felicity was sitting cross-legged in the center of the bed, her back to me. She was still clad in one of the pairs of flannel pajamas I'd packed for her days before.

She didn't reply.

My wife's original accommodations had seemed more like a small hotel room than something you would find at a hospital—sparse, but comfortable, furnished with a bed, dresser, some chairs and a small table. The bathroom was utilitarian but fairly spacious. She'd even had a television and large windows looking out onto a garden courtyard.

This room, however, made that look like a plush suite. Her furnishings consisted of little more than the hospital bed upon which she was now perched and a basic, straight-backed chair in the far corner. Gone was everything else, with the exception of the view. Of course, we were several stories up, and the thick windows were sandwiching heavy-duty safety wire, ostensibly to prevent suicide attempts. At least the walls were a calming, pale blue instead of the stark white so often depicted in movies. Still, that was of little comfort.

I stepped a little farther into the room and spoke a bit louder, "Knock knock."

"So, what do you think of the new place?" she asked. "I just moved in, so I haven't had time to do much with it."

Her voice was flat, emotionless, with more than just her usual Celtic lilt accenting the words, probably because she was tired—a lingering effect of the sedative. Her attempt at humor was even cliché, which was just more evidence of that fact.

I could easily detect a note of hoarseness that was most likely the result of her crying fit combined with the dozen or so hysterical screams I'd been told she'd treated them all to.

After another long pause, she replied, "It happened again, Row. She came back."

"Yeah, I heard," I replied, stepping in just a little further.

"See? I told you it would be safer this way."

"Yes, you did, but I'm still not necessarily convinced."

"Well, you aren't acting much like it then," she remarked.

"How so?"

"You can come closer. She's not here now, and I won't be biting you."

"I didn't think you would."

"And, so you're standing all the way over there for what reason?"

"I didn't want to startle you."

"Aye, are you certain it's not because you're afraid of me?"

I shifted my focus and realized she had been watching my reflection in the windowpane all along. I couldn't help but crack a thin smile. That was just like my wife, always aware of her surroundings even if she didn't appear to be.

"No," I said, shaking my head as I moved forward, skirting around the end of the bed and drawing closer to her. "Just giving you a little space is all."

After a thick pause, she looked up at me, her eyes tired and bloodshot. "I've had enough space for one day," she said, her voice low. "I'd much prefer it if you would just hold me for a while."

She slowly unfolded her legs and scooted toward the edge of the bed. In a single fluid motion she slipped her arms around my waist as I wrapped my own about her shoulders and pulled her close, stroking her hair. She didn't begin to cry, but then, I suppose she might not have had any tears left.

We stood there for what seemed like several minutes, simply gripping one another tightly. No words came from either of us, as everything we had to say at that moment in time was communicated by the embrace.

Finally, Felicity spoke. "Rowan, am I insane?"

"No, honey," I soothed. "You aren't insane."

"You aren't just saying that, are you?"

"No, sweetheart, I'm not just saying that."

"Because you would. I know you."

"Yes, you're right, I would. But, I'm not now."

"Make her stop."

"I'm trying."

Her grip on me finally loosened, and I guided her gently back onto the bed before retrieving the chair from the corner and pulling it up in front of her.

"So, do you want to talk about it?" I asked.

She shook her head. "There's really nothing to talk about. I don't remember anything."

Before I could reply, the warbling tone of my cell began ramping upward. I ignored it.

"Aren't you going to answer that?" she asked.

I shook my head. "Whoever it is can leave a message."

"What if it's something important?"

"You're what's important right now."

The insistent tone reached a climax then abruptly ended as the caller was shunted off to my voicemail.

She looked down into my eyes with a sad expression then reached out and touched my face. "Aye, this isn't working, *Caorthann*."

"What isn't working, honey?"

"This," she murmured. "I think maybe you're wrong. Maybe I am insane."

"No, you aren't," I countered, adding a mild insistence to my voice.

"Then why is this happening to me?"

"I don't know, but you've seen it happen to me and I'm not insane. Neither are you."

"Says you."

"And Helen," I offered. "This is magick gone awry and you know it."

"I'm beginning to wonder."

"I know you are, and believe me, I've been there, more times than I can count. But you were there for me every time, and I'm here for you now. We'll get through this."

"Maybe it runs in the family."

"What?"

"Insanity."

"Dammit, Felicity…" I mumbled as I screwed up my face and shook my head.

My cell phone emitted a muffled chirp from my pocket to let me know I had a new voice message, but I continued to ignore it.

"Well, my sister must be," she whispered.

I still hadn't grown used to hearing her say "my sister" even though she had spoken the words several dozen times since Maggie had dropped the story in her lap. Even so, I had been under the impression she had taken it well. But now, I was beginning to wonder.

"That has nothing to do with you," I objected.

"Aye, it has to. She gets inside me and makes me do things. We're bound by blood. Maybe we are bound by madness as well."

"You're going to have to stop talking like this, Felicity," I told her. "You aren't her and she isn't you. This is a *Lwa*, and it's taking the path of least resistance."

She shook her head slightly. "This isn't just the *Lwa*. It's her too. You know that."

"Even if it is, so what?"

"You said it yourself."

"What?"

"The *Lwa* is taking the path of least resistance. What better choice than someone who is insane?"

"Honey, we can't have this conversation. You aren't being rational."

"Aye, you're right. Maybe you should go."

"Excuse me?"

She hung her head, avoiding my eyes. "You should go now."

"Felicity..."

"No," she choked. "Go. Please."

It took a pair of minutes before I could bring myself to rise from the chair. Felicity still hadn't lifted her head, and it became obvious that she was done with the visit. No amount of pleading was going to bring her back into the conversation, not right now anyway. Her stubbornness would see to that.

I was worried, angry, hurt, and confused all at once, but there was nothing more I could do here. I just kept telling myself that she was safe and that Helen would take care of her. Maybe tomorrow she would be ready to talk again.

I leaned forward and kissed her on top of her head.

"I love you Felicity Caitlin O'Brien," I whispered, lingering for several heartbeats before turning and walking to the door.

It took a moment before the attendant answered my knock and unbolted the barrier. On my way out I paused, looking back toward my wife. She had drawn her legs back up and was sitting again, just as I had found her when I walked in, although this time she was no longer watching the window.

"Dammit, Helen, she thinks she's insane!" I almost spat the comment across the desk. My pain and confusion had given way to anger before the elevator doors had ever closed. Now that I was standing in the office she kept at the hospital, it had begun to boil over.

"Rowan," she replied calmly. "I told you that everything we had accomplished thus far was completely negated by the incident this morning."

"But she thinks she's insane!"

"She thought she was insane the day you admitted her," she replied matter-of-factly. "She simply had not told you as much."

My cell phone chirped again. My awareness of the tone had been drifting in and out, so I'd lost count of how many times it had reminded me to pick up my voice mail. I snatched it from my pocket, angrily stabbed some buttons to silence the annoyance, and then shoved it back into the darkness from whence it came.

"Well, there's got to be something you can do," I demanded.

"Yes, Rowan, there is. Continue her sessions and keep her safe and comfortable until you find the rogue spirit that is causing her this strife. Then, and only then, real healing can begin."

"Dammit, Helen, this is fucked up."

"Yes, it is."

I rubbed my hand across the lower half of my face, pinching my cheeks together and pursing my lips as I contemplated the situation. Stubble had already begun to sprout around my goatee, and it made a soft swishing noise as it dragged against the ridges on my fingertips.

"I'm sorry," I finally muttered.

"I understand, Rowan," she replied. "And, apology accepted."

We sat in silence for a long while. I could feel the ever-present throb in my head beating out a rhythm all its own. I'd grown used to it these days. Enough so that I pretty much ignored it unless it got worse.

"I guess I'd better go home," I finally said.

"That would probably be a good idea," Helen replied. "I would not normally do this, however, under the circumstances I am willing to make an exception. Would you like for me to prescribe something to help you sleep?"

"No." I shook my head. "I'll be fine."

I hadn't been in my truck for more than five minutes that my cell phone began to ring. I finished backing out of the space and levered the vehicle into drive before fishing around in my pocket for the device and pulling it out. Stabbing it on, I placed it against my ear, holding it tight as I swung my gaze left and right before pulling out of the parking lot.

"Rowan Gant," I half-barked into the device. Right now I didn't care who I alienated.

"Rowan, it's Velvet," a Southern drawl rolled into my ear. "Did you get my message?"

"No," I returned, fighting to soften my tone.

"Is something wrong?"

"Yeah, actually. Felicity experienced another possession by the *Lwa* this morning," I explained. "It wasn't good."

"Did anyone get hurt?" she asked, genuine concern in her voice. I had confided everything in her to date, so she was well aware of how bad things could get.

"Physically, no, but my wife is now convinced that she is insane."

"I'm sorry."

"Thanks, but I don't intend to let her travel that road for very long. But anyway, you said left a message? Tell me it's good news."

"Yes, I think it might be. I just might have found something."

"If you did, I'll put you on my goddamned altar as my personal Goddess."

"Let's not go that far just yet," she replied. "I put some feelers out in the *Vodoun* community and started getting a few interesting calls. But, one that came in yesterday really stuck out, so I ran it down. There's a tomb in New Orleans that has been having offerings placed on it on a fairly regular basis starting a few years ago. Not unusual in itself, but none of the locals were familiar with the ancestor, so that was curious. Still, not that big a deal, but then over the past year, they noticed that the activity had increased significantly."

"Did this tomb survive Katrina?"

"Yes, it is in a part of the city that didn't flood."

"Has there been activity there since the disaster?"

"Yes, actually."

"Okay, sounds promising. So, in your opinion do you think this might mean someone has made this ancestor a personal *Lwa*?"

"It's possible, but let me finish because here's the interesting thing. The tomb had been damaged at some point, so the name was only partially legible, but it started with an M and an I..."

"You're getting damn close to a place on that altar, Velvet."

She ignored the comment and rushed into an explanation. "Just to cover the bases, I went ahead and got the location for the tomb and had a friend with the Louisiana Division City Archives look into it for me. Listen to this. The remains interred in there are of one Miranda Blanque, date of death on or around September fourteenth, eighteen fifty-one."

I felt the thud in my skull ramp up a notch then send a hard stab of pain lancing beneath my scalp. A wave of gooseflesh followed it as the hair along the back of my neck rose to attention. I knew then that this wasn't a case of finding *some* thing.

This was *the* thing.

It was she.

"How does it feel?" I asked.

"How does what feel?"

"To be a Goddess," I replied. "Because you just got a promotion."

Wednesday, November 30
7:17 P.M.
Lambert Saint Louis International Airport
Concourse C, Gate C3
Saint Louis, Missouri

CHAPTER 34:

Felicity had been in much better spirits when I had visited her earlier in the day. Apparently, a good nights sleep and some time chatting with Helen had done wonders. I didn't want to second-guess someone with a laundry list of credentials that I, myself, didn't possess, but I was betting my wife had far more resilience than she'd been credited.

Helen had objected to me coming to the hospital at first, feeling that my presence might upset some of the balance they had reached. For once, I actually agreed on that point and would have bowed to her wishes had it not been for the fact that I needed to seek my wife's permission. Not exactly like a child seeking endorsement from a parent, but I needed to make a trip to New Orleans. There was no way around it. Unfortunately, I was having trouble making myself leave Saint Louis with Felicity locked away in the psychiatric ward of a hospital, even if she was under Helen's watchful eye.

I knew I had no choice, and so did they. In fact, the prospect that I had most likely found the *Lwa* served to brighten my wife's mood even more, turning her underlying sense of despair into a newfound hope. But, in the end it still took both of them better than an hour to convince me that it was okay for me to leave and that she would be all right.

I looked at my watch and shifted in my seat. The entire row of chairs was interconnected, and they rocked slightly as I moved, shifting back and coming to a rest with a mildly jarring clunk. The lady sitting two seats to the left of me instantly shot me a hard glance. Her face was creased with a thin frown as she made a show of tugging at her yarn and settling back in to crochet whatever oddly shaped project she was attempting.

"Sorry," I mumbled then tried to sit still. The seat wasn't exactly comfortable, so I couldn't say how long that was going to last.

My trip through the TSA security checkpoint had been much quicker than I expected, so I had ended up sitting here way too long. It was one of the things I hated most about air travel, especially since 9-11. It had become a terminal case of hurry up and wait. Of course, I had hurried, and now I was waiting. I'd been planted in this spot long enough now that my buttocks were going to sleep, and I still had a plane ride ahead of me.

According to the time on my watch, I had a good twenty to thirty minutes before they would even begin boarding. In fact, the plane hadn't even arrived yet, and in my experience if they said they were going to board at 7:45 that really meant 8:05. I knew I was going to be miserable if I didn't at least get up and move around a bit.

I turned my head slightly to the side and watched the woman with the crochet hook stabbing away as she poked it through one loop, hooked a strand, pulled, then repeated, twisting and fiddling as she went. Eventually, she stopped and gazed intently at a folded magazine in her lap. I assumed it was a pattern of sorts.

Either way, pattern or not, I took the opportunity to get up from my seat and heft my carry-on from the floor next to me. The row of joined chairs rocked and thumped once again, and even though she wasn't actually working on the project at the moment, the lady shot me another disgusted glare.

This time I didn't bother to apologize. I simply shrugged and walked away.

Hooking the strap of my backpack over my shoulder, I started across the concourse, dodging travelers as they endeavored to run over one another with their wheeled luggage in tow. After running the gauntlet, I ducked into the coffee shop that sat diagonally across from my gate. I ordered a large coffee with a double shot of espresso and then, after glancing at the refrigerated case, had them add a cheese Danish onto the tab. I suddenly realized that I hadn't even given thought to eating before I rushed to the airport. There'd been too much to do with getting the last minute plane ticket, arranging for our friend

RJ to watch the animals, canceling a meeting with a client, and trying to pack for the quick trip.

The shop was bustling, just as it was any other time I'd had occasion to fly, so it took a few minutes for my drink to get done. I simply stood away from the crush of people, holding my pastry-filled and logo-adorned bag in one hand, with the thumb of my other hooked through the shoulder strap of my backpack. Eventually, my name was called, and after an aborted attempt or two at reaching the counter, I managed to get my hands on my coffee.

I had kept an eye on my gate and thus far saw no one exiting the jetway, so I figured there was plenty of time before I would be called to board. I exited the shop and found that one of the small café tables in front of it was free, so I parked myself there, dropping my carryon to the floor and sitting back. The chair wasn't any more comfortable than the one I had been sitting in before, but at least it wasn't connected to anything else, so the only person I could disturb was myself.

I was just pulling the Danish out of the bag when my cell phone started to warble. I dropped the pastry onto a handful of napkins then pulled the device out of my pocket and answered it.

"Rowan Gant."

"Where the fuck are you?" Ben's voice hit my ear.

"Actually, I'm at the airport."

"Why in hell are ya' at the friggin' airport?"

"You don't want to know."

"Well where ya' goin'?"

"Like I said, you don't want to know."

"Dammit, Row, is this somethin' ta' do with that Voodoo stuff? Are you doin' somethin' stupid like I told ya' not to?"

"Do I need to say it a third time, Ben?"

"Fuck me."

"I'd rather not. So, did you just call me to brush up on your suspect interviewing skills, or was there some greater reason?"

He adopted a snide tone. "I dunno, are you sure *you* wanna know?"

"Hey, you called me."

"Yeah, I did."

"So?"

"So I got a piece'a news for ya'. Are ya' sittin' down?"

"Actually, yes."

"Good, 'cause guess what? We found your goddamned sister-in…half sister-in…aww, hell, whatever-the-fuck-she-is-in-law."

I instantly sat up straighter in the chair. "You found her? Where?"

"Well, not 'zactly found. But, we know who she is."

"Who?"

"Her name's Annalise Devereaux," he replied. "I'm lookin' at 'er driver's license photo right this minute. And, Row, you ain't gonna believe this. She's the fuckin' spittin' image of Firehair."

"Where is she, Ben?" I pressed.

"Right now, we don't know, 'cause of Katrina."

"What do you mean?"

"The address on 'er license is in a section of New Orleans that got totally flooded out, so there's no way to know where she is at the moment. But, obviously we know she survived."

I sat there staring into space for a moment, feeling my headache creep up another notch.

"Row…" Ben's voice flooded into my ear. "Hey, Row, you still there?"

"Yeah," I finally said. "So, Ben, you wanted to know where I'm going?"

"Yeah, I do, but I seem ta' recall you decided ta' be an asshole about tellin' me when I asked."

"Well, it's my turn to tell you something *you* won't believe. I'll give you three guesses where I'm going, and the first two don't count."

Friday, December 2
3:11 P.M.
St. Louis Cemetery #1
New Orleans, Louisiana

EPILOGUE:

"**D**o you have any change with you?" the woman asked.

The man dug in his pocket and extracted a handful of coins, spread them out with his index finger, then displayed his palm to her. "This enough?"

"It's really not as much about the amount as the effort and respect," she replied, nodding toward the assortment in his hand and then showing him the few she held in her own. "Just let them know you have a gift for them and ask permission to enter."

The pair was standing on the sidewalk in front of the cemetery gate. The walls surrounding the plots showed their advanced age but were obviously maintained as best they could be. The iron gates were propped open in an eerily inviting manner.

"I can't say that I've ever done this before," he replied.

"Have you gone into cemeteries before?" she asked.

"Yeah, of course."

"Then I suspect you've offended a few ancestors."

"Great."

"Don't worry about that now. You'll all get over it," she told him with a quick shake of her head. "Just do it right this time."

"Anything special I'm supposed to say?"

"No, just speak from the heart. Tell them you're bringing a gift and ask permission. It's not hard. It's like showing up at a dinner party with a bottle of wine and knocking on the door."

"And then I just walk in?"

"You'll know what to do," she said with a slight smile. "Believe me, if they don't want you to come in, you'll know it."

"Okay," he replied, an underscore of apprehension in his voice.

He stood at the gates and gathered his thoughts for a moment, then looking in through the opening at the closely arranged rows of tombs, he began to speak.

"Greetings…" he started hesitantly.

He glanced over at the woman for reassurance but saw that she had her eyes closed, and her lips were moving as she silently greeted the spirits herself.

"Greetings," he began again. He continued speaking aloud though he wasn't quite sure why. "My name is Rowan, and I've come to visit you…for…well, for some very important reasons. I've brought you this token…"

Not quite sure how to proceed, he held his hand out, displaying the coins to the unseen spirits.

The day was pleasant with the temperature resting in the upper fifties. The sun was shining, and there'd been no reason for anything more than a light jacket. Even so, a slight chill ran up his spine causing him to shiver. It lasted only a moment then was immediately followed by soothing warmth that enveloped his entire body. His earlier anxiety was instantly replaced by comfort.

Just as Velvet had told him he would, he knew he was welcome.

"Put the coins over here," she said, placing her own in a receptacle just past the gates.

He followed suit, mimicking her overt motion that made them clatter noisily. He looked to her with a raised eyebrow, and she easily read the unspoken question in his face.

"You want them to hear it," she explained. "They need to know you are actually leaving the gift you promised."

He nodded but remained silent.

"Rowan," she said with a slight smile. "You can talk here. It's okay. Just keep your voice low."

"Okay," he replied. "I just wasn't sure."

"Well, you can. Oh, and in case I forget, don't just walk out the gates. When we leave, we'll say goodbye, thank them, and then back out."

"Back out? Like walk backwards?"

"Yes."

"Okay. You're the expert."

The woman looked up and to the right, pointing as she mumbled something to herself. A second later she took his arm and pulled gently.

"The tomb should be this way, near the back."

They had only been walking for a minute or two, carefully making their way along the narrow paths, when the pain started to intensify. The man stumbled and caught himself as the hard stab drove deep into the base of his skull.

"Are you all right?" the woman asked.

"Something's wrong," he replied, reaching up to rub the back of his throbbing head.

"We're almost there," she told him. "Are you going to be able to handle this?"

He gave her a slight nod. "I have to."

They started forward again, rounding the corner of a large, family tomb, the woman in the lead.

"Someone's here," she whispered.

The man looked up and saw a petite woman with fiery red hair cascading down to the middle of her back. She was standing with her forehead pressed against the stone of a tomb some thirty-odd yards away.

They stopped dead in their tracks and simply stared.

As if she could sense that she was being watched, the red haired woman pushed back from the tomb and slowly turned to face them.

There was the distance to consider.

And, there were even the oblique shadows from the closely spaced stone mausoleums.

But still, the resemblance was beyond uncanny.

At that moment, if Rowan Gant didn't know for a fact that his wife was almost seven hundred miles away in Saint Louis, he would have sworn she was standing there, staring directly at him, with a look of abject fear distorting her face.

A legacy of darkened desires and well-intentioned magick
gone awry…If Felicity is to heal, a forgotten spell must
first be broken. Only then will she be able to meet the
darkness on her own terms…
Whether Rowan wants her to or not.

THE END OF DESIRE
A ROWAN GANT INVESTIGATION
BOOK THREE OF THE MIRANDA TRILOGY

Number Eight In The Best Selling
RGI Suspense-Thriller Series

Coming To Bookstores Nationwide
2007

The Rowan Gant Investigations

Sometimes, it takes more than a detective to stop a killer...

ISBN 0-9678221-0-6
EAN 9780967822105
$8.95 US

MURDEROUS SATAN WORSHIPPING WITCHES

When a young woman is ritualistically murdered in her Saint Louis apartment with the primary clue being a pentacle scrawled in her own blood, police are quick to dismiss it as a cult killing. Not one for taking things at face value, city homicide detective Ben Storm calls on his long time friend, Rowan Gant—a practicing Witch—for help.

In helping his friend, Rowan discovers that the victim is one of his former pupils. Even worse, the clues that he helps to uncover show that this murder is only a prelude to even more ritualistic bloodletting for dark purposes.

As the body count starts to rise, Rowan is suddenly thrust into an investigation where not only must he help stop a sadistic serial killer, but also must fight the prejudices and suspicions of those his is working with—including his best friend.

THE RETURN OF THE BURNING TIMES

In 1484, then Pope Innocent VIII issued a papal bull—a decree giving the endorsement of the church to the inquisitors of the day who hunted, tortured, tried and ultimately murdered those accused of heresy—especially the practice of WitchCraft. Modern day Witches refer to this dark period of history as "The Burning Times."

Rowan Gant returns to face a nightmare long thought to be a distant memory. A killer armed with gross misinterpretations of the Holy Bible and a 15th century Witch hunting manual known as the *Malleus Maleficarum* has resurrected the Inquisition and the members of the Pagan community of St. Louis are his prey.

With the unspeakable horrors of "The Burning Times" being played out across the metropolitan area, Rowan is again enlisted by homicide detective Benjamin Storm and the Major Case Squad to help solve the crimes—all the while knowing full well that his religion makes him a potential target.

ISBN 0967822114
EAN 9780967822112
$8.95 US

PICTURE PERFECT

Rowan Gant is a Witch.
His bane is to see things that others cannot.
To feel things he wishes he could not.
To experience events through the eyes of another...
Through the eyes of victims...
Sometimes, the things he sees are evil...
Criminal...
Because of this, in the span of less than two years, Rowan has come face to face with not one, but two sadistic serial killers...
In both cases he was lucky to survive.
Still, he abides the basic rule of The Craft—Harm None.

This predator could make Rowan forget that rule...

ISBN 096782219X
EAN 9780967822198
$8.95 US

LET THE BURNINGS BEGIN...

In February of 2001, serial killer Eldon Andrew Porter set about creating a modern day version of the 15th century inquisition and Witch trials. Following the tenets of the *Malleus Maleficarum* and his own insane interpretation of the *Holy Bible*, he tortured and subsequently murdered several innocent people.

During a showdown on the old Chain of Rocks Bridge, he narrowly escaped apprehension by the Greater St. Louis Major Case Squad.

In the process, his left arm was severely crippled by a gunshot fired at close range.

A gunshot fired by a man he was trying to kill. A man who embraced the mystical arts. A Witch. Rowan Gant.

In December of the same year, Eldon Porter's fingerprints were found at the scene of a horrific murder in Cape Girardeau, Missouri, just south of St. Louis. An eyewitness who later spotted the victim's stolen vehicle reported that it was headed north...

ISBN 0967822181
EAN 9780967822181
$14.95 US

Photograph Copyright © 2004, K. J. Epps

ABOUT THE AUTHOR

M. R. Sellars has been called the "Dennis Miller of Paganism" for his quick wit and humorously deadpan observations of life within the Pagan community and beyond. However, his humor is only one facet of his personality, as evidenced by the dark, unique thrillers he pens. That face has earned him another name—the "Pagan Tony Hillerman." Even with all these comparative monikers, he still likes to think of himself as just another writer trying to eke out a living doing what he loves.

All of the current *Rowan Gant* novels have spent several consecutive weeks on numerous bookstore bestseller lists. *The Law of Three*, book #4 in the saga, received the *St. Louis Riverfront Times People's Choice* award soon after its debut.

An honorary elder of *Mystic Moon*, a teaching coven based in Kansas City, an honorary member of *Dragon Clan Circle* in Indiana, and an elder of *The Grove of the Old Ways*, Sellars is actually for the most part a solitary practitioner of an eclectic mix of Pagan paths, and has been since the late seventies. He currently resides in the Midwest with his wife, daughter, and a host of rescued felines. His schedule never seems to slow down and when not writing, researching a project, or taking time to spend with his family, he can be found on the road performing workshops and book signings nationwide.

At the time of this writing, Sellars is working on several projects, as well as traveling on promotional tour.

For more information about M. R. Sellars and his work, visit him on the World Wide Web at www.mrsellars.com and sign up for his e-newsletter, *RGI: Beyond the Blotter*.

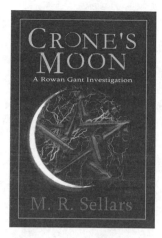

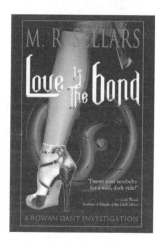